*Fo*

# TRIPL

Three beloved authors bring
you three compelling,
breathtaking romances

*We're proud to present*

# MILLS & BOON SPOTLIGHT™

*A chance to buy collections of bestselling
novels by favourite authors every month –
they're back by popular demand!*

## January 2010

### Desiring the Reilly Brothers
by Maureen Child

*Featuring*

*The Tempting Mrs Reilly
Whatever Reilly Wants...
The Last Reilly Standing*

### Triplets Found

*Featuring*

*The Virgin's Makeover* by Judy Duarte
*Take a Chance on Me* by Karen Rose Smith
*And Then There Were Three*
by Lynda Sandoval

# TRIPLETS FOUND

## JUDY DUARTE

## KAREN ROSE SMITH

## LYNDA SANDOVAL

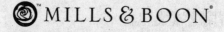

TRIPLETS FOUND © Harlequin Books S.A. 2010.

First published in Great Britain 2010
Harlequin Mills & Boon Limited,
Eton House, 18-24 Paradise Road, Richmond, Surrey TW9 1SR

The publisher acknowledges the copyright holders of the individual works, which
have already been published in the UK in single, separate volumes, as follows:

*The Virgin's Makeover* © Harlequin Books S.A. 2004
*Take a Chance on Me* © Harlequin Books S.A. 2004
*And Then There Were Three* © Harlequin Books S.A. 2004

Special thanks and acknowledgement are given to Judy Duarte,
Karen Rose Smith and Lynda Sandoval for their contributions to the
LOGAN'S LEGACY series.

ISBN: 978 0 263 88029 8

64-0110

Printed and bound in Spain
by Litografia Rosés S.A., Barcelona

# THE VIRGIN'S
# MAKEOVER

BY
JUDY DUARTE

**Judy Duarte**, an avid reader who enjoys a happy ending, always wanted to write books of her own. One day she decided to make that dream come true. Five years and six manuscripts later, she sold her first book to Special Edition.

Her unpublished stories have won the Emily and the Orange Rose awards and in 2001 she became a double Golden Heart finalist. Judy credits her success to Romance Writers of America and two wonderful critique partners, Sheri WhiteFeather and Crystal Green.

At times, when a stubborn hero and a headstrong heroine claim her undivided attention, she and her family are thankful for fast food, pizza delivery and video games. When she's not at the keyboard, she enjoys travelling, spending romantic evenings with her personal hero and playing board games with her children.

Judy lives in Southern California and loves to hear from her readers. You may write to her at: PO Box 498, San Luis Rey, CA 92068-0498, USA. You can also visit her website at: www.judyduarte.com.

To the special ladies who love my youngest son as their own: Lydia Bustos, a wonderful sister-in-law and *tía* who spends hours at Chuckie Cheese and pretends to enjoy some of the same movies, over and over. Sheri Marotte, a talented teacher who became my friend and overlooked more than a fair share of tardies when my early-morning writing time went into extra innings. Soledad "Chole" Mendez, a great baby-sitter and friend who provides me with immeasurable peace of mind whenever my little boy is in her care. Thank you, ladies, from the bottom of my heart!

# *Prologue*

*Portland, Oregon—1976*

"**I**'m pregnant."

Jared Cambry's gut clenched as he looked at Olivia in disbelief. "But we only did it once. Are you sure?"

The sixteen-year-old blonde glanced down at her worn leather sandals and kicked at a dandelion that grew in the grass at the park where they'd met. She looked up and caught his gaze. "Yeah. I'm sure."

Jared wanted to bolt, wanted to call her a liar. Instead, he blew out a ragged breath. "I don't know what to say."

"I was surprised, too," she said. "I guess neither of us planned on having a baby."

She could say *that* again. He'd just been accepted to Arizona State. And last time his parents had taken him to visit, the football coach had said that he had a good shot at a quarterback position in the fall—maybe even first string.

He looked at the teenage girl who'd just given him the worst piece of news he'd ever heard.

"I know we're young," Olivia said.

Young? Heck, he'd only had his drivers' license for a little over a year. And though old enough to drive, she still rode a bike. They should be thinking about college. And summer vacation. Not a baby.

Besides, it's not as though they'd ever dated. They'd met at a party a couple of months ago, and it had just happened.

Two weeks before the party, he and Megan Phillips, a pretty, redheaded cheerleader he'd gone out with since the fall, had broken up. He was still nursing a broken heart and a wounded pride. And he wasn't in the party spirit—until Olivia had come along, holding two glasses of cheap, fruit-flavored wine.

Olivia had a pretty smile and a way of making him forget about the obnoxious college guy Megan had dumped him for.

Neither of them had been virgins, but the experience had still been awkward. And Jared had a feeling she'd been disappointed.

He'd driven her home afterward, and they'd exchanged phone numbers. But he hadn't called her.

And when she'd asked him to meet her today, he'd been surprised.

"We could maybe date for a while, get to know each other better," she said.

They could date? His mom and dad would come unglued if he brought home a girl from the wrong side of the tracks. They had their hopes set on their only son meeting a debutante, or at least someone whose parents belonged to the country club set.

And even if Jared was willing to go out with Olivia, his family was relocating to Scottsdale about the same time he moved to the dorms at ASU. They said the move was for business purposes, although he suspected they wanted to be near their only child in Phoenix.

"What are you thinking?" she asked, eyes snagging his and demanding some kind of answer.

Heck, he was thinking about all kinds of things. College. Playing football. Maybe taking some pre-law and business courses.

And the sudden realization that his once charmed life was going to hell in a broken-down baby buggy.

Only one solution came to mind. "I'll pay for an abortion."

"What?" Olivia asked, voice raised an octave.

"An abortion. I'll get the money. And I'll drive you there and wait while it's done. That way, your mom won't find out."

"No way. I know having a kid isn't convenient for either one of us. But I'm keeping this baby."

She couldn't be serious. Olivia and her mom lived in a rundown, rusted-out trailer on the outskirts of town. How the heck was she ever going to raise a kid?

And even if he got a part-time job flipping burgers while attending school, he wasn't going to be able to contribute too much. Her keeping the baby was a bad idea—for both of them.

"You've got your whole life in front of you," he said. "Why would you want to tie yourself down?"

"Because babies are a blessing. And God wouldn't have let me get pregnant if there wasn't a good reason for it."

Jared rolled his eyes. He didn't think God had anything to do with the mistake they'd made. And he couldn't see how having a kid at his age would bless his life.

Not now.

Not ever.

# Chapter One

*Portland, Oregon—2004*

"**I**'m pregnant."

Lissa Cartwright, who'd been slouching in a cushioned patio chair on the deck, nearly dropped her morning cup of coffee and sat up straight. "You're what?"

"Pregnant," her bright-eyed sister said.

"That's great. Congratulations." Lissa managed a smile. She couldn't be happier, yet the excitement had an ambiguous edge.

Last year, her sister had married the love of her life, a man who adored her. And having a baby had always been Eileen's dream.

Lissa's too, she supposed. That's what made the news so bittersweet.

"You look surprised."

No, Lissa wasn't actually bowled over by the announcement, but as usual, when her sister achieved one of those heart-touching milestones, Lissa felt a wee bit envious. "I just didn't expect to hear it so soon. Or so early in the morning."

Eileen laughed. "You didn't think I'd drive all the way out to the vineyard for breakfast, did you?"

"No." Lissa adored her younger sister, but Eileen wasn't a morning person. Not like Lissa.

In fact, the two young women weren't anything alike, but there was a good reason for that. Seven months after Lissa had been adopted as an infant, her mother had given birth to Eileen.

Lissa wasn't sure when she'd begun to feel like an outsider. Maybe on the day her parents sat her down and told her about being special, about being chosen. About her being their very first baby girl.

That's when Lissa began to take a good hard look at the differences between her and her sister.

Eileen was petite and vivacious, a strawberry blond, just like their mother. And Lissa was tall and introspective, with plain brown hair. God only knew who she resembled—certainly not anyone on the Cartwright family tree.

Still Lissa had to give her mom and dad credit for trying to be fair. They were great parents. And they were good to her. She had no complaints.

After all, how could they not love their *real* daughter more?

Besides, Eileen was everything Lissa wasn't. And their differences went beyond appearance—something Lissa had learned in the fall of first grade.

One day after school, their mother had enrolled them in a dance school and bought them new black-patent-leather tap shoes. Mom's enthusiasm had been contagious, and both girls had been ecstatic and ready for their very first lesson.

Before long, Eileen was dancing her little heart out—Shirley Temple style. All the while, Lissa clomped around like a pack mule in army boots.

Fortunately, Ken and Donna Cartwright had done a good job of pretending to be equally proud of both girls. But the tap instructor hadn't been quite as tactful.

But who could blame her? Lissa had seen the proof played out loud and clear on the family home videos of the dance recitals.

Yet that didn't overshadow one important fact. The girls shared a genuine love for each other—and for their parents.

"Have you told Mom and Dad?" Lissa asked.

"Not yet. I will, as soon as they get in from their morning walk."

From her seat on the deck, Lissa scanned the rolling hillsides of Valencia Vineyards, where sturdy vines nourished premium grapes. She loved the fertile land and the bounty it produced. The vineyard was the one place where she actually belonged, where she could thrive and be herself.

That's why she started each day with breakfast on the backyard deck, under the protection of the over-hang when it rained and out in the sunshine when it didn't.

She spotted her parents near the new, state-of-the-art winery, walking hand-in-hand, their love for each other impossible to ignore.

Maybe that's what Lissa envied. The sense of truly belonging. Of loving and being loved.

"Look." Lissa pointed toward her parents. "They're coming this way."

"Good. I can't wait to tell them, especially Mom. You know how she is about babies." Eileen rolled her eyes and laughed. "Remember how embarrassed we used to get? I've never known another woman to get so goofy whenever she spotted a little one at the mall or in the grocery store."

"I remember," Lissa said. "And you're right. Mom will be thrilled to have a grandchild."

Especially since Eileen's baby would be a *real* grandchild.

The old insecurities seemed to settle over Lissa, but she adored her sister. "I'm so happy for you. I know how much you love Dan."

Eileen reached across the glass tabletop and squeezed Lissa's hand. "I really hope that you find a special man someday. Someone who appreciates you."

"Thanks," Lissa said, although that wasn't likely. Her shyness made her steer clear of serious relationships.

And at this point, it seemed that life—and love—had passed her by. After all, how many twenty-seven-year-old virgins were still walking the face of the earth? Not many, she would wager.

And since she rarely left the vineyard or winery, Lissa would probably go to her grave never having experienced a night of romance or passion—other than in those books her sister gave to her.

Of course, she didn't admit that to anyone. Not even Eileen.

Instead, Lissa said, "There aren't too many special guys who come around here."

"Well, you need to get out more. You've become a workaholic since I got married."

That was true. Lissa had poured her talents into running the vineyard—from farming to the business end. Deep down, she hoped to prove herself, although she wasn't sure who she wanted to impress. Her parents? The world? The faceless biological parents who'd given her away? Or maybe just herself.

Either way, she'd dedicated her life to the family vineyard and winery. And she was good at what she did. She had a head for business and had soaked in every bit of knowledge her dad shared with her as a vintner.

A muted little bark sounded from the sliding door,

and Lissa spotted her new puppy scratching at the glass, trying to get out.

"Looks like Barney woke up and is raring to go." Lissa glanced at her watch. "I hate to leave you on the deck alone, but I have to go to work."

"Don't you want to be here when I tell Mom and Dad?" Eileen asked.

Lissa gave her sister a kiss on the cheek. "I've got a business meeting in a few minutes, and I've got to look over a few files ahead of time. This is your special moment with Mom and Dad. You can tell me all about it later."

"Who are you meeting?" Eileen asked.

"A business consultant."

"A man?" Her sister sat up straight, nearly knocking over her glass of fresh-squeezed orange juice.

Lissa clicked her tongue. "Don't get your hopes up. His name is Sullivan Grayson. Doesn't that sound a bit old and stodgy? Besides, Dad met him in some tournament at the country club. And you know most of the guys he plays golf with are retired."

"And married," Eileen added. "Okay, so maybe another interesting man will come along for you."

"Yeah. Maybe," Lissa said, not at all convinced. Then she took her dishes into the house, eager to get back to work, to return to the world where she could shine.

Once inside the kitchen, she put the dishes in the sink, while the rascally pup jumped at her feet, trying to get her attention by whining and yapping. When her hands were free, she picked up the little dog.

Barney nuzzled in her arms, then gave her several wet kisses on the cheek.

"I love you, too, little guy." Lissa smiled wistfully.

At the rate things were going in her life, the closest thing to a baby she would ever have was this wet-nosed bundle of joy.

And the closest thing to romance and lovemaking she'd ever experience was waiting for her in one of the paperback novels on the nightstand in her bedroom.

Thirty minutes later, in the wood-paneled vineyard office where Lissa spent most of her time, she heard a car pull up and assumed Sullivan Grayson had arrived. She quickly organized the files she'd spread across her desk, ready to meet the man her father had hired to help the vineyard over a financial slump.

With the assistance of the topnotch consultant and investor, they hoped to create a marketing strategy to promote the new blend of varietals Lissa had developed and jumpstart the struggling, family-owned vineyard.

A light rap sounded at the door.

"Come on in," she called.

As a tall, broad-shouldered man entered, the dark walls seemed to close in on them, and Lissa nearly fell out of her swiveled desk chair.

From the open doorway, the morning sun highlighted a dark shade of burnished-copper in his hair and gave him a rugged, mystical aura that stirred her imagination. His face and stance reminded her of a young Scottish laird.

He wore khaki slacks and a green button-down shirt, open at the collar. No tie. Yet, for a moment, she wondered what he would look like in a kilt, with a broadsword in hand.

"Hello." He flashed a crooked smile. "I'm Sullivan Grayson."

There had to be a mistake. She'd expected an older gentleman who'd been doing business long enough to achieve the mile-long résumé of successful ventures her father had shown her. Not someone whose lively eyes and flirtatious smile made her feel like a gawky adolescent.

A hodgepodge of words seemed to jam in her throat, but she cleared her voice and uttered a belated, "Hello."

"You must be Lissa Cartwright," he said, picking up the conversational ball she'd dropped.

She nodded, then stood and extended an arm across the desk in greeting. "How do you do?"

Gosh, could she get any more stiff and formal than that?

Sullivan gave her hand a gentle squeeze, sending a tingle of warmth to her core.

Her knees wobbled, but she didn't think he'd noticed, and she tried desperately to regroup, to swallow her surprise and ignore the heady attraction to a man who was *way* out of her league.

Still, she couldn't help staring, taking inventory, so to speak. Nor could she help thinking of him as a Scottish highlander standing on a windswept moor— ready to battle a foe of the clan. Or to tease the lassies.

Oh, for Pete's sake. She scolded herself and tried to rein in the silly fantasy provoked by those historical romances her sister had given her. Lissa knew better than to waste her bedtime hours reading that unrealistic fluff, no matter how much she secretly enjoyed them.

She slowly pulled her hand from the Scotsman's grip, aware of the calluses on his palm that belied the image of the manicured businessman she'd expected. "Won't you have a seat?"

He took the leather chair across from her, then shot her another grin that continued to rock her usually calm nature.

Where in the world was her dad? He'd get this conversation on the right track.

"My father will be coming along shortly," she said, reminding herself that this was a business meeting. Nothing more. Nothing less.

Besides, what would a good-looking, successful guy like Sullivan Grayson see in a woman like her?

He scanned the room until his gaze landed on the tri-colored bundle of fur chewing on a red rubber doggie ball by the potbellied stove in the corner. "You have a cute puppy."

"Thanks. His name is Barney."

"I like dogs." Sullivan flashed her another one of those grins that rattled her senses. "And dog-lovers."

She cleared her throat, hoping it would also clear her mind of a fantasy that had become far too vivid. "We can wait for my dad. Or we can get started. Your choice."

"Whatever you're comfortable with."

She wasn't comfortable at all. Not with him or this meeting.

"Your father mentioned you've developed a new wine," he said.

"Actually, it's a new blend of varietals." Lissa clasped her hands on top of the desk, glad to steer the conversation and her thoughts away from the Scottish highlands and back on Valencia Vineyards, where they belonged.

Men like Sullivan Grayson didn't take a second look at women like her. And if he did? Good grief. She wouldn't know which way to run.

Sullivan studied his new client's daughter. Lissa Cartwright was an attractive woman, even though she didn't seem to know it. Or maybe she preferred a plain-Jane image, intentionally downplaying her looks by wearing her hair in a bulky, spinster-type bun and hiding her figure behind baggy gray slacks and a lackluster blouse.

She wasn't a beauty, but he'd still felt a spark of attraction when he'd first spotted her behind that desk. Maybe it was those mesmerizing green eyes that held his attention and made him want to tease a smile from her, just to see them come alive.

He figured she'd felt something for him, too. At least her nervousness suggested she had.

But Lissa Cartwright was definitely off-limits. After all, Sullivan never mixed business with pleasure. And since he was working for her father on a family-owned vineyard, he'd put his interest on permanent hold.

Besides, she had business savvy. And from what he'd learned after researching Valencia Vineyards, she was too serious-minded to be considered dating material, especially for a man who'd learned the hard way to keep his relationships light and meaningless.

Since his divorce at the ripe old age of twenty-five, Sullivan preferred his women to have nothing more going for them than a pretty face, a great body and an impressive rung on the social ladder.

The door opened, and Ken Cartwright entered the office. He extended a hand to Sullivan. "Forgive me for being late. My daughter, Eileen, just announced she's expecting a baby. And, needless to say, I couldn't disappear until my wife stopped bouncing off the walls."

Sullivan smiled. "I take it that she's settled down now."

"She's still a bit giddy." Ken chuckled. "You have no idea how much my wife loves babies."

"And you don't?" Lissa elbowed him, her lively green eyes taunting her father.

"Okay," Ken said. "I admit it. My wife and I are both suckers for toothless grins."

"I wonder how they'd fare in an old folks' home?" Lissa asked, flashing a smile at Sullivan that sliced right through him.

He couldn't seem to escape her gaze. She had the most amazing eyes he'd ever seen. And when she smiled, her face lit up.

"Shall we get down to business?" Ken asked.

"Yes," Sullivan answered, a bit too quickly. He needed to focus on what he'd been hired to do, and not on a fascinating pair of verdant green eyes that were more than a little distracting.

At lunchtime, Lissa's mother, Donna, and her sister, Eileen, brought a tray of sandwiches and a pitcher of iced tea for them to eat in the office. Eileen kept making goofy, isn't-he-perfect-for-you faces, mouthing things like, *You go, girl* and pointing toward Sullivan when he wasn't looking.

Lissa wanted to clobber her sister. For goodness' sake, it didn't take a brain surgeon to see that the man was a looker. But she also knew he wouldn't be the slightest bit interested in her.

Of course, she'd gotten used to Eileen's efforts to help. In high school, Lissa had become a bookworm and an honor student, but she'd had very few friends. And no dates to speak of, other than Milt Preston, the guy who played Ichabod Crane in the "Legend of Sleepy Hollow" play.

Eileen had talked Milt into asking Lissa to the Christmas formal. As awkward as the experience had been, Lissa had appreciated her sister taking on a matchmaker role back then, but she didn't really appreciate those same efforts now.

When her mother—thank goodness—finally managed to drag Eileen back to the house, Lissa blew out the breath she'd been holding.

For Pete's sake. She was nervous enough. She certainly didn't need a cheering section at a game that was lost before it even began.

Fortunately, her dad and Sullivan had been oblivious to the girl talk, or so Lissa hoped. And the three of them had eaten lunch while talking over business strategy.

By four in the afternoon, the initial meeting finally ended.

Ken was the first to call it a day. "Lissa, I promised your mother I'd help her grill steaks this evening. Will you take Sullivan to the guest house and help him settle in?"

"I'd be glad to." Lissa still felt uneasy around the man. But she'd best get used to it. Sullivan would be staying at the winery until they'd hammered out the details of the new marketing plan. Then his work at

Valencia Vineyards would be finished. And he'd leave without a backward glance.

"You two may as well get to know each other," Ken suggested. "I have some family obligations to take care of, so you'll be spending a lot of time together."

Don't remind me about dealing with the consultant on my own, Lissa wanted to say. Instead, she offered a pleasant grin—the kind she'd practiced over the years when asked to do something she wasn't comfortable doing and would prefer to delegate to someone else.

"My father's favorite uncle fell and broke a hip," Lissa explained to Sullivan. "And there were a few complications, so Dad will be going to San Diego soon, and you'll be working with me."

"Not a problem." Sullivan flashed her another smile that accelerated her pulse.

She called Barney, who'd been chewing on the frayed edge of the throw rug that sat in front of the potbellied stove. When the pup continued to ignore her, she scooped him up, carried him outside and deposited him on the ground, where he immediately began to sniff around until a twig caught his attention.

Sullivan followed behind. "I need to get my bags out of the trunk. Is it a long walk? I can take my car, so it'll be parked near the guest house."

"No, it's just ahead. And you really can't park any closer than this. See the little suspension bridge that leads to the big house?"

"Yes."

She pointed beyond the wooden structure that spanned the fishpond, toward the quaint guest house she'd always thought of as a cottage. "It's just across the lawn."

They stopped long enough for Sullivan to retrieve a suitcase from the trunk of a sporty, silver-gray Mercedes and for her to snap a leash on Barney.

"Lead the way," Sullivan said, with that flirtatious grin that made her heart rate go bonkers.

Was it her imagination? Or did he keep sliding a glance her way?

No way. It had to be her imagination. Maybe he found her an oddity. Or a novelty of some kind. That had to be it, because she never harbored any unrealistic expectations when it came to men.

"It's nice out here," he said, scanning the lush lawns that surrounded the house.

"I can't imagine living anywhere else." And she couldn't. Living on the vineyard, being a part of the land, was one of the best things about being adopted by the Cartwrights. Their love, of course, was another. Even if Lissa didn't quite fit in, she never doubted their affection.

As they reached the wood-planked front porch of the guest house, she turned the antique brass knob and opened the door. "It's not much, but it's cozy."

Actually, Lissa thought the little house was pretty special. She and her mom had decorated it in a country French decor, with café-style window coverings, a blue plaid sofa and a coordinating floral, overstuffed easy chair.

"It gets pretty chilly at night." She pointed to the thermostat on the light-oak-paneled wall. "You can adjust the heat to your comfort."

He nodded toward the stone hearth that boasted a stack of firewood, kindling and matches. "I'd rather have a fire."

So would Lissa, if she were staying in the cottage. A fire was cozier. And more romantic.

Darn it. Those blasted romance books were getting to her again. And the sooner she could box them up and chuck them into a blazing fire, the better off she'd be.

"There's a kitchenette," she said, "in case you prefer to take your meals alone. But knowing my mom, she'll insist that you join us."

"I eat most of my meals in restaurants, so I'll be looking forward to some home cooking."

"Well, good. Mom will be pleased." Lissa would be, too, but she battled the girlish rush of excitement. "I'll show you the rest of the place."

As she entered the hallway and glanced through the open doorway to the bedroom, her gaze landed upon the blue-and-white checkered comforter on the double bed she'd made up yesterday.

She caught a whiff of his musky, highland scent— mountain fresh and wild—and felt his presence close in on her, as though she might find him inches away, if she turned around.

Her pulse and her breathing seemed to escalate, but her feet remained rooted to the spot.

"Nice room," he said.

Unable to help herself, she turned and caught him merely inches away.

Watching her.

And he wasn't smiling—at least, not in a teasing sort of way.

Something passed between them, although she wasn't sure what it was. Could it be sexual awareness?

Nah. Impossible. Not on his part, anyway.

She cleared her throat, which seemed to be another habit she'd mysteriously acquired today. "The bathroom is down the hall, next to the linen closet. The cupboards and shelves are stocked, so you should find everything you need."

"Thank you." His voice wrapped around her like a tartan plaid on a winter night.

Oh, brother. Those books were going right into a moving trash truck the first chance she got.

"Well," she said, trying to ignore the rush of sexual awareness she didn't know how to deal with. "I guess I'll leave and let you get unpacked."

"Don't," he said.

Huh? "Don't what?"

"Don't leave yet." He tossed her a boyish grin. "I spotted a bottle of wine on the kitchen counter."

"It's our sauvignon blanc. I thought you might like to have a glass now and then."

"That sounds good now. Will you join me? On the front porch?"

The offer took her aback. But it also excited her.

She tried desperately to tell herself it was a continuation of business. A way of relaxing over drinks. The kind of things businessmen did all the time.

Yet she couldn't help making just a wee bit more out of the invitation than was probably wise for someone with a virgin heart—just ripe for the picking.

And ready to bruise.

## Chapter Two

The wooden deck in front of the cottage overlooked the main house, as well as the fertile vineyard.

Sitting at a glass-topped, wrought-iron table, Sullivan and Lissa enjoyed a stunning view as they shared a glass of wine and watched the sun sink low into the western sky.

"Your sister doesn't look anything like you," Sullivan said by way of small talk. He'd noticed how much Eileen and her mother had resembled each other when they'd brought lunch down to the office.

In fact, Lissa didn't look much like her father, either. Ken Cartwright was short and stocky, with a receding blond hairline and a ruddy complexion. He wasn't much to look at, but he was a hell of a nice guy.

Lissa fingered the stem of her wineglass, as though his comment might have bothered her. And he was sorry he'd brought it up. If he could, he'd reel in the thoughtless words.

She looked up and caught his eye. "I don't look like my family because I'm adopted."

Whoops. He hadn't meant to get so personal. And he wasn't sure how to make up for the klutzy attempt at conversation, so he merely nodded and said, "You've got a nice family."

"Yes, I do." She took a sip of wine. "Do you have any brothers or sisters?"

"Nope. I'm an only child."

"That sounds like it might have been sad growing up."

He shrugged. His childhood had been pretty crappy, but not because he didn't have siblings. "I had a lot of cousins to play with."

"Tell me about your family," she said, settling into the chitchat.

Sullivan rarely talked about himself. Nor about personal matters. But maybe because he'd accidentally prodded the adoption revelation out of her, he felt as though turnaround was fair play.

"My folks both loved me, I guess. But their relationship was stormy, and their marriage ended in divorce before I hit middle school."

"That's too bad."

It was. From an early age, Sullivan had dreamed of belonging to a stable family. Maybe that's why he'd married so early. He'd been ready for kids, picket fences and family vacations. But his wife had refused to consider having his baby, then had left him for another man.

Her leaving had not only dashed his unrealistic dreams and damaged his heart, but it had been a real eye-opening experience. She'd taught him a simple lesson. Sullivan wasn't, and maybe never had been, destined for family life.

"It was no big deal," he lied. "Some people shouldn't ever get married."

"What kind of people?"

Her eyes held a naïveté that surprised him, but he smiled and filled in the blanks as generically as he could. "The kind of people who make promises they don't keep."

His parents' marital nightmare had been brutal for a kid to endure. And his own divorce—six years ago—had been pretty tough.

But hey. He'd bounced back quickly.

His first effort to rebound was by having a few relationships, mostly with shallow socialites who would never tempt him to put his heart on the line again. And it had helped. A lot.

"Funny thing about my folks," he said, wanting to focus his thoughts on his parents' divorce and not his own. "My father's family had money and status. And they could trace their lineage back to the *Mayflower*. But that never seemed to be good enough for my mom."

"Why not?"

He would have shrugged off her question, tried to avoid getting into a conversation that was too deep, one that reminded him of his own failed marriage and was too damn revealing. But for some reason, he cut to the chase. "Some women want more than some men can provide."

She furrowed her brow, but didn't respond. And he wondered whether she had any idea what he was talking about.

Probably not. But that was as far as it would go.

It was bad enough that Sullivan had to relive history in his mind. He didn't need to open himself up to memories best left forgotten.

Lissa wasn't sure what Sullivan meant. And maybe she should ask. But the fact was, they had nothing in common. Nothing on which to build any kind of relationship.

She was adopted and didn't know her biological parents, and he had a lineage tracing back to the *Mayflower.*

He was outgoing and worldly—or so it seemed. And she was as plain and boring as a dust mop.

Still, she was impressed by his business sense and flattered by his charm.

Just then, Barney growled, as though facing a monstrous foe, then began tugging at Sullivan's pant leg.

"Oh, Barney!" Lissa set down her wineglass and

picked up the pesky pooch. "Don't chew on people. That's why you have toys."

Sullivan didn't appear to be bothered by the possibility of a rip or tear in what had to be expensive slacks. "He's a cute little guy. Looks like he has a little collie in him."

She laughed. "And a little beagle and Australian shepherd. In fact, it wouldn't surprise me if he had a bit of dachshund thrown into the mix."

Sullivan chuckled. "He *is* pretty long and close to the ground. Where'd you get him?"

"At the dog pound. His number was up, so I guess you could say I saved his life. They were going to put him to sleep if no one adopted him by the end of that day."

For a moment, Lissa thought about how her parents had chosen her over other orphaned babies.

As a child, she would fantasize about her biological parents, the people who'd given her up. She often thought of them as young lovers, forced apart like Romeo and Juliet.

Once she'd imagined herself as the daughter of royalty, stolen by gypsies and taken to the Children's Connection, where her adoptive parents took pity upon her.

But as she grew older, she put away her childhood fantasies, accepting the fact that her biological parents just hadn't wanted to be bothered with a baby.

Or, more important, that they hadn't wanted to be bothered with *her*.

That didn't, of course, mean that she didn't ever think about them. That she didn't ever wonder who they were or where they lived.

Or whether they ever thought about her.

Jared Cambry sat with his wife behind the closed doors of his home office and studied the telephone he'd just hung up. He glanced at Danielle, who stood beside him, silent and hopeful. Her puffy, red-rimmed eyes undoubtedly mirrored his own.

"What did Dr. Chambers say?" A sense of expectancy lingered in her voice, although her expression reflected the fear and despair they'd been living with since shortly after moving back to Portland.

Jared cleared his throat, trying to break free from the emotion lodged in his chest. "He said that the preliminary tests prove that none of us are a match."

Danielle let out a sob she'd been holding back, and Jared quickly reached her side, taking her in his arms, trying to offer whatever support he could.

"We're going to lose him," she cried. "I feel so helpless."

So did Jared.

Before the diagnosis, their lives had been perfect. Charmed.

He and Danielle were crazy about each other and had a great marriage. They'd thought their family was complete with a son and a daughter. But just eight years ago, they'd been blessed with an unexpected baby they'd named Mark.

Even as an infant, Mark had a joyful heart and a smile that lingered on his lips. He was a loving child, and he soon became the light of their lives.

As Danielle cried, Jared stroked her back, nestled his cheek against the dark-brown curls of her hair. Closed his eyes and blinked back his own tears.

God, this was hard. Brutal.

He held his wife close, trying to share his strength—or maybe to absorb some of hers.

Danielle was an admirable woman. And devoted to her family. At times, he felt as though she was the one who held them all together.

She had teaching credentials—high-school history—but since the birth of their oldest child, she'd been a stay-at-home mom who thrived on being the kind of mother every kid deserved.

Three active children kept her calendar full and her days busy, as she chauffeured them to orthodontic appointments, school events, piano lessons and Little League games. But she still found time to volunteer as a tutor in the adult literacy program at the library.

Jared looked at his wife, unable to tell her everything would be all right. How could he when he didn't know if that was true?

"I'd thought Shawna would be the one," she said. "She and Mark are so much alike."

At fifteen, their daughter promised to be a lovely young woman. But the match could have easily been seventeen-year-old Chad, who was already proving to be a fine athlete, as well as a scholar.

They'd been blessed with three beautiful children. But all of that paled against the stark reality that had rocked their entire world during a youth soccer game.

While playing halfback for the Dragons, eight-year-old Mark had collapsed on the field. Jared had missed the game, since he'd been away on a business trip. But Danielle was there. And she'd rushed Mark to Portland General Hospital, where it was determined the boy had a rare blood disorder.

Without a bone-marrow transplant, their youngest son wouldn't live past the age of ten.

Jared and Danielle had been devastated by the diagnosis but had immediately had the entire family tested as potential donors. Unfortunately, it turned out no one was a match.

"What do we do now?" she asked. "Besides pray that a suitable donor is found in time."

Jared knew there was one last family member out there—somewhere. Someone who might prove to be a match. But finding him or her might be as difficult as finding an unrelated donor in the bone-marrow registry—possible, but against the odds.

"Sit down, Danni," Jared told his wife. "I have something to tell you."

She took a tissue from the wad she'd recently begun to carry in her pocket, wiped her eyes, then sat on the tufted leather seat near the lamp. She didn't say anything. She merely twisted the tissue in her hands and waited for Jared to speak.

"When I was seventeen, I had a one-night stand with a teenaged girl that resulted in pregnancy."

Her brow furrowed, and she looked at him aghast, as though she'd been slapped. "How could you have kept that from me?"

"The girl just disappeared," he said, wishing he'd said something to Danni sooner. They didn't keep secrets from each other. Except for this one, he supposed. But he hadn't known how to tell her, so he'd kept putting it off. "Her name was Olivia. And I'm not sure where she is, or whether she kept the baby or not. But that means we have one more possibility of finding a related match."

His pretty dark-haired wife looked shocked, disappointed and more than a little bit angry. And he couldn't blame her for feeling that way.

"You got a girl pregnant?" she asked. "And you don't even know what she did with the baby?"

"That's the size of it. At this point."

Years ago, Olivia had told him babies were a blessing. Jared hadn't realized she'd been right. Not until Danni had given birth to Chad. And even though he'd been caught up in the miracle of his son's birth, he'd been reminded of his firstborn—a child he'd suggested Olivia abort.

His conscience did a real number on him.

And each time he'd held Danni's hand during the birth of his next two children, thoughts of a faceless newborn came back to haunt him.

Why hadn't he looked for Olivia sooner? He'd intended to.

As the senior attorney in his own corporate law firm with successful offices in several states, Jared had recently moved his family back to Portland, where he'd been born, in order to establish an Oregon-based office.

He'd actually planned to look up Olivia and ask about the baby. And although he didn't usually wade into psychological waters, maybe that was the underlying reason he'd wanted to open the Oregon office himself, rather than send one of his partners. But Jared hadn't gotten a chance to look for her yet.

"When Olivia told me she was pregnant, I offered her money for an abortion, but she refused it. She told me she wanted to keep the baby." Jared rested a hip against the polished, hardwood desk. "When I got settled in the dorms in Phoenix, I called her a couple of times. She was thinking about giving the child up for adoption, which would have been a better idea for her."

"So what did she decide to do?" Danielle asked.

"I'm not sure. I called her again to ask how she was doing and offer her some money." Jared raked a hand through his hair and sighed. "I wasn't working, but I had a small savings account I could drain. Anyway, I pressed her to give the baby up for adoption, which I thought was the best solution. But she flipped out, saying she didn't need my help, then hung up on me."

"And that's how it ended?"

"No. I called her back the next day. Her mother took the message, but Olivia didn't return that call. Or the next one."

"So you just let her go?"

"Not exactly. I figured the baby would be due in the spring, so I called again. But their phone had been disconnected, and there was no forwarding number."

"So how do we go about finding her now?" Danni asked. It seemed that her sense of betrayal had been overcome by her concern for Mark.

"I've got my work cut out for me, but with my investigative skills and enough money to hire the best PI in Oregon, I'll find Olivia and the child."

Jared just hoped he would find them in time.

Dinner around the Cartwright table was a pleasant experience, and Sullivan was glad he'd taken his clients up on the offer to join them.

They dined on grilled filet mignon, tossed salad with an incredible—and undoubtedly homemade— vinaigrette dressing, twice-baked potatoes and a crusty loaf of bread that had filled the house with a warm, yeasty aroma.

Donna Cartwright might be closing in on sixty— or maybe even past it—but she was an attractive woman, with shoulder-length strawberry-blond hair like Eileen's.

And she was a darn good cook. If Sullivan hadn't

already complimented her several times, he'd do so again.

"Tell me," Donna said, resting her elbows on the linen-draped table and eyeing Sullivan with a warm smile. "Where are you from?"

"Originally, I'm from Charleston. But I've been living in Portland for the past five years."

"Oh, really?" She appeared interested. Almost too interested, it seemed. "Does your family still live in Charleston?"

"Yes, they do." His mom and dad kept separate residences in the same prestigious part of town. And in spite of their efforts to avoid each other at all costs, they wouldn't ever move. They had too much invested in the land, the community—the banks.

"That's nice," Donna said. "Why did you choose to move to Oregon?"

Uh-oh. Was she making small talk? Or fishing for information about his marital status and eligibility, like some mothers of single daughters did? After all, she still had one more to marry off.

He ought to give Donna the benefit of the doubt, but he couldn't help staying on his toes, ready to make a mad dash for cover. "I moved to Portland for business reasons." *His* business—and nobody else's.

If Sullivan had to see his ex-wife on Gregory Atwater's arm at one more society function, he might have done something to embarrass himself. It had been tough enough living down the fiasco that sent his parents' marriage spiraling into court, so as soon as his divorce had become final, he'd gotten the hell out of Charleston. And five years later, here he was. He'd moved practically from one corner of the United States to another.

Could he have gotten any farther away from his ex or his war-torn childhood?

"Portland is a nice city," Donna said.

Sullivan nodded. "I like it."

Her blue eyes sparkled in a doting mama way, and any red-blooded single man could see her cogs and wheels turning, could sense her maternal game plan. So he braced himself for another round of the bachelor two-step, a defensive move he'd quickly mastered.

He took a sip of wine and savored the taste of the Valencia merlot that was every bit as good as Ken and Lissa had told him it was.

"Are you married?" Donna asked.

Ah, he'd been right. The tenacious woman had finally gone for the jugular. Fortunately, he'd become adept at maintaining his privacy and his happy-go-lucky bachelor status. "No, I'm not married."

"It must be lonely for you."

Lissa, who'd just lifted her wineglass for a sip, choked momentarily, then pressed a white linen napkin to her mouth before saying, "Excuse me."

Sullivan stole a glance her way and realized she wasn't at all comfortable with her mother's shift to yenta mode. He sympathized with the young woman who probably was as happy to be unattached as he was. If she weren't, he suspected she'd dress differently.

"I enjoy the freedom to come and go as I choose," he told the mother.

"Well, that's wonderful," Donna said, although Sullivan had a feeling she thought it was wonderful that he was a bachelor. And that she'd quickly put aside the fact he liked being single.

The older woman tucked a wavy strand of shoulder-length hair behind her ear and continued to hone in on her target. "Surely a man like you must be seeing someone special."

Sullivan had been down this road many times before. "I date several ladies, Mrs. Cartwright. And each of them is pretty special."

"You'll have to forgive my wife for prying into your life," Ken said, with a chuckle. "She thinks everyone needs to be as happily married as we are."

Yeah, well Sullivan's experience told him that many women liked to play matchmaker, whether they were happily married or not.

For some reason, the female of the species seemed to harbor a happily-ever-after fantasy, but he didn't hold on to that illusion any longer. Katherine and Clarence Grayson might have been proper and genteel when they socialized with Charleston's wealthy families. But behind the walls of the family estate, they hadn't behaved any differently than a warring couple in the seedier part of town. The broken dishes and figurines merely cost more money to replace.

"I'm afraid growing up in the midst of marital misery has made me gun-shy," Sullivan said.

Donna seemed to take his statement into consideration and didn't immediately speak.

Sullivan slid a glance at Lissa, who sat up straight—much like a rocket ready to blast off. She probably needed a break as badly as he did.

He shifted in his seat toward Ken, intending to send the conversation in a safer direction, and caught the vintner's eyes. "This merlot is excellent. I think we'll need to work the marketing strategy around it, too."

"I thought you'd like it." The older man leaned back in his chair. "But you haven't tasted anything until you try Lissa's new blend."

"I'm looking forward to it." This time, when Sullivan glanced at Lissa, she didn't seem to be quite as tense. Maybe more like a firecracker than a rocket.

He didn't usually sympathize with single women whose mothers were dead set on seeing them in white lace and a veil, but shy and unassuming Lissa tugged at a sympathetic vein in his heart.

Besides, from what he'd learned while researching his new clients, Lissa loved the vineyard and had a real head for business. The people he'd spoken to referred to her as a career woman, with nothing on her mind but the success of the family vineyard.

And that assessment had been validated by what he'd observed earlier today. He figured she meant to make Valencia Vineyards her life.

Apparently, her mother hadn't wanted to accept that decision.

"Can I get anyone seconds?" Donna asked.

"Not me." Sullivan leaned away from the table. "I haven't eaten this well in ages."

Again, he looked at Lissa, who seemed to be studying her plate. Unless she'd gotten a full heaping of seconds when he wasn't looking, she hadn't eaten much at all. He had a feeling the mother-hen inquisition had annoyed her, too.

And why shouldn't it bother her? She had a business relationship with Sullivan to think about. And they had a lot of work ahead of them. Romantic thoughts would only get in the way, distract them from their focus.

As soon as he could get her alone, he'd have to let her know that this stuff happened to him all the time, and that she shouldn't be the least bit embarrassed, not on his account.

"Decaffeinated coffee anyone?" Donna asked, obviously in her element as a gracious hostess.

"I'll have a cup," Ken said.

The attractive older woman tossed Sullivan a pleasant smile. "How about you?"

"No thank you." Sullivan was ready for the evening to end, especially since he wasn't about to lay himself open for any more questions. And he didn't particularly like seeing Lissa look as if she were sitting in a dental chair, waiting for a root canal.

The dark-haired young woman gathered her nearly

full plate and silverware, along with those of her father and Sullivan, then went into the kitchen, followed by her mother.

Minutes later, when they returned with coffee and slices of cheesecake with a raspberry sauce, Donna wore a solemn expression.

Had she been chastised by her daughter? Probably so, because Lissa looked a bit more comfortable than when she'd been seated at the table.

No telling what—if anything—had gone on in the kitchen, but Sullivan had a feeling Lissa had asked her mother to back off. He hoped the older woman's curiosity had been sated. For everyone's sake.

Actually, Donna Cartwright was a nice lady. Just determined to marry off her last daughter, he supposed.

But Sullivan wasn't in the market for a wife. Not now. Not ever. And the sooner the Cartwrights understood that, the better.

Lissa couldn't wait for the horrible evening to end. What must Sullivan think of her—or her mother?

She knew her mom didn't mean any harm, but if Lissa ever decided to go on a manhunt, she didn't want her mother to pave the way.

At least after their little chat in the kitchen, Mom had gotten the message that Lissa wasn't looking for a husband.

Of course, if she'd been more like Eileen, Sullivan Grayson would have made a great catch. But she wasn't anything like Eileen. And besides, he'd made himself clear. He was happy being a bachelor.

"The cheesecake was delicious," Sullivan said. "In fact, the entire meal was out of this world. I'm going to put on weight while I work here."

Donna beamed like a Girl Scout with a new merit badge. "Well, I'm glad you decided to join us."

Relieved to see the stressful dinner conversation winding down, Lissa pushed her seat away from the table. "If you don't mind, I'll slip into the kitchen and wash the dishes."

Sullivan stood and reached for his desert plate and fork. "Let me help you."

Lissa nearly dropped the cup and saucer she'd picked up, but for the life of her, she couldn't speak, couldn't object. Of course, knowing her mother, she wouldn't have to.

"How thoughtful," Donna told Sullivan, even though it was her habit to shoo off any guest who volunteered to help in the kitchen. "Ken and I will just go on to bed."

At seven-thirty?

Ken glanced at his watch, furrowed his brow, then cocked his head. "It's pretty early for bed, don't you think?"

Lissa didn't take time to listen to her mother's explanation. Instead, she disappeared into the kitchen.

Unfortunately, Sullivan followed her.

She wanted to tell him that she needed some time

alone, to regroup after her mother's lame attempt to find her a husband. But she kept her mouth shut for a while, until she could figure out what to say.

"I noticed how uncomfortable you were in there," he said.

Lissa stood at the sink, her hand frozen on the faucet, warm water flowing from the spigot.

"But don't let it get to you," he said. "I'm used to that kind of thing."

What kind of thing was that? Mothers who tried to find husbands for their spinster daughters?

For goodness' sake. Even if Lissa had been willing to accept her mother's help, the least her mom could do was find a man who actually wanted to settle down.

She turned around to face him, catching a whiff of his taunting highland scent and falling into his hazel gaze. Her heart skipped a beat, and she tried desperately to hide her feelings, her insecurities, all of those things that had worked against her since meeting Sullivan.

"Just so you know," she said, "I have no plans to get married. Ever."

Okay, so she lied. Sort of. She had dreams, of course, enhanced by the stack of romances on her nightstand. But no *plans*. She knew better than to believe a frog could turn into a princess.

"I had a feeling you felt the same way I do," Sullivan said. "Don't you hate it when people try to screw up our contentment?"

She nodded, even though she wasn't all that contented. But at least she didn't have to deal with embarrassment.

Sullivan slid her a crooked smile that made her knees go weak. What an interesting mouth he had.

A mouth that undoubtedly knew how to kiss a woman.

Milt Preston had kissed her once, after their date to the Christmas formal. Lissa had actually been looking forward to it, since Eileen had told her about making out with Jason Crowley in the back seat of his Mustang.

But her first kiss hadn't been anything like her sister's romantic experience. In fact, it had been just plain awful.

Instead of taking it slow and easy, Milt had opened his mouth and zeroed in on her, slapping a wet tongue across her lips, trying to poke and prod his way inside her mouth. She'd pushed him away, but the kiss had left her feeling dirty, sticky and wet.

Disgusted and disappointed, she'd left him standing on the porch and escaped inside the house, where she dashed upstairs to brush her teeth and rid herself of his taste.

Her efforts hadn't worked, so she'd tried a shower. But not even hot, sudsy water could wash away the yucky memory.

As Sullivan squeezed a squirt of dish soap into the sink, his presence closed in on her. The side of his arm brushed against her shoulder, leaving a warm tingle after he moved away. "Would you like to wash or dry?"

"It doesn't matter," she said, trying to focus on the mundane household task. "Which would you rather do?"

"Since I don't know where anything goes, I'll wash."

As the soap formed a frothy foam, Lissa's thoughts drifted from the kitchen sink to a bubble bath in a candlelit bathroom. She'd read a book once where the hero and heroine had showered together, lathering each other until their passion blazed.

Oh, for Pete's sake. She was letting her imagination and her hormones get the best of her.

Sullivan handed her a rinsed plate, and she quickly wiped it dry. They didn't talk much, and before long, the kitchen was back in order.

"I'll see you tomorrow morning," he said, before leaving her alone with her thoughts.

Or rather with her adolescent hormones raging.

What would she have done if the guy had actually come on to her?

She would have skedaddled like a scaredy cat, no doubt.

But Lissa couldn't help wondering what Sullivan's kiss would be like. She had a feeling she might like to let his tongue inside her mouth, but she shrugged off the possibility. A woman like her knew better than to dwell on an impossible dream.

Or to dwell on a handsome bachelor with a playful smile and more than his fair share of pheromones.

## Chapter Three

At nine the next morning, Sullivan met Lissa at the vineyard office, a small, wood-paneled room that held file cabinets, a computer and an expansive antique desk. It looked like the usual workplace, but a mauve, overstuffed sofa against the far wall and a kitchenette in the corner suggested Lissa spent a lot of time here.

And so did the little puppy that lay curled up on a doggie bed by the potbellied stove.

Sullivan watched as Lissa made a pot of coffee from beans she'd ground only a moment ago.

As she had yesterday, she wore a plain, loose-fitting blouse and the same style of baggy trousers—this time a drab brown.

Why did she choose such dull colors when green or blue would highlight those expressive eyes?

Her mother and sister dressed stylishly, so he had to assume that Lissa preferred to be nondescript. Was that so she would be taken more seriously in the business world? Maybe. It made sense.

As she worked, he watched her from behind. She'd woven her hair into a long, single braid that hung down her back. He figured the strands might reach her waist, if she let it free.

Lissa turned, facing him. "How do you like your coffee?"

"Sugar," he said. "No cream."

He'd expected her to turn around and return to her work, but she didn't move. She just stood there like a deer in the meadow, head raised, eyes focused on a potential foe.

"What are you looking at?" she asked.

"Nothing." He hadn't meant to be gawking. But long hair on women had always fascinated him.

If he and Lissa were dating, and his opinion meant something to her, he'd suggest she wear it loose, over her shoulders and down her back. But they weren't dating, so he kept his opinion to himself.

Still, he had half a notion to tease her a bit, to see if she would loosen up. He was flirtatious by nature, and the playful banter between a man and a woman came easily to him. But he'd better back off. His relationship with Lissa was strictly business. And he'd be wise to keep it that way.

The coffee began to gurgle and sputter as it dribbled into the pot, and soon, the aroma of a robust brew permeated the room.

Lissa withdrew a crystal sugar bowl and two mugs from the small overhead cupboard, and he watched the braid swish along the curve of her back. Yesterday she'd worn her hair twisted in a knot. Did she prefer it trussed up and out of the way?

Maybe she disliked it long, but was too busy to go to the salon for a cut and style. It didn't matter, he supposed. But the woman intrigued him for some reason.

Her shyness maybe? Her focus on business and finances? Or maybe because he suspected there was a lot more going on behind those vibrant green eyes than most people knew.

As she handed him a cup of coffee, their fingers brushed, and something passed between them. A soft and gentle awareness, a lingering connection of some kind.

Had that initial little spark of attraction he'd felt for her grown?

If so, he wouldn't act upon it. Lissa Cartwright was too complex, too real. Too rooted in family and responsibility. When he'd been younger and more naive, she would have been the kind of woman he could have cared for—before he'd learned not to believe in romantic dreams.

She snagged his gaze. "Did anyone ever tell you that you have the most interesting eyes?"

*He* had interesting eyes? Hell, she was the one with

eyes that would stop a man dead in his tracks. But he didn't want to go there.

"My eyes aren't anything special," he said. "They're just brown—or hazel, I guess."

"The sunlight is coming through that window." She nodded to the pane of glass on the east wall. "And it highlights little gold flecks. The color is really unusual."

Sullivan stiffened. He wasn't comfortable with her looking at him like that, as if he had something she'd never seen before, as if she thought he was someone special. But he quickly scoffed it off.

She'd only noticed his eye color because of the way the morning sun poured through the window. And she'd merely made a comment, which for some goofy reason, he continued to ponder.

Did his eyes really have gold flecks? If he had a mirror handy, he'd take a peek, just to see what she saw.

"The color is beautiful," she said, her voice going kind of soft.

"Just in the sunlight." He cast off her compliment and tried to shift the focus away from himself. "You're the one with a stunning pair of peepers."

She cocked her head slightly, as though trying to decipher his words. "Me?"

"What's the matter? Surely, you've had tons of compliments over the years."

"Mostly from my mom," she said, cheeks starting

to flush. "Although maybe some lady in a grocery store said something once or twice."

Well, now. See? *That's* what happened when a person tried to downplay their looks so no one would notice them. Sometimes it worked.

"You do have pretty eyes," he told her. "Whether you believe it or not. They're the color of new leaves."

Great. Now he was talking like a friggin' poet.

She thanked him, yet still appeared skeptical.

"By the way," he added, reneging on his earlier decision to keep his opinion to himself. "You ought to wear green or blue. To bring out the color of your eyes, you know."

She glanced down at a pair of brown, rubber-soled loafers—shoes that looked a lot like the ones his great-aunt Clara wore. Then she looked up at him with a doe-eyed gaze that reached deep into his chest.

Whoa. That was a little too close for comfort.

He took his mug, then turned and strode toward the sofa—but only because it was on the far side of the room. Away from her, away from the weird stuff he felt whenever she looked at him that way.

Lissa Cartwright was *not* the kind of woman he pursued. And she was certainly off-limits until his business with the vineyard was over.

From across the room, and from a much safer distance, he turned, took a sip of coffee then asked, "How about a tour of the vineyard?"

"Sure. After we go over the guest list for the dinner

party tomorrow night. I'd like you to know who'll be there ahead of time.'' Lissa reached into the top desk drawer, withdrew a sheet of paper and set it upon the oak desktop.

''What's the purpose of the gathering?'' he asked.

''We want to start a buzz about the new blend. So we've invited several local vintners and a reporter from *Through the Grapevine,* a local magazine that has expanded its circulation and should bring in more tourists and interest in the wine region.''

While Lissa described each guest and gave Sullivan a rundown of their holdings and achievements in the industry, they finished their coffee. Then, leaving the puppy to snooze on its bed, they set out to see every nook and cranny of the vineyard.

The air was fresh and clean from a rain they'd had a couple days before, and as they strolled through the parklike grounds, Sullivan was amazed at the beauty of the place. Besides row upon row of grapes that grew on the rolling hillsides, the lush property displayed a stone-lined fishpond that hosted several mallards and two black swans.

The manicured lawns nearly begged for people to sit and relish the peaceful sight.

''Why haven't you opened up Valencia Vineyards for visitors and tastings?'' he asked. ''The grounds are beautiful, and I think you could really draw in a fair number of tourists each month.''

''We've thought about it,'' Lissa said. ''But we've always preferred our privacy.''

"You called me in for advice," he reminded her.

"And my father and I intend to consider everything you suggest." She led him into the new winery that had replaced the older facility they'd used in the past.

"The construction of this building was a major expense," she explained. "And some hidden costs depleted our funds more than we're comfortable with. That's the primary reason we brought you in as a marketing consultant."

"Then you're in luck. I'm always glad to offer my services."

She bit her bottom lip and looked at him out of the corner of her eye. She wore an interesting expression.

One that seemed to ask how far he'd go to offer his services.

After they'd explored the new winery, Sullivan said, "You've done a wonderful job creating a modern and efficient operation."

Lissa thought so, too. "Thank you."

"And if you decide to open the vineyard and winery for tours, word will quickly spread."

"You're probably right." She'd have to discuss it with her father. After all, he was the one who valued his privacy.

"So, where's that killer new blend I've been hearing about?" Sullivan asked. "Do I have to wait for that dinner party tomorrow night?"

"No. I can let you have a taste now."

"Great." He flashed her a smile that made her

heart skip a beat, which was surprising, since she'd grown a lot more comfortable with the man over the past few hours.

Lissa led him to the tasting room, then took two glasses from the stash they kept in a solid oak cabinet. The walls were lined with wine bottles tucked into crisscrossed shelves. But her special blend remained in an oak barrel that appeared to be only a decoration. She pulled the tap, filled both glasses and offered one to Sullivan.

Before taking a drink, he clinked his goblet against hers and offered a toast. "To the special lady who made this wine."

Lissa appreciated his thoughtful gesture, but didn't take a sip. Instead, she watched for Sullivan's reaction, studying the good-looking man over the rim of her glass.

She guessed he was a bit of a playboy. But how could he not be, with those sexy eyes and that flirty smile?

Sullivan Grayson was too darn attractive for his own good. Or rather, for her own good.

Yet he also had a wealth of sexual experience and could make a woman's first time special. At least, she suspected he would.

If Lissa had any courage at all, she'd suggest a brief affair. After all, who would get hurt? Not her. She had no illusions about falling in love.

And he certainly wouldn't get hurt, since he'd probably never given a thought to settling down. Besides, once his job with Valencia Vineyards was finished, he'd be on his way. And that reason, on top of her fierce attraction, made him a perfect first-time lover—if she were inclined to act out the silly fantasy.

For Pete's sake. What if he wasn't the least bit interested in being her one-time lover? And if he were, her attempts to please him would be clumsy at best. Either way, she'd be embarrassed. Humiliated. Mortified.

Fortunately, she was too shy to even suggest it.

Sullivan closed his eyes and appeared to be savoring the taste of the wine.

She held her breath, waiting for him to comment.

When his gaze locked on hers, his expression grew serious. "Lissa, this is incredible. I'm no expert, by any means, but I know what I like."

She blew out the breath she'd been holding. "Really?"

"It's great." His eyes verified his sincerity. "With the fresh, unique taste we'll need a name, something that will reflect the newness, as well as the appeal."

"I agree." Both she and her dad hoped that the wine would increase sales—with the right marketing strategy. "Any ideas?"

He thought for a while, then broke into a lazy grin. "There's one word we need to use in the name."

"What's that?" She took a sip from her glass.

"Virgin."

*Virgin?* Lissa choked, sputtered and coughed.

"Are you okay?"

She cleared her throat. "I'm fine. I guess it just went down the wrong pipe."

The explanation seemed to appease him, although she really hadn't swallowed wrong. His comment had surprised her. Heck, the way Sullivan said *virgin* made it seem as though he thought virginity held some kind of merit, some value.

If that were the case, maybe her inexperience wouldn't scare him away.

The idea of losing her innocence to Sullivan made her imagination soar. Of course, he'd probably be shocked if she suggested it—assuming she had the nerve to broach the subject. After all, she'd never been suggestive or forward—sexually speaking.

Besides, Sullivan had his share of beautiful women. What would make him settle for a nobody like her?

She could, of course, dream. Couldn't she?

Lissa had become good at fantasizing. Which certainly helped, because the thought of going to her deathbed as a virgin was downright depressing, if she dwelled upon it.

"Virgin Mist," he said. "Now, *that's* a name that would appeal to the masses. It promises something new and fresh. What do you think?"

Before she could tell him it worked for her, the big, oval-topped door opened, and her father walked into the tasting room.

"How'd you like the tour?" he asked Sullivan.

"It was great. Enlightening. And the tour director

really knows her stuff.'' Sullivan shot Lissa a smile that nearly wobbled her knees.

''Well, she ought to. Lissa loves the vineyard.'' Ken slid an arm around her shoulder and gave her a squeeze. ''In fact, she's the daughter who takes after me.''

Sullivan chuckled, and Lissa smiled.

It was nice when her father said things like that, when he seemed to forget that she was adopted.

But they both knew there was another man out there—somewhere. A faceless man who could actually lay claim to her genetic makeup.

In his Portland law office, Jared studied a legal brief, yet his mind wasn't on his work.

He was still reeling over the fact that the clock was ticking. That he still didn't know anything about Olivia Maddison or her child. That the PI he'd hired had been due to check in ten minutes ago.

Just as he glanced at his gold wristwatch, a beep sounded over the intercom system.

''Mr. Cambry?'' his secretary asked.

''Yes.''

''Mr. Hastings with Investigative Specialties is here to see you.''

''Send him in.'' Jared was eager to know what the investigator had learned, whether he'd found Olivia yet.

Moments later, Sam Hastings entered. He was a big

man with a full head of blond hair and prominent brows that shaded pensive eyes.

Jared stood and reached across the table to shake hands. "Any news?"

"Yeah. I'm afraid so." Sam blew out a sigh. "Olivia is dead."

Dead? Jared slowly dropped to his seat. "What happened?"

"Car accident. Twenty-seven years ago."

"And the baby?" Jared asked, heart pounding. Had the child died, too?

"It was made a ward of the state and put up for adoption."

"Now what?" Jared asked.

"Well, let me tell you what I've learned, what we've got to work with." Sam took the seat in front of the desk, as though the revelation might take a while. "Olivia and her mother were involved in a traffic accident. Mrs. Maddison was killed instantly, and Olivia was critically injured. Paramedics took her to Portland General Hospital, where she remained in a coma until she died a few weeks later."

"So, what do the hospital records show?" Jared asked.

"That's the problem." Sam took a deep breath, then slowly let it out. "A few months after Olivia's death, a severe storm caused a power surge through-out the county. The hospital's backup generator kicked on a few seconds later, and the patients were okay. But because the computers are old and the hospital birth clinic lacked funding until the new owners, the Logans, came on board, the computer files were either lost or are nearly impossible to retrieve.''

''But surely there are paper files, not just the computer entries,'' Jared said, hoping his efforts to find his firstborn hadn't struck out completely.

''I'm afraid not. When the power surged, it caused a circuit breaker in the clinic to spark. Some of the sparks landed on a cutesy wall hanging they used as a nursery decoration. A fire started, eliminating a number of paper files regarding adoptions, foster care situations, fertility information and other things.''

Jared could hear his pulse pounding in his ears, could feel his palms growing moist, his stomach knotting. ''Are you telling me that we can't find out what happened to the baby?''

''The child survived the accident, was born prematurely and put up for adoption through the Children's Connection. What we've got are bits and pieces of information.''

''Like what?'' Jared asked, his hopes resurrecting.

''A name, an address, a gender...but I'm not sure what matches up.''

''Let's see what you've got, and we'll take it from there.''

Could that baby he'd fathered twenty-seven years ago be the miracle they needed?

That evening, as Lissa prepared for bed, she couldn't find Barney. And when she asked her folks, neither of them had seen him, either. Obviously, the rascally pup had sneaked out again. But it was too dangerous for him to stay outside all night.

She grabbed her robe and put on a pair of slippers, intent on searching the grounds.

As she stood on the front porch and scanned the lawn and the pond, she spotted Sullivan sitting quietly on the deck of the cottage, her puppy in his lap.

"Looking for this little guy?" he called out.

"Yes." She touched the sash of her blue chenille robe, checking to see that it was snug, then fingered the edge of the lapel, making sure it covered her flannel nightgown.

She walked across the grass, then made her way over the small, wooden bridge.

All the while, Sullivan watched her.

She felt weird letting him see her like this, yet she was probably more bundled up than in her street clothes.

When she neared the guest cottage, he asked, "Why don't you join me for a while?"

Join him? Sit down on one of the padded, wrought-iron chairs on the wooden porch and chat? She really ought to take Barney and go back to the house, yet something urged her to stay.

"All right," she said. "Just for a few minutes."

He glanced into his lap, where the puppy rested. "This little rascal was chasing a duck, who didn't take too kindly to being barked at."

Lissa laughed. "Barney has a lot to learn."

"But he's brave. Instead of running back to the house with his tail between his legs, he wandered over to me."

"You were sitting out here?"

He nodded. "I like sitting outside when the day is done."

She didn't tell him, since it seemed like an insignificant thing for two people to have in common, that sitting on the deck in the backyard was how she always started her days.

"My great-aunt Clara has a front porch like this. It overlooks the stream that runs through her property." Sullivan shot her a crooked grin. "You have a lot in common with her."

"How so?"

He shook his head and chuckled, but didn't answer.

For some reason, she had a feeling he wasn't being complimentary. And that the commonality she shared with his aunt wasn't something to be proud of. But curiosity got the better of her. "Speak up, or I'll take my dog and go home."

His eyes crinkled with mirth. "She wears comfortable walking shoes like yours. And she wraps herself in chenille and flannel before going to sleep."

So, Lissa had been right. He *was* making fun of her. Yet there wasn't a cruel edge to his laughter. And she chose not to be offended by his teasing. Heck, there was nothing wrong with choosing comfort over glamour and style.

"What would you prefer I wear?" she asked. "Stiletto heels and a silk scarf?"

His eyes lit up. "Do you have them hidden in your bedroom?"

She swatted at his arm. "No. But I've got drawers full of flannel and chenille."

"Too bad." He slid her a playful grin.

The conversation had turned a bit sexual, which might have excited her, had she been dressed in satin. But her chenille robe weighed heavily upon her shoulders.

"Well," she said. "Those few minutes have flown by. And it's time for me to turn in."

"I hope you're not mad. Great-aunt Clara is a great gal. And she's got more spunk than her eighty-five-year-old sister."

Lissa arched a brow. "How old is your aunt?"

"Ninety-seven. And she still mows her own yard and works in the garden."

"Impressive. Then there's hope for the flannel-and-chenille crowd."

"Great-aunt Clara has a boyfriend, too." He tossed her a dimpled grin.

"You don't say." Lissa figured she'd be ninety before a guy noticed her.

She glanced toward the house and saw that her parents had turned off their bedroom light. Her mother's doing, no doubt. Trying to give Lissa a little push toward romance.

When she looked at Sullivan, he was gazing at her.

"Are you involved with anyone?" he asked.

The question took her aback—in part because the truth was too revealing. She didn't mind if he knew she chose sensible shoes. Or that she wore flannel to bed. But she didn't want him to think of her as the awkward virgin that she was.

So she said, "No one at the moment."

He didn't comment, merely studied her.

But she was afraid he'd see through her half truth, so she stood. "Well, I really need to go. Don't let the bed bugs bite."

He stroked Barney's head. "I'll see you in the morning."

She nodded, then reached to pick up the sleeping pup. As she did so, their hands touched, and a warm shiver shimmied through her veins.

Before she could react—or run—Sullivan tugged gently upon her braid. "Do you ever let your hair down, Lissa?"

"Never," she said, her voice a near whisper.

"You ought to." His words settled over her like a cloak of crushed velvet.

She slowly straightened, pulling her braid from his hand. "Good night. I'll see you in the morning."

As she strode toward the house, she tried to shake the adolescent fascination with a man who was out of her league.

Yet she couldn't shake the thought of letting her hair down—for him.

# Chapter Four

*Do you ever let your hair down?*

Lissa stood before the antique floor-length mirror in her bedroom, studying the brown mop that hung over her shoulders and down her back.

Why didn't she just go to the salon in town and have it all chopped off?

Because she'd become so good at braiding it, so used to twisting it this way or that. Shorter hair meant styling gel, mousse, curling irons and spray—stuff Lissa had never been adept at using. Of course, she could always plop a hat on her head.

But not on a special occasion like tonight.

She'd dressed in a black, A-line dress with three-quarter length sleeves and a hem that reached midcalf. The simple style suited her.

Now, the only thing left to do was her hair. For a moment, she considered letting it hang loose—as Sullivan had suggested. But she felt incomplete, exposed. And far too vulnerable for a night like this.

Her dad planned to serve the new blend Lissa had created as a prelude to a bigger unveiling later this month. But with the exclusive guest list of local vintners and wine connoisseurs, Lissa felt this dinner party was critical and her nerves were on edge.

And to add more stress to the evening, her dad had invited that reporter from *Through the Grapevine* magazine to record everyone's reaction.

Normally, Lissa preferred to blend into the crowd, to be discreet and unnoticed. But her basic shyness didn't surface while she was making wine or discussing the vineyard she loved. So, for the first time in years, Lissa had actually primped—a little.

She decided upon a French braid that hung down her back. The style might be a bit more elegant than she was used to, but tonight called for something special, out of the ordinary.

If Eileen were here, she'd insist Lissa put on some makeup. A while back, her sister had given her a monstrous palette of colorful goop for no reason at all, volunteering to help her choose the perfect shades. Unfortunately, Lissa had declined the lesson.

She glanced at the unused palette that sat on the bathroom counter. As klutzy as she was, she'd probably smear on the stuff and look like a clown. Yet a tiny spark of vanity surfaced, and she picked up a tube of lipstick, lifted the lid and rolled out the stick. A pink gloss. She could handle something simple like that.

And what was in this blue tube? Mascara? Maybe a dab would be okay. She unscrewed the top and pulled out the small, curved brush. Leaning toward the bathroom mirror, she stroked the bristles along her lashes.

Gosh, this was tough. And some women fussed with makeup every day. Talk about gluttons for punishment.

Her mouth opened on its own, which seemed to help with her aim. Maybe a little to the left.

Ow! Damn. Right in the eyeball. Ouch. And it stung. By the time she rubbed and blinked, two black smears made her look like a raccoon.

Forget it. Vanity was definitely overrated.

Somehow, she managed to get her face washed, but her eyes still looked a bit dark around the edges. Well, that's what she got for trying to be somebody else— somebody feminine and attractive.

She looked at her watch. Six forty-five. Oh shoot. People would be arriving any minute. She slipped on a pair of low-heeled black pumps—sensible shoes like good old Aunt Clara wore, she supposed—then headed for the kitchen to give her mother a hand.

Donna had hired a caterer for this evening, so there probably wasn't much left for Lissa to do, other than greet everyone.

Just as she stepped away from the foot of the stairs,

a knock sounded, alerting her to the arrival of the first guest. Showtime. She strode across the carpet to the polished hardwood entry and opened the door.

Sullivan stood on the porch, wearing expensive-looking black slacks, a white shirt—open at the collar—and a stylish sports jacket. A *GQ* cover boy come to life.

He flashed her a playful grin. "You look great this evening, Lissa. Nice dress."

"Thank you." Did he really think she looked nice? Or was that just the standard how-do-you-do comment that folks made at dinner parties?

"You did something to your eyes," he said.

"Yeah. During a moment of weakness, I nearly blinded myself. But it won't happen again. Come on inside." She stepped away from the door and led him through the living room. "Can I get you a drink?"

"How about Scotch and water?"

"You've got it."

Within moments, the house began to fill with the local vintners and wine connoisseurs they'd invited. Lissa milled around, making cocktail-hour conversation.

The next doorbell announced the arrival of the last guest, or so Lissa hoped. The reporter from *Through the Grapevine* magazine had yet to arrive.

Her name was Gretchen, which was all Lissa had been told over the telephone. No one had prepared Lissa for the voluptuous blonde in a traffic-stopping red dress revealed when the door swung open.

The word *tacky* came to mind, but that wasn't really true. The blonde merely had a sophisticated style and a healthy dose of self-confidence.

But heck, Lissa would feel confident, too—if she had a face and figure like that.

More than a few men turned to gawk, as the statuesque woman stepped into the foyer. Unable to help herself, Lissa peeked at the woman's feet, expecting to see high heels. Wow. Those red strappy sandals weren't exactly stilettos, but they were pretty darn close. They also showed off a pedicure and cherry-red toenail polish.

Lissa glanced at her own size nines. At least the dependable pumps were comfortable. And who needed bunions and foot problems later on? Heck, Sullivan's Great-aunt Clara probably had gorgeous feet—wrinkled, maybe. But not all crippled up from years of abuse.

Gathering the hostess skills her mom had taught her, Lissa extended a hand and introduced herself to the attractive reporter. "You must be Gretchen Thomas."

"Yes, I am. Thank you for inviting me." Gretchen's lively blue eyes quickly scanned the milling crowd, then landed on Sullivan.

And wouldn't you know it? The sexy *GQ* hottie had spotted her, too.

"Who's that man near the bookcase?" Gretchen asked. "Is he one of the local vintners? I don't believe I've met him."

"He's a business consultant," Lissa said.

"Interesting."

Yes, wasn't it? Lissa wanted to place the sole of her sensible shoe on the blonde's shapely backside and boot her out of the house before the reporter and the consultant had a chance to exchange telephone numbers.

But why bother?

Lissa didn't need a crystal ball or a cup of tea leaves to see how the evening would unfold. She could sense what was coming down the pike.

Well, *c'est la vie.*

Here today. Gone tomorrow.

*Que sera, sera.*

With hormones dancing in her eyes, Gretchen threw back her shoulders, lifted her chin and made her way toward the only eligible bachelor in the room. Well, the only bachelor in the twenty- to forty-something range.

One of their guests, Anthony Martinelli, a longtime friend of her father's and a successful local vintner, had lost his wife last winter. Rumor had it he was looking to find love again. But the older man, while handsome, was probably too tame for a woman like Gretchen.

On the other hand, Sullivan was more the reporter's style. And the lady in red appeared to have staked her claim.

So much for Lissa's silly hope of having a one-time fling with the consultant. She had a feeling Sullivan would be taken before the night was over.

But why should she give a flying leap about that? She'd known nothing would ever become of her silly fantasy. Still, as she watched Sullivan smile at the blonde's swivel-hipped approach, an ache settled in her chest.

Get over it, she told herself, shoving aside the sting of disappointment and hiding behind an I'm-not-the-least-bit-interested stance.

Anthony Martinelli approached her little corner of the world, interrupting her thoughts.

"Hello, Lissa." The handsome older man, who wore his Italian heritage well, flashed her a charming smile that crinkled along the edges of his sharp blue eyes. "You look lovely tonight."

Lissa didn't warrant the "lovely" comment, although she had tried to look her best this evening. But she appreciated Anthony's kindness, especially as she watched her hopeless romantic fantasy go up in a sensuous swirl of smoke. "Thank you. You look rather dashing yourself."

Anthony must have been a real lady-killer when he was younger, because he was one of the most attractive middle-aged men she knew. Many of her father's friends and business associates developed a paunch, a softness. But the widowed vintner didn't appear to have aged in all the years Lissa had known him.

The silver at his temples merely gave him added charm, while a trim, solid physique and a sun-deepened olive complexion suggested he still did a lot of the physical work on his vineyard.

"I hear you're about to introduce a new blend this evening," Anthony said.

Lissa smiled, glad to focus on her work. "We're calling it Virgin Mist."

"Sounds intriguing. And appealing."

So Sullivan had been right. The name was perfect in a marketing sense.

"We wanted our closest friends to be the first to taste it," she added.

"Then I'm especially happy you've included me." Anthony cast her a charming Al Pacino smile. "I've been meaning to call you, Lissa. I'm not sure what your calendar looks like, but I'd like to take you to lunch or dinner someday soon."

The comment took her aback. Had the widowed vintner taken an interest in her?

A romantic interest?

Surely not. He probably wanted to discuss business.

"I'll have to check my calendar, but since my dad is leaving for San Diego in the next day or so, I'll be pretty busy."

"What's in San Diego?"

"He needs to get his uncle situated in an inter-mediate-care facility." She didn't want Anthony thinking she was trying to blow him off, so she added, "While Dad's gone, I'll be working with the marketing consultant we brought in, but after he goes home, I should have some time.''

''Good. I'll give you a call next week,'' Anthony said, his blue eyes vivid and...

And what?

Flirtatious?

Not likely. Ever since Sullivan had arrived on the scene, Lissa's schoolgirl imagination had certainly taken her on a romantic joy ride.

Still, she liked the idea that someone might have found her attractive—even if he was more than twenty years her senior.

Gretchen Thomas had latched on to Sullivan for the cocktail hour and it appeared she planned to stay that way until after breakfast tomorrow morning.

She was an attractive woman, aware of her beauty and adept at showing off her double-D assets to the fullest. Sullivan might have taken her up on the unspoken offer of sex, had they met while he was on vacation. But his only interest in Gretchen this evening was the article she would write about Virgin Mist.

Her lips curled into a smile. ''Maybe we can sit together during dinner.''

''Mrs. Cartwright has probably assigned place settings.'' At least Sullivan hoped so. It would make things easier for him if Gretchen latched on to someone else for the remainder of the evening. Otherwise, he'd have to make sure he rejected her affections with grace and charm. If he failed to do that, things could get really hairy.

A woman scorned was one thing. But a female reporter scorned was something entirely different.

He tried to remain cordial and keep things on an impersonal level, but Gretchen wasn't making things easy.

"I have no qualms about moving a couple of name tags," she said, with a cherry-red smile.

"That sounds appealing, but it's my job to rub elbows with some of the vintners this evening." Sullivan scanned the mingling crowd, looking for Lissa. He could use a little help slipping away from Gretchen.

Several times during the past half hour, he'd searched the room and caught Lissa's eye, only to have his gaze ricochet off an unreadable expression.

Was she mad about something? Did she think he'd dropped the ball because he'd been lusting after the busty reporter who'd tried to attach herself to his hip?

Lissa needed to understand this thing with Gretchen wasn't going anywhere, that as attractive— and obviously willing—as Gretchen was, Sullivan wouldn't let things take a sexual and unprofessional turn.

"Excuse me," Ken Cartwright said, addressing his guests. "May I have your attention?"

Ah, a way out. Thank goodness.

People gradually grew silent and turned toward their host, allowing Ken to continue his speech. "My daughter Lissa has worked with me for years, learning everything I know about wine. And I think she's surpassed anything I've ever done.''

The guests smiled and looked at Lissa, then at her father.

''My daughter has created a new blend called Virgin Mist,'' Ken said, pride evident in every word. ''And we'd like you to try a glass before we officially unveil it later this month.''

As the catering staff carried in silver platters laden with glasses, offering Virgin Mist to each guest, Sullivan couldn't help but study Lissa. She worried her bottom lip, undoubtedly waiting for the reaction of her peers, waiting for their response.

Sullivan should be at her side. It was his job to support her.

As glasses raised, a few murmurs rippled through the room. Anticipation grew steadily.

Taking the chance to untangle himself from the determined blonde, he said, ''It's been great talking to you, but it looks as though I'm back on the clock. Will you please excuse me?''

The woman gave him a sad-eyed pout, which he quickly dismissed. Leaving Gretchen, he made his way toward Lissa, but before he could reach her side, an older man eased close to her. It was the guy he'd seen her talking to earlier, although both seemed friendlier now.

The man was expensively dressed and the picture of refined charm. Handsome.

And he was also old enough to be her dad.

He whispered something that lit up her eyes. Complimenting her wine, Sullivan realized, as the other guests burst into nods and smiles.

Lissa appeared to be pleased with the attention. But Sullivan spotted masculine interest in the man's gaze, in his stance.

Ever since his ex had dumped him for a rich guy who was old enough for Medicare—or so Sullivan thought—those May-December things stuck in his craw.

What attracted a young woman to an old duck like that?

He'd always suspected Kristin had gone for Atwater's bucks. Not that Sullivan hadn't had money when they'd first married. He'd had a ton of it—all tied up in a trust fund, which his father had refused to release until after Sullivan had earned his first million.

And Kristin, apparently, had gotten tired of waiting.

Yet Lissa didn't seem to be the kind of woman who was attracted to a hefty bank account.

Maybe it was the father-thing, her being adopted and all. But even that psychological stretch didn't help Sullivan understand. Or make it any easier to accept.

The older gentleman intimated something to Lissa, and she laughed. Sullivan supposed the friendly exchange shouldn't bother him. The guy was probably one of the vintners in this region. A successful man, no doubt.

But as the evening unfolded, he learned a little more about the man who'd set his sights on Lissa.

Martinelli's second wife had died in a skiing accident last year, while vacationing with friends in Canada. The woman had also been fifteen years younger than Martinelli.

Why didn't the guy go after women his own age?

Not that Sullivan had staked any kind of claim on Lissa. Nor did he intend to. But there were plenty of guys in their thirties who would appreciate her, who were better suited.

Sullivan decided Anthony Martinelli was too old, too charming, too…too wrong for Lissa.

Much later, after the last guest had said goodbye at the door and Ken and Donna had disappeared upstairs, Lissa joined Sullivan near the fireplace. "So? What do you think?"

He thought that Gramps was making a play for her, but he knew that wasn't what she meant. "Everything went exceptionally well. Word will spread about Virgin Mist. And when we have the official unveiling later this month, Valencia Vineyards should become a force to be reckoned with in the wine industry."

A slow smile lit up her face, warming the emerald flecks in her eyes to a brilliant gleam. "Anthony said the same thing."

So, Sullivan had been right. The old guy had charmed her.

Normally, Sullivan didn't involve himself in his clients' personal affairs, but he couldn't help commenting this time. ''Martinelli was making the moves on you all evening. And you're young enough to be his daughter.''

She bristled.

Okay, maybe he shouldn't have said anything. But it was too late to backpedal now.

''Anthony was the epitome of grace and charm this evening,'' she said. ''But on the other hand, that buxom reporter kept thrusting her chest at you and making a scene.''

''I admit, Gretchen was pretty brazen. But I didn't take her up on her offer.''

''She offered you sex?''

''Not with words.'' Sullivan crossed his arms, unsure of how or why they'd gotten into this conversation. But for some reason, he couldn't back off, couldn't keep that old baggage from surfacing. ''But, in case you didn't notice, ol' Dapper Dad had the same idea. He just had more class and style.''

Lissa blew out a heavy sigh. ''You're crazy.''

Maybe he was. But like a bulldog with his jaws locked on a meaty bone, Sullivan couldn't seem to let it go, let it drop. ''Are you interested in him?''

Her brow furrowed, as though his question offended her. But she seemed to recover. ''I might be interested. Anthony is a nice man.''

''And he's old enough to be your father.''

''So what?'' She crossed her arms. A spark of anger brought a fire to her eyes. "Lots of women like older men."

"That's because they're either after money or a father figure."

"I'm not after anything."

Sullivan realized he should have kept his opinions to himself and wished he'd never brought up the subject. "I'm sorry. This really is none of my business. And the conversation is way out of line."

"You're right."

"Forgive me?" Sullivan asked, tossing her a playful grin meant to appease her.

She paused for a moment, as though giving it some thought. "Apology accepted," she said. "It's been a long and stressful night. Maybe we should start fresh in the morning."

"Good idea." Sullivan placed a hand on her shoulder, felt the tension ease. "I won't say anything else about your choice of men."

"Thank you."

"I'll see you in the office at nine," Sullivan said, before turning and heading out the door.

Lissa watched him go. The words they'd spoken still hung in the air.

*Lots of women like older guys.*

*They're either after money or a father figure.*

Money had never been important to her. Not so important that she'd be attracted to a man's financial portfolio. So there went the first of Sullivan's theories.

And she had a wonderful father, a man who'd been good to her, even if he wasn't her *real* father. And that took care of Sullivan's other older man/younger woman theory.

Besides having a lot in common, she found Anthony attractive and his attention flattering.

Yet another explanation rose to the forefront.

Anthony was the first man who'd taken an interest in her, and that had to count for something.

No, the "father thing" had nothing to do with it.

## Chapter Five

Jared slowed his black Lexus at the fork in the road then followed the route he'd mapped to Valencia Vineyards. The damaged files from the Children's Connection had raised a lot of questions, and he hoped this two-hour trek from Portland would provide some answers.

From the bits and pieces of charred paper the private investigator had painstakingly studied and put together, Jared learned that Olivia had given birth to a boy named Adam Bartlite. And apparently, Adam had grown up on a vineyard. At least, that's the address his adoptive parents had given the clinic.

A search of county land records revealed that Ken and Donna Cartwright had owned the property for nearly forty years. For that reason, Jared suspected that Adam's father was probably the caretaker or another employee who was provided with family lodging on the property.

After proceeding a mile down the road, a big Ponderosa-style sign told Jared he'd found the place. He turned in and followed a long, winding drive past rows upon rows of grapevines growing on the rolling hillsides.

He assumed Adam had grown up on the vineyard, although there was a good chance the young man no longer lived here. His parents could have retired or moved on. Or he might have gone off to college and settled into a career near his alma mater, as Jared had done. But surely someone at the vineyard would remember the Bartlites, even if the family had moved away.

Jared wasn't sure how his firstborn would take the surprise appearance of his biological father, but they'd have to deal with that when the time came. The first step was locating the boy—or rather the man.

As he pulled up to the house, a large, wood-and-glass structure with an A-framed entry, Jared parked and climbed from the car. His pulse raced with anticipation as he approached the front door.

At seventeen, Jared hadn't been ready to take on the responsibility of being a father, nor had he wanted to marry a teenage girl he barely knew. But now that he'd matured and had a family of his own, he felt as though he'd let the kid down, even if Adam had been raised in a happy home.

Jared would like to make amends—somehow. Not that he had any legal responsibility; but morally, he did.

He knocked on the door. When no one answered right away, he rang the bell.

When was the last time he'd felt so nervous? He couldn't remember.

A petite older woman with strawberry-blond hair answered the door.

"Mrs. Cartwright?" he asked.

"Yes."

"I'm Jared Cambry. And I'm looking for Adam Bartlite."

She furrowed her brow. "I'm afraid I don't know anyone by that name."

A dead end?

Sam Hastings, the private investigator, had photocopied the charred scraps of paper, all that remained of a file on Olivia Maddison. Had this address been part of another adoption case? He supposed it was possible.

"There was a fire at the Children's Connection clinic that destroyed many of their records, so my information is sketchy at best. But this is the address that was in the file." Jared tugged at the knot in his tie.

The woman straightened and tucked a strand of hair behind her ear. "We adopted our daughter from the

Children's Connection. But we don't know anyone by the name of Bartlite.''

Maybe Adam and his parents had only lived here a short while and she'd forgotten.

''My son would be twenty-seven years old,'' Jared said, trying to jar the woman's memory, hoping he hadn't hit an insurmountable wall.

''Our Lissa is twenty-seven.''

A coincidence? Or merely a mix-up of the scanty records they'd pieced together?

Grasping for a straw, Jared asked, ''Do you know anything about her birth parents?''

''Not much. Just a few details. But that's because an old high-school friend of mine worked at Portland General for a while. I was curious, so she gave me a bit of information.''

''What did you learn?''

''Lissa's mother was only seventeen. She'd intended to keep her baby, but was involved in a car accident that left her in a coma. The doctors delivered Lissa prematurely, and the poor mother died shortly after the birth.''

Hope jumpstarted Jared's pulse. ''Was the mother's name Olivia Maddison?''

Mrs. Cartwright sobered, furrowed a delicate brow and held on to the doorjamb. ''Lissa's mother's name was Olivia. But that's all I know. What's all this about?''

''I think I may be Lissa's biological father.'' The revelation made him feel grossly inadequate. Why hadn't he come looking for his child sooner? Come before a crisis made him look as if he would have stayed anonymous forever.

"But you were looking for Adam Bartlite," she said, as though trying to negate his tie to her daughter.

"I'm not sure where or how Adam Bartlite fits into the picture. Maybe he was a child whose records had been mixed with Lissa's when the clinic staff tried to salvage what they could."

It really didn't matter. Not anymore. He'd found what he was looking for—his child. A daughter.

Mrs. Cartwright pursed her lips and looked at him as if he were the angel of death. "What do you want from us?"

"Nothing," he lied, not ready to reveal his purpose. "I just want to meet her, maybe get to know her."

The woman who'd nurtured his child studied him critically. Assessing his character, he supposed. And maybe trying to spot a telltale resemblance. When she caught his gaze, her mouth parted. "Your eyes are the same shade as hers."

"Was she born on January the thirteenth at Portland General Hospital?"

The woman nodded, but didn't speak. She didn't have to.

Jared tried to keep the excitement—and hope—from his voice. "Is she here?"

"She's down at the vineyard office."

Apprehension slammed into him. And so did shame. He should have looked for her sooner.

What if she wasn't happy to see him? What if she thought he was using her? In a sense, he was. Questions bombarded him. But the biggest one rang loud and clear. What if Lissa didn't care about the life-or-death situation facing her biological father's family?

"How do you think she'll feel about me showing up unannounced?" he asked, hoping the child he'd given up wouldn't harbor any ill feelings.

"I'm not sure."

"Maybe she'll resent me for not being a part of her life," Jared said, revealing his fears. "Resent me for giving her up."

"Lissa is a lovely young woman. And there's not a day goes by that I don't thank the Good Lord for giving her to us. I'd been unable to get pregnant for years, and I'd wanted a baby desperately." Tears welled in her eyes, and she tried to blink them back.

"I don't want to interfere in her life or take her away from you. I'd just like to get to know her."

Mrs. Cartwright nodded. "I can't blame you for that. It might have been more difficult for me had you come looking for her while she was still a child."

Jared tried to put himself in Mrs. Cartwright's shoes. If someone showed up on his doorstep wanting to lay claim to one of his kids, he'd be concerned, too. "Thank you for loving her, for being her mother."

"It's been a joy and an honor, Mr. Cambry." Then

she grabbed a sweater from a coat rack in the hall. "Come along with me. I'll introduce you. The rest is up to Lissa."

She had that right.

How would Lissa react when she met him? And more important, what would she say when he asked her to be tested as a bone-marrow donor?

He would find out soon enough.

Lissa bent over the desk where Sullivan had displayed a marketing plan he'd developed. She might have put away any romantic ideas involving the handsome consultant, but she couldn't overlook his musky, mountain-meadow scent, couldn't ignore the brush of his arm against hers, the heat that raced through her blood. Nor could she keep her eyes off him.

He'd dressed casually today in jeans and a white dress shirt. Rolled sleeves revealed muscular forearms and an expensive gold watch.

"So, what do you think?" he asked.

Okay. Mind back on business. "As I've already mentioned, I think your idea of opening the vineyard and winery for tours is a good one. I'll discuss it with my father when he gets back from San Diego."

Sullivan nodded, as a light rap sounded at the office door. Before Lissa could answer, her mother turned the knob and let herself in. A tall, dark-haired stranger followed her.

"Honey," her mom began. "I know you're busy, but there's someone I think you should meet."

Lissa straightened and approached her mother and the middle-aged man. His eyes seemed to study her with more curiosity than was the norm. Who was he?

"I'm Jared Cambry." The man extended a hand in greeting, his green eyes scanning her face, her expression.

His name didn't sound familiar, but Lissa shook his hand. "Lissa Cartwright."

"You look like your mother," he said.

Lissa glanced at Donna and wrinkled her brow. Eileen was the one who favored their mother. Was the guy blind?

"He means Olivia," Donna said, her voice soft. And a little wobbly.

Olivia was her birth mother's name. Did this guy know her real mother? Her real parents? A multitude of questions tumbled forth. But, for the life of her, the words wouldn't form.

"I have reason to believe I'm your father," the man said.

Lissa found it difficult to speak, to think. To react.

She finally said, "I'm a bit overwhelmed." But flabbergasted was more like it. As a little girl, she'd always envisioned her real parents coming for her, but they usually arrived in a coach like Cinderella's.

"I can understand your surprise," he said.

Could he? As a kid, she'd dreamed of this day. Lived for it. But now? She wasn't sure. Why had he come looking for her? To assuage his guilt? To satisfy his curiosity? Had he thought about her often? Prayed she was loved and cared for?

A childlike hope sprang from nowhere, wishing he'd say that he'd been searching for her for years, that he'd never meant to give her away.

"I'd been meaning to find you," he said, "ever since moving back to Portland last year. But I hadn't gotten around to it. I'm an attorney, and I've been trying to set up a new office. Now my family is faced with a crisis. And I'm hoping you can help."

Did he want money? She quickly scanned his length, taking in the expensive, gray three-piece suit, the pale yellow shirt. The classy tie.

He didn't appear to be poor or struggling.

"What kind of crisis?" she asked.

"My youngest son, your half brother, was diagnosed with a rare blood disorder. And he needs a bone-marrow transplant."

A myriad of emotions swirled in her heart. Surprise that he'd walked into her life. Curiosity, too. But it seemed as though he'd only come looking for her because he stood to lose something. Someone special to him.

He hadn't been looking for *her*.

"Mark is only eight years old." The man pulled a wallet from the inside pocket of his jacket, withdrew a photograph of a kid in a soccer uniform and handed it to her. "He's a bright and loving little boy—the greatest kid in the world. Without a transplant, he won't live to see his tenth birthday.''

She looked into the smiling face of a dark-haired child with a splatter of freckles across his nose and a bright-eyed grin.

Her brother?

Her *half* brother.

This was all so overwhelming. She needed time to think. To react.

As though wanting some direction, some guidance, she glanced at her mother. The poor thing looked as though she was about to fall apart.

Lissa's gaze drifted to Sullivan, who stood on the sidelines watching the scene unfold. She supposed it might have been better to meet privately with Mr. Cambry. But in a way, she welcomed the presence of others, appreciated their silent support. An audience made holding back the tears much easier.

''Whether you're a match or not, I'd still like to establish a relationship with you,'' Mr. Cambry...Jared said. For goodness' sake. What was she supposed to call him?

Torn in a hundred different pieces, Lissa again looked to her mother, as though Donna could save the day, as she'd always done in the past. But this was a decision Lissa would have to make on her own. At least the father-daughter-relationship stuff.

She wouldn't, of course, refuse to help his son. She glanced at the photo she held in her hand. The boy's name was Mark. And he was much too young to be facing death.

Jared scanned the small, woodsy office, as though noticing the others for the first time, then focused on Lissa. "I'm sorry for blurting out news I should have revealed in private. But I've been so eager to find you...."

Because of the boy, she realized. Not because of her.

"Maybe we could have an early lunch together and discuss this further?" he asked. "We can drive into the nearest town. I noticed several cafés and diners as I passed through."

"I'm afraid not," Lissa answered. "I'm much too busy to take a lunch break today. But I'll have the required testing done in the next day or so. Just let me know where I need to go. And if I'm a match, I'll donate bone marrow to your son."

Her brother.

"Thank you," Jared said. "I can't ask for more than that. But I really meant what I said about having a relationship with you—regardless of how everything else works out."

She nodded, but again her voice failed her. For some reason, she didn't want to make promises—or accept any—that might not pan out.

Her mother finally spoke. "I'll walk you back to your car, Mr. Cambry."

"All right." Jared withdrew a business card from his wallet, wrote down several phone numbers. Then handed it to Lissa. "Please call me. Anytime of the day or night."

Again she nodded, but when she returned the photo to him, he refused to take it. "Please keep it. I'd like you to have it."

Lissa stood like a concrete angel in the center of a cemetery until the door shut behind her mother and her father—or rather, the guy who'd provided half her genetic makeup.

And, in spite of a determination to keep her feelings locked inside where Sullivan would never see, the tears slipped down her face. She set the picture of the boy—Mark—on the desktop, then wiped her eyes and nibbled at her lip.

*Oh, God. Don't let me fall apart here, in front of Sullivan.* She could only imagine what the consultant was thinking of the surreal event that had just taken place.

Sullivan had been watching the awkward meeting, but only because he couldn't find a graceful way to leave the room. He'd never been a sucker for tears, but as Lissa's pain became evident, washing a path down her cheeks, it was tough to remain silent or invisible.

"Hey, if you'd like some time to sort through all of this, I understand. I can go for a walk." He nodded toward the doggie bed on the floor. "I can even take Barney."

"That's all right," she said, sniffling. "We've got a lot of work to do."

Yeah? If the situation were reversed, Sullivan would need time to regroup.

Did she expect to switch gears and keep going? Apparently so, because she stood over the desk and began to peruse the paperwork he'd already laid before her. But before they could return to the business discussion they'd been having, another wave of tears surfaced.

"I'm sorry." She sniffled and wiped her face with the back of a hand.

"It's none of my business," he said, "but it seems to me as though you don't want to talk to the guy. I'd think you'd be curious about your roots."

"I *am* curious. But what if I reach out to him, and then he disappears from my life when the tests show I'm not a match for his son?" She blew out a ragged sigh. "To tell you the truth, I'm afraid of getting close, then having him turn his back on me after he gets what he wants."

If anyone understood rejection—the fear of loving someone and having them walk out—it was Sullivan. Without a conscious thought, he slipped an arm around her and gave her a friendly squeeze. He didn't say anything, though. Hell, he didn't have any training in this kind of touchy-feely stuff.

But apparently, he'd lucked out. Lissa hadn't needed any words of wisdom, because she leaned into his embrace, drawing comfort he didn't usually offer anyone.

They stood there for a while, not talking, not really moving. But something weird began to happen. The friendly hug triggered a powerful awareness of Lissa as a woman.

She fit nicely in his arms. A little too nicely. Sullivan couldn't help savoring her scent—something that reminded him of a peach orchard in the spring. And he grew pleasantly aware of the softness of her breasts as they pressed against his chest.

Without a conscious effort, his hands slid along the contour of her back, offering comfort, while providing proof of the curves she hid behind loose-fitting clothes.

He had an unwelcome urge to brush a kiss against her hair, to nuzzle her cheek. But he refrained. And even though he meant to keep things between them on a business level, he continued to hold her, unwilling to let go until she'd had her full dose of compassion and pulled away.

Lissa could have remained in Sullivan's arms all day and into the night.

His musky scent taunted her. While he held her against his hard, muscular chest, she fought the urge not to nestle against him.

His hands slid up and down her back—in an effort to comfort her, no doubt. And she found her body stirring, her hormones begging for more than a friendly touch.

But there was too much going on in her life right now, too many emotions running amok. She didn't need to shoot herself in the foot by reading more into his embrace than he intended.

She took a deep breath, stepped out of his arms, then let the air go, deflating her lungs and her silly dreams. How could she make something out of his efforts to be kind and supportive?

"I'm sorry for falling apart in front of you." She offered a wobbly smile. "You're proving to be a friend, as well as a business associate."

He nodded. "Are you sure you don't want to take the guy up on the offer to talk?"

No. She wasn't sure about anything.

"We can discuss marketing later," Sullivan added. "Even if you don't want to see him, maybe you need to take a walk or something."

It wouldn't help. The questions that had been brewing for years, the questions she hadn't asked her father while he was here, would only prod her into doing what she needed to do.

She reached into her pocket and pulled out the business card he'd given her. She flipped it over and spotted the home and cell phone numbers he'd written on the back.

He couldn't have gotten far.

She placed a hand on Sullivan's cheek. "Thanks for understanding."

Then she picked up the telephone and placed a call to Jared Cambry's cell phone.

Lissa and Jared sat across from each other at the Golden Corkscrew, a trendy little restaurant that offered the best food and drink the Pacific Northwest had to offer.

For the most part, their plates remained untouched, a silent testimony that they had too much to talk about, too many reasons not to eat.

Lissa agreed to have her blood drawn at the Portland General annex lab located at the clinic in town, before heading back to the vineyard. And Jared promised to let her know as soon as he'd heard anything.

But their conversation didn't end there, and Lissa believed he might be telling her the truth, that he might actually want a relationship with her, whether she was able to donate bone marrow or not.

He'd shown her photos of his wife, Danielle—a pretty woman with curly brown hair that reached her shoulders. From the way he talked about the woman, Lissa suspected they had a loving marriage, just like her parents had.

She still had the photograph of Mark, the boy who needed a bone-marrow donor. And through wallet-sized pictures, she met her other two siblings—seventeen-year-old Chad, who wore a football uniform and held his helmet, and fifteen-year-old Shawna, a pretty girl with braces.

"That's an older picture of Shawna," Jared said. "She's had her braces off for about six months."

"I'd like to meet them," Lissa said. "Someday. I'm pretty busy right now, with the launching of the blend."

Jared smiled warmly. "Your parents must be very proud of you. I certainly am. And I'd like to order a case of Virgin Mist as soon as it goes on sale."

She returned his smile, glad that he'd recognized her accomplishment and wanted to be supportive. "It'll be on the market after the reception later this month."

"Well, I hope the unveiling is everything you want it to be and more."

"Thanks. It will be a pretty special event. And I'll probably have to break down and go shopping." She blew out a sigh. "I hate dressing up."

"Why?" he asked. "Most women love that stuff."

"Dressing up just draws attention to me and makes me feel awkward."

"I don't know why. You're a beautiful woman, Lissa."

Her mother had said as much on many occasions. Her dad, too. But for some reason, hearing Jared compliment her made it almost seem true.

"I've got a ton of self-confidence when it comes to the vineyard, to farming and making wine, but…" She let the words drop.

Jared reached across the table and took her hand. "You and I are going shopping. I'm going to buy you a whole new wardrobe, one that makes you feel good enough to stand out in a crowd.''

"Oh, no," she said. "You don't need to do that."

"But I want to. It's a very small way to make up for not being there for you." He gave her hand a squeeze. "Please? It'll be fun."

She didn't know about fun. But it might be interesting to go shopping with the man. Her dad never liked that sort of thing, leaving all the household and family purchases to her mother.

Jared motioned for the waitress and asked for their check. "I'm going to spring for a whole makeover, starting at that hair salon down the street."

The salon? Lissa lifted her hand and fingered the heavy bun resting on top of her head. She hadn't had a trim in ages. Of course, she'd never agree to a full-on haircut unless a personal beautician or a step-by-step styling lesson came with it.

"You're a lovely woman, Lissa. And it's only right that you let an expert enhance your basic beauty."

Was he right? Did she have something a stylist could work with?

Jared's excitement and sincerity were hard to ignore. What would her mother say when she returned home in a new outfit and a different hairstyle—one she could handle on her own.

Or better yet, what would Sullivan say?

Would it make a difference? Would he find her attractive? Someone he wouldn't mind taking to bed?

"All right," she said, her attraction to Sullivan influencing the crazy decision.

"Great. Let's get started."

The first stop was a dress shop, where Jared took an active part in choosing a new wardrobe, one with bright colors that set off her green eyes and showed off more of her body than she'd otherwise been comfortable revealing.

The last purchase was a green silky top that hugged her waist and a formfitting black skirt.

"Can she wear that out of the store?" Jared asked.

"Certainly," the happy sales clerk said. "I'll cut off the tags."

"Thank you for doing this," Lissa said. "It's been kind of fun, actually."

"My pleasure," he said. "I've enjoyed watching you blossom. Now let's go to the salon."

Lissa glanced at her watch. It was getting late. And she probably should head back to the office, where Sullivan would be waiting for her. "That's not necessary."

"Indulge me," Jared said, green eyes shimmering.

Oh, what the heck. "All right."

Two hours later, Lissa sat before a mirror in the beauty salon, unable to believe the change in her. Of course, she'd sometimes had two people working on her at a time, but she'd managed to squeeze in a manicure and a pedicure.

Antoine, the male stylist, had used a henna rinse to bring out the natural color of her hair. He trimmed the ends and talked her into some layering that created a full, flowing effect, insisting that one of her most attractive features, other than the big green eyes, was her waist-length hair.

The talented stylist had created a miracle, leaving Lissa with a sensual look she'd never expected.

"You can still twist it and braid it," Antoine said, "but wear it loose whenever you want to make an impression on people, particularly men."

*Do you ever let your hair down?* Sullivan had once asked her.

A burst of confidence bubbled forth. What would he say, when she returned to the vineyard? Would he be pleased? Aroused?

And if so, then what?

Would she have the courage to flirt? To actually offer herself to him?

She turned her head, watching the strands flow gracefully down her back like a long, silky veil.

Funny, but she didn't feel vulnerable or exposed now. Not at all.

"Renee," Antoine called the makeup artist who'd been waiting nearby. "We're ready to add the finishing touch."

When Renee finished instructing her in the art of makeup application, as well as adding lipstick, blush and mascara, Lissa couldn't believe her eyes.

She looked like a new woman.

Heck, she even felt like a new woman.

A beautiful woman.

Lissa couldn't wait to see the look on Sullivan's face when she knocked upon the cottage door and asked if he'd like to share a glass of wine and watch the sunset.

And if he appeared impressed?

Who knew what else she might ask him to share?

*Chapter Six*

Before climbing from her silver Honda Prelude, Lissa couldn't help but take one last look at her reflection in the rearview mirror.

For the first time in her life, she saw a stylish woman gazing back at her. The light application of sage-colored shadow and dark-brown mascara highlighted the green of her eyes. And a feathered layering of the hair at the side of her face softened the plain, yet harsh style she'd worn before.

Jared had been right.

The makeover had done wonders for her appearance. And it raised her confidence level to an all-time high.

She slid from the car, then tugged at the short,

black skirt, making sure it hadn't hiked up, revealing a pair of thong panties the sales lady insisted all the young women were wearing.

"I don't want Shawna ever learning I bought you those," Jared had said with a smile. "She's growing up too fast as it is."

Well, it seemed as though Lissa had grown up overnight. Or rather, during the course of an afternoon in town with her biological father.

They'd driven to Valley View Clinic, which housed an annex lab of Portland General Hospital. A technician drew the necessary blood for the preliminary testing, and Lissa signed a form allowing the results to be divulged to Jared.

After giving Jared a hug, Lissa promised to come to Portland soon. Meeting with him had answered a lot of her questions about her origin and her feelings of abandonment.

Jared hadn't been ready to marry a girl he hardly knew, a teen who refused his calls. And although he'd wanted to provide for Olivia and her baby, Olivia had shut him out.

It was anyone's guess what would have happened had Lissa's birth mother lived.

But one thing was certain. Lissa's life would have been dramatically different from the one that she knew. And to be perfectly honest, she couldn't imagine not having Ken and Donna Cartwright as parents. Or Eileen as a sister.

In many ways, Jared still seemed like a stranger,

but she sensed they could become friends. Or maybe something more—given time.

Once in her car, she picked up the cell phone and called home.

"I was so worried," her mother said. "Mr. Cambry looked like a decent sort, but you never know."

"Actually, he was very nice, Mom."

"Will you be seeing him again?"

"I may drive into Portland and meet his family later in the month, but I have too much going on even to consider it until after the reception next week."

"I'm making a pot roast for dinner," her mom said. "Your favorite. If you see Sullivan, tell him I'm setting an extra plate."

"Will do. I'm going straight to the office when I get back, since Sullivan and I still have a lot to get done today."

"You work so hard, honey. I wish you would take more time for yourself."

Lissa planned to take her mom's advice as soon as she got back to the vineyard, if everything worked out. Because even though she and Sullivan had a lot to discuss, her first order of business was gauging his reaction to the new Lissa.

When she arrived at the vineyard office, she found Sullivan and Barney gone, so she headed to the cottage, where she assumed he and the puppy would be. As she strode across the small suspension bridge in a brand new pair of high heels, she realized even her walk had changed since the afternoon makeover.

Had she acquired a swivel-hipped swagger like

Gretchen's? Amazing. And she didn't feel the least bit klutzy.

Yet, as she approached the deck in front of his house, a brief wave of nervousness swept through her tummy. But she managed to get a grip on it.

For goodness' sake, it's not like she was going to seduce the man. All she really needed to do was get an idea of how he might react to the idea of making love to her. She could always broach the subject another day.

Or change her mind completely.

This was merely a little sexual experimentation. She certainly didn't intend to pounce on Sullivan before dinner.

She'd probably start by asking about Barney. Then she'd thank him for encouraging her to meet with Jared. And if that went well, maybe she'd suggest a glass of wine on the porch.

Of course, she wasn't sure how far she'd go with a sexual proposition. She'd have to play that by ear. Asking a man to be her one-time lover might be awkward, but she was determined not to be a virgin the rest of her life.

And that meant taking control of her destiny, even if she took a tumble. What was that they said about falling from the horse? Well, she'd just climb right back on.

With her new confidence riding high in the saddle, Lissa rapped soundly upon the door.

*Cowgirl up.*

Moments later, Sullivan answered, wearing a pair

of faded jeans and a white T-shirt. Gorgeous, as usual. But it wasn't his casual, playboy stance that tickled her arousal. It was the expression on his face.

"Lissa." His eyes widened and his jaw dropped. "I...uh...wow."

She'd caused him to stutter. Imagine that. And it was a good kind of stutter. His eyes swept over her, and, without a doubt, she knew he liked what he saw.

His reaction was empowering.

Lissa had never evoked that kind of wide-eyed effect on anyone, let alone a man she found so darn attractive. Her confidence soared, and she felt like singing "Yippee-Ki-Yay." But there was no reason to let him think she'd had a makeover with him in mind.

"I went shopping for an outfit to wear to the reception and decided to have my hair done while I was in town. Since Virgin Mist is so much a part of me, I thought we both needed a fresh package. Do you like my new look?"

"Like it? It's great. *You* look great." He raked a hand through his hair, then seemed to regroup. He opened the door and stepped aside. "Come on in."

Before she could ask about Barney, she spotted the pup curled up on the sofa, chewing on one of Sullivan's socks.

"Thanks for babysitting."

"No problem," he said, his eyes still scanning her from head to toe and back again. The heated gaze caressed her, causing her heart to flutter, her blood to warm, her courage to soar.

She placed a hand on her hip, feeling the sleek green fabric that outlined her shape. "I'm glad you suggested I talk to Jared. It did me a lot of good."

"I can see that," he said, his eyes following her hand movement. "It must have been one hell of a conversation."

It was working. She'd caught his interest. So why not push the envelope a little further? "How about a glass of wine before dinner?"

"Yeah. Sure." Sullivan went to the kitchenette, pulled a bottle of wine from the fridge, then fumbled through the drawers, looking for a corkscrew.

Was he nervous?

Because of her?

That was encouraging—to say the least.

"Let me," she said, entering the small, confined area. The dinky kitchen was barely large enough for one, let alone two. But she liked the idea of rubbing elbows with Sullivan, of bumping him with her hip, brushing her shoulder against his upper arm.

He must have liked it, too, because he just stood there with a mesmerized look on his face.

Merely inches apart, neither of them moved. Their gazes locked, and she could almost hear his heartbeat, feel him breathing. He reached out and took a lock of her hair in his hand, fingering the silky strands. "I'd wanted to see it loose like this."

As her hair slid through his fingers, his eyes darkened, and his expression sobered.

Lissa had read about that kind of heated reaction in romance novels and had seen it on the big screen at the movie-theater in town. But she'd never experienced it firsthand.

A woman could sure get used to seeing desire brewing in a man's eyes, to seeing the hunger. Especially if that desire and hunger were for her.

According to the books she'd read and the movies she'd seen, Sullivan should take her in his arms and kiss her about now.

Was he thinking about it?

Or did he need a cue?

Lissa didn't want to be part of the audience any longer. Nor did she want to let life—or rather a once-in-a-lifetime opportunity—pass her by. She placed a hand upon his jaw, brushed a thumb across the faint bristle of his cheek, felt her body coming alive.

He did nothing to stop her, nothing to let her know she'd overstepped her boundaries. So she slid her hand to the back of his neck and drew his lips to hers.

And just as she'd seen lovers do on the silver screen, she closed her eyes, waiting for the world to spin out of control.

And boy howdy, did it spin.

Sullivan had no idea where his business ethics had run off to, but when Lissa pulled his mouth to hers, he'd nearly come unglued at the seams.

This was crazy. Foolish. But he couldn't seem to stop the kiss. Nor could he keep from dipping his tongue into her willing mouth, exploring the wet, velvety softness that opened for him.

Her hair flowed around them like a sensual veil.

And desire shot right through him. He pulled her flush against a demanding erection and caressed her back. But that wasn't enough. He wanted to touch more of her, to experience all she had to offer.

His hands sought her breasts, and all the while, his tongue explored her mouth.

Had any other woman tasted so sweet?

Just hours ago, he'd found her interesting. Admirable. But how in the world had this beautiful, sexy woman mystically evolved from a mild-mannered, levelheaded businesswoman?

Ah, man. Business.

What had Lissa done to him? And where was his body taking his mind?

With reluctance, his hand withdrew from the fullness of her breast, and he ended the kiss, trying to break the spell that had clouded his mind and turned him inside out. "I...uh...don't know what got into me. I make it a point not to mix business with pleasure."

"What can I do to change your mind?" she asked, her voice husky. A red flush on her neck and chest told him the startling kiss had aroused her, too.

"I shouldn't change my mind," he said. *Shouldn't.* But he sure as hell wanted to.

The minute she'd entered the guest house, he'd lost sight of anything but the stunning woman who'd made a swanlike transformation. The change had unbalanced him, and he struggled with fascination, with attraction—not to mention a mind-boggling case of lust.

"I realize a full-blown affair might make things sticky," she said. "But what about a one-time fling? If we kept it a secret between the two of us, no one would ever need to know."

She was asking him to make love to her?

The suggestion both startled and aroused him. He probably ought to decline, but for some reason, the words didn't form.

As her fingers fiddled with the top button of her blouse, he found it even more difficult to speak.

Her hands dropped to the next button, and he realized she was undressing. Or was she just teasing him?

Two buttons undone.

She took it slowly, as if it was her first time taking off her clothes in front of a man. The act of innocence taunted him, tempting him to distraction. But she knew exactly what she was doing, had probably done it many times before. And it was working on him. Big time.

Hell, he'd been so busy these past couple of months that he couldn't remember the last time he'd had sex. Maybe that's what had gotten into him, pumping his blood, making his hormones take control of his body.

Three buttons.

Her slow, sensuous efforts revealed a black satiny bra.

Sullivan liked the feel of satin, liked the look of black underwear on fair skin. But he also liked to avoid commitment-bound women looking for a husband.

Of course, Lissa was a career-minded woman, not a nester. And right now, she was behaving more like a player.

Four.

Only two more to go. She wasn't going to stop, was she?

"Lady, you're driving me crazy. And making it difficult to keep my mind on business."

A smile tickled her lips, revealing that she knew exactly what she was doing to him. And that she was well aware of the blood-pounding effect it was having on him.

*Put a stop to this,* his conscience demanded. But a rebellious erection refused to listen.

As the last two buttons bit the dust, Sullivan sucked in a breath. What he wouldn't give to reach inside her open blouse, touch her skin, tease her the same way she was toying with him. But she'd set a strip-tease in motion, and for the life of him, he couldn't stop the show.

She slid the green, slinky material off her shoulders and let it slip to the kitchen floor. Next came the formfitting skirt. She unzipped it at the side, then pushed it down her hips. When it dropped to the linoleum, she kicked it aside.

Her hair hung over her shoulders and to her waist, but it couldn't hide the black bra and...oh, wow...a skimpy pair of black thong panties.

And to think, she'd been hiding that beautiful figure behind dull, baggy clothing—which was a real shame, as far as he was concerned.

As she silently offered her body, he sensed a slight hesitation, a gaze seeking his permission. Her sensual act of innocence enflamed his libido.

"Ah, Lissa." Her name slipped out of his mouth in near reverence.

She unhooked her bra and let it slide away, revealing two near-perfect breasts with taut nipples begging to be touched, stroked, kissed. And as she removed the little black panties, he was lost in a swirl of heat and desire.

"You don't make it easy for a guy to be ethical," he said, entranced by her beauty, by the gift of her body.

Like Lady Godiva, she stood before him, awaiting his acceptance with springtime-green eyes that promised renewal and awakening.

"I want you to make love to me, Sullivan."

Unable to fight the blood-pounding arousal any longer, he took her in his arms and claimed her mouth as his own. The kiss deepened, with tongues mating, hands seeking. Passion ignited and burned out of control.

A groan sounded low in his throat, as he tried to remove his clothes without taking his mouth from hers, without removing his hands from her silky skin, from her beaded nipples, her full breasts.

Finally, he had to pull away, his breath coming out in pants. "Did you bring any protection?"

Her jaw dropped, and her eyes widened. "You don't have any?"

"I came here for business purposes," he said, hoping and praying he still had a spare condom in his shaving kit. He'd thought about tossing it out ages ago, but for some reason, had left it there. For an emergency like this, he supposed.

He took her hand and led her into the bathroom. As he fumbled in the black leather bag, his fingers struck pay dirt, and he let out a sigh. "We're in luck."

Then he withdrew the worn foil-wrapped treasure, and took her to his bed.

He supposed there was time to back out, to change his mind. But better judgment be damned. He'd deal with the repercussions later.

After quickly shedding his clothes and shielding himself with the condom, he urged her onto the bed, then quickly made up for lost time. His hands slid along her silky skin, appreciating each gentle, womanly curve. He kissed her throat, her chest, her belly.

He ought to take it slow, savor her taste. But he was ready to explode. And if he didn't bury himself deep within her soon, he'd die from want of her.

Passion brewed in those big green eyes, begging him to love her thoroughly. Had it been that long for her, too?

He hovered over her. "Are you sure about this?"

She nodded. "More sure than you'll ever know. I want to feel you inside of me."

And that's just where he wanted to be. But as he entered her, she caught her breath.

Was she a virgin? She must be. She was so tight, ready but unyielding.

Damn it. And she hadn't told him, warned him. He started to pull back, to withdraw.

"Don't stop," she said, holding him close. "Don't you dare stop."

"It's your first time," he said. "And it's going to hurt."

"I don't care." She tilted her hips, making her needs and desires known.

Sullivan didn't think there was a man alive who could have reined in his passion and heeded his conscience at a time like this, so he thrust forward, breaking any resistance and completing the act she'd set into motion.

So tight, so willing.

He increased the tempo, and she arched up to receive each of his thrusts until he reached a mindspinning, body-trembling climax. When the last wave of pleasure had passed, he continued to hold her, afraid to face the moment of truth.

In a way, he felt honored, as though he'd been given a gift he didn't deserve. But he also felt trapped.

He'd never made love to a virgin before. Wasn't there some kind of responsibility or obligation a woman's first lover was supposed to assume?

Sullivan didn't have a clue, although he felt some kind of moral responsibility that put a guilt trip on him.

And to make matters worse, he'd always prided himself in knowing the lady in his arms had enjoyed lovemaking as much as he had. There was no way it had been good for her, so in effect, he felt like a failure.

He was drowning in guilt and remorse. Fear, too.

Because he wasn't sure what she'd expect from him now.


As Sullivan rolled to the side, taking Lissa with him, she was caught up in a whirl of feelings she hadn't anticipated.

Making love had been better than she'd expected. Yes, there'd been pain. But there'd also been a rush, a feeling of power, of entering the realm of womanhood. And she'd experienced heat and desire, things she'd only read about before.

And once wouldn't be enough—especially with Sullivan working so closely with her for the next few weeks.

"Why didn't you tell me you were a virgin?" he asked.

Had she not measured up? Had he found her less desirable? "Would my virginity have made a difference?"

"I would have been more careful." He placed a hand on her hip, caressed it softly. "Are you okay?"

"I'm fine." She offered him a smile meant to absolve him from guilt. "It really didn't hurt much. And it should feel better next time."

"Next time?" he asked, his expression growing serious. "I thought this was a one-shot deal."

"Of course," she said, trying hard not to show her disappointment. "But *I* intend to have a next time."

He didn't answer.

Okay, so she desperately wanted to make love again. *With him.* But she'd only asked for a one-time fling, and she needed to let him off the hook.

She swallowed her disappointment and tried to save face. "I don't expect this to affect our business relationship."

"I won't let it," he said.

"Good." Then she rolled away from him and climbed out of bed.

"Where are you going?" he asked, still lying amidst rumpled sheets.

"To freshen up. Mom's having pot roast for dinner. And she's setting a place for you." She tossed a strand of hair over her shoulder, then went to retrieve her clothes from the kitchen.

She hoped her carefree departure left him with the idea that their lovemaking hadn't fazed her in the least. God forbid he got the idea that it had turned her life upside down. Or that he suspected she'd wanted to stay in bed with him until tomorrow morning. And maybe the next.

Or that he knew how badly she'd wanted him to ask her not to leave yet.

She freshened up in the bathroom and tried to put herself back together so her mother wouldn't suspect what they'd done, wouldn't lecture or—worse yet— start thinking about another wedding in the family.

A quick glance in the mirror revealed a red rash on her cheek, where his beard had chafed her. Great.

Well, there wasn't much she could do about that. Maybe her mom wouldn't notice.

Lissa conjured a light-hearted expression before leaving the bathroom. She found Sullivan sitting in the living room. He hadn't put on his clothes. She supposed they no longer had any reason to be modest.

"I wish it had been better for you," he said. "But for the record, it was good for me."

She offered him a smile. "I'm glad. And believe it or not, it was good for me, too."

"Tell your mother I'll be up as soon as I shower and change."

Lissa nodded, then picked up Barney from behind the recliner and walked out the front door.

Originally, she'd hoped to lose her virginity. Nothing more. Nothing less. But now she realized there was more to her game plan.

Making love to Sullivan had merely been the first step. Reaching an orgasm would be the next. But she couldn't imagine experiencing that with anyone other than Sullivan.

And she wondered what he'd do if she went back on her word and tried to seduce him again.

## Chapter Seven

From the moment she and Sullivan entered the main house for dinner, Lissa acted as though nothing had happened between them. And Sullivan followed her lead.

It hadn't been an easy pretense, especially when her mother nearly dropped a bowl of mashed potatoes onto the carpet when Lissa walked into the dining room.

Mom stood near the table, the china bowl now clenched safely against her chest. "Oh my goodness, honey. You mentioned getting your hair done and buying a new dress, but you've...you've...blossomed."

"I thought that the wine and I could both use a

fresh new look.'' Lissa offered her mother a smile. It took all she had not to glance at Sullivan and check out his expression.

Was she afraid of what she might see? Or of what she might reveal?

Their lovemaking had touched her on a very personal level, making her complete. Making her feel like a desirable woman.

Had it been a positive experience for him, too?

''I can't get over it,'' her mom said, turning to Sullivan. ''Lissa is absolutely beautiful. Don't you agree?''

So much for avoiding eye contact with the man who'd sent her senses reeling, who'd helped her touch the moon and reach the stars.

Maybe it was her imagination but, for a moment, she thought she saw a glimmer of emotion in his eyes. But it quickly disappeared, as if it hadn't been there at all.

''She looks great,'' Sullivan said, sincerity in his gaze and truth in his tone. But not a hint of anything more.

It would have been nice to know what he was thinking or feeling, but he'd rolled back any evidence of his thoughts or emotions, tucking them way out of sight.

Well, what did she expect? She'd told him it would be their secret. And that she only wanted a one-time fling.

Hadn't he said he wouldn't allow their lovemaking

to interfere with business? And hadn't she agreed to do the same?

But Lissa hadn't realized how difficult that would be. She couldn't seem to get the smile-provoking memory of her first sexual encounter out of her mind.

The physical intimacy made her realize she wanted a man in her life, a lover. Not that the man had to be Sullivan, but that's who came to mind.

Could another lover replicate Sullivan's heated caresses and knee-buckling kisses?

She didn't think so.

And as much as she hated to admit it, her feelings had been affected by their lovemaking. In what way, she couldn't be sure.

Had Sullivan felt something, too? Something unexplainable?

She might never know, since she'd set the ball in motion by pretending they hadn't done anything special. But her course was set.

If they ever were to make love again, Sullivan would have to make the next move.

"Have a seat," her mother said, while placing the bowl of mashed potatoes onto the dining-room table. "I hope you like roast beef, Sullivan."

"I appreciate home-cooked meals, since I rarely get a chance to enjoy them." He took the seat across from Lissa. "And for the record, roast beef is one of my favorites."

Lissa wondered what other meals he liked. In spite

of their intimacy, there was a lot she didn't know about the man. A lot she'd like to find out.

Her mom returned to the table with a platter of meat and a bowl of vegetables. "Lissa, your dad called. He talked Uncle Pete into selling the house and moving to Oregon."

"Uncle Pete practically raised my father," Lissa said to Sullivan.

"There's a convalescent hospital not far from us," Mom added, while taking her seat and addressed Sullivan. "So we can be close enough to visit. Uncle Pete's wife died last summer. And since they'd never been blessed with children, he only has us."

"I think we need to bring him home to live here," Lissa said. "That way we can look after him."

"But what about his medical care?" Mom said.

"I'll be more than happy to help take care of him. And we can hire a nurse, if we need to. But I think Uncle Pete needs to spend the rest of his life with a family who loves him."

"I'm sure your father will agree," Mom said. "I'll talk to him about it after he gets home."

As Lissa passed the platter of beef to Sullivan, her mom clicked her tongue, slowly shook her head and grinned. "I can't get over the change in you."

Making love to Sullivan had been a stellar, life-changing event. Was the loss of her virginity as obvious as it felt?

Mom scrunched her eyes and cocked her head to

the side, her gaze still focused on Lissa. "What's that?"

"What's what?" Lissa picked up the bowl of gravy to hand to Sullivan.

"That red splotch on your face."

Oh, Lordy. Her mom had spotted the faint abrasion from the light stubble of Sullivan's afternoon shadow. Would she guess what they'd done this afternoon? Maybe insist upon having a little talk about sex being special and reserved for marriage?

Lissa's grip on the bowl froze and she stole a peek at Sullivan, as though doing so would help her concoct a plausible explanation—other than the truth, of course. Her parents were pretty old-fashioned.

"You're right, Donna." Sullivan's brows knit together. "Her face does look red and irritated."

The big oaf. At first, Lissa thought seriously about kicking him under the table, but refrained.

He knew perfectly well what had caused the light abrasion, but was playing dumb rather than acting guilty and drawing more curiosity. Could Lissa play the game as easily? She'd never been very good at that sort of thing. Maybe because she couldn't lie to save her soul.

She didn't feel the least bit guilty for what they'd done, even if it didn't mean anything to Sullivan. But she wasn't in the mood for a well-intentioned lecture after her lover went back to the guest house.

Since Lissa couldn't remember which cheek was red, she lifted her hands and touched them both. "I do feel kind of itchy. Maybe it's an allergic reaction to the makeup they applied at the salon.''

''That's possible,'' her mom said, craning her neck to get a different look at the red, telltale splotch. ''You might want to wash your face and apply some cortisone cream.''

''Good idea,'' Lissa said, hoping the subject had died an easy death. ''I'll do that after dinner.''

Mom took a sip from her water goblet, then focused on Sullivan. ''How are things coming along? Will you be ready for the reception two weeks from now?''

''We've got our work cut out for us, but I think we'll be ready. Of course, that means rolling up our sleeves and doing some of the physical labor ourselves.'' He shot a glance at Lissa. ''Are you up to the task? More important, are you able to stay focused?''

Donna laughed. ''You must not know my daughter very well. If anything, she's a workaholic and too focused on the business.''

*Are you able to stay focused?* Lissa knew exactly what he meant. Could she stay focused on the task at hand, and not on pleasure? She had to. And fortunately, all the preparations for the Virgin Mist unveiling would keep them busy, which would help her keep up pretenses.

Of course, that didn't mean that each time she looked at him her heart wouldn't go topsy-turvy— like it was doing right now.

"Focusing will be easy," she said to Sullivan. "This reception and the unveiling is a high priority in my life. And I won't have any problem putting everything else on the back burner." Where it would undoubtedly simmer to the boiling point, if she let it.

"Good." Sullivan was glad Lissa knew what he meant, and that they were in agreement. He carried a ton of guilt over what he'd allowed to happen. It wasn't like him to let his libido take over his business sense and his good judgment.

Getting involved with Lissa wasn't a good idea. It complicated things. And it also distracted him with thoughts and urges best left for a less-complicated woman, best left to a time when he was off duty and prepared to play.

"Speaking of the reception," Donna said. "Which label did you two settle upon? I really like the artwork on that gold-and-black sample."

"I didn't think any of them were good enough," Sullivan said. "Not really."

"But won't you need to display the bottle for the unveiling?" Donna looked at Lissa, then back to him.

"I would have preferred to have the bottle or at least the artwork for the reception, but it's important that we choose just the right label, Donna. I don't want to sell Virgin Mist short. We can work around not having the finished product available by display-ing the wine in the oak barrels, which only makes it look new and fresh."

"Well, I suppose you know best."

*About marketing strategy and business?* That was true. But Sullivan wasn't so sure about anything else.

For one thing, he'd always prided himself on being a good lover, a considerate lover, able to pleasure the woman in his arms. But that hadn't happened with Lissa. It hadn't been good for her, not as good as she deserved.

If she hadn't left his bed, he would have ended things by giving her an orgasm to remember. But as it was, Sullivan felt negligent, as though he owed her an earthmoving climax.

In his defense, he could argue that her virginity had surprised him. And so had her hasty departure. But that didn't absolve him from guilt.

At the time, after the last wave of his release and as his head cleared, Sullivan had worried that Lissa might make more out of their lovemaking than she should have. Especially with it being her first time and all. And to be honest, he really hadn't looked forward to having the standard, after-the-loving chit-chat with her—since it was tough letting a woman down easily.

But then she'd climbed out of bed and practically dashed out of the guest house, leaving him unbalanced.

He'd let her go and gone along with her let's-keep-things-casual, no-big-deal attitude.

It was over and done. End of story.

Yet something told him it wasn't over yet.

And for some reason, he wasn't quite sure whether he wanted it to be or not.

The act of indifference, as far as Lissa knew, had worked. Her mom hadn't picked up on the possibility that her oldest daughter had more than a business interest in the handsome consultant. And with each day that passed, Lissa grew more certain that her feelings for Sullivan were becoming personal and complicated.

Her dad arrived home, tired from his trip to San Diego and emotionally drained, but relieved to have his uncle's affairs in order and to have Uncle Pete in Oregon and settled in a private facility only twenty minutes away. If the hip healed sufficiently, God willing, and the doctors released him, they could bring the sweet elderly man home to live with them.

Dad had been pleased to know Sullivan and Lissa had carried on without him. And he'd been proud of their efforts to make the vineyard and winery look festive and inviting.

The landscapers worked double shifts all week. And yesterday, Lissa had gone to town and purchased a case of white twinkling lights to put around the trees that grew in the yard and up near the road. There'd been a ton of work to do, and both Lissa and Sullivan had jumped in to share it.

And now, as Lissa and her dad got ready for the first guests to arrive at the Virgin Mist reception, they surveyed the handiwork from inside the tasting room of the new winery.

They'd contracted the same caterer they'd used in the past. But this time, rather than choosing a wine to complement the meal, the woman had prepared appetizers and a menu that would enhance the taste of the wine they planned to launch.

"What do you think?" Lissa asked her dad.

He slipped one arm around her waist, gave her a gentle squeeze and kissed her cheek. "I think you're absolutely the most beautiful woman in the state. And I can't get over the change in you."

"That's not what I meant." Still, she flushed at his compliment. The poor man had nearly lost his false teeth when he'd returned home to find Lissa in one of the short skirts and formfitting tops Jared had purchased. He'd also noticed that she'd let her hair down, something she'd refused to do in the past.

"I guess I should have taken you on a shopping spree years ago," he said, with a smile that seemed wistful and a little sad.

"Ah, Daddy. The makeover was long overdue. And if you'll remember, I always dreaded shopping trips in the past. Something just clicked inside of me."

She didn't want him to think she'd cast him aside. Jared might have fathered her, but Ken Cartwright would always be her daddy—he'd earned that special place in her heart.

The heavy-set teddy bear of a man had given her

pony rides on his back until his knees had grown sore and red. And he'd stayed by her bedside whenever she'd been sick, unable to sleep until he'd known she was feeling better and was on the mend.

In fact, doting father that he was, he'd shared every single germ either of the girls brought home. He'd caught a mild but itchy case of chicken pox from Lissa, two bouts of strep throat from Eileen and every childhood illness that cropped up. And he'd never complained.

"I still feel as though I should have taken an interest in your shopping and stuff," Dad said, "like Mr. Cambry did. Your mom wanted me to, many times, and I should have put forth the effort."

"You didn't fail me in any way, shape or form, Daddy. The makeover had nothing to do with a man taking me into a dress shop." Her new look had more to do with the business consultant waiting at home, but she wasn't about to admit that to anyone. "It was just a matter of timing. I was ready to blossom."

"I want you to know something, honey. I love you—in the bud stage or fully bloomed."

He placed another kiss on her cheek, and she gave him a hug. "I know, Daddy. And I love you, too."

"You and Sullivan have done a great job with the unveiling. I just wish we could have displayed the bottled wine."

"We narrowed it down to three different labels, all of which were pretty good. But Sullivan wasn't happy with any of them. He says we need something better, something more intriguing.''

"That's why we brought the man in, honey. He understands marketing better than we do.''

Lissa agreed. So far she'd been impressed by Sullivan's business savvy and innovative ideas. "He suggested, for tonight, that we display the oak barrels in a way that portrays the wine as fresh off the vine and something to be treasured.''

As the door opened, Sullivan sauntered into the winery wearing a tuxedo and looking like the heart-throb who starred in one of her more recent dreams.

With those red highlights in his brown hair, Sullivan still reminded her of a Scottish laird who'd traveled through time. And when he slid her an appreciative smile, dropping the business-like expression he'd hidden behind these past two weeks, her heart threatened to burst from her chest.

"You look great tonight, Lissa.''

"Thank you.'' She refrained from telling him he looked like a broadsword-yielding warrior on a wind-swept moor. And that she'd love to swing onto the back of his steed and ride off to his castle in the highlands.

Having sex was supposed to make those fantasies disappear, not make them more vivid, more intense. More complex.

Ken greeted Sullivan, then looked at his wristwatch before excusing himself. "I'll be back shortly. I have to see what's taking my wife so long. The guests will be arriving soon.''

After he'd gone, Sullivan's eyes lingered on Lissa's hair, her face, her gown. ''That's a pretty dress. I like the color. And the fit.''

''Thank you.'' She wore an outfit Jared had purchased, a sea-green gown with a slit up the side for easy movement. Jared had said the men wouldn't be able to take their eyes off her, and she'd hoped he was right.

''I'm glad you didn't put your hair up again,'' Sullivan said, his gaze warming her from the inside out. ''I like it loose.''

She'd used pearl-and-silver clips to pull the sides of her hair back, but the remainder flowed down her back. And when Sullivan looked at her—his eyes filled with sexual awareness—she felt special, self-assured.

Before Sullivan had arrived at Valencia Vineyards, Lissa had felt confident about her knowledge, about her work as a vintner, about the blend she'd created. But thanks to Sullivan, she felt good about herself as a woman—one who'd touched the heavens.

She'd intended to steer clear of the handsome man this evening, to make him think that she didn't want to be at his side, that she didn't want more than she'd asked for. But after seeing the way he looked at her, she wasn't so sure that was the right approach.

Maybe, after the reception ended and the last guest

went home, Sullivan would be able to put business aside—one more time.

Because Lissa wanted another chance to touch the moon and stars, even if she couldn't call them her own.

As the evening progressed, Sullivan found it difficult to remain aloof and unaffected by Lissa's smile or the sparkle in her eyes as she made her way through clusters of people who'd come to Valencia Vineyard to celebrate the launch of Virgin Mist.

But it was pretty damn hard to keep his mind off the lady when she'd knocked the socks off every man at the reception. More than a few moved in on her, even some of the guys who'd brought wives or dates. Their words remained polite and cordial, but Sullivan could see the interest in their eyes.

They, too, were mesmerized by the metamorphosis.

Had they noticed the change in her personality, too? She appeared more confident. More daring.

She even carried herself differently than before, reminding him of the playful socialites he chose to date in an effort to keep his relationships light. Or at least, that's the excuse he gave himself for dogging her all night long, trying to keep the wolves at bay.

When Anthony Martinelli approached her by the display of oak barrels, Sullivan was hard-pressed to remain at a distance, so he moved closer, joining them.

"You've done a wonderful job with the reception,'' he heard the older man tell Lissa. ''And an even better job of creating a full-bodied wine sure to be a hit. Virgin Mist is delicate and rich, elegant and forward, fruity and complex.''

''Thank you.'' Her eyes brightened, setting off a display of emerald fireworks.

Martinelli nodded at Sullivan, acknowledging his presence, then resumed his conversation with Lissa. ''Have you come up with a label?''

''We're designing it now.'' She flashed Sullivan a smile, including him in the conversation.

''I suggest you consider a sketch, using your profile as a model.'' Anthony reached for a strand of her hair. ''Wearing it like this, of course.''

As much as Sullivan hated to admit it, hated to see the old buzzard fondle Lissa's hair and caress her with his eyes, the guy had a hell of an idea.

Sullivan could see the label now—an image of Lissa, with her Lady Godiva hair sparking a man's imagination, his thirst. A virgin walking in the mist.

It took all he could to keep from pulling her aside to let her know Martinelli's comment had set his imagination soaring, and that he had the perfect idea for the label.

''If you want the name of a renowned artist who specializes in sketching the human face, I'd be happy to give you a referral.'' Martinelli cast an appreciative smile at Lissa. ''The only thing drawing more attention from the wine this evening is the elegant vintner who created it.''

Sullivan wanted to clobber the guy for being so damn poetic and gallant. Lissa wasn't going to fall for that mush, was she?

Not that she didn't look hot. And not that her image wouldn't make a killer label for a dynamite wine. But Martinelli was too old to be making a play for her.

Hell, the vintner's interest in her had been obvious before, but now he was moving in for the kill.

Sullivan wanted to grab the guy by the lapel of his expensive tuxedo jacket and tell him to back off.

But Lissa wasn't Sullivan's woman. And Martinelli wasn't doing anything wrong. Not really.

It just didn't feel right to think of them together.

Maybe Sullivan still bore a trace of the old jealousy he'd been left with after his ex had left him for an older lover.

That was the only reason Sullivan didn't like the idea of Martinelli making a play for Lissa.

That and the idea Lissa might fall for the guy.

Two hours later, after the last guest had left and the catering staff had the bulk of the clean-up complete, Ken approached Lissa and Sullivan, where they stood beside a stack of oak barrels. "You both did an incredible job. The reception was a huge success."

"Thanks, Dad." Lissa turned to Sullivan and smiled. "I have to give our consultant a lot of credit for that. I didn't realize he would roll up his sleeves and get to work the way he did."

Normally, Sullivan left the physical labor to others.

But working side-by-side with Lissa had been tough, and he'd needed to exert some pent-up sexual energy. Besides, he also wanted Virgin Mist to get the kick-off it deserved. "Lissa put in more than her share of sweat, too."

"Well, I appreciate everything you did." Ken took Donna by the hand. "Hon, are you ready to turn in for the night?"

"Yes, I am. It's been a long day, and I'm exhausted." Donna turned to Lissa. "Did you want to walk up to the house with us?"

"If you don't mind," Sullivan said, "I'd like to talk to her about a few things."

"Certainly," Ken said, leading his wife to the door. "Good night."

When they were alone, Sullivan leaned against a barrel. "Martinelli had a good idea. You should be the model on the label."

"I don't know about that." Lissa scrunched her pretty face. "I don't want my image displayed on wine bottles."

"I'm not talking about a photograph, just a gold-embossed sketch. You'd be walking naked in the mist, your hair covering most of you."

She shot him an incredulous glance. "If you think I'd model in the nude, you're nuts."

He wasn't crazy at all. But she had a point. He didn't like the idea of her posing naked. The very thought of her removing her clothes in front of someone else reminded him of the sensual striptease she'd done for him. And for some reason, he'd like to think of that as his own private show.

"The artist can put your face and hair on another woman's body," he said, unwilling to let her veto the idea.

"In that case, I'll consider it." She flashed him a playful smile. "I suppose we'll need to thank Anthony for the idea."

Sullivan didn't want to thank the guy for anything. "He only mentioned your face. I had the idea of incorporating the mist. And the naked body."

"I'll have to thank him tomorrow evening."

"Why tomorrow?"

"He asked me to go to dinner."

Dinner? A knot formed in Sullivan's gut. "And you accepted?"

She crossed her arms and lifted her brows. "Is that a problem?"

Uh-oh. Time to backpedal. He had no claim on Lissa. And he didn't care who she dated. It was just that the guy bothered him. That's all. "No. It's not a problem. You can certainly date whoever you want."

She eyed him carefully, as though she didn't buy his explanation or his fancy footwork. "You're not jealous, are you?"

"Of course not." If she wanted to date anyone else but Martinelli, it wouldn't have bothered him. At least he didn't think it would.

She studied him for a moment, as though she could

see something he couldn't. "You really don't like Anthony, do you?"

"No." But not because the guy had done anything wrong. He was just too old.

And too interested in Lissa.

She edged close to him, her peachy, orchard-fresh scent accosting him and setting off a flurry of pheromones.

His reaction should have scared him, but he didn't back away. And although he'd kept his thoughts to himself—for the most part—he slowly let down his guard.

What would she see in his eyes? Jealousy?

No way. Martinelli just reminded him of Kristin's lover, the guy she'd chosen over Sullivan.

Lissa placed a hand on his lapel, close to his heart. Could she feel the acceleration of his pulse?

"Was once enough for you?" she asked.

He'd thought so. He'd hoped so. But the fact was, he'd found it difficult to sleep in the bed they'd shared. Her scent had remained in the bedding for several days. And the image of her striptease lingered in his mind.

"Was it enough for you?" Believe it or not, he actually hoped she'd say no and complicate his work at the vineyard, at least one more time.

She smiled with both innocence and seduction. "I wouldn't mind doing it again."

*With him?*

Or was she thinking about Martinelli?

The past-his-prime vintner would probably be happy to take a pretty young woman like Lissa to bed, to kiss and stroke her to her first climax. But Sullivan wanted to be the one who saw that first orgasmic pleasure in her eyes.

Otherwise, she'd be comparing their first time to her next sexual encounter. She'd be comparing him to someone else. And he'd be damned if he'd let her think that Anthony Martinelli was a better lover than him.

Pride took over, and in spite of his better judgment, Sullivan took her in his arms and lowered his mouth to hers, claiming her.

Just for tonight.

## Chapter Eight

Lissa leaned into Sullivan's embrace and lost herself in his kiss. She hungered for his taste, his breezy, highland scent, his touch.

As tongues mated and hands roamed, their breathing grew ragged and hot. The kiss intensified, playing upon her senses, fanning her desire.

Sullivan caressed her derriere with both hands, then pulled her flush against him. She felt his hard arousal, and nestled against it, letting him know she wanted him, too.

Lissa might have been inexperienced before, but not any longer. She knew what to expect, what she wanted. And what she needed to fill the ache of emptiness in her core.

Her pulse raced, and heat settled in her belly. She wanted to peel off his clothes—hers, too—and feel him skin to skin, breasts to chest.

Maybe they'd make love right here, in the tasting room, on the floor. And, interestingly enough, she found the idea of making love in the winery erotic. Exciting.

Besides, it would take too much time, too much effort, to walk across the grounds and into the cottage. And Lissa wanted Sullivan, wanted this.

And she wanted it now.

A loud clamor echoed in the room, alerting them both to the presence of someone else.

She tore her mouth from his, only to notice the assistant caterer stoop to pick up a stainless-steel pan he'd dropped onto the polished concrete floor.

"Sorry." The young man, his eyes wide and cheeks flushed, clutched the pan to his chest. "It slipped right out of my hands."

"No problem," Lissa said, although the annoying and embarrassing interruption had made her jump like a skittish cat.

The bungling caterer looked ready to bolt. And she couldn't blame the poor guy. The heated kiss he'd witnessed belonged behind closed bedroom doors.

"I...uh...left this pan behind." The young man nodded toward the door, moving backward for a quick escape. "I'll just let myself out. We're leaving now, if that's okay."

"Fine." Lissa looked at Sullivan, trying to read his

thoughts. Had he changed his mind? Not that he'd actually suggested anything, but that kiss had nearly sent her soaring through the rooftop, and she figured it had affected him, too. At least, she hoped so.

When the caterer shut the door, Sullivan raked a hand through his hair. "I guess I'd better walk you back to the house."

"Yours or mine?" she asked, afraid he'd send her home. To bed. Alone.

He blew out a heavy sigh. "Back to your house, now that I'm thinking straight. I don't have any more condoms, so that kiss will have to do until I can pick up a box in town."

"Remember when I went into town and purchased those little white lights?"

He nodded.

She slid him a slow, playful smile. "I stopped by the drugstore that afternoon. Just in case."

Just in case? Sullivan should have been concerned about her premeditated purchase, since he really hadn't wanted their relationship to go any further. But right now, in the blood-pumping afterglow of a hungry, insatiable kiss, he was glad to know they had protection at their disposal.

The condom they'd used before had been old. Maybe expired. So even if he had another one left, he wouldn't feel good about using it. He certainly didn't want to risk a broken rubber in the midst of passion.

And to be honest, Sullivan was glad that Lissa

wanted to make love again, glad that he had the chance to make things right—before any comparisons went into effect.

"So, where'd you stash the condoms?" he asked.

"I hid them between the box spring and the mattress in my room."

"We're not making love there." Not in her parents' house.

"I didn't expect us to." She crossed her arms. "I couldn't very well carry a box of condoms with me tonight. And I wasn't sure whether we'd need them or not."

"We'll need them." He ran the knuckles of one hand along her cheek, felt the silky-soft skin he'd marred last time with his afternoon stubble. "While you get the condoms, I'll shave. I don't want to leave any marks on you this time."

"It didn't hurt," she said. "And neither did the one you left on my breast."

He gently tugged at a lock of her hair, then let the silky strands slide through his fingers. "Well, I'll be careful this time." Careful to make sure she enjoyed it every bit as much as he did. Even more.

Sullivan took her by the hand and led her to the entrance of the winery, then waited while she turned off the inside lights and locked the door.

As they walked along the roadway, their feet crunched along the pavement, and an owl hooted in the distance. The fertile scent of farmland filled the crisp, nighttime air, and a blanket of stars cast a romantic spell upon the entire vineyard.

Sullivan slowed his steps near a young maple tree, its branches sprinkled with small, twinkling lights. He drew her to a stop.

"Tell me something. Were you planning another seduction?" His lips quirked, casting a crooked grin her way.

"You kissed me first," she reminded him. "I just wanted to be prepared."

"And I appreciate your foresight." He cupped her cheek. "Come on. Let's make it quick."

She stood on tiptoes and brushed a kiss across his lips. "Good idea."

Sullivan sure hoped so.

The only thing that seemed to matter was taking her back to his bed, bringing her unexpected pleasure, making things right. And after she'd cried out with fulfillment, he'd bury himself deep within her.

He wasn't going to worry about business and ethics until tomorrow, after they'd both been sated. Then, maybe he could get pretty Lissa off his mind for good. A heavy-duty relationship with her wasn't going anywhere. For more reasons than one.

And she seemed to know that, too.

Sullivan had a well-established and successful consulting business that required him to travel for weeks on end. And Lissa was firmly rooted on the vineyard. It was the perfect setup for infidelity and heartbreak.

And he ought to know. He'd seen it happen to his parents, and he'd experienced it firsthand.

It was best to keep things light. Unencumbered. And then he'd be on his way.

They crossed the small bridge and the lawn, but before they reached the steps of her front porch, she paused and said, "I'll stay inside until I'm sure they're asleep."

"Fair enough." He watched until she disappeared into the muted light of the quiet house. Apparently, she was determined to keep things a secret between them, as she'd said.

He was okay with that. It would make things less complicated when he left.

Taking a deep breath, Sullivan glanced at the crescent-shaped moon. Too bad it wasn't full. Lissa deserved the best that Sullivan *and* the night had to offer.

He turned and walked back to the cottage, where he would wait for Lissa to come to him.

Like a virgin in the mist.

An hour later, Lissa slipped out of the darkened house and headed across the lawn, toward the bridge that led to the cottage. She hadn't wanted her parents to know she was sneaking out to meet Sullivan. Not that she was doing anything wrong. But to be on the safe side, she'd waited until after they'd gone to sleep.

No need to worry them. Or to provoke any questions she didn't want to answer.

She'd taken off her dress, since she assumed it would end up in a wad on the floor. In its place, she'd slipped on a pair of flannel night shorts and a one-size-fits-all T-shirt. Unfortunately, her shopping spree with Jared hadn't included a skimpy nightie. And this was the best she could do.

It was chilly outside, so she'd put on a robe. As she neared the cottage, she contemplated running back home and changing her clothes. Surely, she could find something more alluring, more sexy than this.

But knowing her and the insecurities that had been known to plague her, she'd be hard-pressed to find something suitable. And by the time she settled on the proper garment to wear to a tryst, Sullivan would probably be sawing logs.

Soft light poured from the cottage window, as she approached. Rather than knock, she opened the door and let herself in.

Candles flickered on the coffee table. A fire glowed in the hearth, and a sensuous tune played on the stereo—Kenny G, at his best.

Sullivan sat upon the sofa in the cozy living room, wearing a pair of slacks and a lazy smile. No shirt. No shoes. No pretenses.

She flipped a strand of hair behind her ear, a little more nervous than she'd expected.

He stood, then moved toward her and took her hand. "Want to sit by the fire for a while?"

No. She wanted to feel his arms around her, to taste

his kiss. But she nodded and let him lead her to the overstuffed sofa.

"Why don't you take off the robe?" he asked.

She slipped out of the worn chenille housecoat and draped it over the easy chair. Then she took a seat beside him.

He took her hand and held it in his lap. His thumb made a slow circle on her skin, sending a warm rippling tingle along her arm. "We rushed into things last time, and I intend to take it slow this evening."

How slow? She wasn't sure whether she could wait patiently, without pouncing on him, trying to revive the heated kiss they'd shared in the winery.

The fire licked the logs on the grate in the hearth, while the sounds of a sexy instrumental filled the air. The ambiance heightened her senses, her sexual awareness. Her anticipation. And she realized Sullivan knew exactly what he was doing, where he was taking her.

The lovemaking had already begun.

He gave her hand a gentle squeeze, and she looked at him, caught the passion in his gaze.

Then he kissed her. Slow and gentle at first, but deepening the kiss until she thought she'd go wild. Desire nearly consumed her, and she ached to have him inside her, where he belonged—if only until the end of the month.

Somehow, and she wasn't entirely sure when, she ended up lying on the sofa, with him hovering over her, caressing her, taking her places she'd never been.

Sullivan wrestled with his desire, trying to keep it at bay, while he slowly removed her shirt, baring her breasts for him to caress and kiss. Her nipples had already beaded, and a flush crept over her chest—a sure sign that his efforts to arouse her had been rewarded. But he wouldn't stop the foreplay yet, wouldn't press for more.

They made out like a couple of teenagers exploring their sexuality, their bodies' reactions. And even though Sullivan had a lot of experience, he still found it exciting to learn what pleasured Lissa, to watch the passion glaze her eyes, to hear her whimper.

He used his hands and his mouth to bring her to the precipice of her first climax. And he nearly beat his chest in primal pride when the waves of pleasure took her over the edge.

"Oh, wow," she said, her eyes wide in awe. "I've read about those, but never had any idea it would be so nice."

"Nice?"

"Much better than nice," she said, a sated smile curling her lips.

"They'll only get better," he said.

"Next time?"

"As the night progresses."

Sullivan and Lissa made love on the sofa. And on the living-room floor. And finally, sometime before dawn, they found themselves on the bed, in a room lit only by lilac-scented candles Sullivan had found in the linen closet and used to set the mood throughout the house before she'd arrived.

He knew they'd both be wiped out tomorrow, as they tried to focus on the work still left to be done. But tonight he didn't care.

As they lay amidst rumpled sheets, among the blended scent of their lovemaking and fields of lilac, Sullivan ran a hand along Lissa's hip, taking time to savor the silky texture of her skin.

Lissa might be new to the world of sex, but she was a fast learner.

"I'd like to ask you a question," she said.

Uh-oh. His hand slowed, his fingers resting upon the edge of her thigh. "What do you want to know?"

"How do you feel about us having a discreet affair, one that'll end when you leave?"

Normally, he would have run for the hills at a time like this. But even though he was wary of entering a committed relationship, the one she proposed didn't seem too scary, especially since he had an out. He was leaving in two weeks—maybe less.

And she was only suggesting a short-term affair, which is all his relationships ever were.

If he told her no, he'd have a hell of a time keeping his hands to himself while they continued to work together. And quite frankly, he didn't want to. Not after the last mind-spinning climax they'd shared.

Funny, but the idea of a one-on-one until he left the vineyard didn't bother him—too much.

Some women got pretty territorial when it came to

the men they were sleeping with. Except, maybe, for the ladies he dated.

But Lissa wasn't like any of the women he'd gone out with in the past. And he wasn't sure whether that was a good thing or not. Still, he'd be a fool to think he could remain at the vineyard without wanting to make love to her again.

"A two-week affair?" he asked. "One we keep secret?"

She nodded.

"I think that can be arranged."

She smiled, green eyes dancing in the candlelight. He felt a tightening in his chest, just at the thought of having her to himself. Heck, he might even get a little territorial—for the next couple of weeks.

That was one way to put the kibosh on ol' Dapper Dad's program.

"What about Martinelli?" he asked, hating himself for doing so. But he wanted to hear her say the dinner date was history before it even started.

"What about him?" Lissa asked, tracing his eyebrow with her finger.

"Are you going to cancel your dinner plans?"

"Why should I?" she asked.

"Just wondered. That's all." He tried to keep the reaction from his face, the furrowed brow, the frown. The surprise. Disappointment, too.

*Lissa was going out with the guy anyway?*

She brushed a lock of hair from his forehead, her fingers lingering on his skin. "I know you don't like

Anthony, although I can't figure out why. It's only a dinner. Besides, you'll be leaving soon.''

And that meant she'd have another lover waiting in the wings.

Sullivan's gut knotted. But only because his successor might be Anthony Martinelli. That's the only reason.

He didn't want her to go, but what was he supposed to say? *I want you to myself?*

No way. Sullivan wasn't into promises and commitments. Not with women.

Not even when the lady looked as good as Lissa and fit so nicely in his arms.

Besides, his work here would be over soon. And if she was taking the affair this casually, all the better for him. All the easier his leaving would be.

So why did he still feel like clobbering the old guy?

Like a masochistic fool, Sullivan sat on the porch of his cottage, waiting for Martinelli's car to pull up. He still couldn't believe Lissa hadn't called off the date. Hell, she'd even left the vineyard office early to get ready.

And here he was—babysitting the darn dog like a lovesick clown.

What kind of deal was that?

In the wee hours of the morning, before she'd left to sneak back into her house, Sullivan had again asked her if the dinner was still on. He'd expected her to tell him she would call Martinelli and cancel.

After all, it didn't seem right to spend the night making love with one man, then go out to dinner with another when the sheets were hardly cold.

"Anthony and I have known each other for years," she'd told him. As if that negated what Martinelli had up his sleeve.

"We're just friends," she'd added.

Oh yeah? Well somebody ought to tell the old buzzard that. Martinelli wanted more from Lissa than friendship.

The puppy growled, then barked and tugged on his new yellow leash, trying to get Sullivan's attention. Barney wanted to go for a walk near the pond, as they'd done in the past. But Sullivan wasn't going anywhere.

He preferred to stew on the porch about something that shouldn't bother him at all.

When a champagne-colored, late-model Lexus pulled up, Sullivan tensed his jaw. He watched as Martinelli climbed from the car and headed to the house, all decked up in a classy suit. Suave and sophisticated. Tall and lean.

The guy looked good for his age. Too good. He probably had a gym in his house. And steered clear of fats and carbs.

Sullivan grumbled under his breath. Maybe he ought to just take the dog for a walk, watch Barney chase one of the old ducks that waddled in and out of the pond.

If Lissa weren't in danger of falling for another old duck, he would.

Well, hell. Someone had to look out for her. She might have lost her virginity, but she was still innocent, as far as Sullivan was concerned.

He'd unleashed a lamb into the wild, so now it was his responsibility to look after her.

And for that reason, he planned to sit right here until Martinelli brought her home.

## Chapter Nine

Lissa peered at her reflection in the mirror and sighed at the sight of puffy, dark circles under her eyes. They really didn't surprise her. She'd spent most of last night in the cottage with Sullivan, which had left her sexually fulfilled, but exhausted.

She glanced at her wristwatch. Nearly five-fifteen. Anthony would be here any minute, if he wasn't downstairs already. She probably should have canceled the date with him. And she wasn't entirely sure why she hadn't.

Maybe because Sullivan expected her to. And maybe because she didn't want her lover to think she was making more out of their relationship than it was, or that she expected more than he was willing to give.

There was, of course, another reason she'd agreed to go out with Anthony. Other than that high-school fiasco with Milt Preston, Lissa had never been on a real date before.

Besides, Sullivan would be leaving soon. So where would that leave her? She had a life to think about, a future.

"Lissa," her mom called from the living room. "Anthony is here."

She took one last glance at the mirror, then headed downstairs. She'd chosen the same black dress she'd worn to the dinner party, rather than one of the more stylish outfits Jared had purchased. She looked all right—and certainly not like a woman who was having a heated affair on the sly.

A yawn slipped out, as she entered the spacious living room, where her mother and Anthony chatted on different sides of the sofa. She would definitely have to make this an early night.

"I'm sorry to keep you waiting," Lissa told Anthony.

"No problem." He stood and cast her a charming smile. "You look lovely."

"Thank you."

His gaze caressed her and lingered longer than was appropriate for a business dinner. She might have downplayed his romantic interest before, but she saw it now. Clearly. Sullivan had been right—about Anthony's interest in her, but not about his character.

Anthony Martinelli was a very nice man. Too old

for her, she supposed. But a good conversationalist. And handsome.

Who knew what might develop down the road. Wasn't that why people dated? To learn more about each other? Of course, in Lissa's case, she still had a lot to learn about herself—at least in affairs of the heart.

She turned to her mother, wondering whether her mom had picked up a vibe that this evening was a date and not at all business-related.

Mom merely smiled at the old family friend. "I hope you two get a chance to enjoy the meal, Anthony. Lissa has been so focused on Virgin Mist that she hasn't taken any time for herself."

Apparently, her mother thought bags under the eyes were the result of burning the midnight oil and not from making love until dawn.

"Shall we go?" Anthony asked.

"Do try to have some fun," her mother said, as she walked them to the door.

"I'll make sure of it, Donna." Anthony placed a gentle hand upon Lissa's back and escorted her out of the house and to his car.

"How do you think your parents will feel about us dating?" he asked, as they approached the top-of-the-line Lexus.

So, there it was. Out in the open. This was definitely a date.

"I'm not sure how they'll feel, Anthony." For

some reason, Lissa wasn't concerned about her parents' reactions right now.

But shouldn't she feel at least a tingle of excitement at his interest?

She glanced at the guest house, where Sullivan sat on the porch, and gave a little wave to acknowledge him. He didn't act as though he'd seen her, but she suspected he had. And the scowl he wore told her he wasn't a happy camper. Was he grumpy because he disliked Anthony? Or was it more than that?

A niggling sense of guilt swept over her.

Okay. So maybe she should have feigned a headache and canceled.

But it was too late now.

"I thought we'd have dinner on the coast," Anthony said. "I hope that's all right with you."

"It sounds nice." Lissa hadn't made the thirty-mile drive in ages. "I didn't get a lot of sleep last night, though. So I'd better warn you. I might start winding down early."

"I'll try not to keep you out too late," Anthony said, appearing a bit disappointed but understanding.

Just before six o'clock, they arrived at Café Europa, the restaurant Anthony had chosen. Lissa found the small, intimate dining room with white plaster walls and dark wood beams quaint and appealing.

The maître d' greeted Anthony like a favored customer, then sat them at a linen-draped table that displayed a crystal votive and a vase of tulips. A large bay window provided a majestic view of the rocky bluff, as well as the ocean.

"This is one of my favorite places to dine," Anthony said, as he took the seat across from her.

"I can see why. The atmosphere is incredible."

During the cocktail hour and dinner, Anthony was a perfect gentleman. And they spent a pleasant hour or two in conversation.

"How was your salmon?" he asked.

"It was wonderful. And so was the service. I'm surprised there isn't a line waiting to get in."

"Not many people know about this place—yet. But word will spread." He scanned the interior. "I like the European flair."

She smiled. "The atmosphere suits you."

"It suits you, too." A smile crinkled his eyes, yet he still didn't look his age.

When the waiter returned with the processed credit card, Anthony added a tip and signed the receipt. "I suppose I'd better get you home."

"That's probably a good idea." She'd hate to fall asleep in the car. He might think that she found him boring, which wasn't the case.

He reached across the table and took her hand. "You know what they say about all work and no play."

Yes, she did. After the reception, she and Sullivan had played all night long. But that would remain her secret. "As soon as we've officially launched Virgin Mist, I'll consider a vacation."

"Good." He smiled and released her hand. "Are you ready to go?"

"Yes. Thank you. I had a wonderful time." And she had. All in all, the evening had been much nicer than she'd expected. But she was glad it was over.

Nearly forty minutes later, they pulled into Valencia Vineyards and followed the long drive to the house. As Anthony parked, Lissa looked at the darkened cottage.

Apparently, Sullivan had gone to bed. He had to be as tired as she was. Maybe more so. She'd dozed off once or twice last night, in a pleasant afterglow. And each time she'd opened her eyes, she'd found him wide awake, watching her.

Anthony slid from the driver's seat, then circled the car and opened her door. "I have tickets to the theater next Saturday. And I'd like you to join me."

He took her hand and helped her from the car. His manners impressed her, flattered her. But that didn't mean she felt good about going out with him again. Not while Sullivan was still working for the vineyard and living on the property. And even after Sullivan moved on, she suspected his memory would hold her back as well.

"I'm going to be pretty busy with Virgin Mist for the next couple weeks," she said. "Maybe another time?"

"Of course."

Again, she glanced at the darkened cottage. If truth

be told, she was glad Sullivan had turned out the lights and gone to bed. It made things easier that way.

Who needed to hear an ''I told you so,'' even if it came from her own conscience?

She'd just leave Barney at the guest house and talk to Sullivan in the morning.

At the front door of the family home, the porch light glowed in a golden welcome.

''Would you mind if I kissed you?'' Anthony asked.

The question took her aback, and she wasn't sure what to say. In a way, she wondered how Anthony's kiss would compare to Sullivan's. The only other kiss she had to measure it by was the wet and sticky one she'd shared with Milt Preston on this very porch.

''No, I wouldn't mind.''

With a debonair smile, he took her in his arms and lowered his mouth to hers.

It was a nice kiss, cloaked in the fresh fragrance of his musky aftershave. It was a gentle kiss, soft and sweet. All in all, the kiss was pleasant, but it lacked the heat and passion of Sullivan's.

''I'll call you in a few days,'' Anthony said.

''All right.''

He smiled, then turned and walked away. As she watched him go, her gaze drifted to the cottage, where the outdoor light suddenly came on. And a dark figure took a seat on the deck.

What had Sullivan been doing? Sitting in the dark?

Well, it wasn't dark any longer. And she had a feeling the scowl he wore had never left his face.

As Anthony drove away from the vineyard, Lissa headed for the guest house to get Barney. She wasn't in a hurry, though. Something told her she'd be in for a lecture. Or a sullen pout.

Okay. So the date had been a mistake. The kiss, too. But rather than reveal her regret and disappointment, she forced a smile and continued to walk.

Maybe Anthony Martinelli *was* too old for her. Maybe he'd been a family friend for so long she'd never be able to think of him as anything else. But a more likely explanation was that she wanted to see fireworks and feel the heat she'd recently grown accustomed to.

How many more men would she have to kiss before finding one who made her heart flutter and her body sing the way Sullivan did?

Sullivan had dozed off in the chair shortly after Lissa left. And he'd awakened only moments ago.

He hadn't purposely turned the lights off. He just hadn't gotten up to turn any of them on. Not even after Martinelli's car pulled up.

And like a voyeur in the dark, Sullivan couldn't help but watch the couple from his seat on his deck.

*Lissa had kissed the guy.* And not just a peck between friends.

All right. So it wasn't the kind of kiss that got a man's blood pumping, but Martinelli was too suave to press for more on the first date. But that didn't mean the middle-aged vintner didn't want more from her. Or that he wouldn't make a bolder move next time.

A sense of betrayal washed over Sullivan, although he wasn't sure why. He and Lissa hadn't made any lifetime promises. So he suspected it was some of the leftover baggage from his divorce that made him want to throw a punch or two at the salt-and-pepper-haired vintner.

There was no other reason for Sullivan's senseless resentment. So why did he feel an ache in his gut and a hole in his chest?

He watched as Lissa made her way across the lawn and over the bridge. All the while, he sat.

And waited.

"Thanks for looking after Barney," she told him, as she stepped onto the deck.

"You're welcome."

She took Barney from his lap and held the puppy in front of her, like a shield, while the little pup wiggled and squirmed to give her a couple of wet kisses on the chin. "I guess I'd better take him home."

"Are you coming back?"

"Not tonight. I'll see you in the morning. I need to get a good night's sleep."

Sullivan needed a good night's sleep, too. But he doubted he'd get one.

And he cursed under his breath for letting her go without a fight.

\* \* \*

The next day, neither Lissa nor Sullivan brought up the subject of Anthony Martinelli, the dinner date or the disappointing kiss.

Nor did they mention making love to each other again.

Instead, they focused on work, on marketing, on ads and television commercials.

Still, getting back in Sullivan's good graces—and in his bed—was never far from Lissa's mind.

"I've asked an artist to meet us tomorrow morning," he said.

"An artist?"

"To sketch the image of the virgin for the label." He leaned back in his chair. "You're not going to back out, are you?"

"No. I guess not. But you said just my face, right?"

He slid her a playful grin, his gaze warming her straight to the core. "That's what I said. But another female model might not do your body justice."

Her cheeks warmed. And so did her heart. The tension between them was easing, which was good. She didn't like the idea of dealing with Sullivan on a strictly business level.

"Then maybe I ought to pose," she said, wondering if the decision would irritate him. Especially since she suspected the kiss she'd shared with Anthony had annoyed him, even if he never mentioned it. "Are you sure it won't bother you if I do?"

"No. It won't bother me a bit if you strip down in front of the artist."

She found that surprising. And disappointing. The couple of times she'd suspected Sullivan might be feeling a bit jealous had actually pleased her. Not that she wanted him to be a bossy and possessive brute. But maybe, deep in her heart, she hoped their relationship wouldn't be shallow and based only upon lust. Of course, that didn't mean she wouldn't be realistic about the future of an affair destined to end when his job was done.

"I didn't know you'd already started scouting an artist," Lissa said. "Where'd you find him?"

"*Her.*" Sullivan tossed Lissa a crooked smile. "The artist I want to use is a woman. I thought you'd be more comfortable."

Or would *he* feel more comfortable?

Lissa was probably reading *way* too much into this, but it felt good to think Sullivan might be a wee bit territorial about their relationship, their intimacy.

"All right. I suppose modeling in the nude won't be so bad after all." Lissa stood to stretch the muscles that kinked in her neck, then moved to the window to peer outside.

What she needed was some exercise, some fresh air. Being cooped up in the office for days on end was getting to her.

As she walked, a squeak sounded when she stepped on something small and rubbery. Barney had left one of his chew toys in the middle of the floor.

"Hey, Barn, you'd better come get your rubber duckie." She scanned the office, but didn't spot the little rascal. Where'd he go? "Barney?"

Sullivan, who sat at the desk, looked up from the ad layout he'd been working on. "I haven't seen him since this morning. Maybe he curled up and fell asleep."

They scouted around the office, looking in every nook and cranny. But Barney was nowhere to be found.

"Maybe he slipped outside when your mother brought us sandwiches and iced tea," Sullivan said.

"I'd better go look for him." She strode to the door, with Sullivan on her heels.

Twenty minutes later, they still hadn't found the puppy. They'd checked the pond, where every unruffled duck and swan was present and accounted for.

"I don't know where else to look." Lissa tried to keep the worry from her voice, but she'd become very attached to the playful, loving little dog.

"We'll find him." Sullivan nodded toward the house. "Maybe he followed your mother home."

As they neared the side of the yard, the gate was open. Sullivan pointed. "There he is. By the garden shed. But it looks as though he's gotten into something."

"Imagine that," Lissa said. Barney had a penchant for mischief. But as she drew closer, she noticed a frothy green coat of saliva on his snout.

She picked him up, holding him at arm's distance

so the goop wouldn't stain her blouse. "What did you eat?"

Sullivan pulled open the shed door and peered inside. "Bad news. Look." Sullivan pointed to a chewed up box of rat poison.

"Oh, my God. No." She hugged the puppy close, no longer worried about her blouse.

"Come on," Sullivan said. "I'll take you to the vet."

An hour later, Sullivan drove Lissa home. Each time he glanced across the seat and saw her tear-stained cheeks, he wanted to reach out, to comfort her.

"Barney's so little," she said, capturing his gaze. "Do you think he'll be all right?"

"The vet said he'd know more in the morning. I'm sure pumping his stomach will help. It just depends upon how much he ingested before we found him. And how much his body absorbed."

"I know this may sound crazy to you, but I've really come to love that little guy. And I don't want to lose him."

Sullivan knew exactly how she felt. When he was a kid, he'd had a dog who'd been his best friend and his constant companion. In fact, Bandit had been there for him when his parents' marriage hit the rocks, when going home after school would have been otherwise unbearable.

"I've grown pretty attached to the pesky little guy,

too,'' Sullivan said. ''Pets have a way of burrowing their way into our hearts.''

Lissa sniffled, then let out a sob. The tears began to flow all over again.

Sullivan may not have been comfortable with emotional stuff, but he knew how it felt to lose a pet. And how it felt to have no one understand that kind of grief.

He remembered the day Bandit had died, the day he'd cried himself sick. The day his dad had said, ''That's enough, son. Go wash your face and dry your eyes.''

Easy to say, and tough to do when the pain kept twisting a kid's heart and wringing the tears right out of him.

Unsure of what more he could say or do, Sullivan let her cry until they returned to the vineyard. Then, after parking the car, he went around to help her out. He wasn't trying to mimic Martinelli's style and manners. It was more than that. Lissa was pretty torn up about her pet, and he wanted to help. To support her. Or whatever. He wasn't too good at this sort of thing.

As she climbed from the car, he slipped an arm around her, and she leaned into him. He held her while she cried, something he wished his overbearing dad had done. Couldn't the man have understood that a brokenhearted nine-year-old couldn't just suck it up when his family had fallen apart and the only one who seemed to give a damn about him was a dead dog?

"I'm sorry for being such a crybaby," she said. "I don't usually fall apart like this."

"Don't be sorry. I understand."

Did he? Lissa clung to Sullivan, to his strength, his support. The sexy man could turn her inside out with a smile and send her heart soaring with a kiss. Yet now, he stroked her back in a gentle, understanding way. Funny, how her body knew the difference—appreciated the difference.

His compassion touched her. Even more than his flirty smile, quick wit and easy laugh.

If she ever fell in love with a man, she'd want him to be the kind who would stand by her through life's ups and downs. A man who would hold her when she cried, as Sullivan was doing now.

"Want to go to the cottage for a while?" he asked. "Maybe have a glass of wine on the deck?"

She nodded. "Yes. I'd like that." She didn't feel like returning to the office. Not when her heart and mind were at the veterinary clinic with Barney.

As they walked, Sullivan reached for her hand. "I lost my dog when I was just a kid. Cried for three days and refused to go to school."

She sniffled. "What was his name?"

"Bandit. He was just a mutt I'd found wandering the neighborhood. But he was the best friend I ever had. My only friend, for a while."

"What happened to him?"

"He used to meet me at the school bus stop every afternoon. And one day, he wasn't waiting for me at the curb.'' Sullivan took a deep breath, as though re-living his own grief. ''So I called him. He came flying out of the neighbor's yard and dashed into the street. Right in front of a mail truck.''

''I'm sorry.'' She gently squeezed his hand, while wishing she could do more.

When they entered the guest house, Sullivan closed the door. Then took her in his arms and gave her a warm, gentle kiss.

How could he do that? Give her a heated, body-arousing kiss one minute, then one that was comfort-ing and heartwarming the next?

''My folks never understood the depth of my grief,'' he told her. ''They bought me a puppy, a golden lab with champion bloodlines. For some rea-son, they thought they'd replaced Bandit with a better dog. But they hadn't.''

She wrapped her arms around him, trying to absorb a little boy's pain, trying to share her own.

He brushed a kiss across her brow, then gazed into her eyes. They stood that way for a while, caught up in a powerful bond. Something passed between them, something warm and mesmerizing. Something Lissa wanted to hold close to her heart forever.

Was it love?

It had to be.

Without words, without needing any, Sullivan led her into the bedroom, where they undressed, slowly and deliberately. Their joining was gentle, soothing and stirring. And when he entered her, she arched to meet him, taking all he had to offer and giving all she could in return.

The loving rhythm built to a powerful peak, bursting into a star-shattering climax that rocked her heart and soul.

Lissa wanted to say the words, to tell Sullivan what she truly believed—that she'd fallen in love with him.

But she held her tongue and closed her eyes, relishing the moment, the warmth and intimacy. Savoring the aura of promise that surrounded them.

Their relationship had taken an unexpected turn this afternoon. At least it had on Lissa's part.

Did Sullivan feel it, too?

She hoped so. Because the realization that she'd fallen in love with him both touched and frightened her.

What if he didn't feel the same thing for her?

Letting him go after his job at Valencia Vineyards had ended would tear her up.

Especially if he walked away from her without a backward glance.

## Chapter Ten

Long after Lissa left the bed in the guest house and went home, Sullivan lay still, staring at the ceiling.

He always held something back while making love. And he'd never let go like that before. Not even with his ex-wife.

That didn't mean sex with Kristin hadn't been good. It had, at least in the early stage of their marriage. But somewhere along the way things had changed. He'd opened his heart and closed his eyes, blinding himself to reality.

Until he came home that stormy day in November and found Kristin gone.

She'd left a note that was supposed to make him understand why things hadn't worked for her. For them. But her words only brought on a rush of pain, anger and resentment.

Instead of providing answers, her rambling explanation had merely provoked more questions: Why hadn't she wanted to face him? Why hadn't she mentioned her unhappiness sooner?

Even now, Sullivan still wasn't sure exactly when their marriage had gone to hell.

But he knew the affair he and Lissa had embarked upon had just taken a downhill slide.

While making love with Lissa, he'd opened up his heart—this time, just a crack—and closed his eyes. And that's when it happened, when he got that sinking feeling in his chest. The forewarning of disaster.

He wasn't sure how Lissa felt about their little ''fling,'' as she called it. But on his part, there'd been more than lust going on. How much more, he couldn't be sure. But it was enough to scare the liver out of him.

That kind of intimate release led people to ask for promises others couldn't keep, commitments that would only lead to heartbreak and disappointment.

Been there. Done that. And Sullivan wouldn't make the same mistake, wouldn't set himself up for emotional suicide again.

Who was he to think that the career of a traveling consultant would be conducive to a stable relationship? And what about Lissa?

She was on a light-hearted quest for self-discovery.

Why else would she dangle Martinelli on a string while sleeping with Sullivan?

The telephone on the nightstand rang, and he answered.

"Hello," Donna said, her voice as sweet and gracious as ever. "Dinner will be ready in about ten minutes. We're having spaghetti tonight."

Sullivan didn't feel like eating. Not at the family table. The Cartwrights were slowly sucking him in. Making him comfortable. Too comfortable.

He couldn't let that happen. "If you don't mind, I'd like to have dinner alone tonight. I've got another client, one I'll be working with when I finish here at Valencia Vineyards. And we need to have a telephone conference. It'll take quite a while."

If there was anything to the Pinocchio tale, Sullivan's nose would have sprouted a couple of feet by now. Not that he didn't have a client to talk to. But the conversation would take all of three minutes.

"That's too bad," Donna said. "But I understand. I'll have Lissa bring you a plate of food."

"Don't do that," Sullivan said a little too quickly. A little too panicky. "I'm not really hungry this evening."

"Are you sure?" she asked.

"Positive."

He had to pull back. To cut his losses and get out while he could.

After all, Lissa was interested in Martinelli. And

with Sullivan's luck, he'd open his heart to the beautiful, green-eyed Lady Godiva and she'd walk away.

Just like his ex.

And if there was one thing he'd learned through his parents' crappy marriage and the painful reinforcement he'd received from his own marital breakup, it was to keep a sexual relationship light. Unencumbered.

Sullivan had to keep his eyes wide open, if he planned to keep his heart in one piece.

Early the next morning, before Lissa left for the office, the phone rang.

"Honey," her mom called from the kitchen. "Can you get that? I'm wearing rubber gloves. And I'm up to my elbows in oven cleaner, grit and grime."

"Sure." Lissa answered in the hall.

"Miss Cartwright?" an unfamiliar male voice asked.

"Yes."

"This is Doctor Margolis at Hidden Valley Veterinary Clinic."

Her heart dropped to her stomach. "How is Barney doing? Is he going to be okay?"

"He's much better this morning, although not completely out of the woods. Of course, he doesn't like the charcoal we've been giving him to absorb the poison. But he seems to be on the road to recovery."

"Oh, thank goodness." She blew out the breath she'd been holding. "When can he come home?"

"I'd like to keep him just a bit longer. Why don't you pick him up after lunch?"

"Thanks, Doctor. We'll be there around two o'clock."

*We'll* be there?

It was a natural assumption, wasn't it? Sullivan would probably want to go with her. After all, he'd been worried about Barney, too.

Did she dare hope that they'd taken a step toward being a real couple? It sure felt that way yesterday afternoon when he'd supported her through Barney's ordeal. And when he'd made tender, mind-spinning love to her.

Of course, when he hadn't joined them for dinner last night, her old insecurities had flared, suggesting he might be pulling away from her. But she quickly dismissed them. After all, Sullivan had a conference call to make, another client he needed to speak to. And Lissa understood that.

Still, as she'd stared at his empty seat, felt the loss of his heart-tingling smile, she'd realized how difficult it would be to let him go, once his job at Valencia Vineyards was finished. But that didn't mean he wouldn't come back.

Lissa and Sullivan had found something special, something worth holding on to.

Hadn't they?

"Who was it?" her mother called from the kitchen.

"It was the vet. Barney is doing better."

Before Lissa reached the front door, the phone rang again.

At this rate, she'd be late to meet Sullivan at the office. She sighed heavily, then grabbed the receiver from the lamp table near the sofa. "Hello."

"Lissa? It's Jared."

The call took her aback, but only for a moment. She'd talked to the man after the reception, when he'd called to ask how everything went. But she didn't think he'd called to chat today. "Hi, Jared."

Did he have the results of her blood test? Would she be able to donate bone marrow to Mark?

"I have some bad news," he said.

"I'm not a match?" She couldn't imagine any news that would be worse than that, other than a setback in Mark's condition. She said a quick prayer, hoping that wasn't the case.

"No." His voice sounded rough and ragged. "You're not a match."

"I'm really sorry." The words seemed so hollow, so insignificant. But not because they weren't sincere. She knew what this meant to Mark, to Jared, to everyone who loved the little boy. They'd have to search for an unrelated match. And that narrowed their chances of finding a bone-marrow donor in time.

"And there's something else," Jared said. "The paper work we found at the Children's Connection indicated Olivia's child had a different blood type than the lab reported for you."

Her heart went out to the poor man. The records

he'd found had been painstakingly pieced together. But that left all kinds of room for error. "Maybe you were mistaken, Jared. I might not be your daughter after all."

"Actually," he said, "the preliminary tests indicate you are my daughter, but that's where things get confusing."

"What do you mean?"

"Originally, I came to the vineyard looking for Adam Bartlite. His name was listed on one of the scraps of paper we'd found in the salvaged file. Your address was on a different piece. I put those two bits of information together when I shouldn't have."

Obviously. But she understood his desperation, his need to find a donor for his son. "Jared, I'm still not following you."

"There was yet another scrap of charred paper in the file. One that listed the blood type of a child born to Olivia Maddison."

"And my blood type doesn't match that one?" Lissa furrowed her brow. "I don't understand. My parents were told my mother's name was Olivia. And that was before the fire destroyed any of the paperwork."

"I think Olivia may have given birth to twins who were separated at birth—a boy and a girl. Although it's rare, you have different blood types. Your brother was adopted by another family. And his name is Adam Bartlite."

"Are you sure?"

''No. But I intend to find out.''

Lissa leaned against the side of the sofa. Her life had certainly taken a strange twist. Once the adopted daughter of Ken and Donna Cartwright, her family had grown to include Jared, his wife and three half siblings. And that wasn't all. She might have a brother. A *twin* brother.

''I didn't mention this before,'' Jared said, ''because I didn't think it was relevant. But multiple births run in my family. And Olivia told me she'd had a twin who died as an infant.''

''I'm stunned,'' Lissa said. ''To say the least.''

''Me, too. But a twin birth is the only possible explanation.''

''And now you need to find Adam,'' Lissa said.

''Yes.''

Her *real* brother. Did he look like her? Did they share any of the same mannerisms? The same likes and dislikes? Had her twin been blessed with a loving home, as she had?

''I'd like to meet Adam,'' Lissa said. ''When you find him.''

''It may take some time. I just came to this conclusion this morning, after the doctor called to give me the lab results. But I'll keep you posted.''

''Thanks, Jared. And if you need any help looking for Adam, I'll do what I can.''

''I appreciate that.''

When the telephone disconnected, she stood in the

living room for the longest time, trying to sort through things.

There'd been a lot of changes in her once simple life. Her family was growing by leaps and bounds, assuming Jared was right about her having a twin brother.

And then there was Sullivan. Lissa couldn't wait to share the news with the man who'd become so much more than a lover. Did she dare dream that they might create a family of their own?

By the time she arrived at the office, Sullivan was busy working on another ad layout. He glanced up from the desk, no doubt wondering what had kept her. After all, she was never late to work.

"What's up?" he asked.

"Good news and bad. First of all, Barney is doing much better. And the vet thinks he'll make it."

"That's obviously the good news. What's the rest of it?"

She adjusted her hair, then sat on the edge of the desk. "I'm not a match for Mark, Jared's son."

"That's too bad." Sullivan leaned back in the tufted leather desk chair. "What happens now?"

"Well, Jared has reason to believe I might have a twin brother out there someplace. And he's trying to find him."

Before she could go into any further explanation, the office telephone rang.

Now what? She wondered, unable to quell her impatience. Or a sense of dread.

She lifted the receiver and tried to command an upbeat voice. "Valencia Vineyards."

"Lissa, this is Gretchen Thomas with *Through the Grapevine* magazine. I'm sorry about not being able to make it to the reception last Saturday night."

"That's all right," Lissa said, glad the woman hadn't been in attendance. She didn't think she could have stood by watching the reporter make goo-goo eyes at Sullivan. "Sometimes things don't work out. I understand."

"Well, my boss was at the reception and was very impressed with what you've created. He believes Virgin Mist is going to be well received by consumers and connoisseurs alike. So he suggested I do a bigger spread on both the wine and the vintner."

"That's great," Lissa said, although her enthusiasm was muted by the fact she couldn't donate bone marrow to her younger brother. And also by the possibility that she had a twin. Somewhere. For the first time in her life, she found it difficult to focus on business.

"So if you don't mind," Gretchen said, "I'd like to make an appointment to come out to the vineyard and interview you."

"Sure." Lissa glanced at Sullivan. She wasn't excited about watching the reporter flirt and fawn over the man she was sleeping with, the man she loved. But the publicity would be good for the vineyard and Virgin Mist. "When did you want to come out here?"

"The sooner the better. If I can get a photographer

to accompany me, I'd like to set something up for this afternoon.''

''That'll be fine,'' Lissa said, although she'd rather send Sullivan on an errand that would keep him busy until after the blond bombshell had left the premises. Maybe he could go get Barney at the vet—without her.

If she scheduled it right…

''Should we aim for one o'clock?'' Gretchen asked.

The vet was out for lunch between twelve and two. So much for orchestrating Sullivan's absence. But the article was too important. And Lissa's jealousy was silly and misplaced. After all, Sullivan hadn't given the busty blonde much attention when she'd made a play for him at dinner. ''Sure, Gretchen, one o'clock will work out fine.''

''I think Roger, my photographer, is free, but I'll confirm as soon as I know for sure.''

When Lissa hung up the phone, she told Sullivan what Gretchen had said.

''Having the editor of a wine magazine think that highly of Virgin Mist is a real plus. I guess we'd better turn on the charm when Gretchen arrives.''

That's what Lissa was afraid of.

Sullivan would turn on the charm. And since his work at Valencia Vineyards was coming to an end, Gretchen would lure him into her eager arms.

Sullivan tried hard to keep his mind on his work. He needed to tell Lissa that their affair was over. That it was best they end things before he left—which, by the way, would be next week. Hell, maybe sooner than that. Some of the loose ends could be handled over the telephone.

But he thought he owed her more than an It's-been-nice-knowing-you. He wasn't sure just what he owed her, though. More than the Dear John he'd come home to find—that was for sure.

He supposed having an adult conversation over a glass of wine on the deck was better than a discussion over a scarred-oak desk in a stuffy office, so he decided to wait until the workday was over.

Of course, Lissa had been the one to suggest the temporary affair in the first place. And she *was* interested in Martinelli. It was possible that she wouldn't give a rat's hind end if they each went their own way in the next couple of days.

And maybe their lovemaking yesterday hadn't affected her in the same way it had him. She could have been so caught up in emotion over her concern for Barney, that she hadn't felt the same intimacy that he'd felt. The same gut-wrenching fear of getting in too deep.

"Is something wrong?" she asked, when he peered out the window for the fifth or sixth time since the clock had struck one.

"No." He was just edgy. Unsettled. And waiting for the cavalry to arrive.

Where the hell was the *Through the Grapevine*

magazine reporter? She'd take the focus off what had happened between Lissa and him. Although Sullivan still wasn't exactly sure what *had* happened between them.

"Are you looking for Gretchen?" Lissa asked.

Maybe he was. But the tone of Lissa's voice indicated female concern. Jealousy?

"She's late," is all he said. "And you have to pick up Barney."

"Did you want to go with me?" she asked.

"I have some work to do later this afternoon. And I have to schedule my next client."

Her face dropped, and her brow furrowed. Disappointment?

Since when had he not been able to read a woman's expressions and at least have a good idea what she was thinking and feeling?

At a quarter past one, a white van with a grape logo on the side pulled up, and Gretchen Thomas climbed out. Tight-fitting jeans clung to the curves of her hips, complementing her long legs. And a form-fitting pink T-shirt displayed her other assets to their fullest.

Damn. That woman was proud of her figure. Too proud, if you asked him. But that didn't mean he didn't appreciate looking at her.

He shot a glance at Lissa, saw her lean against the desk with her arms crossed and fix a solemn look on her face.

Anger? Hurt? Or was she merely disinterested?

Hell, he didn't know for sure. Working with Lissa after yesterday's killer bout of intimacy-in-the-buff left him uneasy.

Hey, maybe she thought he was acting strangely. And *that's* what he'd read in her expression.

"I'll get the door," Sullivan said. Then he invited Gretchen inside, along with her sidekick, a pudgy male photographer who seemed to be enamored with the sexy reporter. *Good luck, pal. She's way out of your starry-eyed league.*

"It's nice to see you again, Sullivan." Gretchen extended an arm in greeting, giving his hand a warm, lingering squeeze.

"Same here." He still preferred not to mix business with pleasure, but he had a feeling Gretchen wouldn't let that stop her.

"Hello, there." Gretchen slid Lissa a smile, as though finally noting the vintner she'd come to interview. Noting the makeover, too, he suspected. But she didn't acknowledge the change in Lissa.

"This is my photographer," Gretchen said, nodding to the short, stocky man. "Roger Donaldson."

While the men shook hands, Gretchen withdrew a small tape recorder, a pen and a pad of paper from a black canvas tote bag.

Lissa took a seat at the desk, and the reporter sat across from her.

"All right. Let's get started." Gretchen placed the tape recorder on the table and jabbed at the record button. "Tell me, Lissa, what made you want to become a vintner?"

"I've always admired my father. As a small child, I tagged along after him every chance I got. He taught me a love for the land and the vineyard. And naturally, I followed in his footsteps."

Gretchen quickly got down to business, asking questions, scribbling answers. Sullivan had to give her credit. She seemed to know her stuff. And he suspected the magazine spread would be well-written, with the wine and vineyard presented in a positive light.

"How about a tour?" Gretchen asked.

Lissa glanced at her wristwatch. "Sure. As long as we can get it done within the next half hour. I've got an appointment at two."

"I'm sure it won't matter if you're late," Sullivan said. "As long as you get Barney picked up before the vet closes, it should be all right."

Lissa nodded, then led Gretchen and Roger outside. Sullivan followed several steps behind.

Nearly two hours and two rolls of film later, Gretchen seemed pleased with what they'd accomplished. Sullivan had tried to keep a low profile, and surprisingly enough, the reporter had performed like a professional—until she closed her notepad and stuck it in the canvas bag she carried.

"So," Gretchen said, sidling up to Sullivan and slipping her arm through his. "How much longer will you be on the clock?"

"A couple of days or a week. I'm not sure yet."
He looked at Lissa, trying to gauge her reaction.

Surprise, then indifference? Or was the lack of interest merely an act?

Hell, it didn't matter. They had to have that talk soon. Maybe tonight.

"When you're on your own time and free to pursue a little pleasure," Gretchen told him, "I'd like to take you to dinner."

"Sure. I'll have time when my work here is done." Sullivan shot another glance at Lissa, saw a stonelike mask on her face. He hadn't really meant to encourage Gretchen. Or to anger Lissa. But he'd just done both.

He certainly wasn't about to beat himself up over it, though. He and Lissa needed a change of pace.

The intimacy mode he'd slipped into yesterday added to his unfounded jealousy of Martinelli, proving that Sullivan had let things with Lissa get way out of hand.

He slid a look over his shoulder, spotting Lissa walking alongside the photographer. She didn't appear troubled or worried. Maybe she'd come to the same conclusion as he had—that it was time to end things between them.

But the nondescript smile she wore didn't provide any clue as to what was on her mind.

Lissa had been shocked when Gretchen had asked Sullivan out to dinner. And even more so when he accepted.

Of course, the two lovers hadn't acted as though they were anything more than a business consultant and his client, so she really couldn't blame the pushy reporter for stepping on invisible toes.

But that didn't mean Lissa wasn't hurt.

When Sullivan looked over his shoulder and caught her eye, she feigned a smile, hoping to hide the ache inside. He was leaving in a week. Maybe in days. And he hadn't broached the subject with her. Hadn't even asked whether she'd like to keep seeing him.

Gretchen's aggressive style rubbed Lissa the wrong way. But a dagger of grief sliced deep into her chest when Sullivan agreed to go out with the pushy blonde. And not even the afternoon sunshine or the fertile scent of grapes growing on the hillsides could lift her spirits or ease her pain the way it usually did.

They strode two-by-two along the dirt roadway that led to the office, where the magazine's van was parked. Gretchen had taken hold of Sullivan's arm. And Lissa was left to bring up the rear with sweet, chubby-cheeked Roger, who was huffing and puffing like a little choo-choo train saying I-think-I-can, I-think-I-can.

Maybe it was time to end things with Sullivan. But she feared it was too late.

Lissa had fallen head over heels for the playboy business consultant who would soon leave her and her heart in the dust. Like he was doing now.

As they reached the office, Lissa spoke to both

Gretchen and Sullivan. "If you'll excuse me, I need to go pick up my puppy from the vet."

"That's fine," Gretchen said. "I have everything I need from you."

Yeah. And now it was time for the busty reporter to procure what she *needed* from Sullivan. But Lissa refused to let her feelings rise to the surface—not in front of anyone.

In the past, she'd spent a lot of time alone, usually because she was more comfortable staying close to home and out of the limelight.

But this was different, she decided, as a cold cloak of loneliness settled around her. And she knew it would be worse when Sullivan actually packed up his things and drove away.

She entered the office and grabbed her purse, but before heading to the car, she went into the bathroom to freshen up, to wash the emotion from her face.

The paper towels were nearly gone, so she bent to get another roll from under the sink. And there, sitting front and center, was the package of feminine napkins she kept handy—pads she'd be needing soon.

Soon? Her hands froze on the cupboard door, and her mind reeled as she began to count backward.

She was late. About a week. Maybe two. And she'd always been regular. Could she be pregnant? With Sullivan's baby?

Surely not. They'd used condoms.

There had to be an explanation—like anxiety. Lissa

had been under tremendous stress recently, with the unveiling of the wine. And from meeting her biological father. Even the excitement of having sex for the first time might have postponed her cycle.

That had to be it. She shut the cupboard door, leaving the roll of paper towels under the sink. She had to get out of here. Had to get to the vet. And to the pharmacy in town.

Those home pregnancy tests were pretty accurate, or so the ads said. And a negative result would do her nerves a world of good.

The sooner she put the fear of pregnancy aside, the better off she'd be. Lord knew she had enough to worry about, enough to deal with.

Besides, Barney needed her—even if Sullivan didn't.

She peered out the office window, scouting a swift escape. Roger waited in the van, while Gretchen continued to chat with Sullivan. His back was to the office door. So taking that moment to slip away unnoticed, Lissa averted her eyes and quickly jumped in her car. Tears threatened to give way, but she blinked them back.

*You're getting way too emotional about this,* she told herself, as she backed out of the parking space, threw the car into Drive and headed away from the vineyard.

What do you mean, *too* emotional? She'd fallen in love with a man who was slowly pulling away from her. And it hurt more than she could have imagined.

What a fool she'd been.

She'd only meant to lose her virginity. Losing her heart hadn't been part of the plan.

And what if she'd gotten pregnant with Sullivan's baby?

Could things get any worse than that?

## *Chapter Eleven*

An hour later, Lissa returned to the vineyard with Barney. The puppy had whined, piddled on the vet's floor and gone absolutely bonkers when he saw her, which made her feel slightly better.

At least someone loved her back.

She parked her car where the van had once been, then scooped Barney into her arms. Thank goodness, the magazine people had left. It would have been nearly impossible to keep her emotions in check if she'd had to watch Gretchen throwing herself at Sullivan.

When Lissa entered the office, Sullivan looked up from the paperwork on the desk. He broke into a grin at the sight of a wiggly Barney in her arms. "How's that little rascal doing?"

"You'd never know he'd had a brush with death or that he'd had his stomach pumped yesterday." Lissa placed the squirmy pup on the ground and watched him scamper toward his basket of toys.

Sullivan leaned back, the desk chair squeaking in protest. "You know, I think we've done the bulk of the work that needs to be done on the premises. We can probably handle the rest by telephone or e-mail."

Lissa didn't need a psychic to see what was happening. Sullivan was leaving—and ending things. And he was trying to be cool and casual about it. Well, she'd play it his way. Or at least, she'd try to. "Whatever you think would work best."

"I think I can wrap up things here in another two days. Claire is coming tomorrow, and we'll need another full day after that. So let's plan on me leaving by mid-morning on Friday." Sullivan fiddled with the ink pen on his desk, then caught her eye.

Did he see her disappointment? Her heartbreak? She managed a flimsy smile in response. She didn't trust her words to get past the knot in her chest.

"I don't see any need to charge you for on-site consulting when I can advise you from my home office for a nominal fee."

Lissa should probably feel grateful, but she didn't. His leaving might be good for the vineyard—financially speaking—but it was tearing her up inside.

"I appreciate you looking out for our best interests," she said, trying to assume a nonchalant stance, even though her heart and her world were spinning out of control.

She'd never been a good actress, so she made her way to the window and peered out at nothing in particular. The vineyard had always provided her comfort and peace before. Would that continue to be the case, now that Sullivan had come and gone from her life?

It didn't seem likely that things would ever be the same again. She certainly wouldn't be.

"By the way," Sullivan said. "Claire Windsor called while you were at the vet. She's the artist I'd like us to use for the sketch. I've tentatively scheduled a sitting, but wanted to run it by you first."

Lissa, with her back still to the man she loved, stared blankly through the pane of glass. "Whatever you decide is fine with me."

"Don't you want to know more about her? Maybe take a look at her Web site and see a sample of her work?"

"That isn't necessary." She turned and, while leaning against the windowsill, crossed her arms. "You've done the research. Besides, that's why we hired you. For your expertise."

Their relationship had gone back to business mode. And even if Lissa didn't like the way things had turned out, she'd do her best to remain strong. Unaffected. In control.

"Claire can come out tomorrow morning, if that's

okay with you. Otherwise, she's not available until late April or early May."

"Then tomorrow will have to do."

"That's what I was thinking. The sooner we get that label designed and under production, the better."

Yes, and the sooner he would be able to cut all ties to Valencia Vineyards, all ties to her.

The artwork on the label was the only thing pressing—and probably the only thing he felt responsible for, since he hadn't liked any of the samples she and her dad had shown him.

"What time is Claire coming?" Lissa asked.

"First thing in the morning, if I give her the okay." He studied her, as though trying to figure out what she was thinking, feeling.

But she'd be damned if she'd give him a clue. "Then go ahead and confirm, Sullivan. I'll be glad to have the label finished and the wine bottled."

"Great. I'll send her an e-mail and give her directions."

They worked a while longer, their conversation focused on business. But things between them were strained, at least that's how it felt to Lissa.

Some of the strain might be self-inflicted, she supposed, since her thoughts kept drifting to the home pregnancy test locked in the glove compartment of her car.

As soon as Sullivan went back to the cottage, she'd retrieve the test, follow the instructions and put her fears to rest—once and for all.

Maybe then she could get used to living without Sullivan in her life.

She glanced at the clock on the wall. Five-oh-seven. Her mom would be calling soon, reminding them it was time for dinner.

"Are you going to eat with us this evening?" she asked, somehow knowing he wasn't. But as his client and host, she thought it was best to ask. To assume nothing had changed their business relationship, that their lovemaking had never taken place.

"No, I'm not going to be able to join you. I already called your mom and told her. I have some errands to run in town, and it will be easier if I pick up something to eat while I'm gone."

She nodded, realizing he might not have left the vineyard, but he'd already left her.

The lovemaking they'd shared yesterday, the joining she'd thought had meant something special, had merely been his way of saying goodbye.

Lissa couldn't complain, though. She'd gotten what she wanted, what she'd thought she'd wanted—just a one-time fling. And apparently, that's all it had been to him. A fling. A temporary affair. A roll in the hay.

Unfortunately, that fling had meant the world to her.

"I think we can discuss the spring tour schedule in the morning, if that's okay with you." He stood and stretched.

She watched as his muscles flexed, realizing she'd never see him again. Never hold him. Never share a heated kiss or another earthshaking climax wrapped in his arms.

A dull ache grew in her heart, and she tried desperately to ignore it. She gathered her tattered emotions and tucked them deep in her chest. "I see no reason why we can't call it a day."

"All right. Then I'll see you in the morning." Sullivan made his way to the door, but when his hand gripped the knob, he paused and looked over his shoulder. "Maybe tomorrow afternoon, we can sit on the deck and discuss other things over a glass of wine."

*Other things?* Was he going to actually broach the subject of their…affair, or whatever? And if so, did she even want him to? Maybe it was better to let the whole thing die a humane death.

"I'm not sure there's anything to discuss," she said, trying to gain some kind of upper hand on their breakup, trying not to reveal she was dying inside.

That way, when he left, she'd have her pride intact. As well as the memory of their lovemaking to haunt her dreams.

He merely nodded, as though he agreed, as though they had nothing to talk about, which was just as well. The growing pain was nearly unbearable, and she feared the tears would begin to fall before he left, betraying the secret of her broken heart.

Grief lodged in her throat, preventing her from talking. But there really wasn't anything to say, anything to do—other than let him go with all the grace and indifference she could muster.

As the door shut, leaving her and Barney alone, Lissa remained standing like a stone-cold statue with missing limbs. And when she was sure Sullivan had made it into the guest house, she went to the car and removed the small brown bag that hid her purchase.

Once she'd safely locked herself inside the bathroom, she opened the box and pulled out the instruction sheet. Her hands trembled as she set up the plastic apparatus that would display the results. And when she completed the test, she waited.

And waited.

According to the instructions, a little pink dot would form if she was pregnant. So she stared at the small plastic contraption, the seconds pounding out in an agonizingly slow tempo.

Nothing yet.

Thank goodness. She glanced in the mirror and blew out a shaky breath. At least she didn't have to fear telling Sullivan that their little "fling" had left him a father.

She looked down at the pregnancy test one last time and gasped. What was that? Something pale and pink? No, it couldn't be. A dot?

They'd used condoms for goodness' sake. Had they gotten careless? Had one of them sprung a microscopic leak? Lissa knew those things weren't foolproof. But why did *she* have to be a statistic?

Lissa snatched the instruction sheet off the countertop. Maybe she'd read something wrong, done something wrong.

But no such luck.

The proof was in the bright-pink dot that glared back at her.

Still, there might be a mistake. These store-bought tests couldn't possibly be 100 percent accurate all of the time.

In the morning, she'd call the doctor and try to get in to see him, maybe ask for a more extensive lab test.

But deep in her heart, she had a feeling the pink dot wasn't a fluke. And that stress hadn't caused an upset in her hormonal balance.

Somehow, she'd gotten pregnant.

So now what? Did she dare tell Sullivan the news?

Or did she keep her secret to herself and let him leave without a backward glance?

Claire Windsor arrived at the vineyard office just after nine o'clock the next morning. She was a petite woman, with short, dark-brown hair, expressive blue eyes, and a ready smile.

Sullivan thought the stylishly dressed artist looked a lot prettier in person than she did in her Web site photo. The bright turquoise linen jacket she wore made her blue eyes sparkle.

Because of the awards, honors and achievements listed on her site, he guessed her to be about forty or so, although she didn't really look it.

"Did you have any trouble finding the place?" he asked.

"Not at all. Your directions were easy to follow."

When Lissa, who'd been taking Barney for a walk on a leash—or maybe it was the other way around—entered the office, Sullivan introduced the women.

"I can see what you mean," the attractive, forty-something artist told Sullivan, while studying Lissa's face. "She has a perfect profile for what you have in mind. And that hair? Beautiful."

"You came highly recommended," Sullivan told the artist. "I'm glad the timing worked out for all of us."

"I thought you got my name from my Web site," Claire said. "Who can I thank for the recommendation?"

"Anthony Martinelli."

The woman seemed taken aback at the mention of Anthony's name, but her expression eased into a smile. "It's been a long time since I've seen him. Our paths don't cross often. How is he?"

"Maybe you ought to ask Lissa," Sullivan said. "She's the one who knows him best."

Lissa flashed him a narrow-eyed glare. She was annoyed at him, most likely, and wanted him to know. Then she turned a cordial smile to Claire and addressed his comment. "Anthony lost his wife about a year ago, Claire. It was unexpected and a big shock. But he seems to be doing well."

"He's dating again," Sullivan interjected, unable to help himself from throwing a jab.

The vintner sure seemed to bring out that raw bone of jealousy in Sullivan, making him irrational. It shouldn't matter what Lissa did or who she dated. Sullivan didn't want a lasting relationship with her, but for some reason, he didn't want Anthony to have one with her, either.

Lissa crossed her arms and arched a brow. "When did you speak to Anthony about the artwork?"

"At the reception," Sullivan said, realizing he'd better do something to lighten her mood. "Anthony was the one who first suggested having your image sketched on the label. And he mentioned knowing a great artist. Don't you remember?"

"Now that you mention it, I do."

"So when you agreed to the idea, I found his name in your Rolodex and called him. He didn't have Claire's number, but he gave me her name, and I checked out her Web site. I was impressed by her work, so I set up the appointment." Sullivan slid the attractive, older woman a warm smile. "Anthony was right. You've got a lot of talent, Claire. And you'll do justice to both the lady and the wine."

"I appreciate your confidence." Claire turned to Lissa. "Should we get started?"

"Would it be okay if we did this in my bedroom?" Lissa asked.

"The Cartwrights have a beautiful garden," Sullivan said, thinking Claire would find the backdrop inspiring.

Lissa shot him an incredulous look. "I'm not taking my clothes off outside."

"Sullivan suggested I come out to the vineyard," Claire said, "since you might not feel comfortable in my studio. So I'll set up wherever you like. I can improvise the background in my workshop when I complete the project and prep it for use on the label."

"I'd feel better in my room," Lissa said.

"That'll be fine." Claire smiled warmly. "I'll go and get my things so we can get started."

When the artist had gone back to her car, Lissa crossed her arms and gazed at Sullivan. "So you called to get a recommendation from Anthony. Isn't that odd, considering you don't like the man?"

"I can put aside my feelings for the benefit of my client." Sullivan shrugged. "Besides, maybe I was wrong about the guy. You obviously think the world of him. So go ahead and date him."

"I don't need your permission or your approval."

No, Sullivan realized, she didn't. And for some reason, in spite of his determination to end things while his heart was still in one piece, he didn't like the idea of another man sleeping with her. Any man.

After the women walked out of the office, leaving Sullivan with Barney, he and the dog wandered to the pond. He wasn't sure how long he stayed out in the fresh air and sunshine with only Barney to keep him company. An hour? Maybe two?

He'd wanted to stay nearby, to make sure the sketching session went well. Or maybe it was just curiosity about the entire process.

About the time he decided only a fool would continue to hang around a duck pond with a goofy little pup who couldn't stay out of the mud, a champagne-colored Lexus drove up.

Anthony Martinelli.

What was he doing here?

The older man climbed from his car and approached the pond. He nodded toward the muddy pup chewing upon the bright yellow leash. "Part of your job description?"

Sullivan didn't think the guy was trying to be a smart aleck, but the comment grated upon him just the same, and he didn't see any reason to respond.

"I stopped by to see Ken," Martinelli said. "Is he home?"

"No. He and Donna went to see his uncle in the convalescent home. They should be back shortly."

Martinelli nodded, then glanced up. "Did you ever get in contact with Claire Windsor?"

"As a matter of fact, I did. She's here today."

"Oh, really?" Martinelli glanced toward the house.

Before either of the men could say anything more, Lissa walked out the front door, followed by Claire, who carried an oversize black canvas bag over her shoulder, a large black attaché case in one hand and a sketchbook in the other.

Martinelli flashed Claire a warm smile, and when

she shuffled the items she held, he took her hand in greeting. "It's good to see you again."

"It's been a long time." Claire removed her hand, but not her gaze.

That guy sure was suave. Too suave. What was he going to do? Hit on the artist, right in front of the woman he'd been dating?

"I'd love to see the finished product," Anthony said to Claire.

Sullivan tensed. He couldn't really blame the guy for wanting to see the sketch of Lissa without her clothes on. He wanted to see it, too. But Sullivan wasn't nearing the dirty-old-man age. And he wasn't trying to juggle two women at a time.

"Do you mind if I show them?" Claire asked Lissa.

"I guess I'd better get used to people seeing it." Lissa looked at Sullivan, then at Anthony.

Well, Sullivan minded. He didn't want Martinelli ogling Lissa—not even a sketch of her—and he had half a notion to grab the sketchpad and hang on tight. But that was crazy. Her image would soon be on every bottle of Virgin Mist wine.

Still, he wanted to sneak a peek. He wanted to see if the image captured the Lady Godiva essence he remembered.

Okay. So it was good. Innocent, but sexy. And when Claire took it home and finished working on it, the label would probably be dynamite.

"This is great," Anthony said. "You haven't lost

your touch, Claire. I can't wait to see the finished product.''

*The finished product?* Or the real thing? Just watching Anthony gaze at the drawing of Lissa's body tore at Sullivan's gut.

He had to get out of here before he made some stupid, lame, adolescent comment.

''I've got a couple of important calls to make in the office,'' he said, handing Barney's leash to Lissa and excusing himself.

As he strode across the grass, he realized he'd neglected to tell Claire she'd done a fine job capturing the beauty of Lissa's body.

But maybe that's because he was so caught up in the fact she'd caught that same innocent yet sensual expression Lissa had worn the first time they made love.

Lissa watched Sullivan leave, then returned her attention to Anthony and Claire, just in time to see the artist and the vintner exchange a private glance.

It appeared as though the two had a history of more than friendship. And she found her curiosity piqued. ''How long have you and Anthony known each other?''

''We met nearly twenty years ago, but have only seen each other sporadically,'' Claire said, tossing Anthony a charming smile. ''And we've had this…what would you call it?''

''An attraction,'' he said. ''Don't you think?''

Claire smiled. "I guess you could call it that. We met at the wedding of a friend, and Anthony asked me out. But I was leaving the next day for art school in New York. And by the time I returned, he'd married someone else."

"But our timing has always been bad. We've never been single at the same time." Anthony's gaze lingered on Claire. "By the way, how is Derek doing? The last I heard, he'd made a fortune on that business venture in Chicago."

"Derek had to travel a lot—for business purposes. Or so he said. Eventually he found a home away from home. The divorce will be final next week."

"I'm sorry to hear that." Anthony turned to Lissa. "Well, I guess I'd better go."

"I'll tell my dad you came by."

Anthony nodded, then reached into his jacket pocket and pulled out a business card. He handed it to Claire. "Let me give you my number. We've got some catching up to do."

Oh come on, Lissa thought. Who was the man trying to fool? He'd just found out that he and the woman he'd been attracted to for years were, for the first time, both single at the same moment.

But it didn't bother Lissa. Not at all.

Anthony and Claire were probably better suited to each other anyway.

Besides, Lissa wouldn't date the charming vintner again. Not if she was carrying Sullivan's baby.

And even if she weren't pregnant, a relationship with Anthony wasn't going anywhere.

Bottom line? His kiss hadn't measured up to Sullivan's.

And Lissa feared no other man's ever would.

## Chapter Twelve

The next afternoon, Lissa went directly to her room following a visit to the doctor's office, where she'd learned an unsettling fact.

The home pregnancy test she'd purchased had been more dependable than the condoms she and Sullivan had used. And she was definitely going to have a baby.

Fortunately her folks had gone to visit Uncle Pete, so they weren't home to question her about her health or about why a workaholic would leave the hired business consultant to fend for himself in the vineyard office.

She lay on the bed, fully clothed, her hands resting upon a tummy that would expand with the growth of her child. She turned her head and studied the telephone, wondering if she dared make the call. She felt the need to share her news with someone.

But she wasn't yet ready to level with her mom and dad. Or her sister, who had managed to follow the rules and get married before getting pregnant.

She'd tell them all, of course, but not yet. She couldn't bear to see the disappointment in their eyes. Or the pity.

But there was one person whose image kept creeping into her mind. Someone who might care about her dilemma yet was far enough removed to offer wise counsel without making her feel like a fool.

Did she dare call Jared?

Talking to him might quell the overwhelming urge to bare her soul to someone. She rolled to the side, pulled out the drawer on her nightstand and withdrew the business card Jared had given her. What would it hurt?

He'd said to call him anytime, day or night. Had he meant what he said?

She sat up in bed, grabbed the telephone and jabbed a finger at the numbers that would reach him at his law office.

"Cambry, Ames and Walker," a woman said.

"May I speak to Jared Cambry, please? This is Lissa Cartwright."

"One moment. I'll see if he's available."

Lissa didn't have to wait long. Jared picked up almost immediately. "Hey, Lissa, it's good to hear from you."

Thank goodness. She felt a bond of some kind with the man who'd fathered her. And she was glad to know he'd felt something, too. She was getting awfully tired of one-way relationships.

"How's Mark?" she asked.

"He's pale and not as energetic as he used to be, but his spirits are good. And in spite of all the needle pokes, he doesn't complain."

Lissa's heart went out to the man and his family. Watching a bright, happy child grow ill had to be heart-wrenching. "Have you had any luck finding Adam?"

"Not yet. But I've got my investigator working on it."

Her desire to meet her twin brother had been heightened by the need to find a bone-marrow donor in time. And she now understood a part of what Jared had been feeling when he came to the vineyard. He'd wanted to find her after moving back to Portland, but Mark's condition had made finding her critical.

"How is the rest of the family holding up?" she asked.

"We're all trying to keep positive and upbeat around Mark, but it's been tough on us, especially my wife." Jared blew out a heavy breath. "Other than that, everyone else is doing well. And they're looking forward to meeting you."

"I'm glad," Lissa said, before lapsing into silence.

"Okay. What gives?" Jared asked. "I've been a dad long enough to know when someone has a problem and needs to talk."

What would Jared think of her when she told him she'd gotten pregnant and wasn't going to marry the father of the baby? Would he, considering his past mistake, understand?

There was only one way to find out. "I'm pregnant, Jared."

"Pregnant? That's great. Isn't it?"

A tear slipped down her cheek, and she swiped it away with the back of her hand. "I'm going to be an unwed mother."

He didn't speak right away. And she hoped it wasn't because she'd disappointed him. Maybe he was trying to think of something supportive to say. Something wise. Something that would make her believe everything was going to be all right, even if she was hurting to the bone.

"I didn't know your birth mother very well," he said. "But she once told me something I've never forgotten. And if she were alive, I think she'd tell you the same thing."

Lissa sniffled. "What's that?"

"Babies are a blessing."

"Is that how she felt about me?" Lissa hated being a mistake, an inconvenience, but she always tried to keep those old insecurities locked deep inside. So as a second thought and a cover-up, she added, "I mean, is that how she felt about being pregnant?"

"Olivia was only sixteen and not ready to be a mother," Jared said. "But she was willing to do whatever it took to provide her baby with a loving home, whether that meant keeping you herself or giving you up so that a loving family, like the Cartwrights, could have you."

"I've always wondered about her. About you, too. But she didn't have to carry me to term. And I'm glad to know she made me a priority in her life." Lissa blew out a soft sigh.

Her baby would be a priority, too. And fortunately, she was far more capable of providing financially for her child, something sixteen-year-old Olivia hadn't been equipped to do.

"I'm sorry that neither Olivia nor I were there for you when you were growing up," Jared said.

"I understand," she said, although a small, raw part of her was still trying to come to grips with him not being a father to her. But the fact was, she'd been raised in a loving home and had no complaints. "I had a wonderful childhood."

"You have no idea how happy I am that the Cartwrights raised you. I'll be grateful to them for the rest of my life. What did they have to say about your news?"

Lissa bit her lip. "I...uh...haven't told them yet."

"Why not?"

*Because I'm afraid I'll disappoint them, afraid they'll think less of me.*

Gosh, those old feelings were hard to shake. Lissa

was still competing for a place in their hearts, a place right alongside Eileen. "I guess I just wanted to bounce it off you first."

"I'm glad you did. But you also need to share this with your mother, when you're ready, of course. It didn't take me long to see how much that woman loves you. And I'm sure your father does, too."

Lissa nodded. "Yes. And you're right. I do need to talk to them about it. I guess I'm just afraid of letting them down."

"Kids have been disappointing their parents for years. And I'm sure your parents' reactions won't be as bad as you expect. And if they are? They'll get over it. Parents have been doing that for years, too."

"What made you so wise?"

"Disappointing my parents," he said. "And the lectures I had to listen to afterward. And the hugs and tears that followed. It's part of life."

"And speaking of life, I think I'm going to love having you in mine," she said, not quite ready to tell him she loved him, but knowing someday she would.

"I'm glad, Lissa. Just out of curiosity, what did the father of the baby say when you told him?"

She bit her lip and glanced at the antique beveled mirror over her dresser, spotting a lonely stranger staring back at her. "I haven't told him. And I'm not sure whether I will."

"You owe it to the man to tell him."

"It was just an affair. You know. A casual fling." Lissa closed her eyes and blinked back the tears. She hated referring to what she and Sullivan had shared as nothing special when it had meant so much to her.

"I didn't like hearing that Olivia was expecting a baby," Jared said. "Our relationship had been a one-night stand. But I wouldn't have wanted her to keep it a secret. She did the right thing by telling me."

"Thanks, Jared." Lissa wound the telephone cord around her finger, then added, "Just for the record. It was much more than a one-night stand for me. I fell in love with him, but he doesn't feel the same way."

"I'm sorry you're hurting."

"Yeah. Me, too. But that's how we gain wisdom, right? Disappointing our parents and ourselves?"

"And taking responsibility for our mistakes and trying not to make the same ones again."

He was right, and she was glad she'd called him. "I'll tell my mom and dad. And I guess I'll have to tell the baby's father, too."

"You've got me in your corner, Lissa. For whatever that's worth."

"It's worth a lot, Jared."

When the call ended, Lissa hung up the phone and blew out the breath she'd been holding.

In spite of her efforts to enter a no-strings-attached affair, she had fallen helplessly in love with a self-proclaimed bachelor who had no intention of settling down and would probably cringe at the thought of being a father.

But it wasn't her baby's fault. And Lissa would do

everything in her power to make sure her child knew how loved she or he was.

She'd tell her parents the news, of course. And in spite of her reluctance, she'd tell Sullivan, too.

He'd be leaving in the next day or so.

Leaving her forever.

But Lissa wouldn't be alone. She'd have his baby to love.

A child who would depend upon Lissa to make the world a special, loving place to live—even without a father.

"You've been especially quiet this evening," Donna said, as she and Lissa stood over the sink doing the dinner dishes.

"I've got a lot on my mind." Lissa reached for a wet plate from the drainer and wiped it dry. "I'm sure once the label is ready for the bottles and the first group of tourists arrive, I'll be fine."

Her mother bought the explanation, which was a relief, since Lissa didn't feel like talking.

"I sure hope the doctors release Uncle Pete and let him come live with us," Donna said.

"Me, too." Lissa's dad spent a lot of time at the convalescent hospital, trying to make his uncle comfortable after moving from the home he'd lived in for more than fifty years. "Then they could have watched tonight's basketball game here."

Her mom tightened her lips and worried her brow.

"I know. I hate having your dad on the road tonight, especially with that storm coming."

"Daddy is an excellent driver." Lissa placed a hand on her mom's shoulder. "I'm sure he'll be fine."

"You're probably right. But I worry just the same."

They went back to their work and, in no time at all, had the dishes put away and the kitchen back in order.

"I have some chocolate cake left over," Mom said. "Do you want to take a slice to Sullivan?"

Did she? That would give her an excuse to go to the cottage and speak to him about the baby, about the future. With him leaving tomorrow morning, she wouldn't have much chance to talk to him on a casual level.

"All right. I'll take him a piece of cake." Lissa folded the dishtowel and set it upon the clean countertop.

"I'm going to miss that man when he leaves," Donna said. "He sure was nice to have around."

Lissa was going to miss him, too. Not the cool, withdrawn businessman, of course. But she would always remember the charming, witty man who had been her first lover.

Mom handed her a slice of cake on a plate covered in plastic wrap. "Your dad probably won't be back for another hour, so I'm going upstairs to read for a while."

After wiping up the few chocolate crumbs from the counter, Mom rinsed out the dishcloth and draped it over the faucet. "Be sure to take a jacket and umbrella. That storm should hit pretty soon."

Lissa nodded. "I will."

"See you in the morning, Lis." Her mom gave her a kiss on the cheek.

"'Night, Mom." Lissa watched as her mother left the kitchen, then snatched Sullivan's dessert from the counter and strode into the living room.

Through the bay window, Lissa watched a flash of lightning shoot a jagged path across the sky, validating the weatherman's prediction and her mom's reminder.

There was a storm brewing, all right. And not just on the horizon. Lissa's heart ricocheted in her chest, as she set the dessert plate on the lamp table, then took her jacket from the coat rack by the door.

Even though a roll of thunder tumbled through the sky, she nixed the umbrella idea and carried the chocolate cake to the cottage. It's not as though this would take very long. She'd be out of there and back home before the rain came.

As Lissa crossed the bridge, she wished there was another way around the impending discussion. But Jared had been right. Sullivan needed to be told—and the sooner the better. No need to prolong the inevitable. Besides, he was leaving tomorrow morning, and this wasn't the kind of conversation that could be handled by telephone or e-mail, no matter how much easier it would be.

The wind whipped her hair around, and the scent of rain filled the crisp night air, promising a downpour. Lissa wanted to turn around and go home, preferring to curl up with a good book, as her mother had done. But instead of wrapping herself in warmth and comfort, living a fantasy where everyone lived happily-ever-after, she strode toward the cottage, ready to face the cold, stark truth of reality.

As she reached the steps leading to the wooden porch, she paused, taking a breath, sucking in her courage. Then she crossed the deck and knocked on the door.

Sullivan answered wearing only a pair of gray sweat pants. He didn't speak, didn't smile. And she was again reminded of a Scottish highlander, one who'd been caught off-guard and unprotected.

He just stood there staring at her as though she were a marauder.

She managed a smile. "Mom asked me to bring you some dessert."

"Thanks." He took the plate from her. "You didn't have to come out on a night like this."

"I know, but I think there's something we should talk about."

"You're probably right." He stepped aside so she could walk in, then closed the door. "Can I get you a glass of wine?"

She started to say yes, glad to have something to

hold on to, something to ease her nervousness. But wine wouldn't be good for her growing baby. "No thanks. I'll pass."

"Have a seat." He indicated the sofa, then carried the cake to the counter, where he left it.

She sat in the overstuffed easy chair, leaving him on the sofa.

The fireplace blazed, providing warmth and comfort, and her thoughts drifted to the time they'd made love in front of the hearth. She wondered whether she'd ever be able to come into the guest house again without remembering the lovemaking they'd shared, the passion. The wonder of first love. The agony of a broken heart.

"We really haven't ended things right," Sullivan said. "We could both probably use some closure."

He was right. But was there a right way to end a love affair? Lissa wasn't sure.

"We both know things are over," she said. "But it's not over for me."

He tensed. "I didn't make any promises. And with my job, I travel a lot. It's not the kind of life that's conducive to a steady relationship."

She placed her hands on her knees, felt them trembling just a tad. "I'm not asking anything from you. But I do have to tell you something."

Sullivan's stomach clenched. God, she wasn't going to tell him she loved him, was she? Or that she wanted a commitment of some kind? If he could drop his guard and make the same mistake of loving and trusting a woman again, he might take a gamble on Lissa.

But he wasn't up to the task and probably wouldn't ever be. He had too many reasons to believe things couldn't possibly work out. Still, he had to listen, hear her out. "What do you have to tell me?"

"I'm not sure how it happened, but I'm pregnant."

A roar of thunder rumbled across the sky, shaking the roof and causing the windows to shudder. But the reverberating noise didn't shake Sullivan as much as Lissa's announcement.

"You're what?"

"Pregnant. I was late with my...you know, and so I took one of those home pregnancy tests."

"There must be some mistake." He stood and walked across the room, searching for an easy way out, a hole to open up in the floor and let him escape the emotional fall-out of the bomb she'd just dropped.

"I didn't trust the results, either," she said. "So I called the doctor, and he scheduled a blood test. There was no mistake. I'm pregnant." She took a big breath, then slowly let it out. "I'm not asking or expecting anything from you. But I think it's only fair to tell you."

Fair? Hell. A part of him wished he didn't know, that she'd never told him.

But she was right. Sullivan wouldn't want a kid of his running around on earth without him knowing about it.

He raked a hand through his hair. "I don't know what to say."

"You don't have to say anything. I plan to have the baby, though, and raise him or her by myself." She tossed a strand of hair behind her, then clutched her hands in her lap. "I'm not sure how this happened. I mean, we used protection. But I guess it didn't work."

"I didn't feel confident with that first condom. It was probably expired. But I figured using it wouldn't be that risky." He raked a hand through his hair again, thinking it might be standing on end now, much like his emotions.

"Like I said, Sullivan. I don't expect anything from you."

That was good. Because marriage scared the hell out of him. And even if he wanted to lay his heart on the line again, risk betrayal and divorce, he didn't want to subject his kid to any of the things he'd been through as a child, the accusations, the lies, the guilt.

*Where the hell did your mother go?*

*I don't know, Daddy. She went with her cousin, Tom.*

*She doesn't have a cousin named Tom. And don't you dare cover for her.*

Thank God, Sullivan and Kristen hadn't had a child to fight over, a kid that felt responsible for a disastrous marriage, as Sullivan had felt when his folks split up. A nine-year-old boy who had testified in court, betraying both of his parents.

Wouldn't it be better if a kid didn't know his dad at all, rather than go through all of that?

That didn't mean Sullivan wouldn't step up to the plate financially. He wouldn't turn his back on Lissa and the baby.

"I'll pay child support," he offered.

"Whatever you think is fair." She looked like a windblown waif, and he felt as though he should do something, reach out, give her a hug. Something. But he stood rooted to the floor, afraid to do the wrong thing, afraid to open an emotional can of worms.

"I'll start paying before the kid is born," he added, wanting to do the honorable thing while still holding tight to his freedom, his memories, his fears.

"I really don't need anything, but I won't turn down whatever you offer." She stood. "I'd better get back inside the house before the rain hits. We can handle this over the phone and through e-mail."

He merely nodded, like a dummy on the knee of a ventriloquist, wondering if his voice would ever return.

She stopped in the doorway and nailed him with a glimmering, emerald-green gaze. "I'll love our baby enough for both of us, Sullivan."

Then she turned on her heel and left the guest house.

For a moment, he wanted to run out into the night and stop her, have her come back. Hold her in his arms and try to come up with a game plan they could both live with. But the memories of a little boy crying himself to sleep held him back.

Sullivan didn't have what it took to hold a marriage together. And he didn't know many couples who had actually been able to do so.

Lissa had lowered the boom, then let him off the hook. He could leave tomorrow and not look back.

He should feel as though he'd escaped by the skin of his teeth. But he didn't.

His emotions were wound tighter than a spring. Boy, he could sure use a stiff drink right now. Scotch straight up, if he had any available. But he didn't. So instead, he strode into the kitchen and took a chilled bottle of chardonnay from the refrigerator. He pulled the cork and poured a glass.

But somehow, he doubted an entire case of wine would soothe his nerves, still his memories and help him fall asleep.

As Lissa escaped the cottage and stepped into the night air, the wind swept a splatter of rain across her face.

The tears she'd been holding burst free, blending with the first sprinkles of the breaking storm. She'd told Sullivan she didn't want anything from him, but that wasn't true. She loved him and wanted him to love her, too. Just like the fairytales she'd read about, she wanted it all—white lace, scattered rose petals, promises and a happy-ever-after.

But that wasn't going to happen.

By the time she reached the house, the blustery wind and driving rain, along with Sullivan's rejection, had chilled her to the bone.

Shivering and trying to be quiet, she left her wet shoes on the porch, let herself inside and locked the door. Then she carried her damp jacket to the laundry room and hung it up to dry.

Never had she felt like such an outcast, so alone in the world.

As she trudged upstairs, she felt the urge to be held, to be told that everything would be all right, the way her mother had always comforted her in the past.

When Lissa reached her parents' room, she lifted her hand to knock. Paused. Then mustered what little courage she had left and rapped upon the door.

"Come in," her mom said.

Lissa entered the warmth of her mother's bedroom and found Donna sitting up in the king-sized bed, propped up with several fluffy pillows and holding a book in her hand.

"Can I talk to you?" Lissa asked.

"Sure, honey." Her mother set the open paperback down in her lap, then made room on the mattress beside her. "Sit down."

"I...uh...have a problem."

"With the vineyard? Dad's not home yet, but I'll try to help, if I can."

"No. This is a personal problem."

Donna took off her glasses, and closed the book

completely, putting it aside on the bedspread. Then she took Lissa's hand in hers. "What is it?"

"I'm…" She couldn't say it.

"In love?" her mom asked.

Lissa was going to skip the love part and jump right into the unwed-and-pregnant scenario. But love was a much better tack. And it was the truth. She caught her mother's knowing gaze, then nodded.

"Want to talk about it?"

"Not really," Lissa said, "but I think one of your hugs might help."

Her mom swept Lissa into a warm embrace, offering her love wrapped in the familiar scent of gardenia and the softness of a warm, flannel gown.

"Have you fallen in love with Sullivan?" her mother asked.

So much for keeping things a secret. "I didn't know it had been so obvious."

"Not at first, but I could sense the tension between you. It seemed far more personal than business-related. And I could also see the way you looked at each other, when you didn't think anyone was paying attention."

Mom might have seen Lissa sneaking a peek at Sullivan, but those glances couldn't have been mutual. And believing Sullivan felt anything for her would only prolong the pain, the ache.

"He doesn't love me," Lissa said.

"Your hurts were easier to deal with when you were little." Her mom gently tugged a strand of

Lissa's hair, then brushed her cheek with a kiss. "I wish there was some kind of medicine I could give to mend your broken heart, some magic words to make you feel better."

"Does that mean you won't remind me that Sullivan isn't the only fish in the sea?"

"Well, if I thought that were true, or that it would make things all better, I'd probably mention it. But I doubt you're interested in another fish right now."

"You're right. It wouldn't help. And even if I wanted to go fishing tomorrow, I can't."

"Why's that?"

Lissa took a deep breath, then slowly let it out as she prepared to bare her secret. "Because I'm pregnant."

As her mother released her arms and pulled back, Lissa braced herself for a look of shock, of disappointment, of anger.

What she saw was surprise laced with compassion. "Oh, honey. I'm sure it won't be easy to have a child without a husband, but babies are truly a blessing."

Lissa blinked. It was the second time she'd heard that very thing, words both of her mothers believed. "You're not angry with me?"

"For what? I'm not so old that I don't remember how it felt to love your father with all my heart, to offer him my love."

Lissa fell back into her mother's arms. "Thank you for understanding, Mom. I love you."

"I love you, too, sweetheart."

They listened to the sound of the automatic garage door lifting and a car ignition shutting down.

"Daddy's home," Lissa said, "safe and sound."

"Thank the Lord." Her mother froze and took Lissa's hands in hers. "Let's wait to tell him your news until after Sullivan leaves."

"Will Daddy blow his top?" Lissa asked. Her father had a bit of a temper, but usually only toward stubborn home-improvement projects and farm equipment. Never toward his wife or children.

"He won't be angry with you, but knowing your dad and how protective he is, he may want to clobber Sullivan." Mom smiled and cupped Lissa's jaw. "You've always held a special place in your daddy's heart—not that he favors you over Eileen. But you're the one who tagged along after him each day, the one who grew up to be so much like him."

All of a sudden, the adoption issue no longer seemed to matter. And Lissa began to realize she'd always been a *real* daughter. Her misconceived perceptions had thwarted her ability to accept the *real* love her mom and dad had always offered her.

"Oh, my goodness," her mother said, blue eyes sparkling and growing wide as she began counting on her fingers.

"What?"

Her mother clapped her hands and broke into a wide grin. "What a wonderful Christmas we're going to have this year! We'll have two brand-new babies to love and spoil. Two little ones who will grow up close like you and Eileen.''

How fortunate Lissa had been to be adopted by the Cartwrights. Throughout the years, their love had been unwavering. And nothing had changed. They would love her baby, just as they would love Eileen's.

Lissa's child would be blessed with the most wonderful grandparents in the world. And a loving mother. Surely that would make up for an absent father.

Now if Lissa could just figure out how to stop loving a man who didn't love her back, everything would work out fine.

## Chapter Thirteen

*I'm pregnant.*

Those two little words had sent Sullivan's once predictable world spinning topsy-turvy.

Sleep was out of the question, and not just because of the rain pounding on the windows and the wind blowing through the trees. His mind was tossing and turning, and his nerves were on end.

A little after eleven o'clock that night, he threw off the covers and climbed from bed.

Before his marriage to Kristin, Sullivan had actually wanted a family. In his dreams, he'd envisioned two parents playing active roles in their children's lives—reading stories, playing catch in the backyard, that sort of thing.

But he'd quit believing in fairytales the day he'd come home and seen the note Kristin had taped to the bedroom door.

Dear Sullivan,
I don't want to be married anymore. By the time you read this, I'll be in Barbados...

... With someone she liked better. Someone older and richer.

After picking up the pieces that day and facing reality, Sullivan had put away any lingering thoughts of having kids.

Until Lissa made her startling announcement.

In a way, he kind of liked the idea of a little Sullivan running around, especially since his child would have Lissa as a mother. Her compassion was evident in the way she had urged her parents to bring Uncle Pete to live at the vineyard, where he could be loved and cared for by family. And her maternal streak burst forth in her love for Barney, a rascally pup who kept her hopping.

*I'll love the baby enough for both of us.*

And he had no doubt she would.

He figured she'd stay at the vineyard, where she'd raise their child, which is what Sullivan wanted her to do. A kid would be lucky to live here, with Ken and Donna Cartwright as doting grandparents. He imagined Donna would keep the cookie jar filled to the brim with treats.

Sullivan really liked the idea of his and Lissa's

child living at Valencia Vineyards, where the kid would grow up in peace and harmony, something that had been sorely missing from his own childhood.

It was a big relief to know his son or daughter wouldn't wake up wondering whether dawn would bring another godawful fight or a frigid cold war.

Sullivan wanted a hell of a lot more for his child than that. In fact, he didn't mind being a father and taking an active role in his child's life—after it was potty-trained of course. Little babies were scary. But preschoolers were pretty cool.

Maybe Lissa would let him take the kid on weekends and during summer vacations. After all, she was a levelheaded businesswoman, and they worked well together. Why not raise the baby as a joint venture?

*Whatever you think is fair,* she'd said. And sharing the kid sounded fair and right to him.

Yeah, Lissa would be easy to work with—as long as the temptation to make love didn't become a problem. And if it did? A slow smile curled his lips. They were definitely compatible physically. And their lovemaking, as good as it had been, only promised to get better with time. What would it hurt to see their physical needs met every now and then?

The more he thought about it, the more he liked the joint venture idea. It ought to work out just fine.

Unless Lissa got some fool notion about getting married and dragging a stepfather into the picture.

Sullivan's gut clenched at the thought of some other guy teaching his son or daughter how to ride a bike. Or cuddling with Lissa in front of a cozy fire, after the kid went to bed. He scrunched his face, forcing out the image. He didn't want another man to step in and take his place. But what alternative did he have, other than to marry Lissa himself?

*Marry Lissa?*

What kind of crazy thought was that?

She'd never mentioned anything about wanting more than he'd been willing to give. In fact, she'd given him every chance to head for the hills, to escape without having the mistake of their lovemaking haunt him for the rest of his life.

So why didn't he feel like running?

Because he liked it here at Valencia Vineyards. He liked sitting around that big oak table in the evening, enjoying a home-cooked meal, catching Lissa's eye from over the top of a yellow rose centerpiece, knowing she was thinking about the heated kisses they'd shared, the mind-spinning climax they'd just reached.

The last time they'd made love, he'd closed his eyes and let the moment and the lady carry him away. He'd opened his heart and let her slip inside.

And he'd also opened himself up for disaster, for betrayal.

What the hell had he done? Had he fallen—even a little bit—for a woman who was ready to spread her wings and fly? A woman who might move out while he was on a business trip and leave a note, explaining why the marriage no longer worked for her?

Sullivan wasn't sure, but one thing was certain. Lissa wasn't like any other woman he'd ever dated.

He'd seen that from the start.

When he'd first arrived at the vineyard, she'd been a twenty-seven-year-old virgin who loved her family and was dedicated to Valencia Vineyards. Someone who dug in her heels and lasted for the duration.

*I'll love our baby enough for both of us,* she'd said.

That *wasn't* the attitude of a woman who was foot-loose and fancy-free. It was the kind of commitment a loyal and honorable woman made.

Sullivan paced the living-room floor, trying to get his thoughts together.

What did he want out of life?

Once upon a time, he'd wanted the kind of home he hadn't had as a kid. He'd even tried to create a dream family with his ex. But Kristin hadn't been a dream wife.

Was Lissa a better bet?

Could Sullivan and Lissa make that old dream come true?

He peered out the window, saw the trees bend with the wind. Strong, steady. Yet pliant.

Lissa planned to raise a child without a husband. And she would let Sullivan share a part of the baby's life—as much or as little as he wanted.

But did he love her? Even a little?

She hadn't said anything about her feelings, hadn't even given him a clue that she might want a com-mitment of any kind. But now that he was being hon-est with himself, Sullivan had to admit that he'd sensed her feelings ran deep, that she'd closed her eyes, too.

Had she opened her heart? Just a crack?

The last time they'd made love, there'd been something different in the way she'd caressed him, the way she'd kissed him. They'd shared an intimacy, a yearning, a contentment he'd never experienced before.

Was that love?

If not, then why did he have this big, gaping hole in his chest when he thought about leaving the vineyard, about leaving her? And it actually ached even more to think about never holding her, kissing her or making love with her again.

He did love her.

There was no other explanation for the emotional turmoil, for the unexplainable fear he felt at losing her to someone else. And just making the admission seemed to lift a burden from his shoulders.

Now what? Did he march over to the house and bang on the door, lay his heart at her feet and hope she didn't stomp on it?

Sullivan glanced at the clock on the nightstand. 11:43—too damn late to call or go see her. But hell, now that he'd figured out a new plan of action, he couldn't wait until dawn. He needed to talk to her. Now.

He threw on a T-shirt and a pair of slacks, grabbed a jacket from the closet and slipped a pair of loafers on his bare feet.

This was crazy. Stupid. But he couldn't stop himself from going outside in the rain, from trudging across the wet grass, from banging upon the door, then ringing the bell.

No doubt about it, going out in the rain to bare his

heart and soul in the middle of the night was the dumbest thing he'd ever done. But he didn't turn around, didn't rush back to the guest house and hide—not when he'd figured out what he wanted, what he might be able to have.

In what seemed like forever, but was probably only a couple of minutes, a sleepy-eyed Ken opened the door in his robe, looked at Sullivan with a furrowed brow and grimaced.

Well, why not? It was almost midnight, and Sullivan probably looked like hell.

"Is something wrong?" Ken asked.

"I need to talk to Lissa."

Ken glanced at the grandfather clock in the entry. "It's a bit late, son. Don't you think? Can't this wait until morning?"

From the top of the stairs, Donna called out. "Ken, come on back to bed. I'll get Lissa."

But before Donna could take two steps, Lissa poked her head out the bedroom door, looking amazingly sexy and loveable with her hair hanging loose and wearing a pink-and-white flannel gown.

"Sullivan wants to speak to you, honey." Donna opened the bedroom door and gave her daughter a gentle nudge. Then she called to Ken. "Give them some privacy, Ken. You come up here with me."

Ken scratched his head and wrinkled his brow, then climbed the stairs, passing Lissa on her way down.

Lissa glanced at the grandfather clock. Just after quarter to twelve. She wasn't sure why Sullivan had come pounding on the door, why he hadn't waited until morning. After all, he'd made it clear to her that things were over between them.

He looked so...so wet and disheveled.

Was he sick? If not, he was going to be. The rain had plastered his hair to his head. And his jacket and pants were wet.

"I need to talk to you," he said, as she reached the bottom of the stairs. "And it can't wait."

She nodded, as though it all made perfect sense, but it didn't. Was this about the baby news? Or about business? She wasn't sure, but the poor guy looked like a shipwrecked sailor who'd been battered and bruised by a violent storm on the high sea.

"Do you want to sit down?" she asked, nodding toward the sofa.

"Yeah. No." He glanced down at his wet pants and shoes, then removed the muddy loafers, leaving them on the mat by the door. "Your mom would shoot me if I tracked water into her living room. I'd better stand here on the wood floor."

"Just a minute." She hurried down the hall and withdrew a spare blanket from the guest closet, then handed it to him. "You're going to catch cold."

"Thanks." He took the green-and-blue plaid blanket from her, but merely held it. Again, she imagined him a highlander—a wounded Scotsman, clutching his family tartan to his chest.

"What's on your mind?" she asked, afraid of what she might hear, afraid to hope he'd given some thought to their relationship and wasn't ready to end things yet.

"I was a little surprised at the news, so if I reacted like a jerk, I'm sorry."

"I understand."

"But that doesn't mean I don't want to be a part of the baby's life."

"Good." She was relieved to hear that much. "I can't imagine what it would've been like to grow up without having my dad in the house. He and I have always been close."

"It wasn't like that for me," Sullivan said. "My father was never around. And it seemed that both my parents had more important things on their agenda than creating a stable home for the only child they had."

"It must have been tough on you."

"More than you'll ever know." He took a deep breath, then slowly blew it out. "My dad traveled on business, and my mom got tired of waiting for him to come home and escort her to parties and social affairs. So she'd go without him. And if it wasn't a charity event or dinner party, it was a vacation with friends."

"Did your mom take you with her?" Lissa hoped so. Her child would grow up on the vineyard and have a portable crib in the office, a little baby swing, too. And maybe one of those jumpy chairs.

He smiled, yet memories seemed to cloud his gaze. "I had a nanny. Several of them, actually."

Lissa sensed Sullivan wanted to talk, that he

needed to get something off his mind, so she took his jacket and hung it on the coat rack.

"One day, my mom took me into a nearby town for lunch and a movie. We ran into a guy she introduced as her cousin, Tom. Afterward, we left her Mercedes where she'd parked, and he drove us home. But she didn't get out of his car. She sent me inside with the nanny, then they drove off." Sullivan shivered.

From the cold? Or from the recollection? She didn't know for sure, but she let him continue, hoping that sharing the memory would help.

"My dad wasn't due in from Europe for a couple of days, but he came home unexpectedly that afternoon. And when he asked where my mother was, I told him she'd gone with her cousin, Tom." Sullivan shook his head. "How the heck did I know the guy wasn't her cousin?"

"How old were you?" she asked.

"Nine or ten. I don't remember. But I'll never forget what happened."

Lissa stepped closer, took the blanket from him and wrapped it over his shoulders, hugging him without using her arms, without getting too close. "Do you want to talk about it?"

"I've only talked about it once—in court. And I never discussed it again. But maybe it's time to clear the cobwebs out of the attic."

"Maybe so."

"My dad put me in his big, black Caddy and made me point out where they'd left my mother's sporty red Mercedes. It was still in the same spot, so we waited. And waited. All the while, my dad ranted and raved, telling me things about my mother a kid shouldn't have to hear, things about her past and where he hoped she'd spend her future.''

Lissa found it difficult to keep her arms from reaching out to him, from offering comfort. She fingered the satiny edge of the blanket instead.

Sullivan blew out a ragged sigh. ''And when *Cousin* Tom brought my mom back, my dad was waiting for them.''

She was afraid to comment, to ask what happened. So she waited to hear what he wanted to share.

''My dad threw the first punch. And Tom drew the first blood. It got pretty nasty until one of the bystanders called the police.''

''I'm so sorry you had to witness that,'' she said.

''Me, too. Because I had to testify during the divorce proceedings.''

He stood there like a brokenhearted child, and she couldn't help but ease closer, offer him a hug, like the one her mother had given her earlier. And he leaned into her embrace, pulling her close. ''I'm afraid, Lissa.''

''Of what?''

''Afraid of making promises then finding out one of us won't be able to keep them.''

''Promises about the baby?'' she asked.

''No. About us.''

''Us?''

''I think,'' he said, as though choosing his words

carefully, "we ought to consider marriage for the baby's sake."

Her heart went out to him, not only for what he'd been through, but also for thinking of their baby's best interests. "Wanting to do the right thing is admirable, Sullivan. But it's not a good enough reason to get married."

"Why not? I think a sense of ethics belongs in a marriage."

"I agree. But if it's going to last, a marriage needs to be based on love."

"And what if I think I'm falling in love with you?" His voice held a soft, but ragged edge. And his tortured gaze told her the admission had cost him a lot.

She placed a hand on his cheek, felt the light bristles he'd shave off in the morning. And he gripped her wrist to hold it there.

"Do you think you could learn to love me?" he asked. "Given time, I mean."

She didn't say anything at first; she was too amazed by his words, by the evidence of his struggle. "I don't need time, Sullivan. I'm already convinced that I love you."

She loved him? For a moment, a response lodged in his throat, then the past stepped aside, allowing a new day to dawn. "Ah, Lissa. Tell me there's a chance that we can make a go of this."

She wrapped her arms around his neck and smiled. "If you love me half as much as I love you, we can make it work."

The tension and torment eased, and his heart began to swell, to mend, to flood with warmth.

"I love you, Lissa. More than I care to admit." He pulled her into his arms and kissed her, closing his eyes and letting love lead the way.

When the kiss ended, he slid her a crooked grin. "I don't suppose you'd like to go back to the guest house with me?"

"In the rain?" She touched the wet strands of his hair. "I don't think that's a good idea."

"Then maybe you'd better send me away or invite me to stay."

She blessed him with a dimpled smile. "I'm not letting you go anywhere. But if Daddy finds you in my bed, he'll probably shoot first and ask questions later."

Sullivan stiffened. "Do you think your folks will approve of this, of us?"

"Don't worry. They've always supported me in everything I've done, although I've just begun to realize that."

"So now what?" he asked. "I don't want to go back to the guest house alone."

"Then we'd better tell them. That way we can borrow some of my dad's clothes so you don't catch pneumonia."

He kissed her again, long and deep—until he thought his heart would burst. "Let's wake your parents right now."

"Mom will be excited," Lissa said. "And she'll want to start planning a wedding."

"Don't let her get too excited. I want to marry you as soon as possible, and we don't have much time to make things elaborate."

"How much time do we have?" she asked.

He kissed her brow. "My kid will probably be good at math. And I don't want him thinking I took advantage of his mom. Besides, I want to make love to you again and I'd rather not have to worry about getting shot."

"Is Saturday soon enough?"

"No, but that will give me time to reschedule my calendar and plan a great honeymoon. Any idea where you'd like to go?"

She tugged at the plaid blanket draped over him, then broke into an easy smile. "It's probably too late to pull it all together, but I'd like to walk with you on a Scottish moor."

"That can be arranged." Then he kissed her again, letting go of the past and embracing the future.

Saturday dawned bright and clear, with a springtime promise of new life.

A small, intimate wedding would be held on the grounds of Valencia Vineyards, with only family and their closest friends in attendance.

Sullivan's Great-aunt Clara had been genuinely disappointed to miss the ceremony, but she was hosting a Bingo Marathon at the seniors' center in her hometown. And, interestingly enough, neither of Sullivan's parents could make it. His mother was on a Mediterranean cruise, and his dad had another chance to play golf at Augusta.

Lissa would have felt badly had it been her parents who couldn't attend. But Sullivan seemed a bit relieved. "It's just as well, honey. I never know whether they'll let bygones be bygones, or when they'll make a scene."

From the upstairs bedroom, Lissa stood at the window and looked over the parklike grounds, where the minister stood near a gazebo that had been decorated with lush green ivy, yellow roses and white hydrangea after being set up near the pond.

While a few guests took seats on the white chairs provided by Valley Party Rental, she saw Anthony Martinelli speak to her father, with a smiling Claire Windsor on his arm.

Lissa suspected, by the way the couple looked at each other, that there'd soon be another wedding in the valley.

A knock sounded at the door, and her sister Eileen let herself in. "The Cambrys are in the living room. Should we ask them to take a seat outside?"

"No, I'd like to talk to them first."

Eileen's gaze swept over Lissa. "You look absolutely beautiful, Lissa. I'm so happy for you."

"Thanks, Eileen. This is almost too good to be true."

"I felt the same way."

Her sister broke into a big grin, then gave Lissa a gentle hug, one that wouldn't wrinkle the dress Eileen had worn down the aisle last year, the very same dress

their mother had worn more than forty years before that.

Moments later, Lissa entered the living room and
found Jared talking with her mom and dad. Two teenagers stood beside him, a girl with straight brown hair
and green eyes that seemed to be a Cambry trade-
mark. The boy had hair the color of Jared's, yet
seemed to favor someone else. His mother, probably.

"I'd like you to meet Chad and Shawna," Jared
said.

Lissa shook their hands, welcoming them to the
vineyard. "I'm so happy to meet you. And I'm glad
you could come to the wedding."

"Danielle stayed home with Mark," Jared said.
"Since it's a two-hour drive, she didn't feel comfortable leaving him."

"I understand," Lissa said. "After the honeymoon,
Sullivan and I will come to Portland for that visit."

"We'd like that," Jared said.

There wasn't much time to chat before the ceremony, but one question pressed heavily on her mind.
"Have you had any luck finding Adam?"

"Not yet," Jared said. "But we've got a lead.
Something we hadn't expected. I'll let you know if it
pans out."

Lissa nodded. "Sullivan and I will help with the
search after we get home from our honeymoon."

"I appreciate that," Jared said.

She prayed that Jared would find Adam in time,
and that her twin would be the match Mark so desperately needed.

Ken—her *real* father—took her arm. "I hate to rush you, honey, but Pastor McDonald has another wedding later this afternoon. And since he's squeezing us in as a favor to your mother, we need to get started."

"We'll talk after the ceremony," Jared said. Then he escorted Chad and Shawna outside to take their seats.

As the music began, Eileen, the matron of honor, proceeded down the grassy aisle, while Lissa held her daddy's arm.

"I love you and Mom more than you'll ever know," she told the man who'd always been there for her. The man who would be handing her over to the new man in her life. "And when Sullivan and I become parents, I hope we'll be as wise and loving as you and Mom."

A tear slipped down her father's cheek. "And I hope you'll be blessed with children as special as you and your sister."

She kissed his cheek, gave his arm a gentle squeeze, then set her sights on Sullivan who waited for her at the flower-adorned gazebo.

The sun glistened on the red highlights in his hair, again reminding her of a Scottish laird. Sullivan Grayson, her husband, her life.

In only a few short moments, they would say their vows before God and the world. Love lit his face as he waited for her to join him. And tears of happiness misted her eyes.

Sullivan couldn't believe his good fortune, as the

woman he loved made her way toward him on her father's arm.

Radiant Lissa, dressed in a cream-colored lace gown, had never looked lovelier, happier. His heart nearly burst with pride.

God had surely blessed this day, blessed their love.

Ken placed Lissa's hand in the crook of Sullivan's arm, then quickly swiped a tear from his cheek before taking his seat next to a smiling, teary-eyed Donna.

''Dearly Beloved,'' the minister began.

Sullivan held tightly to Lissa's hand, ready to take the journey together. Never had anything felt so right.

In response to the questions men and women had been asked for hundreds of years, Lissa and Sullivan vowed to love each other until the end of time.

And when the minister told Sullivan to kiss his bride, he did so with all the love he'd found in his heart.

# *Epilogue*

Lissa and Sullivan had arrived in Scotland less than a week ago, and already their honeymoon had proven to be more magical than Lissa had ever dreamed.

They'd spent the first few days in Edinburgh, walking along the streets, visiting museums and art galleries, shopping and going to the theater. Then they ventured to the older part of town, where they toured Edinburgh Castle, which loomed over the city on a high hill.

This morning, they'd rented a car and driven out to Gretna Green, a village on the Scottish border where thousands of underage English couples had eloped over the years to marry legally at the age of sixteen without their parents' consent.

An anvil priest, who was usually a colorful character, would perform the marriage by asking the couple to plight their troth in front of two witnesses. And as quick as the bang of a hammer on an anvil, the marriage was legally bound.

Many an angry father had come racing after a couple, leaving the village a rich romantic history, complete with exciting and sometimes comical tales.

Lissa and Sullivan promised to return someday and renew their vows over the anvil in Gretna Green.

As the sun set on a perfect day, they checked into a local bed and breakfast, then took a walk along the cobblestone path in the lush gardens surrounding the two-hundred-year-old stone cottage.

And now, as they readied for a candlelit dinner served on the balcony of their room overlooking the gardens, Sullivan fiddled with the CD player until the sounds of Celtic music filled the air.

Lissa approached him from behind and slipped her arms around his waist. "You have a romantic streak I hadn't expected. I was the one with the Scottish fantasy, and you've done everything to make this trip special."

He turned to face her. "I never realized I had a romantic streak until I met you."

A light rap sounded at the door, and Sullivan kissed her cheek before answering. "Must be the dinner I ordered."

Instead, the elderly father of the proprietor stood sheepishly in the hall, with a teacart that held two crystal glasses and a bottle resting inside a silver ice bucket.

"Excuse me, sir," the man said, handing Sullivan a folded piece of paper. "This message came for you while you were out in the gardens."

Sullivan took the note, glanced at it momentarily, then passed it to Lissa. "It's for you, honey."

"Oh, and sir," the white-haired man said, handing him the silver ice bucket and glasses. "Here's the bubbly you requested."

"Thank you." Sullivan tipped the man, then closed the door, while Lissa opened the note.

"Bad news?" he asked, undoubtedly noticing her wrinkled brow. He made his way to her side.

"No. It's good news, actually. My mom called and left a message. She wanted me to know that Jared found Adam. They'd had his last name spelled wrong, which led them to a dead end. But now they've found him."

Sullivan sat beside her on the goose-down comforter and slipped an arm around her. "That's great."

"I know." Lissa looked at her husband, the man she would cherish for the rest of her life, and smiled. "I can't wait to meet him."

"Do you want to cut the honeymoon short?"

"Absolutely not." She socked him playfully on the shoulder. "I intend to savor every minute of it."

Sullivan brushed a kiss across her lips. "And I intend to savor every day of the rest of our lives."

Then he opened the chilled bottle of sparkling grape juice and filled two crystal goblets. He handed one to her and lifted his glass. "To a love that will last."

"Forever," Lissa added.

The crystal chimed as they toasted their love, their life and their future.

Lissa smiled over the rim of her glass, locking gazes with the man who'd filled her heart with hope and love.

A virgin's dreams and fantasies didn't get any better than this.

\* \* \* \* \* \*

# TAKE A CHANCE
ON ME

BY
KAREN ROSE SMITH

Award-winning author **Karen Rose Smith** first glimpsed the Southwest on a cross-country train ride when she was sixteen. Although she has lived in Pennsylvania all her life, New Mexico has always called to her. The mountains there have a power and beauty she hopes she managed to convey in this book. Readers can reach Karen at her website (www.karenrosesmith.com) or write to her at PO Box 1545, Hanover, PA 17331, USA.

To Edie, my critique partner, my phone sister, my second set of eyes. I'm so grateful we're friends.

With deep appreciation to my research sources: My Portland contacts – Doreen Roberts and Leah Vale; my transplant experts – Dr Danil Hammoudi, Dr Meir Wetzler; as well as Linda Goodnight and her son Dr Travis Goodnight. Thanks also to Judy Duarte and Lynda Sandoval, who made co-ordination of the books easy.

# Chapter One

CEO Adam Bartlett rose to his feet.

The men and women sitting around the large mahogany table went silent, though Adam's former college roommate and present partner, Dylan Montgomery, winked at him. Adam almost smiled. At twenty-seven, he and Dylan ran the software firm they'd started after college. Who could have guessed they'd be this successful…this rich…this respected?

Towering above his board of directors, Adam glanced down at the papers on the table before him. He didn't actually need notes. "Good morning, everyone. I called this meeting to discuss the success of our latest product line. Our recent endeavors have produced another winner. Since most companies who have networks have jumped on the bandwagon—"

Unexpectedly, the door to the conference room swung open. His pretty brunette receptionist, Darlene, looked harried. Though she'd only been with Novel Programs, Unlimited, for a few months, she knew better than to interrupt his board meetings.

Now, however, she waved her hand toward his office suite down the hall. "I'm terribly sorry to interrupt you, Mr. Bartlett, but there's a man out here who demanded he be shown to your office. He won't take no for an answer. He insists this is a matter of life and death."

Over the years, through his company's meteoric rise, Adam had managed to stay out of the limelight and away from the public. "What's his name?"

"Jared Cambry."

The name wasn't familiar unless Adam had met the man at a conference or a merger meeting. He looked over at Dylan, but Dylan shook his head indicating he didn't recognize the name, either.

"He said he's a lawyer," Darlene added in a rush as if in her agitation she'd forgotten that important detail.

Adam pushed his hand through his thick brown hair, accepting the fact his day was going to take a sharp left turn onto a road he didn't expect. To the board, he said, "Dylan will take over the meeting and keep me posted on everything you discuss. Hopefully I'll be back in a few minutes."

As sandy-haired Dylan took Adam's place at the head of the table, Adam exited the room and started down the hall to his office. The door was ajar, and

Adam spotted a man around his own six-two height pacing the room.

"Jared Cambry?" Adam asked, examining the man's features, his dark-brown hair, thinking something about him seemed familiar. Though the lawyer appeared to be in his midforties, if the tension lines on his forehead persisted, he would age fast.

Cambry stared at Adam for a long moment. "Are you Adam Bartlett?"

"Yes. I only have a few minutes. I'm in the middle of a board meeting."

"This could take more than a few minutes," Cambry said wearily. "Can we sit down?"

"Mr. Cambry, I have a tight schedule today. If you'd like to make an appointment for later in the week—"

"This can't wait. I need to talk to you now. My son is dying." He stopped abruptly, then took a moment to compose himself.

Adam took a few steps deeper into the office, closer to Cambry. "I'm sorry about that, but I don't understand what it has to do with me."

When Cambry squared his shoulders, his expression became unreadable. "I'm your father."

Everything inside of Adam went still. His adoptive mother had only told him his mother's name had been Olivia and she'd been a teenager when he was born. When Adam had searched for further information after he'd turned eighteen, he'd discovered that a fire and power outage at Portland General and The Children's Connection Adoption Center had wiped out hard drives that had stored confidential as well as necessary information.

Adam's childhood with his adoptive family had not been a happy one. How he'd longed to find and know his real parents....

Hope nudged a frozen part of his heart open, but before he could ask any one of the myriad questions clicking through his head, before he could rejoice in the fact that he did indeed have a real father, Jared Cambry told Adam why he'd come.

"My son Mark has a rare blood disorder and needs a bone marrow transplant. His sister and brother aren't a match. Your sister, Lissa, isn't a match."

"My sister?"

This time, obviously not caring whether or not Adam sat, Cambry sank down into the wine leather chair in front of Adam's desk. "When I went searching for Olivia and her baby—" He stopped. "Maybe I should start at the beginning."

Automatically Adam closed the door to his office, feeling as if his whole world had suddenly tilted. He wouldn't be getting back to that board meeting, not until he learned every detail he possibly could about his background from Jared Cambry.

Unbuttoning his suit jacket, he sat on the corner of his desk and waited.

Cambry cut a look toward Adam, another out of the office building's window, then his gaze came back to rest on Adam again. "To put it simply, I got a girl pregnant in high school. Her name was Olivia Maddison. When she told me she was pregnant, I—"

Shifting uncomfortably, he cleared his throat. "I

came from a wealthy family, had plenty of money and offered it to her for an abortion. She wanted to have the baby. Then she told me to get out of her life because she intended to do without me or my money. After my family and I moved to Arizona, where I attended college, I contacted her, but she hung up on me. Around the baby's due date, I tried to call again, but her phone had been disconnected and I couldn't locate her.''

When he looked away this time, Adam wondered what kind of man Jared Cambry was now. Did he still run from responsibility?

''Go on,'' Adam prompted, needing to know the whole story.

''I didn't get married until I was twenty-seven. Danielle and I had two kids, a boy and a girl, who came along eighteen months apart. Eight years after that, Danielle suddenly found herself pregnant again. That's when we had Mark.''

Adam could see how Jared's face lit up at the thought of his younger son.

''Mark was sunshine from the minute he was born, always had a smile on his face, got along with everybody. I'm not sure why—maybe because of my roots and my past—I felt drawn back to Portland about a year ago, moved my family and opened a law office here. We were building a new life…a great life. Mark liked T-ball and soccer and we gave him hockey equipment for his eighth birthday. But then one day, he passed out while he was playing soccer, and we rushed him to the hospital. We learned he had this rare blood disease and without a bone marrow transplant, he won't make it past the age of ten.''

Jared stopped, then pulled himself together again and went on. ''Danielle and I were tested. So were Mark's sister and brother. None of us was a match. I couldn't sleep, couldn't concentrate on anything and then I remembered Olivia…and our baby.''

Adam couldn't imagine any man forgetting that he had a child out in the world somewhere.

''I'd never told Danielle anything about her, but now Mark's life depended on finding Olivia. Danielle agreed we had to do everything possible so I hired a private investigator. Searching newspapers, he found that Olivia and her mother had been in an accident and taken to Portland General Hospital. From obits, he found that Mrs. Maddison died immediately after the accident and Olivia passed on a few weeks later.''

Adam was beginning to get the gist of the search. ''Your investigator went to Portland General?''

''Yes. But the hospital had suffered a fire and power outage that affected not only Portland General but The Children's Connection Clinic attached to it. Most records from that time had been destroyed. We got a break when we found out The Children's Connection personnel in recent years had taken time to input information from burned paper files and now they *did* have some sketchy information. We got bits and pieces—Olivia's name and a partial list of expenses sent to the state.''

When Cambry rubbed his fingers back and forth across his temple, Adam could see this situation was hard on the man.

An instant later, Cambry continued, "We couldn't tell exactly what info matched up. I had what I'd thought was your name—Adam Bartlite—but the address listed Valencia Vineyard about two hours outside of Portland. When I went there, I found Lissa who had been adopted by the Cartwrights. It turned out her birthday was the same one I had for you. With the obvious resemblance, you must be twins. Olivia was a twin—her sister died at birth."

Not only a sister, but a twin. Adam tried to absorb that while he listened.

"Lissa was tested, but she's not a match, either. We finally discovered your last name had been misspelled on the records. My private investigator tracked you down. And here I am."

"Does Lissa still live at the vineyard?"

"She does, and she's interested in meeting you. But she's away on her honeymoon right now." He glanced out the window again, then back at Adam. "I know the chief of staff at the hospital. We can have your testing done today if you agree. We'll know in a week to ten days if you're a match."

Trying to digest all of it piece by piece, Adam kept the impact of the news deep inside. He was used to not showing his feelings. He was used to not sharing what he was thinking about anything but business.

That's just the way it was.

He hated the idea of going back to the hospital where his adopted sister had died twenty years ago—the same hospital where doctors gave impersonal care to patients they didn't think twice about. He avoided memories of that day whenever he could. Over the years he'd learned to eat right and exercise so he didn't have to see doctors. Yet that could all change now if he agreed to do this.

Bringing out a handkerchief, Jared Cambry wiped his brow. He was sweating, and Adam understood why. "Did you say Mark is eight?"

"Yes. He's at home right now. But if you're a match and you agree to donate your bone marrow, he'll have to be admitted to the hospital to be prepped and have chemo and possibly radiation before the transplant."

Adam had been seven the day that the horse he loved had trampled his sister, the day his adoptive father had had the horse put down and Delia had died. At that age it had been close to impossible to understand life and death as well as hospital protocol. How could Cambry's young son deal with the idea of a bone marrow transplant or face the possibility of dying?

No matter what Jared Cambry had done or not done in the past, Adam couldn't know he had a half brother out there and *not* help him.

Looking Jared square in the eye, he decided, "Set up the testing and let's see if I'm a match."

When Christopher Chambers, Chief of Staff of Portland General Hospital, called Leigh Peters to his office, he told her, "I chose you because I knew you could handle this job of liaison well. You're one of the best pediatric oncology nurses I have, and I need you to smooth the waters for Jared Cambry."

Chambers was in his late fifties—tall, lean and gray-haired. Now he moved closer to the window and motioned to the hospital and annexes that made up Portland General's complex. "Jared is a large contributor to Portland General and we want to help him as best we can. As I told you, his son's full siblings aren't a match and neither was Lissa Cartwright. Now he has hope again with another half sibling. I want you to handle everyone concerned with kid gloves to make the process flow as easily as possible for them. Our lab's on alert to expedite matters as it did with Lissa Cartwright. Since you've dealt with Jared, his family and his son Mark on the boy's previous hospitalization, you already have a rapport with them."

"I understand, Dr. Chambers." Leigh loved her work as an oncology nurse in pediatrics. Although her aspirations would lead her to med school in June, a dream her mother had instilled before she was out of diapers, Leigh enjoyed working with people, too. She felt honored that Dr. Chambers had singled her out to help with this family.

"The donor will be here in a few minutes. The transplant counselor will meet with him after today's battery of tests. I want you to be his contact person. If at any time you need my input or authorization, call me, Leigh. Understand?"

She understood. She was supposed to grease the wheel and make sure Jared Cambry's road wasn't any harder than it had to be.

The chief of staff added, "I also want you to have someplace quiet where you can meet with Mark's potential donor. The conference room next to my office is vacant." He pulled a key from his pocket. "The file is already on the table there waiting for you. I don't want Mr. Bartlett to have to wait."

"Bartlett?" That name took Leigh back ten years. Certainly there had to be lots of Bartletts in the Portland area. Certainly it was no connection to Adam Bartlett, the young man she'd left ten years ago so she could have a future that was much better than her mother's.

"I have a meeting out of the hospital now." Chambers gave her a business card. "But here's my cell phone number. Don't hesitate to use it if Bartlett has any questions you can't answer."

Then Chambers walked to the elevator, and Leigh made her way to the conference room next door.

Purposely she turned her thoughts away from the past and what she'd left behind, to her future at Case Western University in Cleveland. Orientation started June fifth. She really should be more excited. Her lifetime goal was within her grasp. But she loved her work here and—

She opened the conference room door with her key and saw the file sitting on the conference table. She'd like to go through it thoroughly before Mr. Bartlett arrived. Leaving the door open, she crossed to the table, pulled out the chair and sat down to look at the file.

Her heart stopped. The name on the manilla folder was Adam Bartlett.

She'd no sooner flipped open the file than she heard footsteps in the corridor. Moments later, a tall, broad-shouldered man stepped inside.

Not just any man...Adam.

He froze when he saw her. His already serious face looked as if it had been carved from stone. "Leigh?" he asked as if he couldn't believe his eyes.

As she stood, his gaze passed over her quickly but thoroughly—her blond hair tied back in a ponytail because it was more sedate and professional-looking that way, her blue pantsuit, her uniform in Pediatric Oncology. She often wore smocks when caring for the kids, smocks that danced with animals or Disney characters or were tie-dyed to bring more color into the ward, but she'd left all those in her locker for this meeting.

"Hi, Adam." Flustered, she motioned to the table. "I just got your file. I didn't realize who I'd be meeting today. You're Jared Cambry's son?"

After a moment's hesitation, Adam shrugged. "Cambry insists that's what The Children's Connection Clinic's records say. Apparently he had a private investigator looking for me. He just found me this morning."

That surprised her. Jared must have really pulled strings to get Adam's testing done today.

As the two of them stared at each other, Leigh easily recognized the boy Adam had been and realized she was even more attracted to the man he had become. His hair had been longer in high school. Today it was crisply cut in a no-nonsense businessman's style. His shoulders were broader now and filled out the expensive material of his suit jacket. The tie was Armani, the trousers perfectly creased. His Italian leather loafers were so different from the worn-out sneakers he'd sported as a teenager. His whole demeanor shouted success, and a hundred questions danced on her tongue. But they weren't here to discuss old times or to play catch up. Yet, she remembered how she'd left him....

His eyes, still so deeply green, had always mesmerized her. Reluctantly she broke eye contact and motioned to the table. "I haven't had a chance to look through your file."

"There can't be much in it unless Cambry did a background check."

Going over to one of the chairs, she opened the folder and sat down.

After a moment he chose the chair around the corner of the table from her. "I don't understand why I'm meeting with *you*. Are you some type of patient advocate?" His gaze took in her uniform again, then returned to her face.

"No, not in the way you mean. I'm an oncology nurse and usually work with the kids. I suppose that's one of the reasons Dr. Chambers chose me to walk you through this. I can explain any aspects of the testing and the transplant, though a transplant counselor will do most of that. But I'm supposed to act as a liaison for you and Mr. Cambry—with the hospital, with the lab, with the doctors—to make sure everything gets done as quickly as possible."

"I see. Cambry told me he's a corporate attorney. I don't know that much about him except that he left the firm in Phoenix to open a branch here in Portland not so long ago. If this hospital is giving him his own personal liaison, I imagine he contributed to it already."

Leigh felt herself blushing and knew there was no reason for it. "I can't really discuss benefactors of this hospital with you."

"No, I guess you can't, not and be a good liaison."

She sensed a cynicism in Adam's attitude, and then she remembered. Actually she'd never forgotten, she'd just put it to the back of her mind. "You don't think much of hospitals and medical personnel."

Leaning back slightly, he agreed. "That's right. That hasn't changed. In fact, this is the first I've stepped into a hospital since the day Delia died."

Leigh ached for the boy who had lost his horse, his best friend in the world at age seven, as well as his sister in the same day.

"How *is* your family?" she asked gently because she felt as if she should. She'd visited the Bartlett farm a few times while she and Adam were dating. She'd seen the strain between him and Owen Bartlett, had felt the distance between him and his adoptive mother and the two sisters who had been first in their parent's hearts, especially after they'd lost Delia.

"Owen died two years ago."

"I'm terribly sorry." Then she asked a question she knew was none of her business. But she was curious about what had happened to Adam. "Had things gotten any better between you and your dad before he died?"

Silence swirled around the room until finally Adam replied, "How could they get any better, Leigh? Owen Bartlett adopted me because he wanted a boy who could do the chores and take over the farm some day. He and my mom never considered me their real son.

You know after Delia got trampled by Lancer, they blamed me for her death.''

He stopped abruptly, then continued, ''Long before Owen died, I made arrangements for someone to manage the farm for him and to do the heavy work. It gave my mom an easier life, too, and I think she appreciates that. Sharon still lives there with her, but Rena went to Australia on a trip and never came back. She's living in the Outback with a sheep rancher and Mom says she's happy.''

Leaning forward, he motioned toward his file. ''But I'm not here to talk about the past, and I'm sure you want to get on with this, too. I think Cambry said there would be special orders there for all the testing I'm to have done today.''

Politely Adam had filled her in and now he wanted to get on with the job at hand, a life-saving job. She couldn't believe she'd detoured from that. Still…seeing him again—

Mark Cambry came first.

Glancing over the information on Adam, she saw it was indeed scanty. ''Before you can get started with the testing, we have to go over the intake form. Then I'll explain what they're going to do in the lab. You'll also have a chest X-ray, and I see there's an appointment for you at three with Dr. Mason for a physical.''

Adam took his cell phone out of his inside jacket pocket. ''I didn't realize I was going to be here most of the day. Before I go to the lab, I need to make a call.''

She reached for his cell phone before he pressed

Enter. "You can't use that in here—not in the hospital."

Her hand had clasped his. His skin was warm and taut, the back of his large hand, hair roughened. Licks of fire shot up her arm as her gaze met his. She thought she saw a flicker of something old and wild there.

Pulling away from her clasp, Adam slipped the phone back into his pocket. "That's damn inconvenient."

She motioned to the phone on the credenza. "You're welcome to use that. Press eight for an outside line. If you need privacy, I can step outside."

"I don't need privacy. I'm just going to clear my schedule."

Clear his schedule of what? she wondered, then caught herself. The job of liaison wasn't to poke into Adam Bartlett's business or his life and she had to remember that.

However, during the intake session she found out exactly what Adam was doing now. She'd given him a few minutes to fill out basic information on the form. Under Occupation, he'd written—CEO of Novel Programs, Unlimited. Novel Programs, Unlimited, was a software firm that had made its mark in the United States. But whenever she saw a clip about it, the article was about product development or the latest software program. She remembered the name Dylan Montgomery being associated with it, but not Adam's name.

When she went over the information with him, she asked, "How long have you been with Novel Programs, Unlimited?"

"Did I miss filling in a blank?" he asked.

"No," she replied, not feeling as self-conscious this time. After all, she wasn't going to pretend as if she hadn't known him, hadn't dated him for three months, hadn't fallen in love and given him up for a dream that had seemed bigger and more important. "I just wondered."

After sitting there for a long moment, he laid his pen on the table. "I used that scholarship I won at the Computer Science Fair to go to Stanford. My room-mate and I developed programs we felt were unique. We started our company in college and went public the summer after we graduated. The rest is history, as they say."

"Dylan Montgomery was your roommate?"

"Yes, he was. He doesn't mind posing for pictures and talking to reporters, as well as being chief financial officer."

"On the other hand, you don't like any of that," she guessed, remembering the quiet and sometimes remote teenager he'd been.

"I like publicity almost as much as I like hospitals and doctors."

"The doctor you overheard after your sister died—"

"Was an unfeeling son of a bitch. His exact words were, 'We shouldn't have wasted our time on her. I knew she was gone when they brought her in.' Even a seven-year-old could understand exactly what that meant."

"You're still bitter."

"No, Leigh. I just know where I can place my trust and where I can't. I'm only here today because there's an outside chance that I can help save Mark Cambry's life. So let's get to it, okay?''

Old hurt crept over Leigh's heart and she ached to clear the air between them. She needed to tell him why she'd broken off their relationship so long ago. She needed to try to make him understand.

Yet she couldn't do that now. It was time to give him a capsulized version of the transplant process and then escort him to the lab. She'd be checking on his progress throughout the day and maybe when he was finished…

From the file folder she took out a sheaf of papers and placed them before him. ''Let me explain what's going to happen next.''

Leigh kept the rest of their session impersonal and then she acted as the guide she was supposed to be a half hour later as they walked down the hall to the elevator.

Adam cut her a glance. ''I can find the lab on my own.''

''I have no doubt of that but this is my job for today, so let me do it.''

Silence reverberated between them as they waited for the elevator.

Finally Adam asked, ''You said you work with kids?''

''Yes, and I love it. I'm going to miss it when I leave for med school in June.''

That brought his gaze to her face. ''Where are you going?''

''Case Western in Cleveland.''

The elevator doors swished open. After they stepped

inside, silence reigned again until they walked down the first-floor hall to the laboratory door.

Leigh handed Adam three sets of papers. "Just give these to the receptionist. She'll buzz me when you're finished. Normally we hold off on the X-ray and the physical until the results come back, but Mr. Cambry is paying for all this, and if you're a match, he wants you ready to go."

"No, he won't be paying for this. *I* will."

"But my notes state—"

"I don't care what your notes state. Make sure you see to it that they're changed. My name goes to billing for these tests."

His jaw was set, his tone resolute. She could see this was important to him and something on which he wouldn't compromise. But she'd have to speak to Dr. Chambers about it and see how he wanted to handle the situation. For now she just nodded.

Adam opened the laboratory door and went inside.

Three hours later, Leigh met Adam in Dr. Mason's office after his physical had been completed. She suspected being here, letting doctors poke and prod him, had been more difficult than she could ever imagine. After they'd dated a few weeks, he'd told her how his parents had brought him to the hospital the day that Delia was rushed here in the ambulance, how he'd seen a trauma team impersonally work on Delia, how they'd attached her to tubes, put her on a ventilator. To a child, that all had to be terrifying. He'd seen all the personnel as unfeeling, mechanical, uncaring. Then when he'd heard that doctor's comments—

His face was grim now as he shrugged into his suit jacket again, then glanced at his watch.

"Still hoping to get some work in today?" she asked. She'd *hoped* they could have a cup of coffee together, and she could explain why she'd written him that note ten years ago.

"I have a conference call in fifteen minutes, but I'll be able to take it in the car."

Some of the offices led directly outside and now she walked with Adam as he opened the door and stepped into the beginning-of-March breeze. The sun was shining brightly today.

He took a deep breath, held his face up to its heat and then gave a sigh. "I don't know how you work in that place. It's so…"

"Clean?" she asked, hoping to coax a small smile from him.

Although the grim expression was gone now, he still didn't smile. "That wasn't quite the word I was searching for."

For some reason she felt she had to change his mind about this hospital and what she did. "Mark's a wonderful little boy, Adam. I cared for him during his last hospitalization. If you're a match, and if we can do the transplant, this will become a life-saving place. Can you think about that?"

At her question, she thought she saw an old tenderness come back into Adam's green eyes. She thought she felt a warmth that at one time had made her believe she belonged in a new place…made her feel as if she weren't alone.

''I *will* think about that,'' he said.

Then Adam Bartlett headed for the parking garage, and Leigh wondered if he'd ever give her the chance to explain why she'd left him so long ago.

## Chapter Two

Adam rode Thunder at a full run in a way he'd never ridden him before. They were chasing the end of day and eluding it at the same time. As Adam leaned low, he and his horse were one. The stallion was always responsive under his hands, always tuned in to his voice.

A few years ago, when Adam had moved from a condo in the city to the ranch, the first thing he'd done was to buy Thunder—even before he'd bought furniture. Cedar Run Ranch was now his haven, and Thunder was his best friend. Part Arabian, the stallion had an intuition that told him exactly what Adam wanted…when he wanted it. Although Adam and Dylan had been friends since college, he didn't even tell

Dylan some of the worries and secrets he confided in Thunder.

Pines and cedars thickened as the brush tore and scattered under the stallion's hooves. Adam slowed him with a touch. The wind that had splashed against Adam's face became gentler, and he sat up straight on the horse's back. He was riding without a saddle, his worn jeans a thin barrier between his thighs and Thunder's sculpted muscles. He hadn't even worn a jacket, just pulled a sweatshirt over his head.

"Slower, boy," Adam suggested to the horse.

The stallion neighed in reply and Adam smiled, his first real smile since Jared Cambry had forced a meeting this morning.

After another quarter of a mile, Adam walked Thunder between moss-covered maples to the bank of a creek. Rain kept it full as it washed over rocks and rippled along the brambled bank. The sound of the water, the rustle of the leaves overhead, Thunder's black mane under Adam's hand, soothed him in a way nothing else could. Yet even that soothing couldn't make him forget Leigh Peters's big, blue eyes. Those damn big, blue eyes.

He remembered the first time they'd stopped him in his tracks. It had been the end of March, ten long years ago. He'd just been putting in time, wanting his senior year over with so he could get away from his adoptive parents' farm, go to college, make a real life. He'd walked down the high school hall, and he'd seen a girl stuffing books and a jacket into one of the senior lockers. She'd looked up when she heard his footsteps, and those eyes…

He had to admit it wasn't only her eyes. She'd had long blond hair that had fallen over her shoulders, a curvy figure that had encouraged his eighteen-year-old hormones to run wild. And she'd just looked lost.

He wasn't sure what had made him stop. He hadn't dated much. Since he was ten and built his own computer, he'd been interested in creating software programs, challenging himself with ever more difficult computer games, staying away from the crowd that went drinking every Saturday night and acted as if going steady were the be all and end all of life. He had plans to make himself into a man whom even Owen Bartlett would have to respect.

Girls had buzzed around him now and then—in the lunchroom, in the gym where he shot hoops whenever he could get a chance. Although experimenting sexually with them might have been fun, he hadn't wanted the complications or the responsibility....

Until he'd seen Leigh, and dreams and life and plans had changed. He'd walked up to her and asked her if she was new at the school. She'd seemed so grateful he'd stopped to talk to her. That's how it had begun. She'd been his first lover, his first confidante, his first hope that a bond with another person wouldn't cause pain.

But after three months of dating, she'd sent him a note. It had said she couldn't see him again and explained nothing. When he'd called her, she hadn't answered. When he'd stopped by, her mother had told him she wasn't home.

It had taken a few weeks for him to get back on track, but then he'd focused on the future again, life without Leigh, a college education that could hand him the brass ring.

Thunder neighed again and tossed his head.

"Yep, she's still beautiful," Adam acknowledged to himself and the horse.

But Leigh had obviously had a reason for walking out of his life back then, and now he didn't care what it was. He didn't care that he'd seen her again today. She was off to medical school in June, and he had Jared Cambry to deal with. All Cambry had cared about was Adam getting to the hospital for the appointed tests. They certainly hadn't had a long-lost father-and-son reunion. Cambry only cared about eight-year-old Mark.

However, Mark Cambry was Adam's half brother. Real family...blood family. Adam had been told it could be more than a week until the test results came in.

And if he was a match?

Although he despised hospitals and what they represented, he would save his brother's life.

An hour and a half later, Adam had finished his ride and groomed and fed Thunder. As he mounted the steps and crossed the porch to his log home, he thought about going back to the office to finish the work that hadn't gotten done today. He'd no sooner opened the front door, inset with a triangular beveled glass window, when his phone rang.

He crossed the wide-planked flooring, scattered with unique brightly colored wool rugs a decorator had found in a small village in Alaska. They were hand-woven, and the greens, browns and blues added color to the room furnished with a supple black leather couch and armchair, as well as a sage-colored recliner. The polished pine lamps with their parchment shades, the wrought-iron tables with their glass tops blended together to make the room homey, comfortable, and tasteful. His state-of-the-art plasma-screen TV and entertainment center looked out of place in the rustic surroundings, but Adam didn't care about that.

Picking up the cordless phone beside the sofa, he answered, "Bartlett here."

"Adam, it's Leigh. Leigh Peters."

As if he didn't remember her last name.

She went on. "I managed to set up an appointment for you with the transplant counselor tomorrow."

He ran his hand through his hair. She'd mentioned she was going to do that. He just hadn't expected the appointment to be tomorrow. "That was quick."

"Would you rather I postpone the appointment for a few days? I could set it up at the end of the week instead."

Whether he was a match or not, he wanted to know more about the transplant process. He'd heard about the donor registry but had never realized what all of it meant. "What time tomorrow?"

"Marietta Watson—that's who you will be meeting with—has an opening at eleven and another at four. Which would you prefer?"

"Four would be better for me. I can go to the office early and get in a full day. I'm surprised you're still at work."

"I was waiting for Marietta to get back to me about appointment times. In the meantime, I visited with some of my patients."

She really *did* like her work. He could hear it in her voice. Suddenly he had the urge to know if she was involved with anyone, if she lived by herself or with a lover. "You don't have anyone at home waiting for you?"

There were a few beats of silence before she replied, "Yes I do—my mom. It's more economical for me to live with her while I'm saving for med school."

Relief swept through Adam, then he reminded himself he had no right to feel it. He remembered Leigh's mother, Claire. She and Leigh looked more like sisters than mother and daughter. He'd envied the close bond the two of them had shared. "I bet your mom's going to miss you when you leave."

"I'll miss her. Though, she might be glad to finally get me out of her hair."

There was affection and laughter in Leigh's voice, and Adam felt himself responding to it. He'd been Leigh's first lover, and she had been his. That was a sense of connection he couldn't deny. Yet he'd felt betrayed when she'd walked away without a word. He'd been a nobody then with nothing but hopes for a better future. Obviously she hadn't been willing to take a chance on him or else she hadn't felt the same depth of caring he had.

"Where is Marietta Watson located?" he asked, getting back to the subject at hand.

"She's on the first floor, the opposite side of the

building from Dr. Mason. I can meet you in the lobby if you'd like.''

''No, that's not necessary. I'll find her. What's the suite number?''

''It's 107. If she's left for the day, I'll leave a note for her that you're coming in at four.''

''Remember, Leigh, the charges for all of this go on my tab.''

''I spoke with Dr. Chambers about that. He said he'd have a talk with Mr. Cambry...with your father.''

It sounded ironic for Adam to hear those words. He and Cambry had parted this morning without any plans to meet again. Yet no matter what the testing revealed, Adam wanted to know more about this sister Cambry had found, too. He wanted to know more about all of it. For now, though, he'd sit tight and wait to see what happened next.

''Thanks for calling, Leigh. And thanks for setting up the appointment. Now you'd better go home and get some supper.''

''Is that what you're going to do?'' Her question showed obvious interest in his life and he didn't know what to make of that.

''No, I'm going to change and go back into the city. I'll pick up Chinese on the way.''

''You don't live in town?''

''No. I have a ranch southwest of Portland. I needed some space around me.''

''You got used to space growing up on the farm.''

''I guess I did. But Cedar Run Ranch is nothing like Owen Bartlett's farm. Believe me.''

''I'm glad you found a home,'' she said, obviously

understanding everything he'd ever felt about Owen Bartlett and his adopted family.

"You enjoy supper with your mom."

"You enjoy Chinese at your desk."

"I will. Goodbye, Leigh."

Then she said goodbye and ended the connection.

Adam switched off the phone, set it on its base, and stared at it for a long time.

Finally, shaking off the foggy fingers of time-passed, he headed for his shower, a fresh change of clothes and a night of the work that had become his life.

I'm his liaison, Leigh told herself the following afternoon as she hurried down the corridor toward Marietta Watson's office.

It was almost five o'clock and knowing from experience that the counseling sessions lasted about an hour, she'd decided to check in on Adam and see how the session had gone.

*Stop kidding yourself,* her subconscious whispered. *You want to see him again.*

It wasn't that she *wanted* to see him. Well, maybe she did. For reasons that had nothing to do with her being his liaison. They had unfinished business and it was time she apologized for it.

When she opened the door to Suite 107, there was no one in the small waiting room. The door was closed to Marietta's inner office, so Leigh sat down to wait. She'd no sooner picked up a year-old magazine to page through when Adam opened the door, and he and Marietta walked out. They were laughing, and Marietta—a pretty brunette a few years older than Leigh—was looking up at Adam as if she found him very attractive.

He was.

He'd always been handsome in a rugged sort of way and had never seemed to understand how that and his broad shoulders and piercing green eyes affected women. At twenty-seven, and CEO of his own company, he must have had lots of affairs. She hadn't. Life had been filled with work and study. Yet to be honest, she'd never found a man she wanted to be intimate with the way she had been with Adam.

"How did it go?" she asked, looking at Marietta's brightly colored dress, wishing she'd had a change of clothes in her locker.

After Adam gestured to Marietta, he smiled. "She's great. She could explain the theory of relativity to a first-grader and he'd understand. I now have a basic grasp of HLA typing, conditioning for the transplant recipient and an overview of the harvesting procedure."

Leigh knew they'd covered aspects other than the technical ones—what the transplant would mean to Mark, how difficult the whole ordeal would be for the boy, as well as Adam's part in it, if it came to that.

"From your questions, I knew you were processing everything I told you," Marietta concluded. "Sometimes the donors I counsel get lost in the stress and can't absorb the information I give them."

Clasping Adam's arm as if she'd known him for years, she added, "If you think of anything we didn't talk about, or if you have any other questions, feel free to call me. Now I have some paperwork to finish before I can leave."

She raised her hand in a wave to both of them and went back inside her office and closed the door.

Adam was studying Leigh curiously as if wondering why she was there. Feeling a bit self-conscious, she explained, "I wanted to make sure your session went smoothly."

"So you can report to Dr. Chambers and Cambry?"

"No," Leigh answered patiently. "I'm not reporting to anyone. I'm just trying to make sure everyone's needs are met."

There was a need that suddenly flared in Adam Bartlett's eyes, and she felt heat creep into her cheeks. "Marietta's good at her job, too. She means it when she says to call her if you have any further questions."

"I researched bone marrow transplants on the Internet last night. That's how I was able to quickly absorb everything she said. It's certainly cut-and-dried when you get right down to it. She did explain how difficult a decision it is for parents to put their child through the ordeal. I didn't understand the implications of that before."

Leigh nodded. "Mr. Cambry and his wife are going through anguish that I hope I never see."

As they both thought about that, Leigh impulsively asked, "Would you like to come to dinner at my place?"

A few prolonged seconds passed, then Adam asked, "Dinner's part of your job, too?"

"Dinner has nothing to do with my job. Mom's working late tonight so we can talk privately."

He cocked his head to study her. "And what do we have to talk about?"

"I thought maybe we could...catch up. I could make pasta and a salad. I bought a loaf of Italian bread at the bakery yesterday. How about it?"

When Adam withdrew, when he decided to keep thoughts to himself, not one iota of what was going on in his head showed. That used to frustrate her, and it did now, too.

After an interminably long pause, for which she realized she was holding her breath, he finally replied. "All right. A home-cooked meal sounds good. What's your address?"

Portland General Hospital was located on the outskirts of the city. When it had been built in the 1940s, it had stood apart from the hustle and bustle. Now urban Portland had almost caught up with it. As Leigh checked her rearview mirror, she caught a glimpse of Adam's BMW as he followed her in the dusk. Her heart raced when she thought about having dinner with him. Her mind went over apologies and explanations that didn't seem to say what she wanted them to. By the time they reached the apartment complex where she and her mom lived, her palms were damp.

The apartment building, like so many of Portland's structures, was built of wood. It was small as apartment complexes went, with twelve units on three floors. There was an old Victorian house to the left of the building, a dry cleaner and bakery to the right. Checking again in the mirror to see if Adam was following her, Leigh drove around to the back where the parking lot for the apartments was located.

After Adam pulled his car in beside hers, they both got out. As they walked to the rear entrance of the building, she said, "We're on the second floor."

Adam was silent as they mounted the steps, and Leigh suddenly panicked. Maybe this wasn't such a good idea. When they arrived at the apartment door, she used her key to open it and stepped inside.

She could almost hear what Adam was thinking. The apartment wasn't any bigger than the one she and her mom had shared when she'd been in high school. It was decorated in a totally feminine way—shades of rose and yellow, flowered chintz slipcovers over an old sofa and chair, cream-and-taupe braided rugs on the painted tan floor. Prints of Monet watercolors hung on two walls in oak frames with a mirror sconce beside one of them. The television, which sat on a bookshelf, was only as large as the computer monitor that was housed with a keyboard on the hutch in the back corner of the living room.

Taking off her coat, Leigh hung it on a peg inside the front door.

After Adam shrugged out of his suit jacket, he tossed it over the armchair. Next he loosened his tie, and Leigh found it hard to swallow. He looked consummately sexy, and his green eyes followed her as she moved into the kitchen.

"You said your mom's working late tonight. Is she still a medical secretary?" he asked.

Leigh removed a spaghetti pot from a bottom cupboard. "Yes, she is. For a family practice."

Adam nodded to the computer. "Is that yours or hers?"

"Mostly hers. I used it in nursing school. She takes in word processing and does that in her spare time." Her mother had worked two jobs since Leigh was twelve, saving money and adding to the medical school kitty. Leigh would never be able to repay her for all she'd done for her.

As Leigh turned on the spigot and held the pot underneath to fill it, Adam was suddenly by her side.

"I'll lift it out for you," he said as the pot became heavier with the water.

The kitchen area was small, the work space minuscule. Adam's arm brushed hers. She could smell his musky scent, a mixture of man and cologne...*Adam* and cologne. His body heat seemed to surround her. Or was it simply her own body temperature rising?

His sideways glance at her was meant to tell her she should let him handle the heavy pot, but she couldn't look away from him. The eye contact brought back memories of other small spaces—his old car, the janitor's closet in the school where stolen kisses had been exciting and wild.

Water poured over the side of the pot.

She licked her lips.

He seemed to lean closer.

But then he straightened, turned away and flipped off the spigot.

Leigh let go of the pot, moved toward the refrigerator, opened the door and gathered chicken breasts and vegetables. She'd sauté them, then toss them with the pasta, olive oil and garlic.

"What else can I do?" he asked as he set the pot on the burner and turned it on, salting it.

"Do you cook?"

"Now and then. Dylan and I had a range but no oven in our apartment at college. We became adept at opening cans and mixing them. We called all the recipes Adam-and-Dylan's goulash."

She laughed. "Did you write any of them down?"

"Are you kidding? That was the mystery of it. We never made the same thing twice."

"So you and Dylan are good friends?"

Adam shrugged. "We're friends, we're partners, we know each other's likes and dislikes, what buttons not to push. But Dylan and I are very different. He likes the city and the night life and crowds and parties."

"And you like to work after everyone else is gone and spend your spare time at your ranch."

"You always were a quick study," he remarked.

She wasn't sure that was a compliment. "I don't know about being a quick study. I've learned how to listen to the kids, or try to hear what they don't say." She took a sauté pan from another cupboard and set it on the stove.

When Adam unbuttoned his cuffs and rolled up his sleeves, she lost track of what she was doing. His hair roughened forearms were muscled, his gold watch masculine against his tanned wrist.

Silence pulsed awkwardly between them along with the sexual tension that had always been there.

She asked, "So what do you have on the ranch?"

"Lots of trees," he responded dryly.

Smiling, she shook her head. "Do you have animals?"

"I have a stallion named Thunder."

Her gaze met his and she realized he'd bought a horse to make up for the one he'd lost.

"What breed?"

"Mixed. Mostly Arabian. He's a beauty, but he's spirited and restless and hard to handle sometimes, at least for anyone but me. I have a gardener who keeps the grass mowed and the weeds in check. He takes care of Thunder when I have to go out of town, but he keeps his distance from him. I suppose that's best, for his own good."

Leigh chopped carrots on a cutting board. "Do you go out of town often?"

"About once a month. Dylan and I take turns with that."

She cut up onion and fennel and saw the water was almost boiling. She told herself to wait until they were both relaxed and eating to explain what had happened so many years ago, but suddenly she felt as if it were now or never.

"Adam, I've wanted to tell you—"

The lock clicked and the door to the apartment suddenly opened. Her mother came in, saying, "I finished at work sooner than I planned. Did you see that fancy car parked in the parking lot? I can't imagine what it's doing here."

When Claire saw Adam standing in the shadows in the corner of the kitchen, she took a step back. "I know you, don't I? Aren't you…?"

Stepping forward, Adam stood before her mother. "Adam Bartlett. It's been a long time, Ms. Peters."

Claire's gaze took a quick appraisal of his silk tie, his quality trousers, the shirt that still had some starch. "Where did you and Leigh meet up again?" She removed her coat and hung it next to her daughter's on another peg.

Leigh noticed her mother had worn a black pantsuit today and tucked a multicolored scarf into the neck. At forty-three her blond hair had a few strands of gray but it looked like frosting. She'd had her hair permed recently, and it waved around her face attractively. She was only forty-three because she'd become a single mom at seventeen. That's why she convinced Leigh to break up with Adam. That's why she'd insisted an involvement that Leigh was too young to handle would ruin her life.

Leigh's job at the hospital required discretion. She wasn't about to tell her mother what was going on in Adam's life. Before she could respond, Adam did it for her. "I ran into Leigh at Portland General."

Claire looked at her daughter then at Adam then back at Leigh. "Well, why don't I stay out of your way. I have résumés to type up for clients. I can work on those until supper is ready."

"Mom, you don't have to make yourself scarce."

But Claire was already walking toward the computer. "I have to get the work done, honey." After she switched it on, it made a noise it had been making the past few days.

Adam went on alert immediately. "That sounds as

if your fan needs to be cleaned. Do you always keep the tower in the enclosed space?''

Clair nodded. ''Yes. Shouldn't I?''

Smiling patiently, he strode to the computer hutch and pulled out the tower from the lower cupboard. ''It needs to be cleaned, now and then, just like anything else. Do you want me to do it for you?''

''Will the machine stop running if I don't?''

''The fan keeps the unit cool so if it stops working, you're in trouble.''

''But you didn't come here for this. I don't want to impose.''

There was uncertainty on her mother's face, and Leigh knew she wondered if Adam knew what he was doing. ''Have you heard of the company Novel Programs, Unlimited, Mom?''

Clair nodded.

''Adam is the CEO.''

The expression on her mother's face was priceless, and Leigh knew Adam was enjoying her mother's astonishment.

''I won't break anything,'' he said with a grin. ''I promise.''

## Chapter Three

Adam was examining research-and-development files when Dylan came into his office, coffee mug in hand. Adam knew his CFO had scheduled a meeting with distributors early this morning, and he supposed Dylan had come in to give him a report on how it had gone.

"Do you have a few minutes?" Dylan asked.

Pushing his swivel chair away from the computer, Adam faced the doorway. He couldn't concentrate on anything this morning after his dinner with Leigh and her mother last night. He might as well consult with his partner. "Sure. Everything go okay?"

"Nothing unexpected." Dylan sank into the chair across from Adam. "I tried to call you. Last night. You didn't even have your cell phone on."

"You didn't leave a message."

"No. I figured we could hash it out this morning. Were you out in the barn or something?"

Adam laughed. "If I'm not here working, then I must be in the barn?"

Dylan shrugged. "Yeah, that about sums it up. Are you telling me you weren't?"

"I wasn't."

"Did you have another meeting with your father?"

Something sharp stabbed at Adam's insides. "You mean Jared Cambry? No, I didn't have a meeting with him. I haven't heard from him. I think he only wants one thing from me, Dylan—bone marrow."

"You don't know that for sure."

"No, I don't." But from Cambry's words and actions, Adam suspected Mark was his sole concern.

"So where were you last night?" Dylan prodded. "Or are you going to be mysterious about it?"

Although Adam had told Dylan about Cambry and the testing at the hospital, he hadn't said anything about Leigh. He'd never told Dylan anything about her. "It's a long story."

"So fill me in. I've been here since 6:00 a.m. crunching numbers and I need the break."

Dylan worked as many hours as Adam did. Maybe if he told Dylan about the situation with Leigh, he could get a better perspective on it. After all, he probably wouldn't be seeing her again. What were the odds he'd be a compatible donor for Mark?

"There's a liaison at the hospital working with me and Jared Cambry to make sure the process runs smoothly. Coincidentally, I knew her in high school."

Dylan's brows rose. "Knew her?"

Adam wasn't sure exactly how much he wanted to reveal. On the other hand, Dylan had had a lot more experience with women than he had. "Yeah, knew her. We dated. I was serious, apparently she wasn't. She broke it off." His pride meant a lot to him, and that was hard to admit, but he'd always been honest with Dylan.

"Don't make me pull teeth here," Dylan pleaded with a grin. "What happened last night?" He raised his coffee mug to his lips.

"I fixed her mother's hard drive."

Dylan had been taking a sip of his coffee, and he choked.

At Dylan's expression, Adam smiled. "I had another session at the hospital and Leigh was there. Afterward she asked me to her place for dinner. She and her mom live together because she's saving money for med school. Anyway, I hadn't had a home-cooked meal in a while, so I went. Her mother came home unexpectedly and had dinner with us. The fan on her hard drive was making noise, so I cleaned it."

"That wasn't any more exciting than grooming your horse in the barn," Dylan muttered.

Adam couldn't help but laugh. "If you want exciting, you're going to have to look elsewhere."

Still, whenever he thought about Leigh, Adam *felt* excited. Whenever their arms had touched, eyes had met, the old attraction had sizzled. Claire had guided most of the conversation at dinner and he'd let her. It had been superficial, polite, entertaining. After dinner, he'd had a second cup of coffee, Leigh had walked him to the door, and that was that.

Except that *wasn't* that. He'd gotten the impression Leigh had wanted to talk to him privately, and her mother's arrival had deprived her of the chance to do that. Maybe it was for the best. Maybe the fire that licked through his blood whenever he was near her shouldn't be fueled by any more impromptu dates.

"So what did you call about last night?"

"I'm having a problem I don't quite know what to do with. It's Darlene."

Darlene was their receptionist/secretary. Adam had hired her a few months ago to replace the middle-aged woman who had been with them the past few years. Janet's husband had decided to take a job in San Diego and after a month's notice, she'd left. Darlene was quite different from Janet, in her midtwenties, a vivacious brunette who seemed to have endless energy. That's one of the reasons Adam had hired her.

"What kind of problem?"

"It's taking forever for her to do my correspondence. When I ask her if it's finished, she says she's still proofreading it. That's what spell checkers are for."

Suddenly Adam realized that Dylan might have dated a lot of women, but that didn't necessarily mean he understood them...or could read them. "Darlene likes you," he said simply.

"That's why my letters are taking forever?"

"You don't get it."

"What don't I get?"

"She tries to make them perfect. That takes a while."

Dylan still looked puzzled. "What does she do with *your* letters?"

"She types them up and sends them out," Adam answered with a wry smile as he decided to enlighten his partner. "She has a thing for you. Haven't you ever noticed how nervous she gets whenever you're around? She drops things, laughs that funny little laugh. She doesn't do that around me."

"You *are* kidding, right?"

"No, I'm not. But it seems to me I've caught you looking in her direction more than once. Maybe it's not all one-sided."

"I'm dating Natalie."

"Yes, you are. Her father has a yacht. She's as beautiful as any Miss America. The difference is—I don't think she has an original thought in her head."

"Hold back on what you think of her," his friend groused.

"I have been. You've been seeing her since Thanksgiving. I've been wondering why."

Standing, Dylan set his mug on Adam's desk and went over to the window, staring at the sky. "She likes to party, so do I." He turned around to face Adam. "But she's not a sparkling conversationalist. On the other hand, I like the rush of every man looking at her when she's on my arm. She canceled our last date, though, and I haven't called her for a week. Maybe we both know our time together is over."

When Adam's intercom buzzed, Dylan returned to staring out the window.

Adam depressed the button and asked, "Yes, Darlene?"

"There's someone here to see you, Mr. Bartlett. A Leigh Peters. I asked if she had an appointment and she said she didn't."

Dylan was facing him now and looking at him with curiosity.

Why was Leigh here? Because last night her mother's unexpected presence had interrupted whatever conversation they might have had? Because now that he was a CEO rather than a poor kid with only a college scholarship to his name, she might be interested?

There was only one way to find out.

Speaking to his receptionist, he avoided Dylan's gaze. "I have a few minutes, Darlene. Send her back."

Expecting Dylan to leave, Adam sat back in his chair and waited, but his partner made no move to exit his office.

A few seconds later Leigh was peeking in his half-closed door. "Adam?"

The kick in his gut when he saw her made him rise to his feet. She looked too damn good. He was used to seeing her in that blue uniform, her hair tied back. Today she wore a pale green coatdress with gold buttons. The green made her eyes even bluer. Her hair, longer than shoulder length, was caught in a gold barrette over her right temple. It waved around her face looking silky and luscious, as luscious as her curves and her long graceful legs.

Stepping around his desk, Adam said easily, "Come on in, Leigh. Meet my partner, Dylan Montgomery. Dylan, Leigh Peters."

Crossing the room, Dylan extended his hand to her.

"It's nice to meet you. Adam told me you went to school together."

Her gaze shot to his as if she wondered what else he'd told Dylan. Then, with the composure she always seemed to possess, she smiled at his partner and slipped her hand from his. "It's good to meet you, Mr. Montgomery. I read the article in the financial section a few weeks ago where you were quoted quite heavily."

"For some reason I still can't understand, Adam always sends the reporters to me."

"You're much more tactful than I am," Adam explained.

"More tactful maybe, but not more knowledgeable. One of these days you're going to have to do your own PR. Speaking of PR, don't forget that cocktail party Saturday night at my condo. I mean it, Adam. You can't duck this one. I have a few guests coming who can take our fall software line into the international markets quickly."

Crossing to the door, he said, "It's nice to meet you, Miss Peters. Adam, let me know if you come up with any ideas about the problem we discussed."

When Dylan exited the office, he closed the door.

"I didn't mean to interrupt anything important," Leigh apologized. "This is my day off and if you have a few minutes, there's something I want to talk to you about."

Curious now, Adam motioned to the chair in front of his desk as he lodged a hip on the front edge. "Something about Mark Cambry?"

"Oh, no. Nothing that important. When I go to

school in June, I'll be taking the computer with me. I'd like to get Mom a new machine for her word processing, and I thought you could make the best recommendation. I don't have a lot of extra money to spend, but I want to make sure she has what she needs as well as a good word-processing program.''

As Adam had indicated, Dylan was the tactful one. He himself always wanted to cut to the bottom line. ''I could have given you that kind of advice over the phone.''

Leigh looked down at her hands, which were folded around her purse in her lap, and then back up at him. It would have been better if he'd stayed on his side of the desk. He was too close to her here. He could smell the gardenia scent of her perfume. He remembered that was her favorite back in high school. He could also see the little trouble lines on her forehead. Worst of all, he could reach out and touch her if he wanted to.

Without any coy maneuvering, she merely said, ''We didn't have a chance to talk privately last night.''

''You said you wanted to catch up. We did that.''

''Maybe. But we didn't clear the air, and I'd like to do that, too. I want to tell you why I wrote you that note.''

''And why you wouldn't answer the phone? Why you hid in your room when I stopped by?'' He told himself he just wanted to clear the air, too, not that any of it mattered now.

''You know what I came from, Adam. It had always been just me and Mom, and we never had much. Mom wanted so much more for me, and from the time that I was little, we talked about me becoming a doctor.''

It was easy to recall her situation back then. "You hadn't been able to afford med school. You couldn't get a scholarship, and loans available to you wouldn't have been enough to fund your education."

"Right. So I was going to go to nursing school first."

He waited.

After a small breath, she continued. "You know how Mom watched us when we were together. She worried about me constantly when we weren't in sight. She finally admitted to me that she'd become pregnant her last year in high school and had barely been able to finish. Although she said many times that she never regretted having me, she also told me the pregnancy ruined her life. She had plans for college that never happened. Day care had always been hard to find, and the responsibility of taking care of a baby was monumental, especially since my father left town. He was the same age she was and not ready for the burden of a baby."

Leigh seemed to hesitate, as if she was choosing her words carefully. "Mom saw the two of us together, the way we looked at each other, the way we held hands, and she didn't want what happened to her to happen to me. She wanted me to have all the schooling I needed to get without any encumbrances. She especially wanted me to live my dreams because she'd had to give up hers. Mom has always done so much for me, working two jobs for as long as I can remember. When she advised me to stop seeing you, it seemed the best thing to do."

While Adam studied her, she didn't look away or

duck her head, and he respected that. "Why didn't you tell me all this then? Why the note?"

"I knew if I saw you again, I wouldn't be able to break it off. We were young, Adam, so young. Mom kept pointing that out. You had won first prize in that computer science fair and gotten a scholarship and Mom was worried about *you*, too. She didn't want me to hold you back, either."

Nothing would have held him back. He would have liked to have taken Leigh along with him, but she'd had other plans, other dreams and maybe now, seeing the success he had made of his life, she regretted that.

His intercom beeped again, and he realized he hadn't told Darlene to hold his calls. When he pressed the button on the intercom, she said, "Jared Cambry on line two."

This was shaping up to be some morning.

Leigh started to get up from her chair as if to leave to give him privacy, but Adam shook his head, indicating that he wanted her to stay as he took the call. "Mr. Cambry, has something happened with Mark?"

"No, nothing's happened with Mark. And it's Jared, Adam."

First names was progress, Adam supposed. "All right…Jared. If you're calling to see if the testing is completed, it is."

"I knew it was. Leigh Peters called me."

"I see."

"I wanted to thank you for going through with it."

"No thanks are necessary," Adam said in a low voice. He might not be a match.

After a moment of silence, Jared explained, "Mark asked me to call you. He'd like to meet you."

"We might not match," Adam said aloud now.

"He knows that. We've discussed as much as we can with him every step of the way. He's having one of his better days today, and you were on his mind this morning."

"You want me to meet him today?"

"I know this is another imposition, but these days we try to give Mark whatever he asks for...whatever we can. Would it be possible for you to clear your schedule this morning?"

Glancing down at the printout Darlene had laid on his desk earlier, he saw there wasn't anything listed that couldn't be postponed. She could juggle his appointments and he could take care of the rest later today.

"Give me your address," Adam decided. He wasn't surprised when the location of Cambry's home was in a section of town where the elite lived. "I'll be there in half an hour."

When he settled the handset on the console once more, he turned to Leigh. "Mark wants to meet me. I'm going to go over there now."

"You'll like Mark. He's mature beyond his years. Mr. and Mrs. Cambry are very open with him about everything. I wonder how he's doing with all this waiting."

"You mean physically?"

"Yes." Her blue eyes were worried and concerned. "If you want to keep this private, I'll understand. But

I could come along with you to assess his condition, to look at how he's doing as a medical professional.''

''Would this be part of your job as liaison?'' He didn't know Leigh anymore and he wasn't sure of her motives.

''That's part of it, but there's more. I'd like to put our past behind us. I thought maybe we could be friends.''

As Adam turned over her words in his mind, he couldn't help but be wary. All the relationships in his past had not led him to trust easily. On the other hand, maybe he was looking at this too deeply. Leigh's expertise would be valuable when he visited Mark, and having her along might ease the awkwardness between him and the Cambrys. He had no idea what to expect when he walked in the door.

''If you have the time, I'd appreciate your coming along. Give me a few minutes to speak to Dylan and my secretary, then we can go.''

The drive to the Cambrys was quiet for the most part, and Adam was absolutely aware of Leigh sitting straight in the leather seat, not very far from him. He wondered what she was thinking about all this, whether she was sorry she was caught in the middle of it, or if she saw it simply as an opportunity to stretch her job a little.

*She's going to be a doctor,* a smart voice inside of his head told him again, as if to stop him from wondering anything about her. Hating that subconscious voice, he thought about Mark instead. Before he and Leigh had left Novel Programs, Unlimited, he'd snatched up one of his cutting-edge laptop computers that only weighed two pounds and a handful of sample disks, stashing all of it into a carrying case. He didn't know if Mark would enjoy the computer games or not, but trapped in bed he might appreciate something to do, not only now but later if he had to go to the hospital again.

Adam didn't want to think about what it would mean if he wasn't a match.

The area of Portland in which Jared Cambry lived was on the way to Adam's ranch. However, when Adam veered off the main road, he took a series of turns that led him past huge estates where chauffeurs, maids, butlers and gardeners were commonplace.

The Cambrys' driveway was a long curved one, lined with pines that added to the sense of privacy. Their house was exceedingly large, Tudor with its wood beams and stucco. It was a traditional house and Adam wondered if Jared Cambry had turned into a traditional man. Maybe Adam would find out something about him today in his own environment.

Adam automatically went around to Leigh's side of the car and helped her out. Her hand felt small, delicate and warm in his. She was wearing an off-white wool coat over her dress and was every inch a lady...always had been. The sun was shining again today though rain was predicted for the rest of the week. Rain in Portland in March was a given. Thoughts of rain got lost as he watched yellow sunbeams play in Leigh's blond hair, making it glisten. He felt himself responding to the feel of her skin under his, the scent of her perfume brought to him on the breeze, the concern in her large blue eyes.

"Are you ready for this?" she asked gently.

"As ready as I'm going to be."

Releasing her hand, he opened the door to the back and pulled out the computer case.

Adam walked the curving path to the door beside Leigh, taking in the huge casement windows, the gables, the pristine outward appearance of everything. At the double-wide, heavy wood doors, he rang the bell.

A few moments later, Jared Cambry was at the door inviting them into the large foyer. A pretty, dark-haired woman, petite and slender, with chin-length wavy hair, came to greet them, too.

Jared dropped his arm around her shoulders. "Leigh, you've met my wife Danielle. Adam, this is my wife."

As Danielle moved closer, Adam could see the circles under her eyes, the paleness of her skin, the worry lines creasing her forehead. He imagined she'd had many sleepless nights and long days of turmoil.

Still, she touched Leigh's arm briefly, and when he extended his hand to her, she put hers in his. "I'm so glad to meet you, Adam. We can't thank you enough." Her voice caught.

Adam had known this meeting would be difficult, but he'd expected awkwardness to come from different reasons than emotion. He didn't want their thanks. He hadn't done anything.

Taking a step back, he lifted the computer. "I brought Mark something. Even if he already has a computer, this one will be chock-full of games and an e-mail program.''

''He has a PlayStation,'' Jared said. ''We haven't gotten him a computer yet, though there's a hookup for one in his room. I have one in my home office, and he can link into my Internet service. He'll probably love it. He's spending most of his days in bed.''

Jared's arm was still around his wife, and Adam could tell they were holding on to each other for support.

''Would you like to see him now?'' Danielle asked. ''He was watching TV when I went up a little bit ago. I'll make some coffee. Leigh, would you like to join me in the kitchen?''

He understood Danielle's intent at the invitation. As Adam followed Jared up the stairs, he was suddenly grateful a crowd wouldn't be around when he met Mark.

The oak steps were plushly carpeted down the middle. The house was tastefully decorated in taupes and mauves with a touch of green here and there. Jared took him to the second door on the right in the upstairs hall.

When he opened it, Adam assessed the room in a second—several posters of Harry Potter, a red-white-and-blue spread with baseballs and bats andcatchers' mitts, a television set on the dresser facing the bed. There were bookshelves not only lined with books, but with replicas of dinosaurs in porcelain, resin and plush. It was definitely a boy's room, and when Adam's gaze met Mark's in the double bed, his heart tripped, and he understood they were connected in a very big way by blood—their father's blood.

Mark was pale, so very pale. His dark-brown hair was straight and spiky, his green eyes the same color as his father's. What stunned Adam most was that Mark looked like he had when he was a boy. If someone had put their eight-year-old pictures together, Adam didn't know if a stranger could tell them apart.

Royal-blue sheets were folded at Mark's waist and he was propped up on three pillows. In spite of that, he sat up straight, glanced at his father and back at Adam. "You're my brother?"

Adam moved into the room and sat on the corner of the bed so that he and Mark were almost at eye level. "It seems like that may be the case. We'll know for certain after the bloodwork results are in."

Mark was studying Adam's face. "You're my brother. I can tell. You look like me."

Adam laughed. "Yep, I've got to admit, there is a resemblance. You have another older brother, don't you?"

"Yeah, but Chad looks like Mom. So does Shawna. I'm the only one who looks like Dad."

As if the talking had tired him, Mark leaned back against the pillows.

Realizing Jared had left him alone with the boy, Adam set the computer on the bed and unzipped the case. "I brought you something. The battery will stay charged up to ten hours and you can use this while you're in bed. From the looks of it," he pointed to the Harry Potter posters and the dinosaurs, "you'll like this new game we've developed. Dino-land."

"I can use it in bed? That's great. I get tired really fast now if I sit at my desk to draw."

Adam glanced at the corner desk and the colored pens and pencils scattered there. "So drawing's a hobby of yours?"

The boy nodded.

"I'm sure I can dig up a program to use on the computer for drawing. It'll be different than doing it by hand."

"That's okay. Anything's good to make the time pass faster. I hate being stuck up here. I hate not going to school. I hate being different from everybody else."

At that moment Adam was sure Leigh could handle this conversation much better than he could. "Do you talk about any of that with your parents?"

Mark shook his head vigorously. "No, they're so worried most of the time. Mom cries…so does Shawna. Chad and Dad just get this look on their faces. After Lissa wasn't a match, Mom's eyes were red for days until the P.I. found you. Did that lady at the hospital talk to you about the transplant?"

"You mean Marietta?"

"Yeah, she's the one. She's cool. She tried to make it sound not too scary. Did she do that for you, too?"

With a smile, Adam nodded. He knew if they went through with the transplant, this was going to be a whole lot harder for Mark than it was for him, that conditioning would involve chemo until all the abnormal bone marrow cells were destroyed. Mark would have to be in isolation before and after, and that was going to be hard on him. Yet Adam could sense this boy had spirit and that would get him through, along with the love of his family.

"How would you like it if I loaded some of these games onto the computer and you can try them out? We can make sure they work before I leave."

"I'd like that."

While Adam worked on the programs, he and Mark talked. Mark asked him where he grew up, and Adam told him about the farm, but not about his family life there.

"I've always wanted a horse," Mark confided.

"I have a horse. His name's Thunder and he's hard to handle, but he's just right for me. I've been thinking about getting a couple more. My partner says he'd come riding if I found a horse that wouldn't run away with him."

Mark laughed, and Adam felt satisfied that he could *make* him laugh. This little boy needed all the smiles and happy thoughts he could get.

"If you get more horses, can I come ride after this is all over?"

All over. *If* he was a match. They wouldn't know if the transplant was successful for two to four weeks. After that, it could be six months to a year for real recuperation. Looking into his half brother's eyes, Adam felt the hope there. Mark had to believe this would be all over and that he would be well again.

"You can come out to the ranch as soon as you're up to it. But in the meantime, when I do buy more horses, I'll take photos and scan them into the computer. I'll be able to e-mail them to you."

"Way cool!"

Adam loaded another disk.

"If you can e-mail me photos, does that mean you can just e-mail me, too?"

"If you'd like me to."

"Especially when I go back into the hospital, it would be nice. Family's great, but they just don't get Harry. And they can't tell a tyrannosaurus from a brontosaurus."

"And you think I can?"

"Can't you?" Mark challenged.

Dinosaurs had fascinated Adam when he was a kid, too. He'd haunted the school library for information and pictures about them. And as far as Harry Potter went, he had to be up-to-date on all the latest kids gimmicks and games and interests in order to create new software for them.

"I think you're older than eight," Adam decided with a chuckle.

Mark shrugged. "Mom says I'm an old soul, whatever that means."

"It means you're grown-up past your years."

"Were you grown-up past your years?"

Adam felt as if he'd always been an adult. "I guess I was."

Although he had been leaning against the pillows, now Mark sat up again. "Adam?" he asked, in a voice that urged Adam's gaze to meet his.

"What, Mark?"

"I think you're going to be a match."

## Chapter Four

A short time later, when Leigh joined Adam in Mark's room, he was grateful. There were too many feelings ricocheting inside, and he needed time to sort them out. Mark was a terrific kid, and when Adam thought about the odds of them actually being a match…

As Adam loaded the last program into the computer, he could tell Leigh wasn't just talking to Mark, she was observing him and assessing him—a touch of her hand on the eight-year-old's skin, a closer look into his eyes, a few questions about how tired he was and if he'd slept last night.

Finally Adam stood and set the computer on the desk. After he plugged into the phone jack, he turned to Mark. ''All set. This has an extra-long cord so it'll reach to the bed if you want to do e-mail there or surf the Net.''

"Thank you, Adam," Mark replied solemnly.

Adam couldn't help going to the boy then. "I have more computers lying around the office than I know what to do with. You'll put this one to good use. But for now, I think you'd better rest."

Leigh stood and smiled at Mark. "That's a very good idea."

"When will I see you again?" Mark asked Adam.

The question tugged at Adam and he realized he truly did have a brother now. "I'll e-mail you tonight to make sure everything's working, and I'll stop by in a couple of days."

"Do you play chess?" Mark asked him.

"I used to. I'm probably rusty now."

"Dad's been teaching me. Maybe we could do that."

"Maybe we can. Now remember you're test driving some of those programs for me. You remember what you like most about them and what you like least."

Leaning over, Adam ruffled Mark's hair. "I'll see you soon." Then he left the room.

After Leigh said her goodbyes, she caught up to him on the stairs.

"How did it go?" she asked as he let her descend the steps in front of him.

"In some ways I see myself in him when I was a kid."

She glanced over her shoulder at him. "Did you connect?"

"Yes, I guess you could say we did. I've never been

around kids much, but we didn't have any trouble talking.''

As they arrived at the bottom of the stairs, Jared came to meet them. ''Did he take to the computer?''

Standing there, Adam looked for himself in Jared. He found resemblance but decided it might be wishful thinking. ''He seemed to. I think he likes the idea of e-mailing.''

''I let him e-mail his grandparents on my computer sometimes.''

An uncomfortable silence fell over the foyer, and Jared motioned toward the dining room and kitchen beyond. ''Danielle made coffee and has some pastries. Come on.''

Adam couldn't seem to find anything to say to Jared as they made their way to the kitchen. He didn't feel like the man's son. He certainly didn't feel comfortable in his house.

Jumping in to fill the breach, Leigh spoke to Danielle as soon as she saw her in the kitchen. She was standing at an island arranging pastries on a dish. Maple cupboards were polished to a high sheen, and the ceramic tile floor and counter surfaces were immaculately clean. ''Your house is beautiful. There are so many lovely touches. I especially like that sculpture of the mother and children on the buffet in the dining room.''

''That's my favorite piece, too. Jared bought it for me when I had Mark.'' She took a deep breath and cleared her throat. ''How do you think he's doing, Leigh? He has a doctor's appointment tomorrow but I worry every minute.''

"I know you do. I think he's doing as well as can be expected. The doctor can tell you more. How's his appetite?"

"Almost nonexistent. The housekeeper's been making him homemade puddings, fruit smoothies, doctoring up the protein drinks, anything to tempt him. Sometimes it works, but sometimes it doesn't." She looked at Adam. "Waiting to hear if you're a match or not is so incredibly difficult."

"I can only imagine."

After they were all seated at the table, Jared sipped at his black coffee then set down the mug. "Lissa will be returning from her honeymoon soon."

"You said the family who adopted her had a vineyard. Does she work there?"

"Yes, that's how she met her husband. They brought Sullivan in as a consultant to help get the vineyard in the black again."

"Do you have a number where I can reach her when she returns?"

Jared took out his wallet and slipped out a card. "This is her cell phone number. I have it on my Rolodex and on the computer, too, so I don't need this." He slid the card across the table to Adam, and Adam picked it up.

Danielle, who had been busying herself getting more coffee, making sure she had enough pastries, came around the table and put her hand on Adam's shoulder. "Lissa is a wonderful young woman. She wanted to find you as much as Jared, not only for Mark but because you're her brother."

After a few moments as Adam savored the idea of

a blood sister—a twin—Danielle moved to sit beside her husband. Glancing at him, she addressed Adam again. "Feel free to stop by whenever you'd like. I'm sure Shawna and Chad would like to meet you, too."

"Do they spend much time with Mark?" He wondered if this family really cared about each other, or if everyone went their separate ways.

"Shawna and Chad both have cut back on their extracurricular activities. They take turns sitting with Mark. We're trying to keep their lives as normal as possible, but that's hard. Shawna turns sixteen in a week and a half. That's important to us, and I don't want her to feel as if we've forgotten about her in our concern for Mark."

It was difficult for Adam to read Jared but he had no doubt that Danielle was a loving, caring mother. Even though the Cambrys were wealthy, it seemed Danielle was a hands-on parent.

Suddenly there was a buzz on the intercom. Pushing her chair back, Danielle went to it quickly. "Yes, honey."

"Can you bring me a glass of juice with ice in it?"

"Sure can. I'll be right up." Already taking a glass from the cupboard, she offered, "I'm going to take Mark a snack, too, and see if he'll eat. Can I get either of you anything else?"

With a shake of his head, Adam pushed himself up from the table. "No, we'd better be going." His gaze caught Jared's. "Thanks for inviting me over to meet Mark."

Jared rose to his feet. After goodbyes to Danielle,

Leigh slipped on her coat and they all walked to the door.

Jared opened it. He said to Leigh, "If you see Christopher, thank him for all his help in this. I know we'll get results from the tests quicker because he's pushing."

Moments later Jared closed the door.

Adam was silent as he strode to the car. Leigh had always had this quiet way about her that made it easy to be with her. He was grateful for that now, grateful she wasn't trying to engage him in conversation. She wasn't asking questions he didn't have answers to.

Once they were buckled in, he started the engine and turned in the circular driveway, heading away from the house.

Leigh shifted toward him. "If you're a match, will you go through with the extraction of bone marrow?"

"Of course I will. How could I not?"

"Some people would think of themselves first, the discomfort, the whole situation they'd rather get away from rather than be part of. Especially in your case, with what happened to your sister—"

"Somehow I have to erase those memories of what happened with Delia. I was a kid then. Maybe I took it all in differently from how I would have as an adult. But I'll tell you one thing. The doctors at Portland General had better be kind to Mark. They'd better not treat him like a number, because I'll be there to make sure they don't."

As they came to a T in the road, he suddenly felt the urge to be at his ranch and to show it to Leigh. "How would you like to see my place? I think I need to breathe in hay and pine before I go back to work today.'' He glanced at her. ''Unless you have plans for the rest of the day.''

''No plans. I have to run some errands this afternoon, but I'll have plenty of time for that.''

In the close quarters of the car, Adam keenly recognized his attraction to Leigh, the sexual tension that always simmered between them. He wasn't sure why he wanted to show her the ranch, but he just did.

As Adam drove southwest of the city, Leigh knew she was making a mistake. Going along with him to see Mark had been a mistake. She was as drawn to Adam Bartlett now as she had been at seventeen. He'd obviously matured. He was more broad-shouldered now, his face more angular, his hair a shade darker. There was a confident air about him now, too, that hadn't been there as a teenager. His business was a roaring success. Of course he was confident! He'd never talked about his feelings easily, but now he was definitely more guarded. Was it just around her, or was it with everyone?

She didn't have the right to ask or to meddle. After all, she wasn't going to get involved. She was involved professionally but wouldn't be involved personally.

So why was she going to his ranch with him?

Because she was curious.

It wasn't long until they'd turned off the main road onto the secondary roads. She and Adam had veered onto a lane that was much different from the winding, pristine one at Jared's house. This one wasn't bordered by trees but rather was open to the ranch's scenery with white fencing, two red barns—one larger than the other—and meadows. There were clusters of trees, mostly alders and maples, with groves of firs here and there. When they came upon the house, a shiny blue pickup truck was parked in the driveway. As Adam pulled up beside it, Leigh saw that his log home fit in with the rest of the landscape perfectly down to the split-rail fence along the walk to the front door. The house was rustically charming.

"How long have you lived here?" she asked.

"Three years this summer. After living on the farm, I thought I'd never want to see one again. But after college, Dylan and I moved into a condo in the city. I felt like I was living in a hermetically sealed bubble. I could see the sky but couldn't touch it. I could see the grass and trees below but not smell them."

"And you can touch the sky out here?" she asked with a smile.

"I guess I'm able to touch the sky when I feel free. When I can look up into the blue and the wind's on my face and there aren't any walls around me," he said, looking uncomfortable. "I've never explained it quite like that before."

"I know what you mean about walls. I love what I do, especially taking care of children. Yet sometimes I work a double shift and can't wait to get outside."

"There's a gloom about hospitals," Adam muttered as he walked up onto the porch.

"We're trying to change that at Portland General," Leigh assured him. "It has to do with the colors on the walls, decorations, less-clinical uniforms. Especially for the kids."

"That might help some." But Adam sounded doubtful as he opened his front door.

When Leigh entered Adam's house, she saw there was certainly no gloom there. The skylight in the dining room added to the daylight already pouring through the windows. Warm wood tones were everywhere, from the rustic walls and beams, to the floor and entertainment center. Colorful rugs brightened the atmosphere even further. She could see Adam's sneakers peeking out from behind the hassock and an empty soda can sitting on the side table. Last night's paper was strewn on one end of the sofa as if he'd looked at it quickly.

"This is beautiful, Adam. You must enjoy spending time here."

"It seems as if I'm always running in and out. I have a state-of-the-art kitchen I hardly ever use."

Turning to her right, she glimpsed pine cupboards, gleaming off-white counters, stainless steel appliances. Had *women* ever cooked in this kitchen? Certainly more than a few had spent the night. She suddenly wanted to know about that...wanted to know about him. But she didn't have any right to ask about other women.

"Do you want to take a walk?" he asked looking down at her black flats.

"Yes. These shoes are comfortable."

"I'll keep you out of the mud," he said with a smile and a twinkle in his eyes.

That twinkle had been absent since their first meeting on Monday. Now her heart raced faster when she saw it again.

Adam's arm brushed hers as they walked across the paved lane to one of the corrals. Suddenly, though, they were confronted with a stream of water three feet wide that flowed at least a quarter of a mile down the lane.

"We could walk around it." Adam's smile was roguish and his eyes were devilish as he added, "Or..." Picking Leigh up into his arms, he easily took a long step over the water.

"What are you doing?" Leigh gasped as she held on.

"Getting you to the other side quicker. It's pretty muddy where the water's running. I thought we'd try to save those shoes."

With her arms around Adam's neck, she breathed in the remembered male scent. Now expensive cologne mingled with it but he was the same. His beard line was starting to show and she remembered how, by the end of the school day, he'd always had a shadow. It had been sexy then and was still sexy now. His arms were strong as he seemed to hold her without any trouble at all, as if she didn't weigh 110 pounds, as if carrying her was the most natural thing in the world.

However, he only took a few steps with her, then set her down. She looked up at him and turned away, facing the corral, unable to tell what was in his eyes or on his face. Her heart was still beating so fast from the effect of him holding her so close that she could hardly catch her breath. He didn't seem likewise affected.

"This is Thunder's corral."

A beautiful black horse, at least seventeen hands high, ran with his tail flying as he caught sight of Adam. He made a circle around the corral and then another, coming to a standstill under a maple. Then he pawed one hoof onto the ground and came running to meet his master.

Adam laughed. "It's never simple with you, is it?"

Slipping a roll of hard candy from his pocket, Adam peeled one off, and held it out in his hand to the horse. Thunder lapped it up and tossed his head, then came a little closer.

"Can I pet him?" Leigh asked.

Adam seemed to think about that. Then he nodded. "Slowly, very slowly, let him smell your hand. If he backs away, then we'll forget it. He definitely likes some folks better than others, and no one ever goes into the corral with him except me."

"Is he dangerous?"

"No, not when handled correctly. But he's a stallion and he's young and he's spirited. That could lead to trouble even with someone he knows."

Slowly Leigh held her hand out to Thunder. He didn't back away, just eyed it, and then her. "Hold still," Adam murmured, his voice soft and gentle as it gave her a chill up her spine—an excited little chill.

The horse's breath blew warm on her hand and then he snuffled her fingers. When he rubbed the side of his muzzle against her palm, Adam murmured, "Just stroke his neck."

Thunder stood perfectly still as her fingers rippled through his coat. Then he backed up and took off at a run again.

With a chuckle, Adam acknowledged, "He likes you. That's his way of showing off for you."

They watched the horse as he streaked across the corral catty-corner.

"How often do you ride him?"

"On weekends for sure. With days growing longer, I'll get more riding time in during the week, too. I'd like to get a couple more horses."

As she glanced around, she saw space wasn't a problem. Yet with Adam's schedule… "Do you have time for that? I mean, they take a lot of care, don't they?"

"I'd make the time."

Suddenly Adam turned and leaned against the fence. Studying her, he asked, "What do you do in your time off, except for running errands?"

His smile had always made her tummy somersault, and now was no exception. "You have to promise not to laugh if I tell you."

"I won't laugh," he assured her.

"I go ice skating over at the mall. I've loved it ever since I was a kid. After we moved here from the Midwest, it was probably what I missed most—the frozen lakes. In another life, I might have been a figure skater," she teased.

In another life…if she hadn't ended their relationship…if she hadn't wanted to be a doctor…

She was looking up at him now, not at the scenery, not at the magnificent forest, not at the mountains in the distance, not at the blue sky. Adam's eyes had always told her that there were depths to him that nobody knew, and she'd always wanted to explore those depths. The times they'd made love were filled with some adolescent awkwardness. But more than that, she remembered the passion in Adam, the way he'd always tried to satisfy her first. They'd even read a book together about it—

"Leigh," he said hoarsely, and she knew he was remembering, too.

His hand slid under her hair as he nudged her closer. The scent of grass and pine and early spring hovered all around her. Her eyelids fluttered closed as his mouth came down on hers.

There was no coaxing gentleness in the kiss, no get-to-know-you-again slowness, no hesitation to make sure she wanted it, too. There was a surety in Adam now, a command that had never been there before. The kiss was a challenge, too, daring her to taste desire with him again.

She'd forgotten all about the taste of desire and how intoxicating it could be. Kisses came and went, but with Adam...

Adam's kiss had always been like a shimmering rainbow filled with so many colors it dazzled her until she got lost in its brilliance. He didn't just kiss her. His tongue slipped into her mouth and he explored her. He savored her. He remembered her. Although she felt terrifically off balance, although her feet didn't really seem to be touching the earth, although the world as she knew it faded away, she was all too aware of everything about Adam. His muscles tensed as they kissed, his body becoming even harder. The taut strength in his arms was evident in the rest of his body as he brought her closer into him, as she felt his thigh muscles against her skirt, as her breasts pushed against his chest. As he grew harder, she felt herself growing softer, molding into him, molding to him.

When the wind picked up and blew through her hair, her arms went around Adam's neck to hold on, to keep her from floating away.

Then abruptly his hands were on her arms, and he was backing away, breaking the kiss, ending it.

When she gazed up at him, she expected to see passion in his eyes, tenderness, something she'd recognize. But she saw nothing. They weren't mirrors to the soul, but simply shuttered windows that didn't reveal anything inside the man.

He didn't appear to be the least bit affected by what had happened when he said, "For old-time's sake."

She wanted to hear some humor in his voice and warmth, something. But it was unemotional, factual, unfeeling even. She felt like a fool.

"Why did you do that, Adam?"

"To see if my memories were true or figments of my imagination."

"It was an experiment?" she asked, angry now and not sure why.

"You could say that. Admit it, Leigh, you were as curious as I was. Otherwise you would have backed away."

He'd hit *that* nail on the head. How could she be angry at him for acting on what she'd been thinking? Still she wasn't angry about him kissing her. She was annoyed that he hadn't felt anything when he had.

Trying to prove to herself otherwise, trying to prove

that his world had shaken a little, too, she asked, "So was your curiosity satisfied?"

"It was."

And that seemed to be all he was going to say on the subject. She wasn't going to poke and prod at him to see if he'd felt sparks and fire, too. "Well, I'm glad. Kissing for experimentation sake will definitely further the study of man-woman relationships." She was babbling and she knew it but she didn't care. Adam's kiss had rattled her much more than she wanted to admit.

Adam glanced at his watch. "We'd better be getting back."

She'd already told him she didn't have that much to do today so it wasn't *her* schedule he was worried about. After all, he was an important CEO. He had responsibilities, duties and a schedule to keep.

Turning away from the corral, she started across the lane and was met by the wide band of water. She was feeling disgruntled, flustered, embarrassed by giving in to an impulse that meant nothing to him. She wasn't about to have him watch her walk the whole way around the water. She also wasn't going to let him carry her across it again. No way, no how. There was only one course to take.

As she slipped off her shoes, she found a spot where she could see the mud halfway across the water. Shoes in hand, she took a leap on to the mound and felt her feet squish down into the brown ooze. Not giving a hoot about that at this point, she jumped clear of the water onto the lane, hurried to the grass and wiped her feet off in it. Taking a tissue from her pocket, she finished wiping her feet the best she could and slipped them back into the shoes, pretending there weren't splashes of mud on her nylon hose.

Adam had leaped over the stream of water effortlessly and was now watching her. She didn't look at him as she balled the tissue, stuffed it into her pocket and then took off toward his car.

With a few long strides he caught up to her and clasped her arm. "Leigh?"

Stopping, she looked up at him. She couldn't quite tell if he was suppressing a smile around the corners of his mouth. The mouth that had taken her back...taken her forward...

"On Saturday night Dylan is giving a cocktail party, and he insists I bring a date. How would you like to go along?"

She should say no. He was making it clear that this was a business event and he needed someone along because that was the proper thing to do.

But maybe he *had* felt something when he'd kissed her. Maybe...

"I might stop in to see Mark again, too, and it would give us a chance to discuss his condition."

So much for maybes. Dr. Chambers had given her the order to be available to Adam as well as Jared and his family. She'd forget about the kiss and go for the experience of the party. She'd also be doing her job as liaison. It had been a long time since she'd gotten all dressed up. In fact, she suspected she'd never been to a party quite like the one Dylan Montgomery would throw.

"A cocktail party sounds like fun. What time should I be ready?"

## Chapter Five

On Saturday when Adam visited Mark, the little boy seemed weaker and paler to him. Because of that, Adam kept his visit short. The eight-year-old was almost asleep when he left.

Adam had just closed Mark's bedroom door when a teenager came running up the steps. She had dark-brown, perfectly straight hair that went to her shoulders, and bangs that fell nearly to her eyes.

Spotting him, she came up short, then mounted the last three steps more sedately.

"You must be Adam," she guessed with a quick smile, reminiscent of Danielle's.

"Yes, I am. You must be Shawna." Adam extended his hand, and she shook it without hesitation as if she was used to meeting adults every day of the week. She was wearing jeans that had their share of holes for effect and a lime-green T-shirt under a crocheted sweater.

With a glance at Mark's door, she asked, "How is he today? I left early this morning before he was up. Mom was out back talking to a neighbor when I came in."

When Adam had arrived earlier, Danielle had told him Jared was at work today. He tried to bring his work home, but some things he just couldn't.

"Mark tired quickly," Adam said honestly.

Shawna sighed and her eyes became moist. "Some days are like that—more and more days. I wish there was something *I* could do for him. I wish I had been a match."

When he'd met with the counselor, Marietta Watson had told him she'd had a few sessions with Shawna and Chad as well as their parents. The situation was difficult for siblings, too. "For some reason you weren't. But you can hope with me that I am."

"Hope with you." Closing her eyes for a moment, Shawna leaned against the banister. "That's kind of nice. Mom goes to church a lot more now to pray, but I can't see that going and saying a bunch of prayers will help anything. I know how to hope, though."

"Then, in your way, you're praying." Not that Adam was an expert at it. He hadn't prayed in years. But the situation with Mark had made him look outward to something much larger than himself.

Shawna didn't seem in a hurry to go into Mark's room or to end their conversation, and Adam wondered if she needed somebody besides Marietta to talk to about all this, too. "I hear you're going to be sixteen soon."

She gave a little half shrug. "Yeah. Mom and Dad are having a party for me and everything. But it doesn't seem right somehow...with Mark sick."

"Turning sixteen is something to celebrate. I'm sure your parents are proud of you, and they want to show you that."

"Maybe. Later today after Dad gets home, Mom wants to go shopping with me for an outfit. She hardly ever leaves Mark now, and I don't know if I want her to go. If something happened—"

"That's why man made cell phones," Adam said with a smile. "I'm sure your mom has one."

Shawna smiled back. "Yeah, she does. I told her I wanted one for my birthday. I told her I'd be responsible with it. Then I could call in and check how things are going."

Simply in the short while he'd talked to Shawna, Adam had no doubt she *would* be responsible with it. "Mark said you'd been helping him get my e-mails."

"I hope you don't mind that I read them." Her face flushed slightly. "But if he's really tired, I download them, then read them to him."

"I don't mind. Do you type in his messages to me?"

She nodded. "He does it himself during the day, or I guess he gets Mom to help. I hope he's not e-mailing you too much. We don't want him to bother you."

At work Adam checked his e-mail often, and if he had a message from Mark, he responded immediately.

They'd gone back and forth three or four times a day since he'd given him the computer.

"He's not bothering me. He can e-mail as often as he likes."

Shawna's gaze passed over Adam's rugby shirt, his jeans, his athletic shoes. "*We're* related, too," she said as if just realizing it.

"Yes, we are. I'm your half brother."

"That sounds silly—half brother, Lissa's half sister. It seems to me you either are or you aren't."

Adam couldn't help but smile at that.

When she saw it, she added, "Well, it's true. When Dad first told us about all this, I was real…real disappointed in him. If I ever dated a boy who got me pregnant and then took off, Dad would want to kill him."

Adam supposed that was probably true.

"Aren't you mad at him?" she prodded.

Maybe he *was* downright, bottom-out angry at Jared. "I haven't had very long to sort it out. Think about how you felt the day your dad told you the whole story."

"Yeah, that was confusing. I could see Mom was upset about all of it but trying not to be. In another way…we were all glad about it because there was more hope for Mark. Do you know what I mean?"

"I know *exactly* what you mean. Probably the reason I haven't sorted it out yet is because I'm thinking about Mark and not much else."

"The waiting is so hard." Shawna looked down at her hand as she rubbed it along the banister.

"I know it is."

Then she looked up, her face suddenly brighter. "I'm going to hope along with you. I'm going to tell Mom and Dad that's what we all should do." She looked at Mark's door again. "Well, I'd better go. I can sit with him even if he's sleeping."

Halfway to Mark's bedroom, she stopped and turned. "Can you come to my birthday party?"

"Are you sure it isn't just for—"

"Family?" she finished with a smile. "You *are* family. It's next Saturday at seven. Will you come?"

It seemed to mean a lot to Shawna. "Check it out with your parents and see if it's okay. And if you still want me to come, e-mail me," he added with a wink.

"I will," she answered enthusiastically and then slipped into Mark's room.

After Adam went downstairs, he saw that Danielle was still speaking to her neighbor in the backyard. He waved, called, "I'll see you soon," and then went to his car. The cocktail party tonight at Dylan's was on his mind. He wasn't sure what had made him ask Leigh. Certainly not that kiss. *That* had been a monumental mistake. He'd given in to an impulse and a need that he usually kept in check.

Why she was still so attractive to him he didn't know. It had been years since she'd first rocked his world, and he wasn't about to let her rock it again. She was leaving Portland in June, and he had to keep that fact firmly in place in his head.

Asking her along tonight had simply been a practical solution to a problem. Usually he went to these parties alone. Sometimes an unattached female would latch on to him, and without an actual date along, it could be hard to extricate himself politely. He really hated the mingle-and-shake-hands parties that Dylan was so good at. Adam would rather give a presentation on new software, go over marketing strategy, analyze focus group results. However, Dylan had informed him that contacts would be at this party that could take new products global.

Having Leigh on his arm could make the night easier.

When Leigh opened her apartment door to Adam that evening, he had to take a deep breath. She looked more beautiful than he'd ever seen her. Her blond hair was arranged in loose curls on the top of her head. The strapless pink cocktail dress had a sequined bodice and a short, straight skirt. Every one of her curves was evident. The only remnant of the girl she once had been were those big blue eyes.

She smiled almost shyly. "Is this appropriate? I wasn't sure what to wear. I just bought it this morning."

"You didn't have to buy a new dress."

"I don't go to many cocktail parties."

He thought about the prom they hadn't attended. Neither of them had been able to afford it. Instead they had eaten at a fast-food restaurant and gone to a movie. Neither of them had minded then...at least *he* hadn't.

She was gazing at the pintucks on his white starched shirt, and a small smile slipped across her lips.

"What?" he asked.

"You look comfortable in that tux. As if you were born to it."

"I consider it a uniform on nights like these. Believe me, I'll be glad to get rid of the tie at the end of the evening."

Motioning inside, Leigh asked, "Would you like to come in for a few minutes?"

"I don't want to intrude on your mom's evening."

"She's not here. She went to the mall with a friend."

With Leigh looking the way she did tonight, he knew it wasn't a good idea to be alone with her. Glancing at his watch, he decided, "We'd better get going or Dylan will be ringing my cell phone."

Leigh lifted her small purse. "I have mine along just in case we get the results of your test. It's early yet, I know. But we can hope."

"I saw Mark today. It wasn't one of his better days."

"I'm sorry to hear that." She was quiet for a moment, then said, "I'm going to be taking a bunch of kids who've been in cancer treatment to the zoo tomorrow. Why don't you come along? It might help to hear the parents' stories and see how well the kids are doing. You also might get a better handle on what Mark's going to go through. Having Marietta tell you is one thing. Actually seeing the kids who've been through it is another. Being with them always gives me a lift. They're such fighters...such survivors."

As if realizing how passionate she'd become about it, she stopped, then added quietly, "We're meeting at the entrance to the zoo at two if you're interested."

"It sounds like a good idea. I met Shawna, Mark's sister, today. She seems like a great kid, too, but she's definitely worried about her brother."

"Why don't I give Shawna and Chad a call in the morning and see if they'd like to come, too?"

"Why don't you do it right now?"

"I thought we had to get to the party."

"This is more important. If Dylan calls, I'll tell him we're on our way."

In Leigh's apartment Adam felt like a bull in a china shop. Everything was so feminine, so delicate, so in place. Also, there was a funny smell in the apartment tonight—like burned…something. Yet it didn't seem to come from Leigh's kitchen area.

He listened while she made the call, and when she got off the phone, she was smiling. "I got hold of Shawna. She said she loves the zoo and wants to come. But she thinks Chad might have plans. She said her father would drop her off, and I told her I'd take her home."

It was best if they went separately tomorrow, Adam supposed. After all, he and Leigh weren't dating.

After Leigh stepped away from the phone, she headed for the living room. "I'm going to crack a window while we're gone. Our neighbor, Mr. Benson, puts supper on the stove and then forgets it's there while he's watching TV. I think Mom said he burned lima beans tonight."

Leigh's shawl, lying over the chair, didn't look warm enough for the cold, damp night. But he knew women often dressed for effect rather than warmth. As she went to the window, she looked so delectably feminine. Unlocking it, she tried to raise it, but apparently it was stuck.

"The landlord painted a few weeks ago," she explained.

Coming up behind her, Adam offered, "Let me try."

The skin of Leigh's shoulders was a creamy temptation as he stood next to her looking down at her. She'd worn a single pearl necklace and tiny pearls at her ears. His fingers itched to brush the skin along her jawline, itched to feel her soft cheek. That kiss had reminded him too much of how they'd been together, how they could be together again. He dismissed that thought as foolhardy.

With his fist, he pounded along the sash, then took hold of the lever and pulled up the window. "A few inches enough?" he asked.

When he glanced at her, she was watching him. He felt that tingling sexual tension he'd never been able to deny between them.

"A few inches is fine." Her voice was low. "It might start raining again."

"Will your mother be back soon?"

"Anytime."

They were making small talk, having a conversation that had nothing to do with the tension in the air, the thoughts they were both having—thoughts that would *not* become reality.

Stepping away from the window and Leigh, he motioned to the door. "We'd better go."

Leigh didn't respond, just crossed the room and picked up her shawl. When she laid it over her arm absently, Adam advised, "You'd better put that on. Warmer weather's supposed to move in but it hasn't yet."

As she unfolded the black velvet, he took it from her. Maybe he was torturing himself, but it was only for tonight. Her scent was so damn sweet, her lips such a pretty pink, her whole look so feminine. His fingers brushed the stray hair at the nape of her neck that had escaped the topknot. As he settled the shawl over her shoulders, he wanted to surround her with his arms the way the material was doing. He wanted to turn her around, kiss her and take her to the bedroom.

But they didn't even know each other anymore. He never went to bed with a woman simply for the sex. It had to be more than that. Even when he thought there was more, the women he'd been involved with the past few years hadn't interested him for more than a couple of months. He wasn't sure what long-lasting, committed relationships were all about. His adoptive father and mother had been together until his father's death, but Adam didn't think they'd ever been really happy.

Picturing Jared and Danielle Cambry, he'd detected silent communication between the two of them and a bond that was strong. How did a man find that?

When Leigh took the shawl from his hands, he released it, as well as thoughts of what he wanted to do with her. As they went to the door, he decided tonight was going to be about business, and Leigh would be the buffer he needed to make it all the more tolerable.

Twenty minutes later Leigh was still trembling inside as Adam escorted her into Dylan's condo. It was a penthouse apartment with windows everywhere. Still, the chrome and smoked glass, the bar with its bartender in the living room, tuxedoed waiters carrying trays of champagne and hors d'oeuvres didn't make the impression they should have. Even the original oil paintings on the walls couldn't snag her attention. All she could do was relive those moments with Adam in her apartment as they'd stood at the window.

Electricity had seemed to spark around them. Then when he'd helped her with her shawl and his fingers had brushed her neck…

The memory of that touch remained just as other memories did. Adam was so controlled, so guarded sometimes. What more could she expect?

He'd cared about her. She had betrayed those feelings by walking away. In June she'd be walking away again. He was right to keep himself removed, and she should do the same.

*He will probably come to the zoo tomorrow.* However Shawna would be there and so would a crowd of other people.

As Leigh glanced around, she saw there was certainly a crowd here tonight—women in sequined and beaded dresses, both long and short, men mostly wearing tuxedos. Everyone seemed to know one another.

Inside the door, a maid took Leigh's wrap. "Do you think I'll be able to find it again?" she asked Adam as the maid walked away.

"When you're ready to leave, Patrice will appear with it as if out of nowhere. Dylan always asks for her because she's good."

"You mean he doesn't have a maid all the time?"

Adam laughed. "Not Patrice, anyway. He has a housekeeper, Mrs. Warren, who cleans, does laundry and makes sure everything stays straightened up. She's a great cook, too."

"Would you like to have a housekeeper?"

"No, thanks. I have a cleaning lady who comes in once a week and a laundry service for the things I can't wash and dry myself. I like my solitude. Dylan enjoys being waited on hand and foot, but I don't."

"Speaking of the devil..." Adam drawled with a grin as Dylan strode toward them.

"Nice to see you again, Leigh."

"You, too," she said sincerely. Something about Dylan was ingratiating. He was the boy-next-door type of friendly that was comfortable.

"I hope you enjoy yourself tonight," he said with an easy smile.

"I'm sure I will. This is a beautiful apartment."

"She's especially impressed by Patrice," Adam joked.

"Uh-oh. I think Adam's telling tales about me again. I do know how to throw a party without a maid and bartender, but it's much easier to do it with them. And since Adam has made me a rich man—"

"You're my partner," Adam cut in. "We do the work together."

"Yes, but you could have done it on your own. I don't know if I would have the vision and the discipline without you." He focused his attention on her again. "Anyway, before Adam contradicts everything I've said, let me get you a glass of champagne. Why don't you come with me, and I'll introduce you to some people.''

''You don't think I can do that?'' Adam asked with a half smile.

''I'm sure you can. But I think it's best if you go over there and talk to Gregory Treporri. He's been itching to meet you, and he can do us a lot of good.''

Adam glanced over at the gray-haired man in his sixties. ''Do you mind?'' he asked Leigh.

She could tell he didn't want her to feel adrift. ''No, go ahead. I'm always eager to meet new people. This should be fun.''

After Dylan introduced Leigh to a group of men and women, one conversation developed into another. She listened to a banker discuss the world's economy, a real estate agent expound on the best deals in Portland and a model describe every detail at a shoot she'd just finished. Looking around every now and then for Adam, Leigh noticed a pretty redhead approach him as he finished his conversation with the first gentleman.

The redhead was much taller than Leigh, much leggier, and had a look of perfection about her. She wore a little black dress that hugged every curve. Leigh attempted to keep her mind on a university professor's remarks about California's next earthquake, but she couldn't help being interested in what was happening with Adam. After the discussion in Leigh's circle ebbed, she went to the bar for an orange juice, then nibbled at the buffet table. She felt out of her element here, and she was. Not that she couldn't intelligently engage in conversation, but she wasn't connecting on a personal level and that was unusual.

Adam was still talking with the beautiful redhead when he caught her eye and motioned to her. Not hesitating for a second, she joined him.

When Leigh stood next to Adam, he surprised her by circling her waist with his arm, his hand distractingly settling on her hip. He nodded to the redhead. "Leigh Peters, meet Nicole Jackson. Nicole, this is Leigh."

From Adam's body language, his possessive arm around Leigh's waist, it was obvious he was telling Nicole that Leigh was his date tonight.

Nicole's smile wasn't quite so bright now as she managed a hello. She asked Leigh, "Are you new in town?"

"Oh, no. I've lived here since I was seventeen."

"Leigh and I met in high school," Adam explained, making it sound as if they'd been together for a very long time.

"I see. Usually Adam doesn't bring a date to Dylan's parties." Nicole was apparently fishing for more information.

"Usually I don't stay at Dylan's parties very long," Adam said.

Suddenly Leigh realized exactly what was going on. Adam wanted to extricate himself from this woman's interest and he was using *her*. He was intimating they were involved when they weren't. Anger bubbled up; Leigh didn't like the idea of being used as a smoke-screen.

Pulling away from Adam's hold, she gave Nicole a

very bright smile. "I just saw Dylan go into the kitchen. Will you excuse me? There was something I wanted to ask him about his decorator."

Before either Adam or Nicole could comment, she was wending through the guests on the way to the kitchen. She had seen Dylan go in there, but right now she just wanted an escape.

However, she'd only just stepped into the gleaming black and tan kitchen when she found Adam beside her, his hand on her arm. "Leigh, are you all right?"

Dylan had turned at the sound of Adam's voice. He'd been looking for something in the refrigerator.

Now he asked, "Is something wrong?"

Holding on to her temper, Leigh managed, "Everything's just fine. You're giving a beautiful party, Dylan."

With a puzzled look, Dylan glanced at Adam and then back at Leigh. "Would you two like some privacy?"

Leigh said, "No" at the same time Adam said, "Yes."

Dylan chuckled and then drawled, "O—kay. I just came in here to look for olives. The bartender said we ran out. But I can do that later." As he left the kitchen, he told Adam, "I'll head off anyone who tries to come in."

Leigh quickly started after Dylan. "There's no need for that. In fact, if you just tell me where the powder room is located—"

This time Adam firmly clasped her arm and didn't let go. "*I'll* show you where the powder room is after we talk."

Wisely Dylan slipped out of the room.

Leigh looked up at Adam. "I don't think we have anything to talk about."

His deep voice was concerned. "What's gotten you so ruffled?"

"I don't like being used. I thought you invited me here tonight because we'd…mended fences and could become friends again. But that wasn't the reason, was it?"

Adam's face had set into an unreadable mask. "No, that's not the reason. I thought you'd make the evening more pleasant."

"Pleasant?"

He shrugged. "I needed a date, Leigh. It was better to come with someone I knew. I could more easily extricate myself from a situation I didn't like— whether it's from a windy investment banker or an account manager from a cosmetics company."

"And you didn't consider how I'd feel?"

"I thought you'd enjoy mingling…that you'd have a good time."

"Did you really? Or was this some kind of payback?"

An emotion flickered in Adam's eyes, but she couldn't tell what it was. Surprise that she'd figured it out?

"I'm not stupid, Adam. You were hurt all those years ago. I'm sorry about that, but can't you see we were too young for whatever was happening between us?"

"We *were* young, Leigh. You left and I got over it. Tonight has nothing to do with that. I look at the world in realistic terms now. Bringing you here tonight was simply practical. I didn't have an ulterior motive.''

Adam had always been honest with her. Yet on the other hand, he'd always been able to deny what was going on inside of him, too.

After he studied her for a few silent moments, he finally admitted, ''Okay, I understand now. No one likes to feel used.''

She suddenly saw that must have been the way he'd felt ten years ago. After he'd taken her under his wing and made her feel at home in Portland, she'd left his life.

''Would you like to leave?'' he asked.

Being with him now was going to be uncomfortable. Since she finally knew the score, though, she wouldn't be distracted by him and could maybe dive into the party with a little more enthusiasm.

''We can stay. But I'm not going to hang on your arm like an ornament. I don't do that, Adam.''

Could she see a smile in his eyes? Did she see respect there? She couldn't really tell. So she turned away and she went back out into the dining room, determined to have fun if it killed her.

# Chapter Six

As Adam started across the street to the entrance of the Oregon Zoo, he spotted Leigh immediately. He'd not been here often, even though it was only five minutes from downtown Portland. He'd brought a date to the summer concert series a few years back. That woman had come and gone, and he hadn't thought much about the zoo after that....

Until Leigh suggested he come today. Adam wasn't sure what Leigh's attitude would be. She was standing in front of one of the ticket booths with children and parents. Last night, her upset with him had surprised him. He'd asked her to Dylan's party for practical reasons. Yet she'd obviously read more into it than that. They hadn't been together much after their talk in Dylan's kitchen, and she'd been quiet on the way home.

He didn't know what she expected from him.

After all, they were strangers now, even though they'd known each other long ago. Their meeting up again had been sheer chance. If she weren't on a determined course toward something much bigger, maybe he'd let old feelings rise again. But she *was* still on a determined course. That kiss at his ranch had shown him he was better off keeping his distance. He didn't *want* to want her again.

As Adam started up the incline, he could see at least five children gathered around Leigh—two were bald, one had a bandanna covering her head, another sported an inch of new hair growth spiking over his scalp. They all wore smiles and gathered close to Leigh's sides as if she were a pied piper.

The smell of French fries and grilled hamburgers wafted to the entrance from a nearby restaurant. Adam stopped halfway up the incline, watching as Leigh smiled at the kids, hugged one, dropped an arm around another's shoulder. She was dressed in a more relaxed fashion today with jeans and light blue hooded jacket. At this time of year rain was always a possibility.

One of the parents—a tall, lean brunette—approached Leigh with a smile.

As Adam walked toward them, he heard the woman say, ''We can't thank you enough for all the care you gave Marcy when she was in the hospital. She still talks about how nice you were, how you read her a book one night when she couldn't get to sleep. You make a difference, Miss Peters. I hope you know that.''

Leigh looked embarrassed and her cheeks flushed.

"I love working with children because they're so appreciative of everything I do. Sometimes they seem so lost in those hospital beds, and I just want to make them feel as if they're not alone."

"You did that for Marcy when we couldn't be with her. She couldn't wait to come today."

Silently Adam stood unmoving until the woman bustled her daughter into the entrance line.

Leigh's gaze came up to meet his as he joined her. Her smile dimmed a bit, and he found he didn't like that. He didn't like that at all. Still, he had to remind himself this wasn't a date. He'd come to be around the kids, hoping they could help him relate to Mark.

"I didn't think you'd come," Leigh said honestly.

"Why not?"

"Mark's not a large part of your life. You don't even know if you're a match yet."

"No, I don't. But even if I'm not a match, I plan to stay in touch with Mark. And if I'm not a match, I'd like to do everything I can to *find* him a match."

When Leigh examined his face, Adam felt as if she saw too much. She knew how unhappy he'd been growing up with his adoptive family. Maybe it was wishful thinking on his part to believe the Cambrys would accept him as family. But right now Mark was all that mattered.

Someone called to Leigh. Adam saw Shawna running toward them, a wide smile on her face.

"Hi! Sorry if I'm late. Dad dropped me off on his way to a meeting in town. I was playing chess with Mark and tried to convince him to eat lunch."

"Did the convincing do any good?" Adam asked.

"Some. Our housekeeper made him some chicken soup yesterday, and he actually ate most of the bowl." Shawna looked at the kids who were milling about. "Are we ready?"

"We're more than ready," Leigh answered. "Come on, let me introduce you to everyone."

The kids obviously loved the zoo. They chattered and pointed and giggled at the first exhibit of mountain goats cavorting on a rocky hill. Several of them pinched their noses shut when they walked down the curved ramp leading to the circular penguin house. They soon forgot the smell as they watched through the knee-to-ceiling window as penguins toddled around on a lifelike iceberg.

The awed expressions on the kids' faces were unmatchable as they entered the polar bears' "ice cave" with its dim blue lighting. Adam wasn't a camera buff but he wished he'd brought one. He saw that many of the parents had theirs. After they stepped outside once again, at their request, he took lots of pictures of the parents with their kids.

When Leigh came up to Adam after he'd taken a few at the elephant exhibit at the far end of the zoo, she gave him one of the smiles he loved. Then she said, "You're helping them keep a picture of a memory forever."

There was a viewing area for the elephants under an arbor. One of the parents slipped a quarter into the magnifying machine for her son. Adam understood that every memory was important to these parents—every smile, every burst of laughter, every wide-eyed look of surprise. He could see now why Leigh had wanted him to come along. Shawna was just as involved with the kids as he was. He watched while she lifted one little boy so he could use the magnifier.

At one point, Shawna walked beside Adam sipping her soda. "I told Mom and Dad I wanted you at my birthday party. They said you're welcome to come and bring a guest. Lissa and Sullivan are supposed to be back. Maybe you can meet your twin for the first time at our place."

Meeting his sister…his twin. It was hard to wrap his mind around the idea.

"I'll be there," he assured Shawna. "I don't know about bringing a guest."

She shrugged. "Whatever. Just so *you're* there." With a nonchalance only a teenager could possess, she added, "So you know, I invited Leigh, too."

Then she gave him a little-sister smile that, in spite of his turmoil about Leigh, made him grin back in return. It was nice knowing Shawna wanted him at the party. It was nice knowing Mark enjoyed his e-mail. Growing up, he'd told himself he didn't need connections, but now the beginning bonds forming with Mark and Shawna felt right.

Most of the group was standing at a concession stand that sold souvenirs. A handsome man who looked to be around forty saw Leigh, called to her and came over and gave her a hug. Adam found himself much too interested in the scene. The newcomer was dressed much as Adam was in jeans, athletic shoes, and a leather jacket. Adam couldn't hear what the man and Leigh were saying, but they were laughing a lot in between the conversational bits. The guy even took

Leigh's hand once and gave it a squeeze, and before he left, gave her another hug and a kiss on the cheek.

Adam felt a knot in his gut and was glad when the group started moving again. A short time later he saw that Leigh was standing alone.

Hands in his jacket pockets, he walked up beside her. "I think they're getting worn-out," he commented. A few of the kids were dragging now, yet they still were having a good time and didn't seem to want to go home.

"They're not the only ones."

She didn't look as if she were dragging, not at all, but she did look a bit distracted. Did it have something to do with that man?

Adam nodded in the direction from which they'd come. "Was that guy back there an old friend?"

She looked surprised he'd brought it up. "Sort of."

When she didn't say more, Adam pressed, "Or is he an old flame?"

"Reed and I met at a workshop a couple of years ago. We dated for a while."

"He's a doctor?"

"He's a psychologist. I liked him a lot, but he was ready to get married, settle down and have kids. I still had too many things I wanted to accomplish. I haven't gotten involved with anyone for that reason."

"You certainly are single-minded." In a way Adam admired that, but in another way… "Leigh, you know being a doctor isn't going to fulfill your every need. Don't you want more than that?"

"After I earn my medical degree, I can *have* more than that. I've known women who had to drop out of school because they couldn't balance work and a family.''

"There should be a happy medium."

"Have you found a happy medium, Adam? From what I've seen of your life, work fills it up. You don't seem to have any committed relationships, either."

"Maybe that's because I've decided getting involved demands too high a price if it doesn't work out."

They gazed at each other then, lost in what could have been.

They might have stood there that way forever, silent, separate, thinking about what had happened ten years before, except for the fact that Shawna came running over to them, all excited as only a fifteen-almost-sixteen-year-old could be. "Mrs. Bristol, Tommy's mom, asked me if I'm free to baby-sit. She likes the way I've been relating to Tommy. Isn't that great?"

Refocusing his attention on Shawna, Adam broke eye contact with Leigh. "Do you baby-sit often?"

She shook her head. "Only with Mark. I told her she could call Mom, and Mom would tell her how responsible I am. I'm thinking about being a teacher because I like being with kids. If I do a really good job, maybe Mrs. Bristol will spread the word and I'll get lots of practice."

Even with the tension zipping back and forth between him and Leigh, Adam couldn't help but admire this teenager. She was everything he'd ever want a daughter of his own to be.

A daughter of his own. Since when had he thought about having kids?

Shawna gave both him and Leigh a quick appraisal. "Is something wrong?"

Leigh's smile was forced. "No, nothing's wrong. I think this excursion has just tired out all of us."

"Yeah, the parents are talking about taking their kids home. Are we leaving, too?"

"That's probably a good idea. Why don't we go over and say goodbye to everybody."

Shawna looked at Adam. "Are you leaving?"

"Yes, I'm going back to my office for a while. Tell Mark to look for an e-mail tonight. I took some pictures of Thunder. I'll download them and send them to him."

"He'll like that," Shawna said with a smile. "Don't forget to put my birthday party on your calendar."

"I won't forget."

When Leigh turned to go, Adam wanted to clasp her shoulder, keep her there, straighten things out between them. But pride kept him still, kept his hands at his sides, kept his guard up.

"Goodbye, Leigh," he said in a low voice.

"Goodbye, Adam," she returned with a bit of sadness.

Then she was walking away, and he stood there alone.

For the past three days, Leigh had tried to think of everything and anything except for Adam. It wasn't quite so difficult when she was working. She'd accepted a double shift yesterday because she simply couldn't keep analyzing what Adam had meant to her and what he could mean to her again.

Actually that wasn't true. He obviously hadn't forgotten and hadn't forgiven her for what had happened ten years ago. How could she blame him? If their positions had been reversed…

Unfortunately, tonight her mother was working late, and Leigh had no distraction at all as she came home, made herself a supper of a tuna salad sandwich, carrot sticks and rice pudding her mom had bought at the deli. After that she thought about her options. She could go out somewhere and try to keep herself distracted, but she'd already shopped for groceries on Monday and had no desire to walk the mall or even go ice-skating. Her other option was to stay in and do something productive—like cleaning. Then her mother wouldn't have to give up the little spare time she had to do it. Decision made, Leigh put her few dishes in the dishwasher, changed into navy leggings and a red T-shirt, then tugged the vacuum cleaner from the pantry closet.

It was almost seven o'clock by the time she finished vacuuming. She was thinking about taking down the curtains and shaking them out outside when the doorbell rang.

Leigh smiled. It was probably Mr. Benson. Often he came over to borrow an egg or a cup of sugar, or to ask to borrow their broom. She guessed he really didn't need anything he borrowed, but rather that he was lonely and he wanted someone to talk to. Leigh always asked questions of the elderly widower—how his son was doing, what new feat his granddaughter had accomplished, when his family would be visiting him next. Tonight she was glad for any interruption that would fill up her time as she quickly went to the door.

However, when she opened it, she didn't find Mr. Benson. She found Adam.

Knowing she looked a mess—strands of hair had escaped her ponytail while she was working—she felt heat flush her cheeks. Unable to contain her surprise, she asked, "What are you doing here?"

He was wearing a blue-and-black rugby shirt and black jeans. His expression betrayed nothing as he asked, "May I come in?"

Not only she was a mess, but the apartment was a mess. She'd moved the furniture to sweep, vacuum cleaner attachments lay here and there, and small throw rugs were draped over the armchair. Recalling their "nondate" Saturday night and the tension between them on Sunday, she replied, "This isn't a good time."

Adam didn't seem put off by her reluctance to let him in. "Is your mother home?"

"No, she's not."

"Then this *is* a good time, Leigh. We need to talk."

It had rained again today and was still raining now. Adam's hair was damp and there were drops of rain on his shirt. He smelled male and damp and sexy. The look in his eyes was so intensely encompassing that all she could do was back up a few steps and watch him enter the apartment.

The chaos inside seemed to surprise him.

"I'm cleaning." It was a lame explanation, but all she could offer for the moment.

"I can see that." However, the chaos didn't deter him, and he went over to the sofa and waited for her to join him.

After she perched near the arm, he lowered himself to the middle, his gaze on her all the while. "I thought about what you said Saturday night—that I'd asked you along to use you...for a payback. I didn't believe that was my intent, but after what came out of my mouth at the zoo, I realized maybe it was. I thought we had *more* than a teenage crush. You were more than a new girl in town who I dated for a while. I had started weaving dreams about us, Leigh. I thought you had started dreaming, too."

"I had," she admitted. "But Mom reminded me my other dreams were important, too."

"You obviously didn't think we could work on dreams together. You didn't have any faith in what was happening between us."

Walking away from Adam had hurt her, but now she realized how all of it had looked to him. "Can we get past what happened?" she asked now.

"I'm not sure there's any point in getting past it. This summer you'll be leaving for Cleveland. But I had no right to say what I did yesterday. I have no right to judge your life. You've set your goals and I admire them. Believe me, I understand about wanting to succeed, about reaching for something more than you had. In your case, you're reaching for both you and your mother."

Adam was on target with that. She certainly

couldn't deny it. "So where do we go from here?" she almost whispered.

He moved toward her then, and her heart pounded so hard she could hardly catch her breath.

"Where do you *want* to go from here?"

"I don't know. I just know I want you to forgive me. I didn't want to hurt you. I—" She couldn't help the quick tears that came to her eyes and caused a large lump in her throat.

When Adam reached toward her, Leigh closed her eyes. She felt him finger a strand of hair along her cheek. Her body trembled as he brushed a few more behind her ear. Then he wiped away one small tear that had escaped from under her lashes.

"Leigh," he said hoarsely.

Adam's kisses had always made her world spin, and now as his palm caressed her cheek, as his lips covered hers, the light and excitement and fire racing inside of her brought alive needs that had been asleep. It wasn't long before his tongue slipped into her mouth.

She reached for him, wanting to relive experiences they'd shared, wanting to touch him again. When she caressed the back of his neck, he groaned. She could feel the same tension in his body that was coiling inside of her. His tongue coaxed hers into a mating that was intimate, seductive and thoroughly arousing. After he pulled the scrunchie from her ponytail, he ran his fingers through her hair, angled her head and ravished her more completely. Although Adam's passion had always been hotly intense, he was incredibly tender, too. That's what made it so overwhelming. That's what made her lose herself in him.

When his mouth broke away from hers, she thought he was going to stop. She knew it was best if he *did* stop. But Adam apparently had no intention of ending what they had started. His lips trailed soft, wet kisses down her throat. One of his hands stroked her midriff, then moved higher to caress her breast. She was being swept away into an erotic watershed of desire.

Mindlessly she arched into his hand, wanting to feel more, do more. But he was in control. He was leading her, and she could only follow.

As his hand left her breast, she opened her eyes and she could see the fierce need in his. Without a word he lifted her shirt up and over her head, then he unhooked her bra. When she made no move to stop him, he cupped her breast in his hand and fingered the nipple, all the while never moving his gaze from hers. She should be blushing. She should be embarrassed. She should be trying to clear her head of the sexual haze to make sense of what was happening. But Adam was filling her world, not leaving any space for anything else, as he took both of her breasts into his hands and thumbed the nipples simultaneously. She felt as if rockets were going off inside of her. With deliberate slowness, he made incredibly slow rotations around her breasts and passed his hands down her sides. His thumbs met at her navel, and they traced her rib cage.

She could hardly sit still. As arousal cloaked Leigh in its excitement, Adam bent his head to her breast. The chaos in the room and in her heart and in her head vanished in an awareness of only him. His lips were masterful as they teased and taunted her and she breathed his name. After he stopped for only a second, he leaned back on the sofa taking her with him, stretching his legs out under her. She realized Adam had gotten terrifically experienced at foreplay, though she didn't know if she could stand much more. His hands slid over her backside, and the stretchy material of her leggings seemed to be no barrier at all. She could feel every stroke as if she were naked. Her breasts pressed against the cotton of his shirt and she could feel each one of his breaths. Most of all, she was aware of his powerful arousal. The heavy denim of his jeans couldn't hide it and she melted over him, wanting to feel more of it.

He brought his arms around her and kissed her again. It was a hungry kiss, marking everything she could give. When she responded with the same hunger, his hands slid up her shoulders into her hair.

Breaking it off, he growled, "I want you."

"I want you, too," she whispered.

Taking her at her word, he hooked his thumbs in her leggings and started to drag them down. She wiggled and slid and helped any way she could until they were around her ankles. Using her feet to kick them off, she started on the buttons on Adam's shirt. They were both breathing hard. They were both in a hurry to get them undressed. They were both aware of an urgency that defied reason.

"I have to sit up to get my shirt off," Adam muttered. Then he gave her a wry grin. "But I don't want to stop this."

"I'll be able to touch you a lot better if your shirt's off."

Her honest words brought a flair of desire to his

eyes, and moments later he was bare-chested and her fingers were sifting through thick brown hair. She looked up and then found herself lost in another kiss.

The phone rang.

Adam didn't break away and Leigh didn't care. She had an answering machine.

His tongue suggestively stroked hers.

The phone rang again.

Neither of them paid it any heed...neither of them cared who was calling.

However, after the fourth ring, a deep male voice said, "Leigh, it's Dr. Chambers. I'll leave a message here, then I'll also try to reach you on your cell phone."

Adam and Leigh broke apart at the same moment. Leigh was on her feet racing to the kitchen as Dr. Chambers went on, "The results of the tests are back."

Her breath coming in short gasps, she plucked the receiver from its cradle and somehow managed to find her voice. "Dr. Chambers? It's Leigh."

"Leigh. Wonderful. I'm so glad you're there. I know you want to give this information to Mr. Bartlett as soon as you can. He's a perfect match."

Adam had followed Leigh to the phone. As she took in the news, she sent up a prayer of thanks. Mark had a chance now, he really did—that is if Adam went through with the harvesting procedure. With the way he felt about hospitals—

"I'll tell Adam...Mr. Bartlett. What about the Cambrys?"

"Officially you can't say anything to them until

Bartlett signs a consent form. That's procedure, Leigh.''

She knew that. She just thought that in this case since everyone knew each other… ''All right. I'll tell Mr. Bartlett that, too.''

''Fine. Call me back after you reach him. The faster he makes his decision, the better for Mark. If he's going to do this, we need to get the boy into the hospital and get him prepped. This is going to be a rough road for Mark, but at least he has a road now. I'll let you go so you can call Bartlett.''

''Thanks, Dr. Chambers. I'll get back to you as soon as I can.''

Although she was self-conscious about her nakedness now, she didn't want to keep the news from Adam any longer than she had to. ''You're a perfect match. The news couldn't be any better than that. Now you have to decide if you're going to go through the harvesting procedure. The sooner you decide, the better it will be for Mark.''

As Adam digested what she'd told him, she hurried to the sofa, slipped on her bra and slid into her panties and leggings, pulling them up quickly. After she tugged on her T-shirt, she joined Adam in the kitchen once again. ''Do you want me to go over everything that will happen?''

She was trying to be professional when all she could do was stare at his bare chest and think about the way he had kissed her, the way he had touched her, the way she had responded with an abandon she'd never felt before. Yet another part of her was relieved the phone had rung. Making love to Adam shouldn't happen on impulse. Not with their history...not unless they were both sure they wouldn't have regrets afterward.

Adam had been staring out the kitchen window. Now he shifted and met her gaze. "Marietta explained it all thoroughly. Since I already had a physical, they'll admit me when Mark is ready for the transplant, prep me and give me anesthesia. Then they'll extract the bone marrow. I'll stay overnight and be discharged in the morning."

Her heart racing, she nodded. "Your hips will be sore, and you'll feel as if you took a bad fall on the ice. Somebody should drive you home. Have you made up your mind you want to do this?"

"I don't have any choice. I couldn't live with myself if I didn't try to save Mark's life. Can we tell him the news?"

"No one can tell him until you sign the consent papers. That's the procedure."

"All right. Fine. Then let's sign the consent papers."

Leigh checked her watch. "It's almost eight. Nobody will be at the hospital—"

"Didn't you say the sooner we do all this, the better for Mark?"

"Yes, I did." She thought about it. "Let me call Dr. Chambers back. If you sign the papers tonight, we could admit Mark in the morning."

Moments later, her conversation with the chief of staff was short and to the point. The administrator agreed to meet them at the hospital in the conference room she'd used before. He would have everything he needed with him.

When Leigh put down the phone, she looked up at Adam. He was standing a good two feet away.

"Dr. Chambers said he'd meet us there. You can sign the forms tonight."

"Good. Then we can tell the Cambrys. Are you ready?"

The sparks in Adam's eyes told her he was looking at her as if he remembered what state she'd been in just fifteen minutes before. She remembered, too. The problem was, though, he wasn't *acting* as if they'd almost made love on the sofa. He was acting as if nothing had happened.

For now, they'd have to forget about the two of them and concentrate on Mark. Maybe that's what Adam was doing and that was the distance she felt between them.

"Give me two minutes. I just want to change my T-shirt and grab a jacket."

As she hurried to the bedroom, she saw Adam move toward the window again. He stared out unseeingly, and she wished she knew what was going through his head.

# Chapter Seven

Shifting gears from almost having sex with a woman to the realization that he was going to become a transplant donor kept Adam from dwelling on either for too long. Although the phone call had seemed to come at an inopportune moment, he was thankful for it now. Leigh's vulnerability had grabbed him in the gut. Impulse and an overstimulated libido had taken over. Frustratingly, he'd wanted her as he had years ago, and he'd acted on that.

However, if he'd given in to fulfilling his physical needs, he would have been sorry. Everything about this situation with Leigh was unsettling. They'd been thrown together and, apparently, neither of them knew how to react to that. Still, they weren't teenagers any longer. They were adults with adult decisions to make.

He wasn't about to become involved with Leigh Peters again when she'd be leaving in June.

After he found a place in the parking garage, they walked across the catwalk to the hospital. It seemed quiet. Adam hated the idea of Mark being admitted here and everything the young boy was going to have to go through. His own part in it...

He'd handle it as he'd handled everything else in his life. He was a master at shutting down his thoughts and doing whatever he had to do. Letting himself remember what had happened to Delia and thinking about what was going to happen next wouldn't help anyone.

They took the elevator to the fourth floor, and still Leigh didn't say anything. He didn't know if she was thinking about her job or what had almost happened on her couch. She'd avoided his gaze as they'd left her apartment.

Maybe the couch was winning.

The fluorescent glitter of the overhead lights on the tile floor brought back too many memories as Adam strode quickly to the conference room. Somehow Leigh kept up. When they arrived, the door was already open and Adam spotted Dr. Chambers and Marietta waiting inside.

"Marietta," Leigh said, surprised. "I didn't expect you to be here."

The counselor shrugged and her answer encompassed both Leigh and Adam. "Dr. Chambers wanted me here in case Adam had any questions. I'll go over the consent forms with you," she added with a patient smile.

Chambers was apparently making sure all of his bases were covered with this one. The success of this whole endeavor could bring more funding to his hospital in several ways. Adam couldn't fault the good business sense in that. It was just a shame that practicing medicine had boiled down to dollars and cents.

Was that true for Leigh, too? Is that why she wanted to become a doctor? She'd told him more than once that she was happy with the work she was doing. Then again, she might be even happier with a medical degree.

Before they took seats at the conference table, Dr. Chambers shook Adam's hand. "This is a fine thing that you're doing. I wish more people would sign up with the registry and realize they could help save lives."

"It's hard to get the word out," Leigh agreed.

After the women were seated, Adam took his chair, too. He glanced at Marietta. "I hope we didn't disturb your evening. This could have waited till morning, but I want to tell Mark and his family that he has a chance."

"I understand completely. You didn't disturb my evening. I was having dinner with my cat."

Her light tone brought a smile to Adam's lips, and he relaxed a bit, realizing that had been her intent.

For the next half hour Marietta explained the consent forms as Adam signed and dated them. In a mere nine days his life had changed drastically. He knew who his biological father was now. He knew he had a twin. Connections to Mark were becoming stronger day by day.

And Leigh?

Leigh was making him need again.

When all the necessary papers were signed, explanations made and questions answered, Dr. Chambers shook Adam's hand again.

"We're going to tell Jared and his family now. That's all right?" Adam asked.

"Yes, that's fine. Jared knows he's supposed to contact Leigh with any questions…or he can always call me. I'll get in touch with him tomorrow because we'll have to admit Mark and get the ball rolling."

Twenty minutes later Adam and Leigh were at Jared's front door. The lawyer himself answered and, when he saw Leigh with Adam, his expression became worried. "Do you have news?"

"Yes, we do," Leigh said as Adam kept silent. "Adam is a perfect match."

For Adam this moment meant everything. Not only could he be a donor for Mark, but Marietta had explained the test results that confirmed he was definitely Jared's son.

Without saying anything, Jared motioned them inside. He looked stunned. "I was afraid to hope," he murmured. "Please come in. I'll get Danni."

Suddenly there was only one place Adam wanted to be—in Mark's room, telling him the news. "Is Mark still awake?"

"Shawna's with him." Jared's gaze met Adam's. "If you want to tell him, go ahead."

When Adam reached Mark's room, the door was ajar and he pushed it open slowly. Shawna was sitting by Mark's bed reading a magazine and the little boy looked as though he were asleep.

When Shawna saw Adam, she came to the door. "He fell asleep a few minutes ago."

"I don't want to wake him. I have good news, though," he added with a smile he couldn't keep in.

"You're a match?" Shawna's voice rose.

"Yes. We just got the news tonight. I signed all the forms, and Dr. Chambers is going to call your dad tomorrow about admitting Mark and getting the conditioning started."

"I wish Chad were here so I could tell him. His way of dealing with this is to hang out with his friends. He's hardly ever home."

"Maybe now that will change."

"Maybe it will. Oh, I can't believe this!" She clasped Adam's arm. "You're really my brother."

He couldn't suppress his grin. "I guess I am."

"I feel like I've been holding my breath ever since you got tested," she admitted.

This teenager was so open, and Adam admired that. In some ways she reminded him of Leigh when Leigh had been in high school. "I feel that way, too. I want to celebrate yet I know we have a long way to go." He was warning her that they weren't out of the woods, and she was intelligent enough to get that.

"I'm going to sit here with Mark until he wakes up even if it's the middle of the night so I can tell him. I'm sure he'll want to e-mail you right away."

"I doubt if I'll get much sleep tonight. If he e-mails, I'll get right back to him."

Suddenly Shawna threw her arms around Adam and

gave him a giant hug. "Thank you. Thank you for doing this."

A tightness wound about Adam's heart and he found it hard to speak. So he didn't. He hugged her back instead.

After Shawna had returned to Mark's bedside, Adam took a deep breath and went downstairs. Hearing voices in the kitchen, he headed that way. When he saw only Danielle and Leigh sitting at the table, he felt disappointed but also relieved. There was always an awkwardness with Jared that he didn't know what to do with.

Apparently Danielle felt she had to explain. "Jared went out for a walk. This whole situation with Mark and with you has affected him deeply. He's not a man who expresses his feelings easily and I think he's just trying to get a handle on all of it. But I certainly don't want you to think he's not grateful because he is. Without you—" her voice caught "—I don't know what we would have done."

Taking a seat at the table, Adam hoped to learn more about this family. "Shawna said Chad's been out with friends a lot. I was hoping to meet him."

"You'll meet him at Shawna's birthday party on Saturday night if not before."

"You're still going to have it?" Adam asked.

"Absolutely. Mark will be in the hospital having tests run, and I'll be with him as much as I can. But I have to be here for my daughter, too. After the chemo starts, I won't be able to be by Mark's side, but I'll stay at the hospital anyway. They'll limit his contact severely...even with us."

"I understand there'll be a few days of testing for him before that starts."

"Yes."

"I'll check in on you whenever I can," Leigh assured Danielle. "We'll have specialized nurses for the transplant-conditioning process he's going through, but I'll make sure he knows I'm there, too."

"Thank you," Danielle murmured and ducked her head.

Adam could see her emotions were very close to the surface, and he wondered how his father dealt with that.

Abruptly Danielle raised her head, wiped a tear from the corner of her eye and smiled at them. "Enough about us. Adam, I want to know about you. I'm hoping Lissa will be home in time for Shawna's party. Maybe you can meet her and Sullivan then."

Maybe. Or maybe he could give his sister a call before then. "Where did she and—Sullivan is it?—go on their honeymoon?"

"Scotland. I think they're coming back Thursday or Friday. I'm sure she can't wait to hear from you. Don't hesitate to call her."

Adam wondered if his father knew what a gem he had in Danielle—she was such a positive woman.

"Mark has been telling me all about your software company and the programs you gave him," she said now. "I even tried the one with dinosaurs. It was fun."

As the discussion moved toward Adam's life, how he and Dylan had started Novel Programs, Unlimited, in college, he glanced at Leigh. She'd been extremely quiet ever since they'd left her apartment. They'd have to talk about what had happened there. They couldn't ignore it. Now that her liaison work was finished, they wouldn't have to see each other if they didn't want to. Adam knew that would probably be best.

As the hour grew later and Jared hadn't returned, Adam and Leigh said their goodbyes.

In the car Leigh turned to Adam. "I think Mr. Cambry was overwhelmed by all of it. I don't think he knew how to thank you."

"Maybe. Maybe he's not thinking about me at all. Mark's the one he's concerned about and he should be. I belong to a time in his life he probably wants to forget."

Talking to Leigh here about what had happened at her apartment didn't seem right somehow, so he waited. However, when they pulled into the apartment's parking lot, she said, "Mom's home."

Adam switched off the ignition and shifted toward her. If they wouldn't have privacy inside, they'd have to have it out here. Rain had begun falling, and it dripped down the windshield in slow rivulets. Adam knew he wasn't great at tact. Dylan was the diplomat.

"I suppose your job as liaison is over now," he commented.

"That depends on Dr. Chambers. He might want me to help keep the Cambrys informed during the transplant process. And then there's your procedure."

Adam shrugged dismissively. "I'll get admitted one day, I'll be out the next. No big deal."

Under the parking lot's lights, he saw Leigh studying him. "What?" he asked, wondering what she was thinking.

"You're a lot like your father."

"Jared?"

She nodded. "It's hard to tell what he's thinking and especially what he's feeling. You're like that, too. You always have been."

Leigh had said it matter-of-factly, but it didn't sound like a compliment. He knew he felt that Jared was shutting him out right now. Did Leigh feel he was shutting her out? Well, he *was*...with good reason.

"I only talk about what I feel is necessary to talk about," he said in a low tone.

"Do you think it's necessary to talk about what happened tonight?" she asked quietly.

He understood the conversation was all about them and had nothing to do with the Cambrys now. "Is that why you've been so quiet? You're thinking about what happened?"

She seemed to take her time answering, as if she were weighing her words. "Mark's situation is serious enough to make me quiet. But, yes, my silence has more to do with what happened with us."

She stopped as if thinking about going on. But then she blurted out, "You acted as if *nothing* happened, just as you acted after you kissed me. I guess I'm wondering if that's really true. I wondered why you came by tonight."

After a few moments of thoughtful silence, he replied, "I came by because I felt I hadn't been fair to you, and I wanted to tell you that. I didn't intend for anything else to happen."

Looking away from him then, she stared out into the black night. "But it did. Were you sorry about it?"

Even when they were teenagers, Leigh had pushed him to examine what he was feeling. Back then it didn't feel quite as uncomfortable as it did now. "It was enjoyable, Leigh."

"Enjoyable? Don't you understand, Adam, that I don't just *do* that with any man? I haven't been intimate with another man since I was intimate with *you*."

Bombshells had been dropping all around Adam for the past week and a half. He shouldn't be surprised that another one had just smashed into his car. "Why not?"

She seemed totally exasperated that he'd asked the question. "Because you meant a lot to me and I never wanted to get involved with a man unless I felt that way again."

His hand tightened on the steering wheel. "Is that the real reason? Or is it just that you're so goal oriented that nothing else could get in the way of the career you want?"

As soon as the words were out, he saw the hurt on her face and he regretted any suspicions he'd had that she might be interested in him now because he was rich. Leigh had never been like that, and she still wasn't after money. She was after success and respect and a career to give meaning to her life.

"I can't dispute that's the impression I've given you, but it was never that simple." She turned away, stared through the windshield, then opened her door. "I'd better go in."

He didn't like the idea of her being hurt. "It's pouring again."

"I won't melt." She hopped out of the car before he could stop her.

Swearing, he decided he couldn't let her go like this. They'd probably be seeing each other at the hospital. The whole situation was tough enough without icy tension between them.

Climbing out of the car, he strode after her and caught up with her at the apartment building's door.

"Adam, there's no reason for you to come in with me." She'd put her hood up, but it had slipped down, and her hair was getting wet. She brushed it behind her ear.

He wanted to run his hands through her hair. He wanted to kiss her again. Time and place and circumstances were against them, just as they'd been long ago.

"It's late, I'll walk you up to your apartment."

Seeing the purpose in his eyes, she gave up with a resigned sigh.

As they mounted the interior stairway, their footsteps echoed against the walls.

They'd just reached her apartment door when it opened and her mother came out carrying an umbrella. "Leigh? I was worried about you. I got your note that you were at the hospital, but your car's still here. I tried to call your cell phone, but I could only get your voice mail."

"The charge probably ran out. I had it on all day in case Dr. Chambers had to get hold of me."

"Dr. Chambers? Is something wrong?"

Leigh looked to Adam and he knew she wouldn't tell her mother anything unless he gave his permission. "Leigh's been acting as liaison and has been on call for the past week or so. I was a potential donor for a transplant patient. We just found out tonight that I'm a match. I had to sign consent forms and then we went to tell the family."

Her mother was looking from one of them to the other, trying to absorb what Adam had said. "I see. So you are going to be a donor?"

"It looks that way."

"Were you matched up with the registry?"

"No. My biological father came looking for me. His son's sick and apparently I can help." It was amazing how something so big could be summed up in so few words.

"I see," Claire said again, opening the door to the apartment wider. "Would you like to come in for a cup of coffee?"

Adam didn't have to look at Leigh to know that wouldn't be advisable. Maybe this was the way it had to end. Maybe this was easier than hashing it all out, repeating what had already been said. "No. No thank you. It's time I get back to the ranch." He couldn't keep his gaze from holding Leigh's. "I imagine I'll be seeing you at the hospital."

She nodded. "Will you keep in touch with the Cambrys about what's happening with Mark, or do you want me to fill you in?"

"I'll be keeping in touch with them. I'm sure Shawna will keep me informed if Jared doesn't."

Then with a last look at the first girl he'd ever con-

sidered making vows to, he said good-night and
headed for the parking lot.

After Leigh was inside the apartment, she took one
look at her mother and knew they were going to have
a discussion. She didn't feel like it. She'd just handed
her heart to Adam and he had handed it back. No
surprise there. Always guarded, he wasn't about to tell
her he felt anything when she would be leaving again.

Her mother opened the closet door and put the umbrella inside. After she closed it, she shrugged out of
her raincoat and hung it on a peg. "I guess that's why
you didn't go into detail in your note. Confidential-
ity?"

Leigh hung her jacket beside her mother's raincoat.
"Yes." Maybe if she kept her answers short her
mother would drop the whole thing.

"It's a nice thing Adam's doing," Claire remarked
offhandedly.

Going to the mug tree on the counter, Leigh took
one of them and filled it with water.

"So you'll be seeing him at the hospital?" her
mother prompted.

In turmoil about everything that had happened tonight, Leigh held on to her patience and set the mug
inside the microwave, pressing the timer. "Yes, in
conjunction with Mark's transplant."

"That's all?"

"What would you like to know, Mom?" she asked
gently, deciding they might as well have this discussion now.

Her mother came around the table. "I guess I want
to know if you're falling for him again."

The microwave beeped and Leigh accepted the in-evitable. "I don't think I ever got over him." That had been obvious the moment she'd set eyes on him at the hospital.

"Maybe you were younger when you knew him before, but nothing's really changed. You have years of schooling ahead of you—"

"I know what I have ahead of me, Mom." She doubted if any relationship could withstand the gruel-ing hours she'd be keeping.

"So you're not going to get involved?"

"I doubt it. But I honestly don't know."

When her mother looked troubled, Leigh couldn't reassure her, because this time the decision wasn't her mother's. It was her own. Did she want an affair with Adam for a few months? Would that be enough? Or after this evening would he shut down whatever feel-ings were between them?

Tonight she didn't have the answers.

When Adam returned to Cedar Run Ranch, he parked in his garage and didn't even bother changing clothes. Instead he went straight to the barn. Thunder was in his stall, although the back door that led out into the corral was open. Sometimes the big horse didn't come in but stood out in the rain or found shel-ter under the trees.

Adam changed into the spare clothes he kept in the tack room, then he mucked out Thunder's stall, fed the horse and left him to his meal. Picking up his clothes and shoes, Adam jogged to the house through the now sparse raindrops and let himself inside. It was quiet as it always was, but tonight it seemed too damn quiet.

Going into his home office, he dropped the clothes and shoes on a chair, then checked his e-mail. Nothing from Mark. He must still be sleeping. But the light was blinking on his answering machine and he hit Play, surprised when he heard his mother's voice.

"Adam, it's your mom. Please call me when you get in. It's important."

Important. That covered a lot of territory—from an increase in salary for the farm manager, to an illness of one of the cows, to a house problem for his mom herself. She was fifty-six now and slowing down. Life on the farm with Owen Bartlett had been tough. Then again, maybe Rena was coming home from Australia. Still…he couldn't see a family reunion in the offing. After Delia had died, it was as if his connection to the farm and the Bartletts had faded away. Owen, his mom, Sharon and Rena had become even tighter.

No point wondering about it. He made the call.

Peggy Bartlett picked up on the first ring. "Hello?"

"It's Adam. I hope it's not too late. I just got your message."

"No, it's not too late. Thank you for calling."

His mother had always been polite with him, if not warm.

"You said it was important."

"I think it is. John thinks it is. I need your help with Sharon."

Sharon was thirty-two now and still lived at home. She worked for an insurance firm in Portland but Adam didn't know much about her life. Sharon had always been the most distant from him, the most resentful that he'd been brought into the family. "What's the problem?"

"Well, uh, it isn't just Sharon. I had some news for you but it's created a problem and—"

Adam waited, letting his mother figure out what it was she wanted to tell him.

"John and I are going to get married." She said it in a rush as if she couldn't wait to get it out.

At first Adam was startled. John Pavlichek, the manager he'd hired, was in his late forties, at least seven years younger than his mother. On the other hand, he'd been living on the property for the past four years. Adam knew since Owen had died, his mother had depended heavily on John. Maybe this was a practical move on both their parts.

"Adam?"

"Yes, Mom."

"Don't you approve, either?"

"It's not up to me to approve or not approve. It's your life. I don't have a say in it."

"But you're funding John's salary. If you don't approve…"

Was she afraid he'd cut off that salary if he didn't approve? Adam paced his office and ran his hand through his hair. "That won't change, unless John has a hidden fortune and he doesn't need my salary anymore."

"He doesn't have much of his own, you know that."

Yes, Adam did know that because he'd done a complete background check on the man before he'd hired him. Pavlichek had worked as a foreman in a textile factory for twenty years. When the factory closed, he'd had trouble finding another job. He'd been working at a fast-food joint when he'd applied for the job as manager of the Bartlett farm. Adam had seen right away that John was intelligent, hardworking and just down on his luck.

"Tell John he doesn't have to worry about being out of work again."

"Thank you, Adam." There was relief in his mother's voice and he was glad to hear that at least.

"I guess congratulations are in order. When are you getting married?"

"We're not sure yet. We're just going to go to a justice of the peace and maybe out to dinner afterward. That's why I called. Sharon won't go. She insists she doesn't want anything to do with the wedding. In fact, she doesn't want John moving into the house with me. I can't make her see reason. I thought maybe you could."

"Why do you think *I'll* be able to make her see reason?"

"Because she respects what you've become even though she's never said it. I don't have anyone else to turn to, Adam. John's going to move in here whether she likes it or not. But I want…I want her blessing."

Sharon had been one of the beloved daughters. Yes, her blessing would be important. Maybe he was still trying to earn Owen Bartlett's approval after all these years, but he couldn't turn down his mother's request. "All right, I'll see what I can do. I have meetings all day tomorrow into the evening, but I can drive up on Friday. Will she be there around suppertime?''

''She should be. I'm not going to tell her you're coming. It will probably be better that way.''

A surprise attack would definitely be better. If Sharon knew he was coming, she might decide not to be there. ''Play it however you think you should. I'll be there Friday around five.''

''We'll see you then, Adam.''

He heard gratitude again in his mother's voice. He was satisfied with that.

As he went to the kitchen to finally make himself something to eat, it wasn't the visit to the farm Friday that was on his mind. For the moment it wasn't even the thought of the transplant and the procedure he'd have to go through to help Mark. Rather, Leigh was on his mind. Whenever he remembered kissing her, undressing her, his blood heated all over again. Most of all he remembered the hurt look on her face in the car. He remembered her saying, ''I haven't been intimate with another man since I was intimate with you.''

And he wondered how in the hell he was going to put her out of his head.

# Chapter Eight

At 2:00 a.m., when Leigh checked the clock for at least the twentieth time, she knew falling asleep was hopeless. Pushing herself up and sliding her feet over the side of the bed, she went to her closet and reached for the string on the light inside. When she yanked it, she blinked against the glare. It was about time she admitted to herself that her feelings for Adam Bartlett had never faded.

Pulling a small step stool from the corner of the closet, she wedged it between her shoes, then stepped onto it so she could reach the back of the top shelf. It seemed everything was stacked on that shelf—from tax returns to a cosmetics case for traveling to a straw hat she wore at the beach. She remembered exactly where the box was that she was looking for. It was in the back left corner, hidden by the teddy bear that had sat in the middle of her bed when she was a little girl. The box was blue, deceiving in its sturdiness. It looked as if it could have held school reports, research notes or stationery of some kind. But it didn't hold any of those things.

With care, she slid it forward, pushing off the stack of magazines on top of it, lifted it from the shelf and took it over to her bed. After she turned on the bedside lamp, she opened it as if it held the secrets to the universe. Actually, it didn't hold any secrets, just memories.

The first memento she saw was a paper napkin from the fast-food restaurant she and Adam had enjoyed most. On it was a note he had written to her and left in her locker. "Leigh—Meet me under the bleachers after school. A."

Just like the supply closet in the school, the space under those bleachers had allowed them to have some privacy, a place to hold each other, a place to kiss.

Beside the note Leigh found three pressed red rose-buds. Adam had given her those the night of their graduation. In addition, within an envelope, she pulled out a photo taken in one of the machines in the mall as well as movie ticket stubs. She'd scrawled on each the name of the movie they'd seen.

Finally she spotted what she'd really been looking for. It was a leather bracelet with her name and Adam's branded into the rawhide. They'd gone to a street fair together and there had been lots of tables with crafts. An old man had made the bracelet and then personalized it while they waited. After Adam had bought the bracelet for her, he'd snapped it on to her wrist, and she had known exactly what that had meant. He was claiming her. He didn't want her to date anyone else and she hadn't. She hadn't even thought about dating anyone else.

Curious to see if the bracelet still fit, Leigh snapped it on to her wrist. Tracing her finger over Adam's name, she felt tears come to her eyes. She'd kept these mementos for one very good reason. She'd never forgotten Adam Bartlett.

But she might have to forget him now.

As Adam drove north on Route 30 on Friday evening, he recalled again the e-mail he'd received from Mark when he'd awakened and Shawna had told him the news. He'd typed *Yes* with five exclamation points and written, *I knew we'd match. Will you come to see me before they start chemo?*

Adam had read the message inside the message. Mark was exuberant that he could have the transplant...but he was also scared. From the quiver in Danielle's voice when she'd phoned to tell him Mark had been admitted to the hospital around noon yesterday, Adam knew *she* was scared, too.

Adam tried to blank his mind to all of it as the countryside sped by. The drive to the farm outside of Warren took about thirty-five minutes. As Adam's tires crunched down the gravel lane, he thought about how well John had handled the farm and its upkeep. He kept up the paint on the barn as well as maintaining the house and the other buildings in good repair. Before he'd been hired on, Adam had had one of the out buildings renovated into a small utilitarian cabin, and that's where John lived. Now he'd be moving into the main house.

As Adam mounted the porch steps, he wasn't looking forward to this confrontation—he was sure that's what it would be. He and Sharon were like oil and water. Glancing to the side of the house, he saw her sedan was parked in front of the detached garage. His mom had wanted this to be a surprise, but if Sharon felt cornered, she'd resent him being there even more.

When Adam opened the wooden screen door, he looked toward the barn and caught a glimpse of John pitching hay into a stall.

It would no longer be the Bartlett farm. It would be the Pavlichek farm. He felt no stirring of regret at the difference.

After Adam knocked on the door, his mother opened it with a worried frown. Her short black hair was streaked with gray, but she wore makeup which was unusual for her. ''Sharon saw you drive up.''

''And?''

''She went up to her bedroom and shut the door.'' His mother fidgeted with the lapel of her housedress. ''I really need you to talk to her, Adam. I've tried. John's tried. Even Rena tried by phone. But we just can't get through to her.''

''If she keeps me locked out, there's not much I can do except talk through the door.''

When his mother looked even more distressed, Adam added, ''But I'll see what I can do.''

The steps were steep, somewhat narrow, and Adam remembered all the times he'd run up and down them as a boy. The same floorboards still squeaked as he crossed the hall to Sharon's room and knocked.

"Sharon? It's Adam. Can we talk?"

When she opened the door, he realized he hadn't seen her since last summer. Since then she'd gotten her dyed blond hair cut shorter and gained some weight, maybe ten pounds. Still wearing her work clothes—navy slacks and a red and navy paisley blouse—she looked him over as if he were a door-to-door salesman. He'd left his suitcoat and tie in the car. He could tell she was assessing the clothes he wore and the probable cost. That was Sharon.

"Mom asked me to talk to you. Would you like to stay up here or go downstairs?"

"I don't want to talk anywhere. What could you have to say to me that would matter?"

Adam had always tried to maintain a politeness between them but too much was going on in his own life and he was tired of trying to be civil when she didn't put out any effort. "Your attitude belongs on a rebellious teenager, not on a grown woman. So why don't you act like an adult for a change and come down to the living room."

Surprised by his bluntness, it only took her a moment to find a quick comeback. "You think you're so smart. You've always thought you're so smart."

"Sharon, my being smart or not has nothing to do with this conversation. Why don't you want Mom to marry John?"

Apparently startled at his continued directness, she blurted out, "I don't want any man moving in here and taking Dad's place."

Before Adam had a chance to respond, she went on, "But you wouldn't know anything about how that feels because you hated Dad."

"I didn't—" He stopped short at the automatic protest. If he was going to get anywhere with Sharon, he had to be honest with her. "All right. Yes, I did hate him at times. He had a mean streak you didn't see. He showed it to me and he showed it to the livestock. You know as well as I do he only adopted me to have someone to work this farm for him. And after Delia died—"

Regretfully, Adam shook his head. "That's in the past now. If I hated him once, I don't anymore. He's gone and no matter what he was or wasn't, Mom deserves to be happy."

Sharon's expression lost some of its defiance. "I don't understand why Mom can't be happy the way things are. She and John—" Sharon stopped and her cheeks got red.

If his mother had been involved with John for a while, she obviously wanted to make it legal now. "Mom wants to be married and that's her right. Maybe if you can't accept it, if you can't accept John in this house, you should move off the farm and find your *own* life."

"That's easy for you to say," she muttered.

"Why?"

"Because you have more money than you know what to do with."

"I didn't have any money when I left for college."

"You had a scholarship."

"Yes, and it paid my tuition. I worked in pizza

joints for the rest. You do what you have to do to find your life, Sharon. You have a decent job. You can certainly afford an apartment. What's keeping you here?''

''*Mom's* keeping me here. After Dad died, she needed me here.''

''Maybe she did, but now maybe you both need something else. Think about it.''

Silence that had always seemed unbridgeable between them still seemed that way. Finally Sharon asked, ''Are you coming to the wedding?''

''I don't know. If Mom asks, I guess I'll try to be there.''

''She's not even going to have a real wedding. They're just going to a justice of the peace.''

''Anytime two people decide to spend the rest of their lives together and make promises to do that, I think it's a real wedding.''

''You know what, Adam? Just because you own your own company doesn't mean you know *everything*.''

Lord, did he know that! He almost smiled. ''I've never claimed to know everything, Sharon, but I do know if you don't support Mom in this marriage, it'll drive a wedge between the two of you.''

Suspecting Sharon wouldn't listen to anything else he had to say, he left her at her bedroom door and returned to the downstairs. She was one frustrating female he would never understand.

Adam's mother was putting a meat loaf in the oven when he entered the kitchen. After she closed the oven door, she asked, ''Can you stay for supper?''

Glancing at the ceramic teapot clock hanging on the wall, he shook his head. "I have to get back to town."

Peggy Bartlett sighed. "Did you make any progress with Sharon?"

"I don't know. I think she feels as if she's being disloyal to...Dad...if she accepts John into your life."

"That's ridiculous."

"That's how she feels."

His mother studied him for a moment. "Are you sure you have to get back?"

"I have to go to the hospital. There's a young boy I want to see there."

"You hate hospitals. You have ever since—"

They'd never talked about that day. "Yes, I do. But I'm going to have to change the way I've always thought about them."

She looked puzzled. "Why?"

"Because my biological father found me. His son needs a bone marrow transplant and I'm a perfect match."

It was obvious his mom was astonished by the news. "Your real father found you? My goodness, Adam."

"He has a family. I've got two half brothers and a half sister. Not only that, but—" he paused a moment "—did you know I had a twin?"

"A twin? No! We told you we didn't know anything much about your family. Just your mother's first name and that she was young and had died. That was all the information they'd give us."

"My father found my sister first. She lives on a

vineyard about two hours south of Portland. Apparently we're twins.''

''Have you met her yet?''

''She was married recently and just returned from her honeymoon yesterday. I'm going to try to get hold of her.''

''When did all this happen?''

''About a week and a half ago. Why?''

''A man called here, and he wanted to know if we had adopted a child from The Children's Connection Adoption Agency twenty-seven years ago. I told him we had. He went on to explain something about a fire and wanting to update records now. He asked where he could find you. I told him you had an unlisted phone number and I couldn't give that out, but when he pressed, I did say you were the boss of Novel Programs, Unlimited.''

''So *that's* how he found me. He was a private investigator working for my father.''

''If I had known he was a private investigator, I probably wouldn't have told him anything.''

''Then I'm glad he didn't tell you. Mark's a great kid and I want to help him if I can.''

''I hope everything turns out all right.''

''So do I,'' Adam said in a low voice, and then he moved toward the doorway. ''I'd better get going.''

His mother followed him into the foyer. ''Thanks for coming out here to talk to Sharon. I know she's not easy to deal with. I know...I know she and Rena weren't the best sisters.''

When he was silent, she went on, ''I know Owen and I weren't the best parents. Not to you, anyway. I felt I always had to do what Owen said, felt I had to stick by him. I didn't really want to care for another child, but he wanted a boy. We didn't adopt you for the right reasons and it showed. I'm glad your real father found you. Maybe you can find with him and his family what you never had with us. Maybe your twin can be the sister that Sharon and Rena never were.''

Suddenly she clasped his arm. ''I want you to know something, Adam. I'm proud of what you've done and who you've become. I'm not just saying that because of all the help you've given me. I think you've become a fine man.''

His mother had never said anything like that to him before. He wondered if this new marriage she was going to enter into had changed her outlook on life…if she decided she deserved to live life instead of just letting it pass her by.

''Will you come to my wedding to John?'' she asked.

''If you let me know where and when, I'll be there.''

''Will you let me know when you go into the hospital? You will have to do that, won't you, to give bone marrow?''

''I'll let you know.''

Then the woman who had always seemed a bit removed, who never seemed to know exactly what to say or do or how to act with him, gave him a hug.

Adam's heart felt lighter than it had felt in a long time as he drove to the hospital.

* * *

Since Mark's family was keeping him company, Adam didn't stay long. The eight-year-old had been subjected to tests all day, and Adam could easily see he was worn out. He'd simply wanted to stop in so Mark would know he was thinking about him.

After his visit, Danielle came outside the room with Adam, telling the others she was going to get something to drink. But as they walked partway down the hall, she turned to Adam. "They're going to start Mark's chemo on Monday. He doesn't know that yet."

"Do you know when they'll be ready for me?"

She shook her head. "It depends on how everything goes with Mark. Dr. Mason will contact you. Are you getting anxious about it?"

Anxious wasn't the word. He just wanted it all to be over and Mark to be okay. "Not really."

Danielle stuffed her hands into the pockets of her slacks. "We're going to go ahead with Shawna's party tomorrow night. We talked to Mark about it and he's okay with it. Chad's going to hook up one of those video phones so Mark can see what's going on."

"The party will help the weekend go faster," Adam offered.

Danielle nodded. "That's what we thought. Did Shawna tell you you're welcome to bring a guest?"

"She told me, but I'll probably come alone."

"We appreciate how you're keeping in touch with Mark, especially by e-mail. It's keeping his spirits up."

"Good. That's what I intended."

"Adam, Jared doesn't say much, but he appreciates everything you're doing, too."

Adam had learned a long time ago not to try to please a father figure. He really didn't care what Jared thought of him. Everything he did was aimed to help Mark. "I'm glad I got a chance to meet Chad tonight."

"So am I."

But as he left Danielle, Adam knew he'd had enough of family for the night and it was time to go back to the ranch and get his head together.

When Adam returned to the ranch, he took Thunder out on a short night ride. The temperature was in the fifties, and a warmer spell was predicted for next week.

After their ride, Adam walked Thunder to cool him down, then spent time grooming him, talking to him, going over the transplant procedure in his head.

It was ten o'clock when he got back to the house. Switching on the computer, he let his home page boot up while he checked the answering machine. At the same time, he flicked on the small television resting on the bookshelf to catch the local nightly news. He was getting deeply involved in research about cheetahs to design a new game for kids when he heard the sound of fire sirens coming from the TV.

Glancing up at the picture, he saw the local news anchor at the perimeter of a fire scene, motioning toward the firemen and a building.

Adam went instantly on alert and took a second,

more careful look at the building. That was Leigh's apartment house, wasn't it?

Turning up the volume, he heard the anchor say, "The fire at Turndale Apartment Complex began around 8:00 p.m. Mr. Benson in apartment 2C apparently removed bacon from a grease-filled pan and forgot to turn off the burner. Then he fell asleep in his recliner. Fortunately he awakened when a neighbor who smelled the smoke banged on his door. The fire had already enveloped his kitchen by then. Once the alarm was pulled, everyone evacuated the building. Only two apartments were seriously damaged, but several families are trying to find shelter for the night."

Adam shot up out of the chair and headed for his car. Were Leigh and her mother one of those families? Were they okay? Had they been taken to the hospital? Smoke inhalation could be serious.

Adam's foot was heavy on the accelerator as he drove into Portland and headed for Leigh's apartment complex. Of course he couldn't get anywhere near it. The street was blocked. After he parked, he jogged to the cordoned-off area. Smoke filled the air as firemen still hosed the roof.

Approaching one of the policemen who was holding a walkie-talkie in his hand, Adam asked, "Where are the families who got out? I want to make sure someone is safe."

The policeman eyed him. "You related?"

"A friend and her mother."

The officer nodded toward the parking lot. "Off in the far corner. We're still trying to figure out who's here and who isn't."

With a wave of thanks, Adam strode toward the parking lot searching every face as he went. When he saw a group of men and women, some with blankets over their shoulders milling about a large van, he ran toward it.

Leigh was standing beside a woman with an official-looking clipboard. He heard her say, "I don't know where we're going to go. We don't have any relatives here. Will we be able to take anything from the apartment?"

"I'm afraid not," the older woman with gray hair and a kind smile answered. "We'll give you a call when you can get back in."

Claire had been standing there, too, and now looked as upset as Leigh. "But we don't have anything. We don't have clothes for tomorrow or nightwear or even our toothbrushes. If we just wait until the firemen are finished—"

Adam stepped closer then. "Your apartment will be a mess from the smoke and the water damage. It might be hard to salvage anything."

Claire looked at him expectantly. "Adam! Maybe you can do something. I don't even have my purse." She turned away so he couldn't see how upset she really was.

Putting his hand on Leigh's shoulder, he could feel she was trembling and as upset as her mother. Looking toward the woman whose name tag said she was Esther Bradley, he asked, "Do they have to stay here?"

"No. They're accounted for. I just need a number where I can reach them."

"Do you have your cell phone?" he asked Leigh gently.

When she looked up at him, her eyes were shiny and she shook her head. "It was on the charger in the bedroom. Mom and I were in the living room watching TV when someone banged on the door."

Turning to Esther, he decided, "You can reach them at my number." He rattled it off.

Claire brushed one hand through her mussed hair. "What good is giving them your number going to do?"

Instead of answering, he asked, "Do you have anyplace to go?"

Leigh and her mother exchanged a glance, then Leigh ventured, "A motel."

"Will your renter's insurance cover that?"

Again Leigh looked toward her mother.

Claire shook her head. "No, we don't know how long we're going to have to stay, either. I heard one of the firemen say our apartment was damaged the worst, next to Mr. Benson's. I guess we'll just have to put it all on Leigh's credit card. She managed to grab her purse on the way out."

"I have plenty of room at the ranch. Why don't you come and stay there until you find another place?"

It was almost a full minute before Claire replied, "We can't impose like that."

Leigh didn't say a word, and when Adam's gaze met hers, he wondered if he had just made the most foolish decision of his life. Even so, he couldn't go back now. "You won't be imposing. As I said, I have plenty of room. There are three bedrooms. You and

Leigh can have your own rooms. You'll even have a private bath. I'm at the office during the day and most evenings. It'll be better than a motel. You'll have a big-screen TV to watch.'' He tried to make a joke of it, hoping to bring a smile to their lips.

''We'd have to pay you,'' Claire insisted.

''No, you wouldn't. I won't take your money.'' When he saw she was about to protest again, he added, ''But I wouldn't mind a cooked meal, now and then, if that would make you feel better about staying there.''

''How far away is your ranch?'' Claire asked reluctantly.

''About twenty minutes out of town.''

''It would only be for a couple of days,'' Claire mused. She looked at Leigh. ''What do you think?''

''I think Adam's offer is kind and we don't have any choice, at least not for tonight. Maybe we can find another apartment quickly, but we need a place to crash in the meantime. Adam, are you sure about this?''

Whenever he looked at Leigh, he wasn't sure at all. But he was positive Claire would be a fine chaperone and she'd watch over her daughter. His primitive urges would just have to sit on the sidelines. ''Yes, I'm sure. Are you okay to drive?'' he asked Leigh.

''Yes, but I have to find my car. One of the policemen moved it.''

Claire said, ''I'll have to buy a few clothes someplace. So will you, Leigh.''

''I have an extra uniform in my locker, so I'll be okay with that. But we're going to need the necessities for tonight. Why don't we just take my car and stop on the way to Adam's. I know how to get there."

"Are you sure you want to drive?" Adam asked again.

Leigh nodded. "I'm fine. And we'll need my car to get back and forth. Mom's car keys are still in her purse in the apartment." She clasped Adam's arm. "Thank you."

He knew they were in the middle of a fire scene. He knew people were milling about. He knew her mother was looking on. Yet none of that seemed to matter. Stroking his thumb along her cheek, he tried to deny everything he was feeling.

Knowing if he kept touching her, he'd want to touch her more, he dropped his hand. "It's probably going to take you a while to get out of all this. I'll stop at the grocery store on my way home and stock up on food. Anything in particular you're hungry for?"

A smile tickled her lips. "Chocolate marshmallow ice cream."

"I should have guessed." It had always been her favorite, and when they had bought one cone and both licked from it...

*Primitive urges belong on the sidelines,* he reminded himself. "Chocolate marshmallow ice cream, it is."

As he stepped away from Leigh, he saw the way Claire was looking at them. It was a disapproving look, a worried look. Before she decided to go to a motel instead of Cedar Run, he made his way out of the bedlam, feeling strangely light, looking forward to having Leigh in his home.

## Chapter Nine

Adam had just finished stowing away the food in his kitchen when his doorbell rang. Already having second thoughts about his invitation to the Peters women he hurried to the door and opened it wide. Both women looked tired beyond measure and carried the discount store shopping bags in their hands.

"Come on in."

Claire's gaze appraised his house as she came inside, and Adam supposed she was still having problems reconciling the teenager he'd been with the man he'd become.

"Let me hang up your coats," he offered, waiting for them to shed their outerwear.

But Leigh shook her head. "You don't want these

hanging with your good clothes. They smell like smoke. If we could just air them out somehow—''

''There's a clothes rack in the mudroom.''

''I need a good airing out as well as my coat,'' Claire told him with a small smile.

''Come on. I'll show you to your rooms. They have a connecting bath. If you want to get showers, you can.''

As they followed him, Adam made a quick decision on which rooms he'd put them in. There were three bedrooms. He showed Claire to hers first. After she went inside, she laid her bags on the quilted coverlet with its navy, burgundy and green mountain scene. The wrought-iron and rattan bed was a double. The rattan dresser and chest were roomy, and oak blinds at the windows were shut.

''This is nice, Adam. You have a beautiful home.''

''Thanks to a decorator,'' he admitted wryly. ''But I like it. It's comfortable, and that's what I'm looking for.'' He opened the door into the bathroom. ''The towels on the racks are fresh and there are more under the vanity.''

Claire nodded absently, and he sensed that she just wanted to be alone so she could absorb everything that had happened, get a hot shower and go to bed. ''Are you an early riser?'' she asked. ''I don't want to disturb you in the morning.''

''I'm usually up around six-thirty on weekends. I'll take care of Thunder and do some chores before I start coffee. You won't have to worry about disturbing me.''

Though his attention had been focused on Leigh's

mother, he was well aware Leigh was standing just outside the door, taking it all in. She looked pale and seemed much too quiet.

"After I show Leigh to her room, I'm going to turn in. Feel free to use the kitchen or watch TV." He guessed they'd be more comfortable if they had privacy.

Claire patted the bed. "I'm going to take a shower so I don't fall asleep in the tub. After that, I'll be asleep in about two minutes. I'll see you in the morning."

Adam had just reached the doorway when she added, "Thank you, Adam, for taking us in. We really appreciate it. I'll make breakfast in the morning if you'd like. Do you have eggs? Maybe some cheese?"

"Sure do. That sounds great. I hope you get a good night's sleep."

When Leigh followed him into her room, he heard the rustle of the bags she carried, the light sound of her footsteps on the hardwood floor. The guest bedroom he showed her to was beside his, but she didn't comment on that or the decor. This room was furnished in lodgepole pine furniture. The full-size bed was covered with a multicolored comforter of turquoise, red and yellow, but he wasn't sure she even noticed that as she went to the dresser and set her bags and purse on top of it. She rummaged in one of the white bags until she brought out a bottle of pink body gel and one of those net balls to use with it.

"Give me your coat," he suggested. "I'll take it to the mudroom."

Still without a word, she slipped it off and handed

it to him. Then he saw her shiver. She was wearing a burgundy sweatshirt and jeans. Wrapping her arms around herself, she looked as if she were cold.

Her back was still to him and he followed his instincts. Hanging her coat over the bed's footboard, he walked up behind her. "Leigh? What's wrong?"

In the shadows of the room he couldn't see her expression in the mirror.

"I know I shouldn't mind about things being gone. Mom and I are safe. Mr. Benson is safe. Everyone else in the complex is safe. But with the fire, smoke and water damage, we might have lost everything. There's no way to know until we can go back in."

His arms went around her then, but as he pulled her back against him, she shook her head. "I smell like smoke."

"I don't care." Tilting his chin down to her head, he just stood there holding her. Finally he tried to reassure her. "Maybe you'll be able to salvage something."

"That depends on what the fire took before they stopped it. I should have grabbed my jewelry box…some things from the closet."

"You had to get out, Leigh. That was more important."

"But the pearl necklace Mom gave me for graduation was important, and her photo albums, and the gifts the kids in the ward had given me, and… It's not that all of it is worth so much, but it all had memories attached."

Memories. Intangible visions. Feelings. Sensations

that came and went like wisps of smoke. He couldn't tell her she'd remember without the souvenirs.

Turning her to him, he took her face between his palms. "You'll make more memories and gather new souvenirs."

Her beautiful blue eyes were shiny with unshed tears. He realized she'd been strong all night for her mother. She was vulnerable now, and he could take advantage of that or do the right thing and walk away.

He just couldn't walk away so he chose the middle of the road. When he placed a gentle kiss on her lips, he felt her start and then her tremble.

Reluctantly, he pulled away. "I'm going to get you some brandy. It will warm you up and help relax you."

However, she shook her head. "I don't need brandy, Adam. A hot shower will work wonders."

"You're sure?"

"I'm positive."

Adam could hear the water running in the bathroom. "I'll let you get ready for bed."

After he picked up her coat, she asked, "Why did you come to the fire tonight?"

"I didn't put any thought into it. I saw the picture on television, realized your building was burning, and before I knew it I was in the car. I guess I wanted to make sure you were safe."

"I'm not used to having someone look out for me," she murmured. "Except for Mom."

"I think you look out for *her,* too."

Before he did take advantage of Leigh's vulnerability, before he did something they'd both regret, he went to the door. "If you need anything, I'll be in my room."

After he left Leigh standing in his guest bedroom, he knew with her in the room beside his, he wouldn't get any sleep tonight. He'd picture her in that bed. He'd think about all the things he'd like to be doing with her in a bed.

*He* was the one who needed the brandy.

Adam was hoisting a bag of feed and pouring it into a bin when Leigh came into the barn Saturday morning, took off her jacket and threw it over a stall. "It still smells smoky," she said, wrinkling her nose.

It was raining again, but she looked like sunshine in her jeans and yellow pullover sweater that she must have bought last night. Her hair was loose around her face, the way he liked it.

Thunder neighed at her and when she got closer, he did it again.

"Does that mean he's glad to see me?" she asked with a bright smile.

"Sure does."

"Can I pet him?"

"Go slowly. The same way as the first time."

Crossing to the horse's stall, she stood before the large stallion, just looking into his eyes, silently communicating with him. After she brought her hand up slowly, she laid it on top of the gate. In a few moments, Thunder lowered his head and snuffled her fingers. She laughed and gently stroked his nose.

"You seem in better spirits this morning," Adam

noted, finishing with the burlap sack and dropping it next to the feed bins.

"I'm trying to put it all in perspective. After Mom makes breakfast, we're going to go apartment hunting."

"I get the feeling she's uncomfortable staying here with me."

"Mom doesn't like to be beholden to anyone. She's hoping we can find something suitable today so we can get out of your hair."

Crossing to Leigh, he stood beside her and ran his hand down Thunder's neck. "Is that the way you feel? You want to get out of my hair?"

When she faced him, her gaze met his. "I always enjoyed being around you, Adam. That hasn't changed."

After Thunder whinnied, he pawed the ground, then turned to the other side of his stall.

"He seems restless," Leigh remarked.

"I'm going to take him out for a ride after breakfast."

"In the rain?"

Adam shrugged. "He likes it, and so do I. I have a slicker in the tack room. It'll keep me dry." Propping one booted foot on the first rung of the stall, he asked, "Are you going to Shawna's party tonight?"

"I thought I'd stop in. What about you?"

"I wouldn't miss it. I managed to get her tickets and a backstage pass to the 'NSYNC concert."

"She'll be thrilled."

After a moment he added, "And my sister Lissa

might be there tonight. I'd like to meet her. The only thing is—''

''What?''

''I hate to think of meeting her for the first time in the middle of a crowd.''

''Why don't you call her and make contact ahead of time? At least that way you might get a good feel for what she's like.''

''She was supposed to return from Scotland this week. I didn't know how soon I wanted to barge into her life.''

''If I had a brother out there who I'd never met, I'd want to hear from him as soon as I could.''

Unable to keep his hands to himself, he brushed a silky tendril of Leigh's hair behind her ear. ''Not all women are like you.''

''I hope not,'' she joked.

But he hadn't been joking when he'd said it. Leigh obviously cared deeply about everyone and everything in her world.

''Maybe I'll call her when I get back from my ride. Do you want to go together tonight?''

When she seemed a bit uncertain, he reassured her. ''I don't have any ulterior motives, Leigh. I like being with you, too. Since we're both going, we can do our part to conserve fuel.''

His suggestion brought another smile. ''All right. I'd like to go with you. Have you heard from Mark?''

''I visited him last night...before the fire. He's scared but he's facing this like an adult. Better than an adult. He just wants to get the whole thing over with. I'm going to stop in and see him again this afternoon. It might be the last time I can visit for a while. They'll move him into isolation tomorrow. Shawna told me that after the party, her mom's going to go to the hospital and stay overnight with Mark.''

"That will be good for both of them."

With Leigh standing so close to him, he wanted to touch her again. The swish of Thunder's tail along with the pitter-patter of gentle rain on the roof were the only sounds in the barn. Leigh's sweater had a rounded neck, and her pulse point above it seemed to vibrate faster. His own heart was pounding harder.

"I can't be around you and not want to kiss you," he said hoarsely.

"I want you to kiss me." Her voice was no louder than the rustle of hay, but he heard it.

When he wrapped her into his arms, he didn't rush any of it. He wanted to savor inhaling her scent. He wanted to remember how fragile she felt held against him. When she looked up at him with eyes as blue as a beautiful clear sky, he wanted her in a way that was primal and aching and deep. He kissed her forehead and her cheeks and finally her mouth. She tasted of mint and coffee and every delicacy he could ever imagine. He was fully aroused as they took the moment and ran with it, melding to each other more completely. Rocking against her, he groaned from the pleasure. When her hands curled tightly on his shoulders, he knew he was giving her pleasure, too.

However, Thunder's snort alerted Adam that something had changed. An instant later, the barn door scraped open on its hinges. Adam prepared himself for the intrusion as he broke the kiss and pulled back but didn't take his arms from around Leigh.

"Are you two soon ready for breakfast? I made our first appointment for nine-thirty." Claire Peters's voice trailed off as she saw the two of them and guessed what they had been doing.

Leigh's color was high but she didn't skitter away, and Adam was glad about that. Instead she merely shifted in Adam's arms.

He answered Claire, "We're ready when you are."

"I suppose I interrupted something," Claire determined matter-of-factly.

Adam released Leigh now and answered for them both. "We were discussing the Cambrys' party tonight. We were both invited, and we're going together."

"I see." Claire didn't look happy about it, but she didn't say anything more, either. Adam guessed that Leigh was going to get an earful later.

For now, though, she smiled at her mother. "After we look at apartments, I need to shop for something simple to wear tonight."

"I'm sure we can find something," Claire decided, although she didn't sound as if her heart were in it.

Leigh touched Adam's arm, and with a smile said, "I'll help Mom with breakfast."

"I won't be long," he replied as he watched Leigh pick up her jacket and leave the barn with her mother.

Two hours later Adam had returned from his ride, still thinking about kissing Leigh. At breakfast their gazes had connected often. They were on the verge of something again, something that was going to hurt them both. He knew that and so did she, but they couldn't seem to help themselves.

As he groomed Thunder, he thought about the party at Jared's, about Leigh's suggestion to call Lissa. If she didn't want to answer the phone, she wouldn't pick up. If she didn't want to talk to him, he'd be able to hear it in her voice. Either way, he'd be prepared for tonight.

The legs of his jeans were wet from the ride but instead of going to the house to change first, he took his cell phone from his belt, searched for the number he'd entered after Jared had given it to him, and pressed Send.

"Hello?" It was a soft melodic voice that sounded a bit sleepy.

"Lissa Grayson?"

"Yes, I'm Lissa. Who's this?"

"Adam Bartlett."

There was a shocked silence, then an exuberant "Adam! Oh, my goodness. I'm so glad you called. I just got back yesterday and I'm not even out of bed yet. Well, I mean…"

He heard a male chuckle nearby.

Although he should feel awkward at this intrusion into her life, he suddenly felt relieved, and a smile came to his own lips. "I should have known better than to call before noon. You're a newlywed."

At that, she said, "Hold on a minute, Adam."

He heard a brief mumbled conversation and suspected she was telling her new husband who was calling. Then she returned to the phone. "Okay, I'm awake and I'm all yours. Are you going to Shawna's party tonight?''

''That's why I'm calling. A crowd didn't seem the best place to make introductions.''

''I hadn't thought of that, but you're right. I can't wait to see what you look like. Ever since I heard I had a twin, my mind's been spinning.''

''I know what you mean. Did you know that I'm a match for Mark?''

''Jared left the news on the machine here at the vineyard. I'm so glad. Everybody was so disappointed when I wasn't a match, and I felt as if I'd let them down somehow.''

''Now you don't have to be worried about it. I know there's no guarantee the transplant will take, but if we all believe it will, that's got to help.''

''I can't believe I'm actually talking to you! Jared called me in Scotland to tell me he'd met you. He said you're the CEO of a software company, but he didn't say much else. Are you single…married…involved?''

Lissa's excitement at finding him and wanting to know about his life created a joy inside of him as he'd never known. She had no ax to grind. She didn't want anything from him. She just wanted to get to know who he was.

Still…answering her question wasn't easy. ''I'm single.''

''Hmm,'' she said teasingly. ''Do I hear something else attached to that?''

He laughed. ''It's a long story.''

''So, tell me about it. Sullivan went out with Barney. He's our dog.''

It was odd, but Adam already felt as if he'd known Lissa for a lifetime. It was unlike him to confide his personal life to anyone, but she seemed to really care. "I have someone staying with me right now. I knew her in high school. She's a nurse at Portland General and has been the liaison during Mark's transplant process. There was a fire in her apartment building, and she and her mom had nowhere to go."

There were a few moments when Lissa seemed to be thinking about what he'd told her. "I think there's a lot you're leaving out since you haven't really told me if you're involved *now*."

"Leigh's coming with me to the party tonight. You can meet her and draw your own conclusions."

Lissa laughed. "I'll do that. I can't wait for you to meet Sullivan."

Then Lissa launched into the story of how she and Sullivan had met. Finally she revealed, "And the best news of all is, I'm going to have a baby. Just think, you haven't even known me a day and you're going to be an uncle!"

An uncle. A real sister. And Lissa cared. It all seemed surreal to Adam but he was slowly getting used to the idea. "Congratulations. You sound happy about it."

"We're both thrilled."

When Adam heard noises in the background again, the barking of an excited dog, he knew her new husband was back. "I won't tie you up any longer right now. Maybe we'll find some more time to talk tonight."

"You can bet we will. And I'm only two hours away, Adam. We can get together anytime we want."

He liked the sound of that. He liked the sound of Lissa, and he couldn't wait to meet her in person.

That evening, the Cambrys' house blazed with light. Cars were parked around the circular drive and on the macadam area beside the garage.

"Full house," Adam commented to Leigh as they walked up to the front door.

"Shawna told me they didn't only invite her friends, but some neighbors, too."

As always, Leigh looked pretty tonight. He could tell she'd shopped frugally and practically but she still looked elegant in her black slacks, white silk blouse and vest with multicolored fringe. On top of it all, she wore a red jacket. He'd seen the sale price on the sleeve before she'd removed it.

After his visit to Mark, he'd been running late, and they hadn't had much time to talk in the car. She had told him Claire had found two apartments she liked. The problem was, the one with the two bedrooms wouldn't be available for another month. The other had a nice location and a reasonable price, but only one bedroom. The one-bedroom apartment was available immediately.

A uniformed maid opened the door before Adam could even ring the bell. Chatter flowed out from inside, and as he and Leigh stepped into the living room, he saw Shawna surrounded by a crowd of her friends. She was wearing black leather slacks and a short pink top with little beads hanging all over it. When she spotted him, she waved.

As soon as the maid took Leigh's coat, Danielle came toward them, hands outstretched. "I'm so glad you could come. The table in the dining room is loaded with food and there's dancing in the family room. Lissa isn't here yet," she said to Adam. "She called, though. She and Sullivan are running a little late. Something about their dog splashed around in a mud puddle and they had to give him a bath."

Adam was smiling as he guided Leigh toward the family room and the music.

"Did you call your sister?" Leigh asked.

"Yes, I did. I can't wait to meet her." Adam had glanced into the dining room and now canvassed the family room. "I don't see Jared. I wonder where he is."

"Maybe he's running late for some reason, too." Leigh had brought a present for Shawna and now took it to a table heaped with gifts. *His* present for Shawna was tucked into his inside jacket pocket.

Adam was about to ask Leigh if she wanted to get something to eat when Shawna breezed in, her hand clasped in a boy's. He was tall and rangy looking. "Adam and Leigh, I want you to meet Peter. Peter Bennett, my brother Adam and a friend of his, Leigh."

The boy gave them an offhanded grin. "Nice to meet you."

"Nobody's dancing," Shawna said, looking around, seeing teenagers in one group of conversations and adults in another. She looked at Adam. "If I put a slow one on, will you two dance?"

"Are you insinuating that I'm too old to enjoy a fast one?" he joked.

Her cheeks reddened. "No, but Peter prefers slow ones."

The boy was looking at Shawna as if he'd rather dance a slow dance with her someplace private. Adam wondered how Jared handled that. That was a part of being a father that would be damn tough.

He glanced over at Leigh. "A slow one okay with you?"

"That's fine with me."

Shawna went to the entertainment center and soon soft strains of a new pop idol's ballad poured from the speakers. It had been ten long years since Adam had danced with Leigh. Now he opened his arms to her.

When she placed her hand on his shoulder, he could feel its warmth through his suit coat. At least he thought he could. Her other hand was so small, so fragile in his, and he closed his hand around hers and brought it into his chest. When she looked up at him, everybody else in the room faded away. It was only the two of them and the music, her perfume and his cologne mingling, the heat of their bodies coming together. Other couples were dancing now, too, but Adam paid them no mind.

As his arm tightened around Leigh, his jaw brushed her temple. "Did your mother say anything about finding us in the barn this morning?"

Leigh's shoulders lifted and fell, then she looked up at him. Her face was only a few inches from his. "She's just worried about me."

"What's there to worry about?"

"She doesn't want me to get sidetracked."

"We're both responsible adults now, not teenagers. Even if we decided to get involved, we can take precautions."

"You mean against pregnancy," Leigh murmured.

"Yes."

The idea of an involvement and what it would mean wisped around them like a cloud. Pictures played in Adam's mind. Was he contemplating an affair with Leigh knowing he'd have to let her go in June?

Usually he could tell what Leigh was thinking, but now she turned her head away and rested it on his shoulder. Was she thinking about the heartache they'd be asking for? Was she imagining sleeping with him? Why was the timing always wrong for them?

One song stretched into two and Adam decided to stop thinking about the future and simply enjoy what was happening right now. Leigh was soft and fragrant and warm in his arms. He was aroused, and he suspected she was too from the flush on her cheeks, the sparkle in her eyes, the closeness of their bodies.

Then suddenly he felt a tap on his shoulder. When he turned, he saw Chad. The teenager had Jared's hair but resembled his mother. Beside him was a beautiful young woman, who looked a bit like Adam did himself.

Chad said somberly, "Adam, Lissa Grayson and her husband Sullivan. Sullivan and Lissa, meet Adam Bartlett and Leigh Peters."

Adam's heart raced as he released Leigh and turned to face Lissa. The next moment his twin was hugging him, and he knew he finally had a real family.

# Chapter Ten

Twenty minutes later Adam decided he liked Sullivan as much as he liked Lissa. Her husband had a quick wit and an easy laugh. It was obvious he adored his new wife, and she loved him.

While Sullivan answered Leigh's interested questions about the vineyard, Lissa tugged Adam through sliding glass doors onto the patio, her long dark-brown hair flowing behind her. She pulled out one of the white wrought-iron chairs at a small round table, and he sat across from her. They just stared at each other for a while and then both of them laughed.

"You *do* look like me," Adam admitted with a smile.

"No, *you* look like *me*." Then her smile slipped away, and he saw that Lissa Grayson could be a very serious young woman, too. "Tell me how you grew up," she prompted.

"Why don't you go first." He'd never really talked about his background to anyone except Leigh, and it seemed odd to do it now. Lissa must have seen that he needed to get comfortable with the idea so she started slowly.

"The Cartwrights loved me. They always have and they always will. But my sister, their biological daughter, was so beautiful, so accomplished, so intelligent that I was always insecure. Until Sullivan came along. Then I felt beautiful and intelligent and special, too." She hesitated a few moments but then went on to tell Adam about growing up at the vineyard and the makeover Jared had helped her with. It seemed she'd connected with Jared, though she still thought of the Cartwrights as Mom and Dad.

She pushed her waist-length hair over her shoulder. Propping her elbow on the table, her chin in her palm, she said, "So now I want to know more about you. Are you and Leigh Peters involved?"

"Just because we were dancing doesn't mean we're involved."

"You were doing more than dancing. I saw the way you two were looking at each other. But if you don't want to talk about it, I'll understand."

Lissa was so ingenuous, so absolutely natural, and he saw that she wanted to know because some part of her already cared about him. Feeling more comfortable now, he told Lissa the story of how he and Leigh had met at her locker in high school, of the note she'd left him three months later. Somehow that led into his life with the Bartletts and how he'd always felt as if he were odd man out.

After he'd finished, she scolded, "You still didn't answer my question. *Are* you and Leigh involved now?" Lissa's green eyes were bright as she asked him for the truth.

"I'm telling myself I shouldn't get involved. I'm reminding myself she's leaving in June."

Just then Sullivan came through the sliding glass doors and onto the patio. Crossing to his wife, he laid his hand on her shoulder. "How are you feeling?"

"I think jetlag is setting in."

"Or pregnancy. Jared said we could stay the night if we'd like instead of driving back. That might be better for you."

"Maybe that *would* be a good idea. I'll give Mom and Dad a call. I'm sure they won't mind taking care of Barney tonight. He's going to love having a baby to romp with." She reached out and covered Adam's hand with hers. "You will be a *real* uncle, won't you? I want you to come visit often."

"I'll come. I'd like to have you and Sullivan out to the ranch. We'll set up a date after the transplant."

Leigh came to the door then, too. "I'm sorry to interrupt, but Jared would like all of you to come in. He wants to give a toast."

To his surprise Adam didn't feel as if Leigh were interrupting. He felt as if she belonged by his side. Yet he knew that wasn't going to happen. Still, as they went to the living room, he took her hand and she smiled up at him as if she were glad she was at the party with him.

As Adam and Leigh stood on the fringes of the crowd in the living room, a waiter made sure everyone had a drink. Jared draped his arm around Shawna's shoulders and ushered her toward the fireplace. There he handed her a glass. "Sparkling cider," he elaborated with a wink.

When she just rolled her eyes, everyone laughed.

Danielle and Chad came to stand beside him. They, too, had glasses in hand.

After Jared was sure he commanded all of his guests' attention, he raised his and addressed the crowd. "This is a happy occasion for us. Shawna has turned sixteen and she's definitely on her way to adulthood. We've never been more proud of her than we are right now. Shawna, happy sixteenth birthday."

After a round of applause, Jared still didn't move away from the fireplace. Rather, he waited until the applause died down, and then his gaze met Adam's.

"There's someone else here tonight who I'd like to introduce to you. I don't know if all of you have met him yet. He's giving us the greatest gift we could possibly imagine. Adam Bartlett is the man who will donate his bone marrow to Mark. He's a perfect match, and we want to toast him and his generosity in helping us save Mark's life."

Again everyone applauded and Adam soon found all eyes were on him. He raised his glass to Jared's, forced a smile and then took a swallow of his drink.

After the applause died down, everyone turned away and began mingling again. A few of the guests introduced themselves to Adam, most were friends or neighbors of Jared's family. They kept telling him what a wonderful thing he was doing, and Adam felt awkward about all of it.

Standing beside Adam, Leigh watched him go still and turn inward. Whether he wanted to admit it or not, she was sure he was hoping Jared Cambry would be the father he never had. But Jared had just blown that idea to bits. He hadn't acknowledged Adam as his son, and she could see the effects of that in Adam's rigid stance as well as in his forced smile as he spoke to Jared's friends and neighbors. Leigh ached for him and understood the child inside of him who'd wanted Owen Bartlett to accept him as a real son. She didn't know what she would have done as she was growing up if she hadn't had her mother's support. Unlike her, Adam had gone it alone from an early age. She admired him for that, but she'd also seen the toll it had taken on him.

After the well-wishers had moved away, he leaned toward Leigh. "I want to find Shawna again and give her her birthday present. Then I'll be ready to leave. Will you?"

"Whenever you're ready." She'd attached a card to her birthday present for Shawna that was on the table in the family room. It wasn't necessary for her to be here when Shawna opened it. The trendy purse had caught Leigh's eye and she hoped Shawna liked it. On the other hand, she couldn't wait to see Shawna's face when Adam gave her his gift.

It took a few moments for them to find and snag Shawna.

"Do you want to do this alone?" Leigh asked

Adam in a low voice as he guided Shawna toward a quiet corner.

"No. I want you to enjoy her reaction, too."

Shawna stopped beside an indoor palm. She was flushed and happy and excited, enjoying every minute of her party. Enthusiasm bubbled over as she asked, "You're not leaving are you?"

"Soon. I wanted to give you your present first. I was afraid it would get lost if I put it on the table."

"You didn't have to bring a present. Just having you here was a gift."

Leigh could see that Shawna's words went a long way to making up for what her father hadn't said to Adam.

"A sixteenth birthday deserves something memorable." Adam took an envelope from his inside jacket pocket. "I thought you might enjoy these."

As Shawna took the envelope from him, she looked puzzled. It was a legal-size white envelope giving no hint as to what it held. When she pulled out the four tickets inside and a square piece of paper, she looked up at them in astonishment. "The 'NSYNC concert! Oh, my gosh! They were sold out before I could get home from school and call. How did you get these?"

"I just happen to know their road manager. My partner invited him to one of his parties."

"Oh, my gosh," she said again. "And is this a backstage pass?"

"It sure is. You'll have a chance to talk with them for a few minutes. Make sure you have your camera so a friend can snap a picture."

"I can take three friends." Suddenly she threw her

arms around Adam's neck and gave him a big hug. "This is *so* cool. Wait till I tell Mark." After she released Adam, she stepped away. "Dad's going to use the video phone and call Mark. Are you sticking around for that?"

"No. Leigh and I are going to leave now. You can tell Mark I'll e-mail him later."

"I'm glad Mom's going to the hospital and staying with him tonight, then he won't feel alone." After she looked down at the tickets again, she glanced back at Adam. "How did it go with you and Lissa?"

"I like her. A lot. We're going to get together after the transplant."

A few minutes later, when Shawna decided she wanted to show her mom the tickets, Adam and Leigh went with her to say goodbye. They found Lissa, too, and Leigh could see that Adam and his twin were on their way to developing a lasting bond.

On the drive back to the ranch, Adam was quiet and Leigh left him to his thoughts. He had a lot on his mind—Mark's bone marrow transplant, his own procedure, the new family he'd met.

When they reached Cedar Run, Adam pulled into the garage. After they went in the side door to the kitchen, they found all the lights still on and the TV playing. But when Leigh's mother heard them, she switched it off.

"Mom. I'm surprised you're still up."

"It's only eleven. I had a call earlier and I needed to discuss it with you."

Shrugging out of his suit jacket, Adam said, "I'll say good-night."

But Claire stopped him. "No, Adam. Stay. This concerns you, too. The apartment manager called—the one who had that apartment we liked with one bedroom. If we don't want it, she has someone who does. I like the section of town it was in, and it was so bright and cheerful. We'll be cramped until you go to school but then you'll be in Cleveland, and I'll be alone. I'd like to take it. Adam will have his place back, and we can get settled in."

Adam looked at Leigh. "Do you have a place in Cleveland yet?"

"Yes. I flew out over the President's Holiday. I'll be sharing an apartment with two other women. Their roommate is moving out at the end of May, and I'll be taking her place."

"I had another call, too," Claire said. "We can get into our old apartment tomorrow and salvage what we can. If we take this apartment, we'll have someplace to move in to."

"It sounds as if your mind's made up." Leigh didn't know how she felt about feeling like a guest at her mother's. But that's what she'd be.

"I guess my mind *is* made up. It will be hard for you now, not having a room of your own. But the one-bedroom is spacious, and we can probably fit your twin bed in with my double. That way you'll have a place to sleep when you come home over holidays, too."

Besides all the good reasons she'd listed, Leigh knew her mother didn't like imposing on Adam. She also knew her mom had a budget she had to adhere to. Yet Leigh felt misplaced, as if she wouldn't really have a home until she got to Cleveland. Then she thought about everything else that would be happening this week—Mark's chemo, Adam being admitted to the hospital…

Suddenly Adam made a suggestion that took Leigh by surprise. "If you're going to be crowded, Leigh, you can stay here until you leave for Cleveland. I've got plenty of room."

Stunned silence met his suggestion until Claire recovered. "That's not a good idea," she snapped.

But Leigh wasn't as quick to dismiss it for a multitude of reasons. "Adam's offer might solve all our problems, Mom. Mark's transplant will most likely happen this coming week. I want to be here with Adam. He'll need someone to drive him home after his bone marrow extraction. And someone should really be here with him at least for the day he's released."

"That's a lot different from staying until June. What would people say?" Claire insisted, obviously concerned with more than propriety.

"What people, Mom? What I do is no one's business but mine."

At this point Adam intervened. "Leigh wouldn't be living with me, per se, Ms. Peters. She'd be sharing my house. We probably won't even see that much of each other with our work schedules. I didn't bring it up to cause friction. I just thought if it was a solution, maybe we should consider it. As far as the bone marrow donation goes, Dylan can drive me home. I'm sure I'll be fine. If you want to stay because it's practical for you to do that, Leigh, the invitation is open. Don't base your decision on what's happening with me. Okay?"

Adam's intent was clear. He was telling her he didn't need her. He was just offering her an alternative to living in a one-bedroom apartment with her mother...an alternative she was seriously considering.

"I'm sure you want to discuss this between the two of you," Adam added. "I'll be in my office. I'm going to e-mail Mark and then work on a few scheduling details for next week."

As Adam hooked his suit coat over his shoulder and strode through the living room to his den, he looked casual and relaxed as if Leigh's decision didn't matter to him at all. Did he care if she stayed with him or didn't he?

Slipping off her jacket, she went to the foyer closet and hung it up.

When she returned to the living room, her mother was waiting expectantly. "You're not seriously considering staying here with *him,* are you?"

If her mother was trying to make Adam faceless for her, she wouldn't be able to do it. "As I said, he might need me."

"You can't expect me to believe that if you stay here, you're simply going to be housemates."

She honestly didn't know what would happen between her and Adam. But she did know one thing. "I'm not going to give up my dreams simply because I decide to stay with him."

"I'm glad to hear it. But the temptation's going to be there, and you *will* get hurt."

Was she ready to face the fact she might? She was.

Her expression must have told her mother what she was thinking. Shooting to her feet, Claire shook her head vigorously. "You can't tell me you're entertaining the idea of an affair. Leigh, didn't I teach you better than that?"

"You can't live my life for me, Mom. I know what you taught me. I know what I believe. But I also know my heart is telling me to stay here with Adam. Part of me has always wondered about him...wondered if he could open up...wondered if he could ever share what he was feeling."

"What if he can do those things? What if you come under his spell again?"

A smile came to her lips. "Oh, Mom. Adam is no sorcerer. I control my own destiny. Can't you see I need the chance to make my own decisions and make my own mistakes?"

"I don't want you to have to *make* mistakes. I made one that cost me my future. *Your* future could be brilliant. Please don't throw that away to live in the moment."

"I'm not going to throw anything away. I'll help you sort through your things and move into your new place. I'll visit you often whenever you'd like. But I'm going to move in here until I leave, and I'm going to tell Adam right now."

Her mother was used to getting the last word, but Leigh didn't stay around to hear it this time. She didn't stay around to be convinced that not seeing Adam anymore would be the better thing to do. Logic just didn't fit into this equation anymore. She had to go with her instincts, and her instincts were telling her to stay.

Her knock on Adam's door was decisive. She heard him call, "Come in." Opening it, she saw him sitting at the computer, his e-mail program on the screen. "Did you hear from Mark?"

"Sure did. And he said his dad's video-phone worked. Shawna showed him her tickets and he's jealous, but she's going to take pictures and maybe get an autograph for him with her backstage pass."

Adam motioned to the end of the letter. "Danielle just got there, and they're getting ready to turn in. I'm glad she's going to be there tonight. It'll do them both a lot of good."

Swiveling away from the computer then, Adam faced her. "I didn't hear any yelling and screaming coming from the living room. Are you and your mom okay? Maybe I should have waited and asked you privately, but I wanted to be straightforward about the offer."

There was no point going into how her mother felt. "I accept your invitation to stay, Adam."

Rising to his feet, he approached her. "I meant what I said about being housemates, not living together. There are no strings attached to this, Leigh."

He was close and he was sexy and she could so vividly remember dancing with him.

"And if you're here after I donate bone marrow, I *don't* need a nursemaid."

Adam had always had a tremendous amount of pride and she respected that. "But you won't mind if I make supper, will you? Just as a thank-you for letting me stay. I *am* going to pay you rent."

"No, you're not."

This time *her* pride was at stake. "There's no discussion on this, Adam."

"Sure there is. I don't want your money. Throw it into a savings account for things you'll need. Or help your mom buy new furniture."

"I can't stay here for free."

"Why not?"

His eyes were filled with humor and something more serious. His tie was undone, hanging around his shirt collar. He'd rolled up his sleeves and unbuttoned the top two buttons of his shirt. He was so unbearably male.

"Because..." She forgot what she was going to say when Adam came even closer...when he bent his head and kissed her. It was a fleeting kiss as their kisses went, yet it was thoroughly arousing nevertheless. When he backed away, she knew he knew it.

Finding her voice, she managed, "I have to feel I'm contributing. What if I make sure there's always something edible in the refrigerator, whether it's from the deli or something I cook?"

After considering her suggestion, he smiled, "That would be a change. I'm a connoisseur of peanut butter and stale crackers."

"Good. That takes care of that." She glanced at the file folder open on his desk. "Will you be up for a while?"

"I have e-mail to take care of."

"Then I'll see you in the morning."

"In the morning," Adam agreed.

When Leigh left his office, she thought about being

in the house with him alone. What if her mother hadn't been here tonight? Would he still have ended the kiss?

After tomorrow she'd know.

On Friday morning Leigh took her break early to check on Adam. He'd gotten a call on Wednesday that his harvesting and Mark's transplant were set for today. They had driven in early this morning from the ranch so Adam could register around seven-thirty. Her shift started at eight. After they'd separated in the lobby and she'd wished him good luck, he'd given her a thumbs-up sign.

When she'd accepted his invitation to stay at his house, she thought they might talk more and become closer. But since Saturday night, Adam had been keeping his distance. With his pickup truck, he'd helped her and her mother move everything salvageable into her mom's new apartment on Sunday. Yet after Sunday, they'd pretty much gone their separate ways. Adam had worked late every night, and she wondered if he was doing it to distract himself from Mark and the transplant or to stay away from her.

Before Leigh had taken a break, she'd called Patient Registration for the number of Adam's private room. Hurrying down the hall, she found the number, then hesitated an instant outside the door. Finally she knocked before pushing it open. She'd expected to see him dressed in a hospital gown and lying on the bed. Instead, he was still wearing a polo shirt and jeans and pacing the room.

"Adam. I thought they'd be prepping you."

"I thought so, too," he muttered with a dark expression. "But there's been a delay. Did you see Mark this morning?"

"I can't go in to see him, but I checked on his condition."

"And?" Adam's eyes said he wanted her to tell the truth.

"And he needs your bone marrow desperately. His abnormal cells have been destroyed, but normal cells have been destroyed, too. Have you heard from Danielle or Shawna?"

"Danielle e-mailed me last night. She's not saying it, but she's scared to death this won't help, that the transplant won't take. She's afraid he might get an infection even with all the precautions. And damn it, Leigh, I can't tell her not to worry because I'm worried, too."

She could see he was, but she suspected there was more to it than that. Visiting Mark had been one thing, getting through today with the doctors poking, prodding and handling him was another.

Eyeing the hospital gown on the corner of the bed, she gently chided, "You should get changed. They'll want to set up your IV soon—"

"I'm not getting into that damned hospital gown until it's necessary."

Keeping her voice calm, she asked, "Have you spoken with the anesthesiologist yet?"

"Yes, he was here about five minutes ago." With a disgusted look, Adam eyed the hospital gown again, then blew out a breath. "All right. I'll get ready. But I'm not getting into bed until they want to knock me out."

"I can try to find somebody to cover for me if you want me to stay."

"No!" was his immediate reply. "I don't need you here, Leigh. I don't need someone to hold my hand. I just want to get all of it over with."

If he didn't need her here, he didn't need her in his life. Was he just being kind by asking her to stay at the ranch with him? Maybe he was just trying to mend fences that had been too broken to repair. That had been his message this week. If she were smart, she'd listen to it.

But she cared too much about him to act indifferent. "I'll stop in before I leave tonight to see how the procedure went. You should be awake by then."

"You don't have to stop in. I'll call you in the morning and tell you what time I'm being discharged. Are you sure you don't mind driving in for me tomorrow? Dylan could take me home."

"I'm off for the weekend, and I really have nothing to do. Mom's apartment is pretty much together now so I'll be around all day if you need me."

Before he could say again that he didn't, in spite of his gruff attitude, she took a step toward him, stood on tiptoe and kissed him on the cheek. "That's for good luck. I'm sure everything will go smoothly. Just remember I'll be thinking about you as well as Mark, and I'm sure the Cambry family will be, too."

Looking down at her, he suddenly enfolded her into his arms and brought her close for a moment. As he held her, she could feel the beat of his heart.

Abruptly he released her and stepped away. When she gazed into his eyes, she saw the turmoil there and knew he was remembering another day and another time, Delia, and everything that had happened with the medical personnel.

"Good people work here, Adam. Trust them."

Then she left his room…because tears were too close to the surface, because she cared too much, because she was falling in love with Adam Bartlett all over again.

## Chapter Eleven

When Leigh arrived at the hospital Saturday morning to pick up Adam, he looked ready to erupt.

"They're telling me the nurse has to wheel me down in the wheelchair like some invalid! Can you believe it?"

In spite of herself, Leigh felt a smile trying to burst from inside her. Adam's procedure had been textbook perfect. Marrow had been extracted from the back of his hip bones. It had taken the doctor an hour and a half to harvest as much as he needed.

She'd called the head nurse on duty last night and found out that Adam had grumbled and barked when the nurse had to remove his bandage and check the area. The doctor's orders stated he should stay in bed last night, and he'd agreed with the nurses about that.

Still, the head nurse had checked on him often to make sure he was listening. They'd supplied him with ice packs every hour, and Leigh knew he was supposed to use them for forty-eight hours, then heat if he still had pain and swelling. Antibiotics and pain medication had been ordered along with a sleeping pill. Thank goodness Adam had taken the antibiotic, although he'd refused the rest. Another of Leigh's friends on his floor had reported that he was listening to orders to drink a lot of liquids, so Leigh had stopped at the grocery store, buying three different kinds of juices as well as wholesome food. As with any procedure, infection could set in and she intended to watch him carefully for a fever, swelling or any trouble breathing.

"Well, I can see you came through the harvesting just fine, but your mood hasn't improved," she noted dryly.

Although she'd never quite seen Adam scowl before, she realized he was doing it now. Dressed in a football jersey and jeans, he moved a bit gingerly as he went to sit in the wheelchair. "Let's just get out of here. Any news on Mark? I feel isolated without my computer."

For Mark, the transplant had probably been the easiest part of his ordeal. The marrow had been introduced into his body through an IV. "He's doing as well as can be expected."

"I'm getting so tired of hearing hospital-speak," Adam grumbled.

"Adam, you know that's all they can tell us. It's going to be two to four weeks before we have real news on whether the transplant took. You're going to have to be patient just like the Cambrys."

"I'm thin on patience right now."

Maintaining her calm, she offered, "Then I guess we'll have to work on that today, won't we?"

She thought he might give her the I-don't-need-a-nurse speech, but instead he remained silent as if he knew that was his best course. Obviously, Adam was one of those men who did *not* make a good patient.

With a sunny smile, a nurse breezed into the room, clutching an instruction sheet in her hand. "You'll be staying with him?" she asked Leigh now.

"Yes. Unless he orders me off his property," she added with a smile, hoping to coax one from him.

His nurse's voice was enthusiastic and clear. "Here are his instructions, not anything complicated. You know what to look for. Make sure he takes the antibiotics and drinks plenty of liquids. He should use ice fifteen to twenty minutes every hour as needed. Switch over to heat tomorrow."

"I'm right here," Adam interrupted, obvious tension edging his tone. "You already told me all this. I even signed a paper that I understood it."

The nurse ignored him and handed Leigh a bag that had been sent up from the hospital pharmacy. "There's an antibiotic and pain medication in there."

After Leigh took the bag, the nurse went around to the back of the wheelchair. "All right, the gentleman wants to leave. Let's make it happen."

When Adam just rolled his eyes, Leigh suppressed another smile.

* * *

After Leigh parked in Adam's driveway, he got out of her Neon almost as quickly as she did. While she watched, he strode to the door with the movement of a man who was acting as if he was perfectly fine. He wasn't. She'd seen him surreptitiously shifting in his seat during the ride. Since the bone marrow extraction, she knew he'd felt as if he'd taken a bad fall.

To her dismay, after Adam unlocked the door, he started for his office. "I'm going to call my mother to tell her everything went okay, then work for a while." The look he gave her dared her to argue with him.

Knowing that argument would be useless, she offered, "I picked up three ice packs at the drugstore last night. They're in the freezer. I also bought a heat pack for the microwave."

She thought he might claim he didn't need those, either. Instead, he went to the kitchen and took two bills from his wallet, placing them on the table. "That should cover it." Then he took an ice pack from the freezer and went to his office.

Leaving Adam to his own devices for the time being, Leigh prepared lunch. Good food would help his recovery. After she put salmon in the oven to broil, she steamed asparagus and sliced a cantaloupe. Everything was ready when the microwave beeped, signaling the rice was finished.

When Leigh went to Adam's den to call him, he was still using the ice pack and staring at the computer screen. She suspected the pain was spoiling his concentration, but he wouldn't admit it.

To her chagrin, all of her attempts at conversation

were thwarted during lunch. She'd had enough psych classes to know that more was going on here than Adam's reaction to a medical procedure.

As he pushed his plate away and stood, she quickly cleared the table. "I think we should talk."

He eyed her warily. "About what?"

"About what's bothering you. It's obvious something is. Are you sorry you asked me to stay with you? Because if you are, I can still move in with Mom."

Running his hand through his hair, he leaned back against the counter and winced. "Damn," he muttered.

"That's exactly what I mean, Adam. You should be resting. You'll recover quicker if you do. Would you be resting if I weren't here?"

With a sigh, he admitted, "Probably. Maybe. I don't know. I just know I don't like anybody seeing me in a hospital gown or lying in a bed, especially you."

"Why, especially me? I'm a nurse, for goodness sakes."

"You're a *woman*. A woman who—" He shook his head. "I don't want you to see me as anything but strong."

"This is an ego thing?" she asked in amazement.

He flushed slightly. "If you want to call it that. I'm never sick. I don't take drugs. I've done everything in my power to stay out of hospitals. For the past three weeks, I've been inside Portland General enough to last me a lifetime."

So *that* was the problem. There was even more to it than that, she guessed. "Adam, I know what you went through. I know they took your vitals and hooked you up to a monitor and IV. I know you felt powerless as they gave you anesthesia, and you hated the nurses checking on you afterward. I know it brought everything back about that day in the hospital with Delia. Don't you realize if you talk about it, it will help? Keeping it all bottled up inside just makes everything worse.''

After he rubbed his hand across his forehead, his gaze met hers again. ''The whole experience brought back every bad memory I'd locked away. I recalled everything I saw that day…everything I felt. And after I woke up in recovery, all I could think about was Mark. What if my bone marrow doesn't take? What if it's not good enough?''

''Oh, Adam.'' She went to him then, put her arms around him and hugged him.

After a moment his arms went around her, too. ''I didn't mean to be such a bear,'' he murmured. ''I just wanted everyone to go away. I wanted to crawl into a cave and pull a boulder in front of the opening. I knew it would all pass eventually, but it's not passing quickly enough.''

Leaning away, she looked up at him. ''It won't pass if you don't talk about it. It will just gnaw at you and stay alive and resurface in the future. Isn't that what it's done since you were a kid?''

''I suppose so. But it's not easy to talk about, so I can't do it with just anyone.''

''So talk about it with me.''

He closed his eyes then and she suspected that if and when he talked about it with her, he felt vulnerable. He felt as if he were letting his guard down, and he didn't seem to want to do that.

"Even if I don't talk about it," he insisted, "I'm glad you're here. Believe it or not, having you at Cedar Run does make it all easier."

Relief flooded through her. "Good. Then I'm glad I'm here. Now would you consider taking one of those pain pills and resting?"

"You're sure that's going to help me recover faster?" he asked with some humor in his eyes now.

"I'm positive. You're in excellent condition and—"

"You've noticed that?" he asked with a smile.

She couldn't help the heat that came into her cheeks. "I've noticed."

When he took her face between his hands, he admitted, "I've been trying to stay away from you. I told you there were no strings attached to your staying here, and I don't want you to think I've changed my mind about that. But every time I'm near you, I want to kiss you."

She wanted to kiss him. He must have seen that because his lips settled on hers with demand and purpose and the intent to find some satisfaction or at least a distraction. After a long while, he broke away.

Forcing a smile, he decided, "I'm going to listen to my nurse's advice." Going over to the counter, he took out one of the vials and popped the lid.

Though Adam's words had pleased her, Leigh wondered if he could ever really let his guard down with her...if he'd ever really trust her again.

* * *

Leigh's company soothed Adam in a way nothing ever had, and he remembered again how much he'd enjoyed being with her when they were kids. He did sleep most of Saturday. On Sunday, when Leigh made a big breakfast, he found he was actually hungry. Checking his computer wasn't such a chore and he found an e-mail from Danielle, assuring him that Mark was holding his own. That was all they could expect right now. The news should have satisfied Adam, but it didn't.

To keep his mind off of Mark, Leigh played chess with Adam and watched an old movie on TV. After checking to make sure he didn't mind, she went to visit with her mother for a while.

When she left, the house felt empty. Adam found he liked having her coat hanging in the closet next to his. He liked seeing her face at breakfast. He liked hearing her sweet voice call to him from another room. Yet he knew he couldn't like any of it too much. Although kissing her was never far from his mind, he didn't act on any impulses.

By Monday Adam was feeling better but decided to work at home. He found himself looking forward to Leigh returning to the ranch after she finished at the hospital…to having supper with her. He was studying sales figures in foreign markets when she came home. Her step was light as she walked down the hall and peeked into his office.

"Busy?" she asked.

He turned away from the screen. "I can take a break. Any word on Mark?"

"Nothing's changed. I spoke with Danielle for a while, though. She's being so strong for all of them. Jared can't bear to hang around the hospital, but she feels that she can't leave. I convinced her to at least take a walk in the sunshine. When she came back, she had gotten a candy bar from a machine."

"Jared should make sure she's eating. He should be there for her."

"Everyone handles these kinds of situations differently. He's coming in tonight to spend the evening with her."

Was he judging Jared Cambry unfairly? What would he himself do in that situation?

He didn't know.

"Did you get the mail?" Leigh asked him.

"I didn't even think about it. I have to go out to feed Thunder in a little while. I can get it then." His gardener had taken care of Thunder over the weekend.

"How are you feeling?"

"Better. I didn't take pain meds today. I needed to see these figures clearly on the computer."

"They didn't affect your cognitive skills at all. You beat me at chess."

"I think that's just because I've played more often than you have. I'll be finished here shortly. I feel a lot better if I don't stay in one position too long. After Rodney took care of Thunder this morning, I told him I could handle him now."

"I think I'll walk down to the mailbox and get the mail. It's such a beautiful day and it'll help me clear my head."

"Of hospital smells?" he joked.

She gave him a weak smile. "No. We have a little girl on the ward who's not doing so well. I just need to get some distance."

"I admire the work you do," Adam said sincerely.

"I usually love it. Today was just…hard."

He might have gone to her then. He might have taken her into his arms and kissed the vestiges of the day away. But she turned quickly and headed for the living room, and he remembered what she'd said about needing distance. He felt each day they were becoming more connected. If he comforted her now, it would just be another string binding them together. They were eventually going to have to cut all those strings, and it wasn't going to feel good to do it.

Leigh took in huge lungfuls of air as she walked down the lane toward the mailbox, the end-of-the-day sun shining on her head. Tears had been too close to the surface in Adam's den and she hadn't wanted him to feel obligated to listen or to comfort.

As she walked, the wind tossed her hair, and she tried to put everything in perspective. By the time she reached the mailbox, she felt as if she'd gotten her equilibrium back, at least where Adam was concerned.

Pulling open the mailbox, she found three bills for him and a long, legal-looking envelope for her that had been forwarded. Tucking Adam's bills into the pocket of her jacket she quickly opened her envelope. Removing the letter, she unfolded it and read it quickly. She'd received a full scholarship to Case Western!

A full scholarship. That meant she wouldn't be as

tied down with loans after she graduated, though she still had those from undergrad school to pay.

She walked much more slowly up the lane than she had walked to the mailbox. Her future was unfolding. So why didn't she feel heady with excitement? Bubbling over with enthusiasm? Impatient to call her mother and tell her?

Instead of going to the house, she stopped by the corral to watch Thunder. Listening to her heart, she knew the reason the scholarship didn't bring her the joy it should have.

Adam.

While she stood at the fence, she watched Thunder run through the grass. A gust of wind caught her hood and whipped it to one side. As she made sure Adam's bills were secure in her pocket, she dropped her letter. The next gust spun it, dancing it into the corral. Believing she'd need that letter for verification of the scholarship, she hurriedly crawled through the fence into the corral.

As if it were playing a game with her, the breeze swirled the letter two feet away and then a few feet more. Finally Leigh snatched it, then raised her head to find Adam jogging toward her and calling to her.

"Get out of there, Leigh. Out of there!" His words were loud and harsh.

She wanted to tell him he shouldn't be running. He was pointing, too, and she realized he was motioning to Thunder.

Then she got it.

The corral...an unpredictable stallion...what had happened to Delia.

Glancing over her shoulder, she saw Thunder was racing toward her. Deep in her soul, she didn't think the big horse would hurt her. She'd made friends with him, gone to the barn to talk to him often. Still, she hurried the ten feet to the fence and slipped between the rungs, breathless.

"I told you never to go into the corral with Thunder unless I was with you," Adam said furiously.

The beautiful black horse came up to them at the fence, snorted, and took off again the way he had come.

"I know you did, but the wind blew my letter inside."

"I don't care what it blew inside, Leigh. The next time, you let it go. The next time, you come get me. You know what happened to Delia." Then as if he couldn't stand to remember, as if he couldn't stand to look at her and be reminded of what had happened when he was a boy, he turned and strode toward the house.

Running after him, she clasped his arm. "Adam, I'm sorry."

"Sorry wouldn't have been enough if I had to call an ambulance and a team of doctors had to put you back together again." Pulling away from her touch, he went inside and she followed.

He was in the kitchen putting on a pot of coffee to brew when she came in, took his bills from her jacket and hung the coat in the closet. Joining him in the kitchen, she laid the envelopes on the table.

Their gazes met and all the anger seemed to ebb out of Adam, replaced instead by an intense concern. Raking his hand through his thick, brown hair, he said hoarsely, "I don't want you to get hurt."

She moved closer to him and murmured, "I know you don't." She longed to touch him with the freedom of a lover, with the freedom of a woman who belonged to him, but neither applied to her. Instead she asked, "Are you hurting after that run?"

"Is that the nurse asking?"

"No, it's your friend asking." She knew they were that now, if nothing else.

Tipping her chin up with his thumb, he responded, "We've always been beyond friends, Leigh, and I've never known why."

"Some people just…connect when they meet."

"We didn't just connect, we sizzled. We still do. We sizzle when we're standing this close. We sizzle whenever I touch you."

He brushed the back of his hand down her cheek and she felt her whole body tremble.

"We sizzle when you look at me with those big, blue eyes and I just want to get lost in them."

"Oh, Adam…"

"We sizzle when my lips get anywhere near yours."

As his words became actions, the sizzle between them was a mixture of chemistry, emotion, and past history. As Adam kissed her this time, his hands passed over her breasts. Through her silky blouse and her filmy bra, his touch was fire. Her nipples hardened and her breath caught.

As if he knew exactly what was happening to her, his tongue seduced her mouth while his thumb teased her nipple. The pleasure was so excruciatingly sweet, her knees felt weak. Backed up against the counter, she was grateful for the support.

"Do you know how much you distract me?" he broke the kiss to murmur in her ear. "Do you know how much you make me forget about everything else going on?"

"Is that good?" she breathed.

"I don't know. It's never happened with anyone else."

That was the first he'd admitted that she threw him for a loop, too. It was the first he'd admitted that he thought about kissing her when they weren't together. It was the first that Adam had given her hope that he still cared for her.

But then she remembered the letter that had blown into the corral—the letter that would make the next few years easier. She couldn't tell Adam about the scholarship...not here, not now, not when they were doing this. But she couldn't keep kissing him, either, going farther, knowing she'd leave him as she had the last time. He'd hate her if she did. She just knew he would.

Breathless, dizzy from desire, wishing everything was different, she rested her hands on his chest.

That was all it took for him to back away. "What's wrong?"

"I...you...your procedure—"

"Kissing seems to make everything else feel a lot better," he assured her with a sly smile.

She wished she could believe that. She wished she could believe an affair with Adam wouldn't hurt either of them, wouldn't leave them broken, wouldn't leave them resenting each other.

"I have to get supper started. I told Mom I'd drive in tonight and help her hang the pictures she found at a flea market."

Adam's gaze was penetrating as it studied her to see if she was lying. She wasn't, though the picture hanging could have waited till another night.

Dropping his hands to his sides, turning away toward the coffeemaker, he stated, "You should have just gone there straight from the hospital. It was silly to drive the whole way out here and then drive back in."

"I wanted to check on you."

His expression now was guarded. The coffeemaker began dripping as he turned to face her. "I told you before, Leigh, it was no big deal. I don't need a private nurse."

She knew he didn't want her professional concern, but it was all she could give him tonight. "Just because you don't want it, doesn't mean you don't need it."

The tension in the kitchen seemed to suck the air out of the room. The coffee dripped, dripped, dripped. The clock on the wall ticked, ticked, ticked. Her heart pounded as she read the desire in his eyes and felt it in her own body.

When the phone rang, she jumped.

Adam looked almost relieved as he said, "I'll get it."

Picking up the cordless phone on the counter, he greeted the caller.

When Leigh went to the refrigerator to pull out ingredients to start dinner, she heard Adam say, "I'm glad Sharon decided to come." There was a pause. "I'll think about that. I'll see you on Saturday."

After Adam returned the phone to its stand, Leigh could feel his gaze on her. She put the carrots on the counter. "That was your mother?" she guessed.

"Yes, she's getting married on Saturday at three. Sharon has promised to be there. Now all I have to do is figure out what to buy them as a wedding present."

As he reached for a coffee mug and poured a cup of coffee, Leigh realized Adam wasn't going to ask her to go with him. Since she'd backed away from him, he might have decided he didn't want her in his life.

What seemed best for both of them didn't seem right.

Could she live with that?

## Chapter Twelve

On Friday after Leigh appreciatively sniffed the chili simmering in the slow cooker, she returned the lid to the crock. Before he left this morning, Adam had told her he'd be stopping to see Mark after work tonight. The chili would be ready whenever he got home.

Taking escarole and endive from the crisper drawer in the refrigerator to make a salad, she set them on the counter to prepare them for washing. She'd turned on the spigot when she remembered the load of laundry she still had to run through the dryer. She was trying to get the smell of smoke out of her clothes—the ones she'd salvaged, anyway.

She'd just turned off the spigot when the front door opened and Adam came in. One look at him told her his visit with Mark hadn't gone well. His shoulders were rigid, his jaw was set. There was a furrow across his brow that she suspected wasn't going to go away easily.

"How did it go?" she asked gently, as she watched him come through the living room.

He was wearing a khaki-colored hooded jacket today. Shrugging out of it, he tossed it over the arm of the recliner. His tan oxford shirt, with its narrow navy stripe, was open at the collar. Adam's jeans fit Adam the way jeans should fit a man. And Leigh found her heart racing as he got closer—the way it always did.

His expression was somber. "My God, Leigh. I didn't expect him to look so...so close to death. The last time I saw him he was pale and tired, but—" He crossed to the dining area.

"He *was* near death, Adam, but he's coming back now. His body's fighting to make him well." Although Marietta had explained the process Mark would go through—the isolation, the special room—Leigh knew no one was really prepared to deal with it.

"I had to wear a mask and gloves and a gown. I felt as if I shouldn't be there...as if I were using the family's time."

"You *are* family, Adam. You saved his life."

"Not yet. If the transplant doesn't take, if he gets an infection—" Adam rubbed the back of his neck "—then there's no justice in this world. There's no fairness. It makes me wonder why we're here—"

She couldn't help but take Adam's hand. "Look at the joy Mark has already brought into your life."

Closing his eyes, Adam took a deep breath. "If he dies…"

Leigh had never been more aware of her deep feelings for Adam. Without hesitation she wrapped her arms around him and held on tight. He stiffened. But after a few seconds he enfolded her in his embrace, too. Their hearts beat in unison.

Adam still smelled of the outdoors. With his strength surrounding her, she could admit to herself how much she wanted him…had always wanted him. When she looked up at him, he gazed down at her with a hungry intensity that rocked her soul. There was a deeper need there, and male desire that wouldn't be eased with a few kisses.

As he dropped his arms, he said, "If I don't let you go now, we'll end up in my bedroom."

Although she released him, too, her eyes stayed on his. "Maybe it's time we gave into this. Maybe it's time we grab what we can now."

"You're not the type of woman who has an affair."

"No, I'm not. At least, not just with any man. But with you… I want to feel you again, Adam. I want to touch your skin and let you touch mine."

"Leigh."

His voice was a sharp warning, and she knew her words were as arousing as anything else they might do. Somehow she managed, "I've missed you, Adam." It had taken her this long to realize the emptiness inside of her had always been her loss of Adam. No other man had come close to filling up that space.

"If I touch you—" His hand stopped in midair.

"Touch me," she whispered.

Instead of touching her, he kissed her. His hand laced in her hair, holding her head, making sure she understood his need as his lips first took hers, and then his tongue invaded her mouth. Suddenly she understood the restraint and self-control he'd exhibited for the past few weeks, and she gave herself up to Adam's need, as well as her own. There was a depth to this kiss that she'd never felt from Adam before. She responded as she'd always wanted to respond—with her whole being.

They couldn't seem to get enough of each other. His hands pulled her T-shirt from her leggings as he kept kissing her. Through the sensual haze, she remembered she wanted to stroke him, too, and her fingers went to his shirt buttons. But their arms were getting all tangled up. They couldn't seem to keep kissing and get undressed, too.

Finally Adam swept her down the hall with him to his bedroom, kissing her the whole way. His bed was the closest piece of furniture. Somehow she found herself kneeling on the edge, staring up at him, unbuttoning his shirt.

Stilling her hands, he said, "Wait." Then he pulled her T-shirt up and over her head.

Adam's buttons took no time at all, but his expression told her he thought it took forever. When she finished, she moved her hands from his belt, up through the soft curly hair to his nipples.

When Adam groaned, she smiled.

"You're having too much fun." His voice was dark, husky, promising her the same fun she was giving him.

Reaching behind her, he unfastened her bra. Then with deliberate, studied slowness, he eased the straps down her arms, finally tossing the filmy fabric away. Taking her breasts into his hands, he let her nipples graze his palms. Then he did it again. Fireworks shot through her, sparking here, there and everywhere, causing small fires to light into a larger one that became her desire as well as Adam's. After he shrugged off his shirt, he sat down on the bed. Without warning, his lips surrounded her nipple. She thought she'd swoon from the pleasure of it.

His hands were tugging at her leggings and panties and soon she was lying on the bed, naked. She heard the clank of his belt buckle as he unfastened it, the rasp of his zipper as he skated it down. Then he was beside her, as naked as she was...as ready for their union as he had ever been. They needed to reaffirm life. They needed to know there was a reason for them being on this earth.

"Oh, Adam," she sighed, as she wrapped her hand around him, making him shudder with the intimate caress.

While they lay there face-to-face, Adam kissed her again, caressing her breasts, sliding his large hand down her hip, eventually slipping it between her thighs.

"Protection, Leigh. Are you on anything?"

"No. Do you have—"

Instead of answering her, he reached in the nightstand drawer, jerked it open and pulled out a foil packet. Then, apparently knowing what she was thinking and wondering, he admitted, "There have been a few women, Leigh. But I've always used protection. I've never taken any chances. Not with pregnancy. Not with anything else.''

If she could believe anyone in this world, it was Adam. Of course he'd had other women. Of course he'd gone on with his life.

At her silence, he tipped up her chin and looked into her eyes. ''We can still stop.''

She knew Adam *could* stop...*would* stop...because that was the kind of man he was. ''I don't want you to stop.''

''Those are golden words,'' he rasped close to her ear.

As he sucked her earlobe, she became so restless she couldn't keep still. Her hands searched his body for a place to land...a place to caress...a place to do to him what he was doing to her. They gave and took pleasure...gave and shared kisses...gave and caressed each other's bodies until they glistened with their desire.

When Adam tore open the foil packet, she asked, ''Can I do it?''

''You've grown bolder over the years,'' he teased with a smile.

''Maybe. Or maybe I know more about foreplay now.''

His eyebrows arched, and he laughed. ''From what you've read in books, of course.''

''Of course,'' she repeated so innocently that he had to kiss her before he let her apply the condom.

As she rolled the condom onto him with the teasing pleasure of a true courtesan, he sucked in a breath.

Then he took her hands, held them under his beside her head and muttered, "Foreplay be damned."

When Adam thrust into her, Leigh met his demand for satisfaction with a cry of pleasure. After that, she was sure she entered another realm. With each thrust she became more united with Adam. Her joy came from more than physical ecstasy, as he sent her spiraling from one peak to the next, each successively higher, each promising so much more. She teetered on the edge of erotic sensation for what seemed like forever, until suddenly she was climaxing, stars bursting all around her.

Adam cried his release.

Leigh loved Adam's weight on top of her...loved being able to nibble at his shoulder...loved licking the salt from his skin.

"Keep doing that, and we'll have to start all over," he mumbled into her neck.

"Would that be so bad?" she asked, wondering if he now had regrets, wondering if he'd landed back on earth as fast as she had.

Where before Adam had been joking, now he raised himself on his elbows and said seriously, "Not bad. But maybe not good for us, either. Maybe now we've gotten this out of our systems."

His expression was unreadable and his guard was firmly back in place. She knew she had to be the one to take the risk. "I don't think it's that simple. I'm not sure you and I could ever get enough."

Adam's expression didn't change as he rolled onto his back, stared up at the ceiling, then pushed himself up and sat on the edge of the bed. "I'll be right back while you think about what tonight means."

As he disappeared into the bathroom, Leigh wondered just what he *was* thinking about. She found out when he returned a few minutes later.

Standing by the edge of the bed, he concluded, "We know where we stand this time, Leigh. We have a little over two months until you leave. It's up to us to decide what to do with it. Your plans haven't changed, have they?"

He was asking her if tonight had changed anything, and it had. It had made her aware of how serious she was about him. It had made her wonder if her dreams were *her* dreams or if they were her mother's. It had made her think about a medical degree and what that would mean for her future. "I received a full scholarship," she said softly. "That was the letter that blew into Thunder's corral."

Perfectly still, he looked away and then met her gaze again. "You're fortunate. Now you won't be in debt for years."

"I still have undergrad loans to pay. But it will make everything easier."

She could see he wouldn't ask her about the two of them. He wouldn't ask her to give up her plans. He wouldn't ask her to have an affair with him until she left. But that's what she was going to do.

Sitting up, she took in the taut muscles of Adam's shoulders, his washboard stomach, his tall, wonderfully built body. Just looking at him made her quiver inside, and she wasn't going to give this up. She wasn't going to give *him* up. Not yet.

Taking hold of all the courage she had ever possessed, all she might ever possess, she asked, "Would you rather sleep alone, or would you like company?"

The green lights in his eyes told her what his answer would be before he said, "I'd like the company, if *you're* the company."

"I'm it." She tried to keep her voice light.

Lowering himself to the bed, he bent to kiss her.

Leigh let thoughts of the future and consequences burn away as their passion consumed them once more.

Pleased that Adam had asked her to go along to his mother's wedding, Leigh had dressed carefully, even though she knew the ceremony would be somewhat casual. She'd managed to salvage an emerald-green dress with a flared skirt and a short cropped jacket. After a few washings and a long ironing it looked good. Adam's expression when he saw her in it told her she'd chosen well.

The justice of the peace was located in a small house. John and Peggy had decided to get married in Portland, go out for a nice lunch afterward, then spend the night in a motel. Adam told her his mother hadn't stayed overnight anywhere—away from the farm—in years.

As the justice of the peace's wife introduced herself at the door, Leigh smiled and followed Chloe Wagner to a prettily decorated room with metal folding chairs and a white lectern. She couldn't help thinking about last night.

And this morning. She and Adam couldn't seem to get enough of each other. After they'd made love the first time, they'd done it again. Finally they'd eaten supper. But dessert had turned into desire and they'd gone back to bed. Eventually cuddling and falling asleep, they'd awakened hungry for each other again. Now whenever Adam looked at her, she knew what he was thinking. He was wishing they were back in bed. So was she.

After Mrs. Wagner left them in the wedding room, she went to answer the doorbell's peel.

Leigh asked Adam, "Are you sure your mom won't mind me coming?"

"I'm positive. She told me to bring a guest to make the occasion more festive. At the time I didn't think I would."

She knew what he meant. There had been so much tension between them before. After last night...

When Peggy Bartlett, soon to be Pavlichek, entered the small room with her fiancé and her daughter, Leigh recognized her immediately. The past ten years showed, but today, in her mauve suit, with an orchid corsage on her lapel and her wide smile, she looked as happy as any bride should look. When she saw Adam and Leigh, her green eyes opened wider.

She didn't hesitate to come toward them. "Leigh Peters?" she asked.

"Yes, ma'am. I hope you don't mind that Adam brought me along."

"Of course I don't mind." She motioned to her fiancé. "Come here, John. There's someone I want you to meet."

Sharon trailed behind the man who would soon be her stepfather. Leigh felt sorry for her. Adam had told

Leigh everything Sharon had said. His stepsister wasn't exactly frowning now, but she didn't look happy, either.

After introductions were made, Peggy turned to John. "Leigh and Adam were friends in high school. More than friends, I think." She sent Adam a knowing smile.

Before Adam could respond, John took him off the hook.

John Pavlichek was a big, burly man with a butterscotch shock of hair and a matching beard. Today he looked uncomfortable in his suit. But his tie was perfectly tied and his trousers meticulously creased. "That stove for your mother was a perfect wedding present. We couldn't have asked for anything nicer. She told me when we get back to the farm, she's going to start cooking up a storm."

Addressing Leigh, he explained, "It's one of those smooth-topped ranges. That oven's big enough for a twenty-pound turkey!"

Although she and Adam had discussed wedding presents briefly the night he'd received the call about the wedding, he hadn't told her what he'd decided. It seemed he'd chosen the perfect present, and a generous one, too. But she'd seen that generosity before— with Mark and with Shawna.

The justice of the peace entered then. He was a tall, thin man with almost no hair. After he made sure the paperwork was in order, he asked, "Shall we get started?"

As Sharon sat beside Leigh during the short ceremony, Leigh thought she saw a tear come to the woman's eyes when her mother made her promises. Leigh could only imagine what was going through her head.

Leigh had never known her own father. Honestly, she'd never wanted to know him, from what her mother had told her. Yet in many ways, she guessed he was like Jared Cambry. As a teenager he'd been afraid of responsibility, and he'd taken off for parts unknown rather than deal with the girl he had gotten pregnant and her unborn child. Years later her mother had heard through the grapevine that he'd been killed in a motorcycle accident. When Leigh learned of it, she had felt lost, even though the man had never been in her life. It was hard to imagine what losing a parent would actually be like.

Her mother had done so much for her over the years....

The vows Peggy and John took resonated with Leigh, and she could imagine saying them with Adam. She could actually see herself doing that. But as soon as the scene played in her mind, she switched it off. That wasn't where she and Adam were headed. His life was here in Portland, where he had grown a business, where he now had a family that seemed to become larger each day. She would be in Ohio. Long-distance relationships didn't work. She knew that. She also knew her hours would be long and not leave free time for even letter writing, let alone commutes home.

The ceremony ended and Mr. and Mrs. Wagner bestowed on the couple all of their good wishes. Leigh watched as Adam congratulated John and his mother.

It seemed there had been some healing there. At least, they all seemed at peace with the past.

Except for Sharon.

She was wearing tan slacks and an off-white blouse, and Leigh wanted to tell her she'd look so much more attractive in colors. Yet she knew the woman probably wouldn't listen or want anyone else's advice.

Adam made it clear that lunch after the ceremony was on him. He'd made reservations at one of Portland's finest restaurants, and Peggy's eyes glistened when he told her. "You didn't have to do that," she mumbled.

"I *wanted* to do that," Adam assured her.

A half hour later they were seated at a round table covered with a pale gray tablecloth. The silverware shone and the crystal sparkled.

They were eating their salads when Peggy asked Leigh, "Where do you work?"

"At Portland General. That's how Adam and I reconnected again...when he became the donor for Mark Cambry's transplant."

"There was an article in the paper about that yesterday," John reminded Peggy.

"Yes," she agreed. "Did you see it?"

Adam exchanged a glance with Leigh. With everything that was happening in their lives, she didn't think he'd even opened the paper in the past few days.

"I didn't see it," Adam admitted, and Leigh shook her head, indicating she hadn't, either. "Why would an article about that be in the paper?" he asked.

"Mr. Cambry is important in this community. And so are you. They talked about how Mr. Cambry's family wasn't a match. Then they wrote about you being his son. They quoted his daughter, Shawna, several times.''

''Maybe she picked up the phone when the reporter called,'' Leigh suggested, knowing how open Shawna was. ''I can't imagine Jared and Danielle giving out that information.'' She knew how Adam hated publicity, but this shouldn't affect him. His receptionist could always field calls he didn't want to handle.

''What work do you do at the hospital?'' Peggy asked, going back to her original question.

''I'm a nurse in the oncology unit. But that will be changing in June. I'll be attending med school.''

''Here?'' Peggy asked.

''No,'' Adam answered for her. ''In Ohio. She has a full scholarship. She has always dreamed of being a doctor, and now that dream is going to come true.''

He said it matter-of-factly, as if he were reminding himself of all of those facts. Although last night had been wonderful, although they'd talked about grabbing the moment and living in the present, she knew Adam. At some point he'd want to protect himself against the pain of her leaving. He'd shut down and close her out. She was sure of it.

''I'm going to be changing a few things in *my* life, too.'' Sharon had been quiet during lunch and it was the first time she had spoken.

''What kind of things?'' Adam asked, giving her his full attention.

''I applied for a promotion to manage the back claims department. I've been thinking about it for some time. I didn't really want to leave the group of people I'm working with in the intake division, but the salary's better. I'd also have another week's vacation.''

''Those are advantages,'' Adam agreed. ''Would you like the work as well as what you're doing now?''

''I think so. It would be less customer service, more of a supervisory position.''

''When will you know if you got it?'' Adam asked.

''I should know by the end of next week. But in the meantime—'' she exchanged a glance with her mother ''—I'm going to be looking at apartments.''

''I told her she doesn't have to move out,'' Peggy said quietly.

''We've both told her that,'' John agreed, letting Adam know this wasn't his doing.

''Yes, you've both told me that,'' Sharon admitted. ''But you two need your privacy. And I think it's time I…try living on my own.'' Then she gave Adam a glance that was a bit defiant but filled with pride, too.

After that, no controversial subjects arose. It was a pleasant lunch, and when Leigh and Adam drove back to the ranch, she thought he looked relieved.

''Your mom and John seemed pleased with the way the day went,'' Leigh commented. ''They seem happy together.''

''I wonder if they got married because it was practical for both of them. Mom is getting older and needs a man around the house. John… Well, he'll have the obvious advantages. Sex. Home-cooked meals.''

''I think it's more than a practical marriage,'' Leigh protested. ''I saw the way he looked at her, and the way she looked at him. I think they're really in love.

When John took her hands so gently in his, when he said his vows so fervently, it seemed he'd found someone he'd needed all his life. It's more than a practical arrangement,'' she said with certainty this time.

"You're a romantic,'' Adam said with a slight smile.

She'd never thought of herself in that way, but maybe she was.

As Adam drove up Cedar Run's lane to the house, they both spotted the silver sedan parked in the driveway.

"Are you expecting anyone?'' Leigh asked.

"No. I don't think it would be Lissa and Sullivan. They'd call before they drove up here.''

"Unless they wanted to surprise you.''

However, when Adam pulled up beside the car, they could see a man, a stranger, sitting inside.

Adam motioned to the man that he was going to pull into the garage and go around to the door. Then he pressed the remote.

A few minutes later Adam opened his front door. "Can I help you?'' he asked the stranger.

Waiting near the sofa in the living room, Leigh wondered if this visitor could possibly be here for her. Not that she was expecting anyone, either.

The man was dressed in a button-down shirt and casual slacks. He was about five-eight, looked to be in his mid-thirties and kept pushing his glasses up higher on his nose. "Adam Bartlett?'' he asked.

"Yes.''

"My name's Randy Seneft. I'm with *Breaking News* on the PQF network. Could we talk?''

After only a moment's hesitation, Adam stepped back and let the man inside.

Seneft glanced over at Leigh and then smiled at Adam. "One of our producers saw the article in the paper yesterday…about you and Jared Cambry and the bone marrow transplant. We think it's a wonderful story and want to do a live interview as soon as possible. What do you say? Will you do the show live with us for millions of people to see?"

## Chapter Thirteen

"I'm not doing a live interview. I'm not doing *any* kind of interview."

Leigh watched Adam's face harden as he realized exactly what the associate producer wanted.

On one hand, she knew Adam hated the idea of his life being opened for all to see. On the other, she knew the donor registry always needed publicity. The more people who signed up, the more lives could be saved. "You know, maybe you should hear him out," she suggested softly.

The bond that had been established between them last night seemed fragile now as his gaze met hers and she knew he wondered why she was even suggesting it.

"Yes, Mr. Bartlett, maybe you should hear me out.

Or at least hear what I'm proposing.'' The producer hurried on so Adam didn't have a chance to stop him. ''We'd like to do the interview at the hospital. I've already gotten Dr. Chambers's okay. We'll show a videotape of Mark—or run a local station's coverage of his soccer games, explaining his condition and what he's gone through. But the other aspect of this we'd like to explore is how Mr. Cambry found you, and of course your part in all this. I understand there was also a reunion with a twin sister, Lissa Cartright Grayson.''

''That's exactly what I don't want,'' Adam snapped. ''Being put on display for the public to see. Forget it, Mr. Seneft, I'm not interested.'' Adam opened the door wide so the man would leave.

As if he was playing his trump card, the producer stated, ''Mr. Cambry has already agreed to this interview and so has his family. They want to tell other parents that there's hope.''

''We don't even know if the transplant took yet,'' Adam said, clearly angry now.

''I understand that. But that's what makes this a good story. The public will follow it—follow Mark's progress.''

''And you don't give a hoot if everything turns out all right or not. You don't care if Mark lives or dies, as long as you get ratings.''

The producer shook his head. ''Ah, Mr. Bartlett. You want to think the media is made up of heartless souls who are only interested in the story and the public's response to it. That's simply not true. Of course we care. We want Mark to make it. And think of all the people he'll have praying for him.''

"That's low," Adam growled. "If you and the Cambrys want to do the story, that's fine. But I won't have any part of it."

Quickly, before Adam could push him out the door, Mr. Seneft took a card from his pocket and shoved it into Adam's hand. "I realize the idea of an interview has all come as a surprise to you, but I want you to think this over. We're planning the taping for Tuesday night. All you have to do is give me a call to tell me if you want to join us."

Adam remained stonily silent.

"Mr. Bartlett, I really think this would just make a heartwarming story. You trying to save a little boy's life. A family reunited. Please think about it."

After a last look at Adam's set expression, the producer turned and left.

As Leigh sat down on the sofa, she could hear the producer drive away. There was so much she wanted to say, yet this was Adam's decision. He had his reasons for wanting to keep his life private. Still...

He was studying her now. After a last look to make sure Seneft was gone, he crossed the room. "Say what you have to say, Leigh. I know there's something on your mind."

Ever since they first met, Adam could read her. Sometimes that was unsettling. When she searched for the right words to use, he shook his head. "Just say it, Leigh. You're talking to me, not one of your patients."

Tact was a part of her profession, and she realized now he didn't want that. He wanted honesty. "All right. I think this is your chance to foster the donor

transplant registry. To get the word out. To bring people in. You're giving up the opportunity before you
even look at what it could do.''

As he shook his head, he lowered himself to the
sofa on the cushion beside her. ''I don't want my life
laid out for everybody to see. I don't want to have to
relive it. I know exactly what will happen if I agree
to this. It won't be the cut-and-dried human interest
story that producer says it will be. They'll sensation-
alize everything. They'll cut and paste and edit until
it looks exactly like they *want* it to look.''

''Do you watch *Breaking News?*''

''No. I've never seen it. I don't have much time or
taste for network TV, for the reasons I just told you.''

''*Breaking News* isn't like some of the other news
segment programs. It's in very good taste. I read an
article in the Sunday paper on how they put the show
together. They look for good, human-interest stories
that don't make national news, but yet carry a load of
impact for the viewing public. They focus on the lives
of whomever's involved, and how the event or the
situation has impacted them. It's about people more
than about the story. I'm sure both you and Jared
would have a say in where you want the focus.''

Adam stared at the dark screen of the television, as
if he was imagining all of it on there, and he didn't
like any of what he saw. ''Publicity can so easily get
out of hand. It's the last thing I want. Even when
Novel Programs, Unlimited's, stock went public, I
stayed in the background and let Dylan lead the pa-
rade. I did it for a very good reason. I didn't want
reporters poking into my life. They'll bother Mom and

John. They might even dig up something on Owen. No one wants to be exposed. I just don't like the whole idea of it. You're the one who wants to save lives. Sometimes I just want to go back to the way my life was before all of this started.''

There was an underlying message in Adam's tone. The past month had caused nothing but upheaval in his life, and he didn't like it. Although he might be grateful Shawna and Mark were in his life now, and Lissa too, he didn't know where any of it was going to lead. Jared hadn't welcomed him as a son into his family with open arms, and since the transplant was over and done, Adam might feel as if he were no longer necessary.

Resurrecting the relationship she and Adam once had and getting involved again hadn't been wise on either of their parts, and yet she didn't regret it. Maybe *he* did.

''Are you sorry I became your liaison? Are you sorry last night happened?''

''Last night happened because we decided to give in to the chemistry between us, and later be damned. But later's going to come, Leigh. I know it, and you know it. If you thought writing me that note was tough, imagine how you're going to feel when you take off for Cleveland.''

Pushing himself up from the sofa, he added, ''Or maybe it won't be any more difficult than the last time. Maybe you let last night happen because you knew that.''

Her heart ached because he was implying she didn't care as much as he did. He was implying that an affair was easy for her, that it wasn't going to tear her apart when they had to say goodbye. She couldn't even find the words to respond. She found all of her feelings were clogging her throat, and she couldn't get even one of them out.

When he rose to his feet, he avoided her gaze. "I'm going to change and then take Thunder for a ride. Rain is rolling in again tonight and I want to take him for a good workout."

She just nodded, overwhelmed with the enormity of leaving Adam again...overwhelmed with the enormity of chasing a dream that she wasn't sure was hers anymore.

The guard in the lobby of the building where Novel Programs, Unlimited, was located nodded to Adam as he let the glass doors shut behind him on the following afternoon. The overcast, gray sky outside fit Adam's mood. Ever since that producer had turned up on his doorstep last night...

Tony Pasqual, sitting behind his desk in his security uniform, gave Adam a wide-toothed grin. "This is a busy place for a Sunday."

That wasn't what Adam wanted to hear. The tension between him and Leigh since their discussion last night hadn't abated. She'd slept in the guest room. That wasn't what he'd wanted. But after their conversation last evening, his pride had kept him silent when she'd told him that's what she was going to do. Their night in bed together had been a denial of reality. Grabbing the moment in the dark of night had seemed like a good philosophy…until they'd looked at it in the light of day.

Do you really want to go back to life as you knew it before Jared's visit? he asked himself.

He'd meant every word he'd said to her last night. Looking at Leigh, the twist of the knife in his gut when he thought about her leaving, had pushed him to answer her as he had. This morning after a ride on Thunder that hadn't helped at all, after Leigh had made brunch and they'd forced conversation, after thinking about Mark isolated in that sterile hospital atmosphere, Adam had decided work would be his salvation today.

But he'd wanted to work alone, and he hoped anybody else Tony had signed in was working on another floor.

The guard turned the log book to face Adam.

Picking up the pen, Adam scrawled his name, the date and the time, seeing that Dylan and Darlene were signed in before him. Terrific.

"So you've had traffic already today?" he asked.

"You could say that. On your floor, anyway. Mr. Montgomery and Miss Allen said that they had correspondence to catch up on that had backed up last week."

Dylan had flown to Chicago earlier in the week and had been tied up in meetings at the end of it. Apparently, he'd enlisted Darlene's help in catching up.

As Adam took the elevator to the fifteenth floor, he realized he hadn't helped Dylan with his problem with Darlene. On the other hand, Adam didn't know what he could do. He wasn't having a problem with his secretary, Dylan was. It had been more than three weeks since his partner had voiced his concerns. Maybe the whole thing had blown over, or Dylan had brought it out into the open.

Bringing everything out into the open wasn't always the best idea, either. Look at what happened when he and Leigh had finally admitted and acted on what was going on between them. Last night Adam's bed had never felt more empty. Last night he'd wished the past had stayed in the past—along with his desire for Leigh.

Fluorescent lights buzzed overhead, shedding their white glow into the hall as Adam stepped from the elevator. The sky looked even grayer out of the windows up here. He wished he'd put Thunder into his stall instead of leaving him in the corral.

Adam stopped for a moment before the glass doors stenciled with Novel Programs, Unlimited's, bold lettering and logo. He had made his work his life until the past few weeks. Hadn't his course been a lot less bumpy that way?

When he stepped into the wine, cream and black reception area, he wasn't surprised not to find Darlene at her desk. If she and Dylan were going over the minutes of last week's meetings and connected paperwork, they'd be in Dylan's office. Better to stop in and make conversation now, rather than to get interrupted later. Once he closed his office door, he didn't want to be disturbed.

The wine-and-black tweed carpeting muffled his footsteps as he made his way to Dylan's office. He heard the sound of Darlene's light laughter, the baritone of Dylan's voice. But as he came to Dylan's office and pushed open the ajar door, he felt like an intruder into a Sunday-afternoon matinee. Dylan was in his office, but he wasn't working. He was sitting in his oversized leather chair with Darlene on his lap! Darlene's hair was mussed, her lipstick smeared, and the buttons of her blouse were open. They both started like guilty teenagers when they saw him.

Adam could have backed out. He could have mumbled an excuse and left. He could have pretended he didn't see what he saw. But he liked Darlene. She was a good secretary, and he didn't want to lose her. If Dylan was just fooling around...

"Have I interrupted something?" he asked, with the nonchalance that widened both pairs of eyes that were on him.

As Darlene tried to scramble away from Dylan's lap, the CFO kept her still. "Don't go anywhere," he mumbled to her as he pulled her blouse together and held the material in his fist. "Adam, if you could give us a minute," Dylan said in a patient tone.

"I think you need more than a minute for what you were into. At least I *hope* so."

A dark flush crept up Dylan's neck. "This isn't what you think."

Now Darlene managed to hike herself off Dylan's lap, quickly buttoned the buttons of her yellow cotton shirt, then shakily ran a hand through her brown hair. Her face had paled.

Squaring her shoulders, she said to Adam, "Mr. Bartlett, I...I'm sorry you found me in this unprofessional…position. I like working for you, and I promise if you keep me on, it won't happen again.''

Dylan was out of his chair in a shot. ''What do you mean it won't happen again? We're dating. Of course it's going to happen again.''

Adam had never seen his friend quite so rattled. ''Darlene, this is Sunday. Your time's your own. I'm not going to fire you. But maybe you could give me a few minutes with Dylan?''

Avoiding Adam's gaze, as well as Dylan's, she skittered to the door. ''I'll be out at my desk.''

''Darlene,'' Dylan commanded, as if he didn't want her to leave.

She said again, ''I'll be at my desk.''

The silence that enveloped the office had never been quite so tense between the two friends. Finally Adam broke it. ''Do you think that's wise?''

''Don't act like a big brother,'' Dylan muttered. ''And don't talk to me about wise, when you have your high school sweetheart living at the ranch and you know she'll be history again in a couple of months.''

Uh-oh. Dylan was on the offensive. For a guy who was usually placid, he seemed undeniably unnerved. Adam didn't take the bait. ''Darlene's a nice woman, Dylan. I'd hate to see her get hurt. She's the one who might be too uncomfortable staying here if you decide Natalie fits your lifestyle better.''

''Natalie's gone. She and I were never…compatible.''

''And you and Darlene are?''

''It might not look like it, but yes, we are. We both went to parochial school.''

Adam raised a brow.

Dylan's hand slashed through the air defensively. "It impacted her more than it impacted me, but the point is we have similar backgrounds. She has as much energy as I do. She's a night owl who can get up at 5:00 a.m. if she has to. She's terrific fun. When I talked to her about the letters, she offered to resign. You were right. She was having a problem with them because she was trying to make them perfect. She admitted she liked me."

Adam smiled at the surprise in Dylan's voice. "You're a likeable guy."

Dylan shook his head. "I mean it, Adam. She likes me for me, not because I'm CFO of this company, not because I drive a Jaguar, and not because I can fly her to Hawaii for the weekend and the cost won't dent my bank account. We've seen each other almost every night for the past week, and all she wants to do is cuddle in front of the TV and eat popcorn with me."

Adam gave Dylan a skeptical look.

"As opposed to having dinner in a five-star restaurant," Dylan explained. "That's what I like about her. No pretense. No edge. And I find that I like staying in with her."

That statement, above all others, impacted Adam. He knew Darlene was a sincere, honest, hardworking young woman. It seemed as if she'd gotten to his partner in a big way.

"Are you telling me this is serious?"

"More serious than *I've* ever been."

"Maybe she should just work as *my* secretary and

you should hire another one. Then, if things don't work out, it might not be so awkward.''

"I'd rather keep her as *our* secretary and think that things *will* work out. Where's your optimism, Adam?''

Adam looked away from his friend and out into the gray sky. "My optimism is in a nosedive right now.''

"Things not working out with trying to be 'just friends' with the former lover?''

Dylan was entirely too perceptive. Adam wasn't about to spill his guts, or admit how unsettled he was about Leigh and everything else that had happened. "This is where I leave.'' He moved toward the door.

"You can poke into my life, but I can't poke into yours?''

"That sounds like a good policy,'' Adam joked.

Dylan shook his head. "One of these days, you're going to realize that all of those safety fences you've built around yourself don't do one bit of good. They might keep people out, but they don't prevent you from feeling what goes on inside.''

"You've missed your calling. You should host a talk show.''

"And you, my friend, need to get honest with yourself.''

Unsure of exactly what Dylan meant, Adam didn't respond. He left Dylan's office, crossed to his and shut the door. The computer beckoned to him, and he liked the familiarity of it. Right now, he liked the idea of losing himself in cyberspace and shutting everything else out.

If Adam thought he could lose himself in cyberspace, three hours later he knew he couldn't. He'd skipped from one project to another all afternoon. None of them kept his attention for very long. All of his thoughts kept coming back to Leigh and Mark and Jared Cambry.

Dylan had stopped in an hour ago and said he and Darlene were leaving. Now, in the silent office building, Adam heard a sound that was unusual for this time of year. The grumble of thunder. Rain was part and parcel of Portland's charm. Once in a while, storms rolled in from the mountains, but that was rare for the end of March. Weather patterns had seemed to change over the past few years, though.

Staring out the window, he thought he saw a flash of lightning. Damn! And Thunder was out in the corral. He didn't like the idea of the horse getting spooked. With the door of his stall open, he could go inside. But *would* he?

Adam shook his head. Sometimes animals didn't know what was good for them any better than humans did.

What was good for *him?* Adam wondered. He simply didn't know anymore.

Fifteen minutes later, flashes of lightning occurred more often as Adam drove home, his foot heavy on the accelerator. Darkness had fallen, and rain was pouring down by the time he had parked in the garage. Lights were turned on in the house, but he couldn't find Leigh anywhere. Lightning cracked, sounding as if it had hit something close by, then thunder rolled over the dining room skylight, threatening and loud. Leigh's car was in the driveway. Going to the foyer

closet, he found her jacket missing. She wouldn't have
gone to the barn. She wouldn't have…

Without even thinking about stopping to grab his
coat, Adam raced outside, across the yard and lane to
the corral. He couldn't believe his eyes. Under the
forceful white glare of the barn's floodlight, he could
see Leigh had her hood up, buttoned around her face,
and was carrying a lead rope in her hand as she made
her way toward Thunder. The stallion stood at the far
end of the corral under the shelter of two maple trees.
Before Adam could move, Leigh was hurrying across
the corral. All he could think about was the day Delia
had opened the gate…had stepped inside—

Lightning seemed to strike a nearby fence. Great
rolls of thunder boomed as Leigh approached the
horse. Thunder reared up, and Adam was moving over
the fence in a leap, then proceeding at a dead run
across the corral. Lightning flashed as Adam relived
the day when he was seven—every emotion, every
fear, every regret. The memories seemed so terrify-
ingly real that when he peered through the rain and
saw Leigh was out of harm's way, he almost couldn't
believe it.

Thunder reared up again, and Adam was afraid she
wouldn't be as lucky the second time…afraid he
couldn't reach her before the unthinkable happened.

Unaware of anything but what she was doing, Leigh
waited until Thunder was on all four hooves again,
then she grabbed his halter, hooking on the lead.

Her hood slipped from her head, and rain washed
down over her hair as lightning lit up the sky a
third time.

Adam reached her and yanked the lead rope from her hand. "What the hell are you doing out here?" he yelled. "Get into the barn. Get away from a horse that could trample you down with one hoof."

"I couldn't leave him out here."

"Get into the barn!" he commanded again and waited until she ran toward the shelter. Then he patted Thunder's neck and ran with the horse into his stall.

Leigh was standing on the inside walkway, and Adam didn't say a word as he unhooked the lead, closed the outside stall entrance and climbed over the fence, landing beside her. Adrenaline was still rushing through him, hard and fast.

He was so furious with her, language didn't come easily. "You could have been killed." The words sounded gritty and harsh. He was soaked and she wasn't much better, but he didn't care about that right now.

"I know how much he means to you," she said, her eyes huge. "I didn't want anything to happen to him. When the storm turned severe, I didn't know what to do. I didn't know when you'd be home because you didn't tell me. You didn't call."

He hadn't told her because he hadn't known. He hadn't called because he hadn't known what to say to her. Now all he could say again was, "You could have gotten yourself killed."

Swiping drops of rain from her face, she looked angry, too, as she returned, "People who care do things because they're right, no matter what the risk."

"Do what's right? You don't want to do what's right, Leigh. You want to do what's convenient. You don't want to do what's right, you want to hang on to a dream that's as old as you are. Is *that* right?''

She took a shaky breath. "It is for *me*. Don't you see this is exactly what I was trying to avoid ten years ago when I wrote you that note? Don't you see it would have been that much harder if we had stayed together?''

"So you took the easy way out? No courage or risk there." He shook his head, knowing what he had to say, but not wanting to say it. He didn't want her to leave, but she was going to go anyway. "You're the one who broke us apart once before, and you're the one who's going to do it again. So maybe we should both take the easy way out. We might as well just end this now."

He spotted the quick glitter of tears before Leigh turned away. He saw the quiver of her chin right before she ran out of the barn.

But he didn't go after her. There was no reason to. She had made up her mind ten years ago, and he was old news. *They* were old news.

Going to the tack room, he picked up a towel to wipe down Thunder, denying the pain in his heart, the tightness in his throat and the burning behind his eyes.

## Chapter Fourteen

It was seven o'clock Monday morning when the phone rang. Leigh was getting dressed, trying to find something in her suitcase on the sofa that didn't need to be ironed. Since her mother was in the shower, she ran for the phone in the kitchen, using every bit of energy she had. She hadn't slept all night. She missed Adam more than she could say. Everything that had happened with Thunder and afterward had plagued her throughout the night as she'd rolled it all over in her head.

Now she tried to shake herself awake as she picked up the phone, hoping desperately it was Adam. Maybe they could work things out. Maybe she could fly to Portland and he could fly to Cleveland. Maybe the hours wouldn't be as grueling as she imagined. Maybe—

The phone rang insistently again and she picked it up. "Hello."

"Miss Peters? It's Jared Cambry."

She tried to find her professional voice. "Hello, Mr. Cambry."

"I didn't know if you'd be at this number or not. I couldn't reach either of the numbers you gave me, and when I called information, they listed this one for your mother."

"Yes, I'm sorry I didn't call you with the new number. There was a fire at our apartment and I…I was staying somewhere else for a while. I lost my cell phone in the fire and haven't gotten another one yet. What can I do for you?"

"I have a request. I was speaking to Mr. Seneft, the producer for *Breaking News*. He told me he spoke to you and Adam."

"Yes, he did. Adam turned down the interview."

"Yes, I know that. This morning I'm going to try to convince him to change his mind. But even if he doesn't, I'd like you to take part. Marietta Watson will be away next week. She won't be able to explain the transplant process on air. We'd also like to promote the donor registry. You're knowledgeable about both of those things. I wondered if you'd consider doing the interview."

"Adam was concerned everything would be sensationalized."

"I know. The producer told me that. But I have Seneft's guarantee that everything will go exactly as we script it. This won't be tabloid news, Miss Peters. You'll have a real chance to get the word out about the good work that's being done. What do you say?''

"Do you think you can convince Adam to do the interview?''

There was silence on the other end of the line for a few seconds. "I don't know. I haven't handled very well anything else where he's concerned lately.''

"You've been worried about Mark.''

"Yes, I have. But Danielle pointed out a few things to me, and I'm going to see Adam this morning. Will you do the interview even if he doesn't?''

She thought about her work in oncology...the children and what she believed in. "Yes, I'll do it. Just tell me where and when.''

A few minutes later when she hung up the phone, her mother came out of the bedroom, dressed for her day. "Before you go to Cleveland, you should think about buying a couple of suits on sale. They're professional, and you might need them. I've also gotten a box together of spare products—shampoos, lotions, that kind of thing.''

When she'd come home last night with her suitcase, Leigh's mother hadn't said a word. She'd accepted her back as if it had been inevitable. Adam's name hadn't been spoken. Now Leigh knew it had to be. In fact—

Ever since she'd moved into her new apartment, her mother had been planning and buying and worrying about everything Leigh should take to Cleveland...about her schedule when she was there...about her trip home over the Christmas holidays if she could get away. For the past few weeks as well as most of

the night, Leigh had thought about the differences between being a nurse and a doctor. She'd thought about
how these days doctors had little time with their patients. What she enjoyed most was working with patients—comforting them, informing them, being a
friend to them. The more she'd thought about what
Adam had said, about her dream being as old as she
was, about becoming a doctor being an ambition of
her mother's, all of it had rung true.

She'd admitted to herself she was falling in love
with Adam again. What she hadn't admitted was that
ten years ago she had loved him, and she loved him
still.

Was accepting the scholarship and becoming a doctor the easy way out? It had seemed ludicrous. Yet it
made sense, too. Why couldn't she trade one dream
for another? Why couldn't she do the work she loved
and have a life with Adam? Maybe he wouldn't still
want her. Maybe she'd destroyed their chance to have
a future by turning her back on him again.

"Leigh? Did you hear what I said?"

"About the lotion and the shampoo?"

"No. About the suits. Ever since last night you've
been so distracted. Who was that on the phone so
early? Was it Adam?"

Her mother sounded horrified at the thought, and
Leigh had to put a stop to that. She had to put a stop
to a lot of things.

"No. It was Jared Cambry. *Breaking News* is going
to do a story about his family and finding Adam and
the transplant. He wants me to be part of the interview."

"Do you think it's wise to get involved with a TV production?"

Taking a deep breath, Leigh said, "I'm going to do it because Jared Cambry's story is an important one. It will give me a chance to talk about the transplant program."

"Well, if you think that's best. I suppose Adam will be a part of this interview?"

"I'm not sure he *will* be. I'm hoping he will because I have a few things I need to tell him. I left Cedar Run last night when I shouldn't have. We had an argument—"

"About what? Did he ask you to stay here? Did he ask you to give up your scholarship?"

"No, Mom, he didn't. And now I realize why. He wants my dreams to be my *own* dreams. He doesn't want to interfere with what *I* really want. Just like *I* haven't interfered with what *you* really want."

"I don't know what you mean."

"Ten years ago Adam and I *were* young. I accepted your advice and your guidance. Maybe I didn't know what I truly wanted then. Or maybe romance looked bigger than life. But you got through to me, and I broke up with him. Now I know I shouldn't have."

Claire looked shocked. "Of course you should have. You're a nurse now, and on your way."

"Yes, I'm a nurse. And even if Adam and I had stayed together, I think I still would have become a nurse. I love my work. I want to care for kids with cancer every day, not spend more years of my life in school. Most of all, I love Adam. I'm not going to leave Portland, Mom. I'm not going to med school."

Though her mother's face had paled and Claire sank down on one of the thrift-store chairs, Leigh went on as kindly as she could. "I know how you've sacrificed for me. I know how you've worked for me. I appreciate all of it. But I'd be doing both of us an injustice if I went to med school because it was *your* dream."

"You could become an oncology specialist and help so many patients."

"I can help patients now…in a different way."

"What did he say to you last night? What did he do?"

"He told me the truth, Mom. He was honest with me. Now I can be honest with myself." Crossing to her mother, Leigh knelt down beside the chair. "Even if Adam won't take me back, even if I can't convince him that we can have a future together, I'm going to stay here. It's what I want to do. Will you accept that? Can you support my decision?"

At first Claire looked as if she were about to protest, about to give a laundry list of reasons why Leigh was throwing her life away. But then she looked into her daughter's eyes. "I guess if your feelings for Adam Bartlett have lasted all these years, there must be something to them."

"And you can still be proud of me if I stay in nursing and forget about med school?"

"If that's what you really want, honey, I'm not going to stand in your way. I don't want to lose you. You're all I have."

"Maybe. Maybe soon you'll have Adam, too."

When her mother didn't look convinced about that, Leigh smiled. Tonight she'd call Mr. Cambry and find out if Adam was going to do the interview. If he was, she'd find a way to tell him everything that was in her heart and hope that he would accept her love.

When Darlene buzzed Adam that Jared was in the reception area, he closed the catalog on his desk. "Send him back."

Did this personal visit mean that Mark was worse? That the transplant wasn't going to take?

Adam was on his feet when Jared entered the office, and his worry must have shown because Jared quickly said, "It's not Mark. I'm not here because of Mark."

There was great seriousness behind Jared's statement, and Adam looked at him curiously. "Why are you here?"

Jared didn't sit down, but crossed to the credenza, picked up the replica of a Model-T Ford, glanced at the Mustang next to it, then took a deep breath and faced his son. "Danni gave me hell after Shawna's party."

"About what?" He knew Danielle could be fiercely protective of her children, but her giving Jared hell painted quite a picture.

"She didn't like the way I introduced you at the party."

Adam remained silent.

"The truth is, I wanted to introduce you as my son, but I didn't know how you'd feel about that. I haven't known what to do about you…and Lissa. I think she and I are finding our way. But *you* and I…maybe it's harder because you *are* a son. Maybe it's harder because I think we're a lot alike."

Jared held up his hand right away. "Oh, I don't mean in the way we've handled our lives. I certainly did a poor job of that at the beginning. But neither of us has said very much about all of this. *I* should have. It was my place. You were my son. Yes, you might have saved Mark's life, and I will appreciate that to my dying day. But you are a gift, too, Adam. A gift I didn't deserve. A gift maybe I still don't deserve." He looked lost for a moment. "I'm saying this all badly."

"No. No, you're not. I mean...you're right. Neither of us knew how to handle this. It seems you've been uncertain in how to react to me, and I was unable to reach out to you. I would have been terrifically proud if you had introduced me as your son."

Adam could see the same emotion *he* felt in his father's eyes. Jared tried to speak and couldn't. Instead he reached out to Adam. "From now on, everyone I meet will know you're my son."

Adam wasn't sure exactly how it had happened, who had taken the first step, but suddenly they were embracing. And, in an odd way, Adam felt as if he'd found a home.

Obviously embarrassed by emotion he wasn't used to exhibiting, Jared released Adam, backed up a few steps and cleared his throat. "I know you told the producer of *Breaking News* you didn't want to be interviewed, but I'd like you to reconsider. You're a member of my family, and I want you to be a part of this."

Because Adam hadn't been able to reach out to his father, today might never have happened. Jared had taken the first step, and Adam saw now that he needed to reconsider a lot of things. He hadn't reached out to Leigh, either. He hadn't admitted that he...loved her. The quiet truth had been there all along; he just hadn't been silent enough to hear it. He'd thought the feelings belonged to long ago. They didn't. They belonged to now. If he had told her he loved her...if he had told her he wanted to make their relationship work...

What was he willing to give up?

He had enough money in his investments and in the bank that he could retire anytime he wanted. He could leave Portland and start up a new firm in Cleveland. They *could* be together, if that's what she really wanted, too. Last night he'd thought only his bed was empty. That was simply the tip of the iceberg. His life was empty without her.

"I'll do the interview if we can sign Leigh on, too. Is that possible?"

His father's smile was knowing as he confessed, "I already did that this morning."

As Leigh entered the lounge on the third floor of Portland General, cameras seemed to be everywhere. So did cords and lights, technicians and microphones. When she'd called Jared last night, he'd told her Adam would be here.

She saw the sofa and chair lined up on the makeshift stage. She saw the other chair and cameras set up for single interviews. Then she saw Adam in a suit and tie, talking to the producer, looking as serious as he had ever looked. She absolutely couldn't go through this taping without talking to him first. She thought she could, but now, seeing him—

They still had a half hour until airtime, and before she could change her mind, she marched over to him and said, "Excuse me?"

The producer gave her an odd look. "I need to give Adam some last-minute instructions, and then it will be your turn."

"I'm sorry, but I need to talk to Adam for a few minutes first." Looking straight into Adam's eyes she said, "It's not about Mark. It's about us."

Adam's green eyes seemed to go a shade darker as the producer glanced from him to Leigh and back to Adam again. Checking his watch, he said tersely, "Five minutes. You have five minutes."

Intending to not waste a moment of that time, she asked, "Will you come with me?"

She half expected him to say no. She half expected him to put her off until after the taping. He was a business-first kind of guy.

Instead of commenting, or answering her, he moved out in front of her and broke a direct path through everyone milling about into the hall. Once there, he glanced down the corridor, apparently finding what he was looking for. "Down here."

She followed him, not caring where they went, eager to tell him what she had to say, desperate to find out if he was going to give her a chance.

To her surprise, he opened the door to a broom closet. It took her back to her high school days, and she hoped this was a good omen. He switched on the light, and after they were both inside, he closed the door.

"I'm not going to medical school," she blurted out.

"I'm not going to Cleveland. I'm staying here. I love you, Adam. I hope I haven't realized how much too late. I just want to keep being a nurse, working with kids and live in Portland with you."

During the moments he didn't speak, tears came to her eyes, and she thought she'd never breathe again. But then he was holding her shoulders, bringing her closer. "You can't give up your dream for me."

"I'm not giving it up for you. I'm just changing dreams, to one of a life for *us*."

"You beat me to the punch," he said with a tender smile that made her heart soar. "I was going to move to Cleveland because I love you and I know we can make anything work. Anything," he insisted, as he tipped her head up and found her lips with his.

Adam's kiss was long and slow and deep. She'd never felt the depth and fervor of his emotion quite like this before. She responded the only way she could—with everything she was and everything she wanted to give him. There was so much more than desire. There were memories and forgiveness and hope and promise.

Reluctantly, it seemed, he broke away, tipped his head against hers and then leaned back. "I've been doing a lot of thinking."

"There's a lot of that going around," she confessed, trying to lighten the mood a little.

He traced his thumb along her cheek. "I love you, Leigh. More than anything else, I want you to be happy."

"I *will* be happy...with you."

"I've been holding back too much. Giving too little.

Not reaching out when I could. That's been brought home to me so many ways in the past month. When I was going over all the scenarios in my head of what could happen today, I had already made a decision about something I wanted to do with Cedar Run Ranch, whether I stayed here or went to Cleveland with you.''

''You don't want to keep it?''

''Oh, yes, I want to keep it. But if I couldn't be here, I was going to hire someone good to run it. However, since you've decided to stay in nursing, would you consider a different kind of work?''

''What work?'' He had her intrigued now.

''What if we turn the ranch into a camp for kids with cancer? You could be the director of the program and the on-site nurse. I could manage the logistics and financial details.''

''What about Novel Programs, Unlimited?''

''Dylan can run it. It can practically run by itself, anyway. I can keep my hand in if I want to. But most of my time would be devoted to Cedar Run.''

''I absolutely *love* the idea. I have so many contacts—in oncology and physical therapy...and in counseling, too.''

''Anybody but that Reed character you saw at the zoo.''

''Were you jealous?''

''Who? Me? Not any more than you were of Nicole.''

''I was not—''

''The truth. Always the truth.''

He was right. If she had been completely honest

with herself about all of this, about her life and everything she was feeling, they wouldn't have had to go through another difficult parting. "I *was* jealous, Adam. And I'm sorry. I'm sorry for everything I've put us through."

This time his finger covered her lips. Then his lips covered her mouth again, and she knew he'd forgiven her for all of it...because he loved her. Her love for him had lasted all these years. Now she knew it would last until the end of time.

# *Epilogue*

The beginning of April in Portland was often as rainy as March. But today the sun was shining as Adam and Dylan entered Cedar Run Ranch's spare barn in tuxedos.

In just a week Adam had hired a decorator to transform the empty space into a wedding chapel. As Adam's gaze canvassed the barn, he couldn't believe what had been accomplished. Rows of white wooden chairs were filled with his and Leigh's wedding guests—everyone from Jared, Danielle, Shawna and Chad, to Peggy and John and Sharon and Claire. Lissa and Sullivan also sat with them. Adam couldn't believe that not only were all these people his family, but they *felt* like family now—even Sharon, who had grudgingly admitted she'd like to attend. Dylan was his best man, and Adam had also invited Darlene—who still seemed to "like" Dylan—as well as employees he valued and Leigh's friends and co-workers.

There were flowers everywhere—white gladiolus, white roses, white daisies. But the most beautiful scent emanated from the gardenia arbor.

The harpist began playing as Adam and Dylan walked up the center aisle to stand by the minister. There was only one person missing today, and that was Mark. They were all still praying for him, hoping with him. The whole country was doing that now. Their interview about the transplant and Lissa and Adam's reunion had caught fire, and they had also all been interviewed on the morning news. In addition, another segment show had aired clips. The whole country was sending their prayers skyward for Mark, and that couldn't do anything but help.

Dylan winked at Adam as they turned to face the back of the barn.

The wedding planner, a woman in her midforties who had been doing this for years, rolled the white runner up the center aisle.

The harp music changed.

Adam felt as if he'd waited for this moment all of his life. As soon as he saw a flurry of white, a bit of lace, his head came up and his gaze sought Leigh.

She looked like a princess. The gown was lace and pearls, full and billowing. She'd told him the train seemed to stretch for miles. He didn't care about that.

He only cared about her. She wore the pearl necklace her mother had given her for graduation. Somehow it had survived the fire and the cleanup. Her hair was arranged on top of her head, and the veil framed her face like a waterfall. Step by step, she moved closer to him, and it was hard to take his eyes from her face. But he wanted to take in all of her. A bouquet of white roses cascaded from her hands.

And then he saw it. Something that seemed out of place. On her wrist...

The tightness in his chest blurred his eyes for a moment as he realized she was wearing the bracelet he'd bought her ten long years ago. She'd kept it all this time. She'd loved him all this time.

When Leigh reached the arbor, Dylan had already stepped aside. Her mother, her matron of honor, took her bouquet, kissed her on the cheek and smiled at Adam. They'd form a friendship eventually, he and Claire. It had already started. Since he was taking care of the wedding, she had insisted on having a dinner for him and his family last night. She'd rented a room in a restaurant and all of it had gone better than Adam could ever have imagined. Everyone had mingled and talked and joked. At the end of the evening, he'd hugged his soon-to-be mother-in-law.

Taking Leigh's hands, he couldn't imagine ever letting her go. They'd decided they wanted a traditional ceremony with traditional vows. Now as he promised to love and cherish Leigh forever, he understood exactly what that meant. She understood, too, as she squeezed his hands, gazed into his eyes and smiled so tremulously. He wanted to kiss her right then.

The ceremony seemed to be over in a wink, and soon they faced friends and family as Mr. and Mrs. Adam Bartlett.

Pulling strings, Adam had managed on short notice to reserve a reception hall at an inn a few minutes out of town. But Adam and Leigh's guests wanted to congratulate them and wish them well now. One after the other they came through a receiving line.

Finally Jared was standing before them. Shawna and Danielle had already given them hugs, and Chad had shaken their hands.

Jared smiled at them now and said to Leigh, "I hope someday my daughter finds a man as good as Adam." Then he looked at his son. "I hope Mark and Chad each find a woman as lovely and compassionate as Leigh. I don't want you two to be strangers, you hear? In fact, we might have to set up once-a-month family gatherings, just to make sure everybody keeps in touch."

"We'll probably be there more than you want us," Adam joked. "Especially after Mark comes home." They were all praying for that day, and Adam was beginning to believe it would happen.

"Even when you get busy with building your camp?"

"Even then," Adam assured him.

"I won't tie you up any longer. I know you want

to get to the reception." He gave Leigh a hug, and then he gave Adam one, too.

When Jared moved away, Lissa and Sullivan took his place. Lissa hugged Leigh, and then with an uncertain smile, she tightly hugged Adam. He squeezed her back, wanting to know so much more about his twin. She and Sullivan had come to dinner one night this week so he and Leigh could tell them about their plans and personally invite them to the wedding. He had a feeling the four of them were going to be good friends.

Lissa leaned away from him, and her smile was so bright, he knew she was thoroughly happy for him. "When are you and Leigh coming to the vineyard?" she asked now.

"We're flying to Hawaii for two weeks. We both want some consistent sun," he joked. "When we come back, I promise I'll bring you a lei and deliver it personally."

"I think I'm going to like having you for a brother!"

After Lissa and Sullivan moved away, he and Leigh were finally alone. Everyone else had gone ahead to the reception.

"Well, Mrs. Bartlett? How does it feel?"

"How does what feel?" she asked coyly.

Wrapping his arm around her, he pulled her close. "How does it feel to be married to me?"

Her teasing tone gone now, she looked up at him

with her big blue eyes and decided, "It feels wonderful."

That was all Adam needed to hear. In the silence of the barn chapel, with the scent of gardenias permeating the air around them, he kissed Leigh as a man kisses his wife. They were united forever...united in soul, heart and body.

And this was only the beginning.

\* \* \* \* \*

# AND THEN THERE WERE THREE

BY
LYNDA SANDOVAL

**Lynda Sandoval** is a former police officer who exchanged the excitement of that career for blissfully isolated days creating stories she hopes readers will love. Though she's also worked as a youth mental health and runaway crisis counsellor, a television extra, a trade-show art salesperson, a European tour guide and a bookkeeper for an exotic bird and reptile company – among other weird jobs – Lynda's favourite career, by far, is writing books. In addition to romance, Lynda writes women's fiction and young-adult novels and in her spare time she loves to travel, quilt, bid on eBay, hike, read and spend time with her dog. Lynda also works part-time as an emergency fire/medical dispatcher for the fire department. Readers are invited to visit Lynda on the web at www.LyndaLynda.com, or to send mail with an SAE with return postage for a reply to PO Box 1018, Conifer, CO 80433-1018, USA.

For Gail Chasan.
Thank you for believing in me.

## Chapter One

Sam Lowery sat, sprawl-legged and guilt-ridden, in the nondescript waiting room of Portland General. He glowered with disinterest at the talking heads on the pole-mounted television in the corner, all the while obsessing over the fact that he was officially the worst father in the history of parenthood.

How could he have thought for a single moment that the mobile home offices of a construction work-site would be a safe place for his two-year-old daughter to hang out while he worked? His rationalization seemed weak at this point: he hadn't wanted to put Jessica in daycare when she was so young and still so traumatized. But he had to wonder if his aversion to daycare said more about him than it did about her.

He shoved his fingers through his hair. The knowledge that he'd placed Jessica in the very type of danger he sought to avoid made his gut clench with pain. He never should've held on so tightly, never should've expected his secretary to watch his daughter. He never should've worked overtime that fateful night six months ago, but hey, that was a whole 'nuther guilt trip, now wasn't it? He had a plethora of them from which to choose.

The musical tones of his cell phone yanked him back to the present. Had to be the job; it wasn't like he had a pack of buddies who rang him up on a regular basis. He pulled the small phone off his belt clip and checked caller ID on the LED screen before answering. The number popped up: Mia, his secretary. Flipping open the face, he lifted it to his ear. "Hey, Mia."

"Oh, Sam." Mia, a married mother of four herself, had been more than amenable to watching Jessica in the offices while Sam was out on the site, but they both should've realized Mia had her own work to do. A curious two-year-old was more than a full-time job. "How is the poor little darling? Did she need stitches?"

Sam ran a hand slowly down his face, feeling sick and trying not to recall the disturbing picture of the deep cut in his baby girl's pudgy little hand. His heart squeezed. "Yeah, they're stitching her up right now."

"I'm so sorry."

"Don't be. It wasn't your fault."

"Well, listen. I just wanted to check in, but I'll let

you go comfort her while she goes through this ordeal.''

''No need,'' Sam said, wryly, lifting one ankle to rest it over the opposite knee. ''To tell you the truth, Doc kicked me out of the suture room.''

''What?'' Mia's disbelief came across loud and clear. ''How can he kick that darling girl's parent out of the room.''

He shook his head. ''Seems I was 'hovering,' and making it worse for Jessica. Agitating her, Doc said.''

Mia laughed, sadly. ''Well, hon, no offense intended, but I can certainly see that.''

Sam straightened. ''What's that supposed to mean?''

''You're not the typical father, is all.''

Sam grew immediately defensive, all the while knowing he didn't need to be. Not with Mia. But, still. ''I repeat, what's that supposed to mean?''

''Oh, don't get your back up. I meant it as a compliment. You do have a tendency to…well, to hover. Nothing wrong with that. Mothers do it all the time, believe me, and you care for that little girl like a mother would is all I'm saying.'' Mia's breath hitched, and for a moment, that old familiar tension hung between them. ''I'm sorry. I shouldn't have said it that way.''

Sam closed his eyes, shaking his head slowly. It had been six months since the fire, and people still walked on eggshells around him as though he could snap at any moment. He couldn't blame them, though. It wasn't like he shared his emotions freely, or let anyone know where he was coming from. To be honest, he preferred it that way. He didn't want anyone too close to him or his world. "Don't apologize. It's a fact, Mia. I have to be both father and mother to her now."

"Well…you don't *have* to." Mia's tone took on a subtle change. "I happen to know there are a lot of women out there who would jump at the chance to be Jessica's new mommy." Her voice took on a softer tone. "Not to mention your new love."

Sam stiffened. He chose to ignore the "new love" half of Mia's preposterous proposition. When he spoke, his words came out ultra-controlled, through a clenched jaw. "Mia, I've told you before, Jessica had a mother—"

"God rest her soul."

*And fry his.* "You can't just replace a parent." He knew that all too well, but held back a scoff of derision.

"Well, I know. But, Jessica was so young when her mama—" Mia sighed. "She could come to love another mother figure. I know you don't believe that, but it's true nonetheless." A beat passed, and in typical Mia form, she decided to push the other issue. "Plus, if you had someone for yourself—"

"Don't even go there." Love? Ha. He hadn't even managed to pull that farce off the first time, when he'd really wanted it to work out.

Mia's exasperated sigh carried over the line. Her desire to see Sam remarried—happily this time—was an ongoing point of contention, but it was an argument the woman would lose. In the stubbornness department, no one rivaled Sam Lowery. He had stuck his neck out once in the love arena and been sadly disappointed. Oh, he respected Jenny as the mother of his child and always would, but it had quickly become clear theirs wasn't the love match he'd dreamed about. Still, he'd said "I do," to the "for better or worse" part that day in the Justice of the Peace's offices, and he'd meant it, even if the worse outweighed the better—which it had, by a long shot. Real men didn't leave their families, no matter how dissatisfying the arrangement.

He certainly hadn't wanted Jenny dead and buried.

A shudder moved through him at the flashback image.

Jenny may not have been the perfect wife, but she'd given him one amazing gift for which he'd always be grateful: their daughter. With Jessica, he knew true connection, true abiding love, for the first time ever. Maybe parental love was the only type he was meant to have in this life. Who knew? If so, fine with him. In any case, he didn't plan to test the theory by traveling the rocky road of romance again. Ever.

"As I've told you a million times, no new women for me. End of topic," he said, in a tone that would brook no argument. He cleared his throat and switched direction. "I'll tell you what I am going to do, though."

"What's that?" Mia sounded resigned.

"I'm going to suck it up and hire a nanny." Sam slid down in the uncomfortable waiting room chair, stretching his legs out in front of him, feet balanced on their heels. "I can't bring Jess to the job site any longer. She's too much of a handful."

"It's probably a good idea, Sam," Mia said, with sadness threading through her tone. "Much as I loved having her here with me…"

"I know. I appreciate everything you've done, but you have your own work to do, and now that she's two—"

"Goodness knows what the Terrible Threes will bring."

"Exactly. It's a recipe for more disaster." He fished the dog-eared business card out of his pocket and studied the face of it. "Bruce Nolan gave me the name of an agency. Supposed to be a good one—"

"Nannysource?"

"That's the one."

"They are good. You can't go wrong there."

Her vote of confidence helped him relax slightly about the whole prospect of some stranger horning in on the raising of his daughter, but only *slightly*. "I know we're working overtime tomorrow morning, but the agency has Saturday morning hours. I guess I'll take the day off tomorrow and set up some interviews," he said, in a glum tone. "Find some sweet little grandmother who'll treat Jessie like her own grandchild."

Another parental guilt pang went through him when he realized Jessie didn't, and never would, have grandparents of her own. His late wife had grown up with a much older single mother who died just after

Jenny'd graduated from high school, and Sam, himself, had grown up—damn quickly—in the foster care system. When he really analyzed it, their mutual lack of familial connections had been most of what brought Jenny and him together in the first place, but time had proven that being orphaned wasn't enough of a glue to bond them forever.

Still, a nice surrogate grandma for Jessica...yes. That would be good. He actually started to look forward to calling Nannysource. "Yes, a nice, old Mary Poppins sort would do."

"I'm sure you'll find the perfect match. Don't you worry about a thing here. Just take care of that sweet baby. We won't even miss you."

A rueful half smile hiked up one side of Sam's mouth. "Gee, thanks. Just what the boss wants to hear."

"Oh, Sam," Mia scolded.

He checked the clock mounted on the wall of the waiting room. How long did it take to stitch up a tiny little hand anyway? He'd arrived at the hospital with Jessie just after 5:00 p.m., and it was a few minutes past seven. "I just hope—" He stopped, pressing his lips into a thin line.

"Hope what?"

He wrestled with the thought, then decided to share it. "That Jessie will tolerate someone new in her life."

"Jessie's more resilient than you give her credit for, hon. She's a people person in baby form."

Sam pursed his lips, not so sure he agreed. Since

the fire, his formerly giggly, sparkly baby had turned reticent and fearful of strangers and new situations. It ate him alive inside, witnessing the manifestation of her fears, especially since he was responsible for her trauma—a fact no one but he knew.

The apartment fire that night had broken out while he'd been working overtime on a job. *Voluntary.* He'd told Jenny it was mandatory OT, but it hadn't been, and he'd had to live with what he'd thought was a harmless white lie on his conscience for six months now. No one but he knew he'd worked so much over-time back then in order to avoid a less than perfect home life, but there it was. The ugly, unvarnished truth. Had he been home that night, like any decent husband and father, he might've been able to help Jenny escape the inferno.

Instead, she'd died protecting Jessica.

His biggest source of guilt, however, came from the fact that he'd actually felt a flash of gratitude that night when he'd learned it was his Jessica who'd sur-vived rather than his young wife. Not that he'd wanted Jenny dead. Not that at all. But if he'd had to choose a survivor…

Sam stifled a groan. What kind of monster was he, anyway?

Sure, he and Jenny had moved from love to a kind of mutual and dissatisfying tolerance before her death, but that damn well didn't matter. He wouldn't wish a death like Jenny's on his worst enemy, much less the mother of his baby girl—a woman who'd sacri-ficed her own life in order to save her daughter's. He would respect her forever for that decision, and he'd feel guilty forever, too.

Guilt. So much guilt. Ah, well, at least he had one constant in his life.

"Oh, honey, I've got to go," Mia said, interrupting his brooding silence. She'd become so accustomed to his drawn-out silences during their conversations, they didn't even faze her. Sam Lowery was a loner, plain and simple, and Mia knew and accepted it. But, the excitement that had crept into Mia's voice made him curious.

"Why? What's going on?"

"They're about to air the segment about those re-united twins on my news show."

He frowned. "What twins?"

She clucked her tongue. "You're so out of the loop. I don't have time to explain. Call me in the morning to give me a Jessie update. Or anytime during the night if you need an ear to bend. You know I'm here."

"I do. And listen, this wasn't your fault."

"Thank you for saying that, but I still feel guilty."

"Yeah, well, join the club."

They rang off, and Sam hooked his phone back on his belt before glancing up at the television. It had to be tuned in to the same channel Mia had been watching, he realized, because the blonde announcer was in the midst of an intro about reunited adult twins. Might as well watch, he supposed, since he'd been banished from his daughter's bedside and Mia thought he was hopelessly "out of it" when it came to current events.

Sam glanced around and spied a remote on one of the unoccupied chairs. He pushed a few well-worn buttons on the control and increased the volume.

The story centered around a man and woman—coincidentally his age—who hadn't even known they were twins. After their young mother died in a car accident, they'd been relinquished to an adoption agency connected to Portland General and adopted separately. A subsequent fire destroyed their birth records, hence they never knew the other existed. But, lo and behold, their biological father saw fit to search for them recently, when his young son needed a bone marrow transplant.

Sam sat back, twisting his mouth to the side and bouncing the remote against his palm. Something about *that* little detail irked the hell out of him. What was it about the first children the man had created that made them unworthy of keeping? Clearly he hadn't had a problem holding on to the second wave of children he'd fathered, or seeking the first kids when he needed something from them. A muscle in Sam's jaw ticked, and he pushed away his distaste. This wasn't about him. Still, he had to admit, it was a sore point. He couldn't imagine ever living without Jessica, giving her up to strangers to raise.

He thought about turning the idiot box off, but the story intrigued him enough to be a distraction, so he refocused on it. Leaning forward, he rested his elbows on his spread knees, the cracked, vinyl chair squeaking beneath him. The announcer finished her lead and brought out the long lost siblings, Lissa Cartwright and Adam Bartlett. The camera panned to a wide shot, as they sat down across from the reporter, and then it closed in on the twins.

Sam's entire body tensed. The hair on his neck raised, and for a moment, he failed to move, to draw a breath, to blink. When his heart actually started beating again, it was a steady, hard drum against his rib cage. A death knell. He squeezed his eyes shut, shook his head, then peered cautiously at the television screen again.

No way. Couldn't be.

Inconceivable as it was, Sam himself could be Adam Bartlett's scruffier, blue-collar double. They were both about six-foot-one, with dark brown hair and green eyes. They were the exact same age. They had both been abandoned by their birth parents and adopted out of the same agency, the Children's Connection, around the same time. Could it possibly be…?

He sat back and crossed his arms over his chest, as if to protect himself from what he was seeing, and shrugged off the eerie sense of realization creeping up his spine. Ridiculous. A lot of men would fit his and Adam Bartlett's description.

But—he squinted at the screen—it was more than a simple height/weight/hair color/eye color connection. The way Bartlett talked, his mannerisms, the shape of his hands. Even the woman, Lissa Cartwright, resembled Sam in a lot of intangible ways.

And then there was the uncanny adoption timeline. Could this story have more layers than the news media realized? Could these reunited twins actually be two in a set of…triplets? Could Sam himself—

No. No. No. Ridiculous again.

The stress of Jessica's accident was getting to him, that was all. He scrubbed his palms over his face, trying to make it all go away. His whole train of thought made no sense.

*Yes, it does.*

"Yes, it does," he said, repeating the words that had whispered through his mind. And it did. It made a kind of sense Sam couldn't explain. Not even a little bit. He had always felt like something was missing, some deep and important connection he had never been able to fully understand. It was more than just having grown up orphaned, more than missing out on his parents while he fought his way through a foster care system that left a lot to be desired. He'd always felt some…stronger connection, more elusive and confusing. And what was it the scientists said about twins? Or triplets? If this wild theory had any merit, he'd been closer to these two strangers than he'd ever been to anyone since. He'd shared a womb with them, for God's sake, and then they'd been unceremoniously ripped apart. Could that account for his lifelong, inexplicable sense of loss? His lack of belonging? His illogical belief that someone, somewhere shared just a little bit of his soul?

He watched a little longer, enough to learn that Adam Bartlett was some bigwig CEO of a company called Novel Programs, Unlimited, and Lissa had lived an idyllic childhood on a vineyard a couple hours outside Portland.

Gosh, how nice for them. An unpleasant emotion welled up inside his gut. If he had to label the sour feeling, he'd reluctantly call it jealousy. Because, if these two truly were his siblings, he'd obviously drawn the short stick at the placement agency. While they were experiencing "Leave it to Beaver" childhoods, Sam had been shuffled from one foster home to the next, some better than others, some so intolerable he'd made it a life goal to block them from his memory. But, all of them had one thing in common: they'd been devoid of true connections.

A sneer lifted his lip. Fate was truly cruel.

Bitterness bubbled inside him, and he let it. He must've been the least attractive baby. But, of course, he wouldn't know. No one in his life had cared enough to record his babyhood on film. Surely Lissa Cartwright and Adam Bartlett had albums full of baby pictures of themselves.

Having seen more than enough and not liking the direction his thoughts were taking, he switched off the television and tossed the remote aside, settling in for some serious brooding. Even if Adam Bartlett and Lissa Cartwright were his siblings—and deep down in his darkest place, he knew they were—he made the decision right then and there, ironically in the hospital in which they'd been born, that no one would ever know it. Not Adam, nor Lissa, and least of all the supposed "father" who'd thrown him to the wolves twenty-seven years earlier. Sam hadn't had family in all those years. As far as he was concerned, he could live without them forever. He had Jessica, and she was all the family he would ever need.

He could only hope that Mia hadn't noticed his resemblance to Adam Bartlett, too. If that happened, he'd be in a world of hurt.

## Chapter Two

The waning evening sun stretched long, low, golden fingers of light across the road as Sam drove Jessie home. She was groggy from her pain medicine, and every time Sam caught a glimpse of that tiny, bandaged hand, he wanted to jump off a cliff. He'd tilted his rearview mirror to allow him a view of his baby girl in her car seat as he drove.

"You okay, honeypot?"

She didn't answer, but her eyes—so much like Jenny's—met his in the mirror. Was it his imagination, or did they look accusatory?

Sam swallowed thickly, his heart thudding. "How do you feel about having a new Grandma, Jessica? Someone to bake cookies with you and play and read you stories."

Jessica just blinked. She didn't even have a frame of reference for the word "Grandma," so how would she know? Plus, she was only two.

"Daddy's going to find you a nice Grandma to come live with us. Okay? You'll love her. I promise."

No response, but he hadn't really expected one.

"I love you, Jessica," he said, his words husky.

"Yuv you," Jessica murmured, before settling her little head against the side of the carseat and closing her eyes. She looked so innocent, so out of it, the sting of unshed tears burned Sam's eyes. He refocused on the road, trying not to think about the fact that tomorrow would bring the second biggest change in Jessica's life, and all of it, thanks to him. He felt like he was parenting blindly, bound in steel cords and fighting his way out of a dark corridor he'd never been in before. If only he'd had a father to teach him how to be a father, perhaps he wouldn't be so lost.

His thoughts jumped back to Lissa and Adam, and their supposed father, Jared Cambry. Biology be damned, the man was no father, and two complete strangers would never be his family. Anger blossomed inside him. It was a good thing Adam Bartlett had been a bone marrow match for the little boy, because Sam would've closed the door in his face had Jared so much as dared to seek him out after all he'd gone through as an unwanted child. Just as quickly as the anger had come, a flash of remorse for his uncharitable thoughts followed. He glanced at Jessica in the rearview mirror. It wasn't true, and he knew it.

As a father, he'd do anything to save Jessica's life if it came to that. He couldn't blame Cambry for his desperation, but he also didn't have to forgive him for the abandonment. Lucky for all of them, the happy little reunited family had no idea Sam Lowery even existed, and he meant to keep it that way.

But, what *would* it be like to have siblings?

They seemed to care for each other. Would they have room in their hearts to care about another brother?

His hands gripped the wheel tighter, and he pushed the preposterous train of thought away. The stupid twin show on TV had him thinking crazy. The "if onlys" would kill him if he let them, and he refused to let them. Sam Lowery was an orphan. Period. He'd made his peace with that fact long ago.

And, as for his parenting skills, he might be a trial-and-error dad, but he'd make damn sure Jessica never felt slighted. He'd do everything in his power to be the best father he knew how to be...which clearly, given today's debacle, wasn't saying much.

Erin O'Grady loved the time she spent at her brothers' homes, especially Saturday mornings, when all the families got together for brunch. At twenty-three, she was the only unmarried O'Grady, and had no children of her own yet. *Yet* being the operative word, because she planned to produce a passel of them as soon as she fell in love with the right guy and got married. But, for now, doting on her nieces and nephews was the second best option, and with five married, Irish Catholic brothers, she had a slew of them.

That Saturday, at her brother Mick's, Erin sprawled happily on the living room floor, trying to catch her breath while a pack of her nieces and nephews climbed all over her. She was perpetually bruised and had taken more than one sharp little elbow in her tender parts over the years, but it was worth it. She loved being the favorite aunt. She even loved being the human jungle gym.

The muffled ring of her cell phone from inside her purse brought her head up. She glanced toward it, but her nephew, Jason, had her in a full nelson.

"Jase, buddy, I need to get that."

"No way!" He giggled. "Say Uncle!"

"Jase, really—"

"Want me to answer it, sis?" asked Mick, who was the closest to her in age, at twenty-five.

"Please do. It might be the agency calling."

"The agency." Her second-to-the-oldest brother, Patrick, rolled his eyes. "I'm still not sure about that."

Erin scowled. "I'm not a child anymore, Pat, and I want to be a nanny. It's not an issue of whether or not you're 'sure' about it, okay?"

Patrick pointed a finger toward her. "You're not a child, but you'll always be our little sister. You have no idea what could happen."

Brothers Matthew and Miles nodded, and she rolled her eyes in response. God save her from her overprotective brothers. Thank goodness Eamon, the eldest, was out of town on a business trip. He was the worst of the bunch. She loved them, adored having a big, raucous family, but the short leash they kept her on could get tedious at times. The bane of being the only girl, she supposed, and the baby of the family, to boot.

When Mick retrieved the cell phone, her heart started to pound in anticipation. She'd only registered with Nannysource three days earlier, but the manager had been extremely enthusiastic about her credentials and said she hoped to place her soon. Erin said a silent prayer of thanks that she'd chosen her particular specialty. Helping kids who'd suffered some sort of trauma seemed to have put her on the A-list of available nannies at the agency.

"Hello?" Erin watched Mick listen, then nod. "No, you called the right number. This is her brother, Mick O'Grady. Hang on." Mick held the phone away from his ear and whistled. "Okay, kids. Let Aunt Erin up. This is business."

The kids grumbled, but they peeled themselves off her, one-by-one. Erin winked at them, then straightened her clothing and stood, reaching for the cell phone.

"This is Erin."

"Erin, I'm so glad I got you," said Karla, the placement coordinator for Nannysource.

Erin broke into a wide grin. "Hi, Karla. I was hoping it was you. Good news?"

"Well, keep your fingers crossed. I have an interview and I think you're perfect for the position."

"That's fabulous!" Erin listened intently while the

manager described the situation: working with a two-year-old girl who'd survived an apartment fire that had claimed her mother, a mere six months earlier. The father had been hesitant about bringing in outside help because the child seemed to suffer some PTSD, or post-traumatic stress disorder, from the incident. The whole scenario sounded perfect to Erin. Plus, it was a live-in assignment, which would work out great since she was having no luck finding an apartment she could afford, and she was tired of living under her parents' roof, God love them both. This was exactly the type of gig she'd hoped to land when she registered with Nannysource.

Erin's excitement grew to the bursting point. She spun around in a circle but fought to keep her voice businesslike. "It sounds more than ideal."

"Well…there's only one problem."

Erin stilled, tucking one wayward lock of hair behind her ear. She sank into the nearest available chair and braced herself. "Uh-oh. Okay, lay it on me."

"He requested…a grandmotherly type," Karla said, her voice turning a bit regretful.

"Oh no! I'm twenty-three!"

"I know. But in light of the circumstances, Erin, I couldn't think of anyone more equipped to handle the job than you. I'm sure you can win him over."

"Gosh, I hope so." Erin bit her lip and said a silent prayer, but her excitement cooled slightly. "Anyway, it sounds wonderful. I at least want to give it a shot." Erin fished in her handbag for a pen and paper to jot down all the information. She hated to think of a sad widower with an emotionally fragile child going it alone. "When would he like to meet? I'm more than ready."

"As soon as possible. This afternoon, if you can swing it."

"Of course. I take it he's not remarried?"

"Nope, single father."

"That makes sense considering he only lost his wife six months ago." Erin studiously ignored her eavesdropping brothers, but she could feel their protective radar kick into high gear. Testosterone snapped, crackled, and popped all around her.

When Erin had collected all the information she needed for the interview and hung up, the four available O'Grady brothers were staring at her intently, suspicion clear on their faces. "What was that all about?" Patrick asked. Well, growled.

"What?" She tucked away her notes, avoiding their glances.

"You're considering working for a single man? As a live-in nanny?" Mick asked, incredulously. He exchanged narrowed glances with Patrick and Matt.

Erin wouldn't be intimidated out of this interview. She raised her chin. "I'm going to be a nanny for a traumatized two-year-old named Jessica—" She crossed her fingers. "—if all goes well at the interview. That's the point."

"I'm not sure I like it," Mick said slowly, clearly chewing on the idea. "Working for a couple is one thing, but a single man? What if it's all a ploy to get a young, naive woman into his home?"

Erin groaned, then pantomimed feeling for walls all around and above her. "Oh, I'm sorry. I'd forgotten I lived in a glass box, Mick. And, newsflash, I'm not naive."

"Don't be flippant."

"Well?" She spread her arms wide. "It's a job, and a good one at that. It's absolutely ideal for me, and I'm a big girl, perfectly capable of making wise decisions."

"You're twenty-three!" Miles leaned forward to make his point. "And you're our baby sister."

"Maybe we should check him out first," Matthew said to the other men, ignoring Erin completely. "Make sure he's not using this nanny thing as a cover to lure young, naive—"

"I am not naive!" Erin shot to her feet and planted fists on her hips. She glared at each of her brothers in turn, then couldn't help but give them a grudging smile. She loved the big, annoying oafs. Can't live with 'em, can't kill 'em. "Gosh, you guys are so friggin' irritating."

"You don't need to swear," said Mick, reproachfully.

Erin ignored him. "I don't need you dogging my every footstep. Do you really have that little faith in my judgement?"

"It's not a matter of faith, Erin," Mick said. "It's a matter of family protection."

"Great, we're in the mob now."

"There she goes, being flippant again."

Erin knew they meant well, but she'd had enough.

She hiked her purse on her shoulder and tossed her auburn hair. "Look, I love you guys, but I don't need bodyguards. Please, just let me do this and trust my instincts. You make me feel like I'm in prison." Wary silence ensued. Erin sighed with exasperation. When it came to her brothers, smothering was an understatement. "I'll check in by phone the minute I get to the man's house and the moment I leave. Will that satisfy you?"

"Nope." Mick lifted his chin toward Matthew, the middle of the five boys and the burliest. "Follow her. Park down the street, and if anything seems out of the ordinary—"

Erin growled playfully. "You're all impossible."

Matthew rose and lumbered off behind her. At the door, she turned and aimed a finger up toward his face. Narrowing her gaze into her best threatening scowl, she said, "Stay out of sight, and don't you dare come barreling into my interview and ruin it. I swear, if you do, I'll go find some Hell's Angels and date every single one of them."

"Okay, okay, go easy. No need to make threats."

"It could take up to an hour," Erin said, still scowling. "I'll program your cell number into mine so I just have to press send if something goes wrong, which it won't."

"I said okay." Matthew turned her toward the door.

She wiggled back around and grabbed his thick arm. "I mean it! I need this job. Don't screw this up for me."

Matthew held two meaty hands up, palms forward. "Just go. Sheesh, sisters. You'd think a little gratitude wouldn't be so far out of the question."

Erin stared at him, dumbfounded, before uttering a sound of disbelief and flouncing out the door toward what she hoped was the most stellar interview of her life. Forget her brothers. Forget everything. She wanted this job.

The doorbell rang, and Sam checked his watch. Excellent start—the nanny was right on time. He appreciated promptness. He took one quick moment to straighten his hair in the hall mirror and smooth his clothing before facing who he hoped would be Jessica's new "grandma."

Fixing an enigmatic smile on his face—not too friendly, not too grumpy—he pulled open the door.

Sam's stomach contracted, and the smile faded. No, no, no. This wasn't right at all. He'd asked for a grandmotherly type, and the enticing young woman standing on his doorstep was anything but. From her stylishly messy mop of red hair to her charming crooked grin, she was the antithesis of what he'd hoped to find waiting on his stoop. Wait—maybe she wasn't the nanny at all. He cocked his head to the side. "Can I help you?"

She straightened her shoulders and stuck out her hand. Her nails, he noticed against his will, were short and neatly manicured. Bare of polish. He'd always found natural nails on a woman very sexy, and his chest tightened. "I'm Erin O'Grady, Mr. Lowery. Nannysource sent me over for the interview."

"Call me Sam. But there must be some mistake. I requested an older woman," he blurted. Then, as if just realizing how rude that sounded, he shook her hand, the very hand he'd found sexy mere moments earlier. Unacceptable.

"Yes, but Karla thought you might change your mind after we talked." She hiked one shoulder. "You see, I specialize in working with children who've faced some sort of trauma. She thought I'd be perfect for what you and Jessica need."

*What he needed.* Something disturbingly feral swirled inside Sam's body as Erin's smooth, warm palm slid from his. Miss Erin O'Grady might be perfect for a lot of things, but caring for his daughter wasn't one of them. And, no matter what Mia suggested, he wasn't looking for those *other* things. What he needed was a grandmother for his daughter, not a too-sexy-for-her-own-good nanny living under his roof, perfuming the air with her laughter and feminine scent. He was only human, after all.

Still, he supposed he should at least feign giving the interview before calling Nannysource later to reject Erin. "Well, come on in then. I have to warn you, Jessica has been reticent since..."

Erin laid a hand gently on his forearm. "I'm sorry to have heard about what happened to Jessica and her mother."

Another zing of attraction moved through Sam at the feel of that smooth palm against his skin. He glanced from Erin's face, to her hand on his arm, and back again. She quickly removed it. "Thank you. It's been...difficult. Mind you, Jessica's a wonderful little girl—"

"I'm certain of that." The unsuitable nanny's face turned all business. "One problem with a child facing trauma at eighteen months or thereabouts is she has enough memory to know and remember parts of what happened, but she doesn't have the vocabulary to talk about it like an adult might. But there are ways we can work with her, to bring her out of her shell."

"And you're familiar with these...ways?"

"Intimately."

Sam eyed Erin thoughtfully. Damn. She would be perfect if she weren't so...young? Attractive? Distracting? He couldn't decide which word described her best, or if all of them combined made her completely wrong for the job. She might be great for Jessica—that remained to be seen—but he couldn't imagine having someone like Erin underfoot 24/7. Yes, he'd sworn off love and he meant it, but he was a red-blooded, American male with needs and desires. A magnetic young redhead was just what he didn't need in his life right now—in any capacity.

"Make yourself comfortable," he said, taking no pains to hide his less than enthusiastic tone. "Let's meet Jessica."

"Can't wait!"

He waited until she was settled on the sofa, then headed down the hall to get his baby girl. He wasn't sure what he'd expected when the prospective nanny met his daughter. Polite conversation, maybe? A few thoughtful compliments—that slightly cheesy way people speak to children—all the while maintaining a businesslike air? Maybe not that, exactly. But he hadn't expected Erin to drop her purse and get right down on the floor with Jessica, speaking to her like she was a little person and not a baby. And he absolutely hadn't expected Jessica to open up to a complete stranger, even one so captivating as Erin O'Grady.

But she did.

"Well, hello, precious girl," Erin said, opening her arms.

Jessica broke into a grin and toddled right over. "See doggy?" She thrust her bedraggled, stuffed St. Bernard into Erin's face.

"He's beautiful. What's his name, Jessica?"

Jessica flashed a questioning smile at her father.

"His name is Doggy," Sam said, almost apologetically, sinking into an armchair to watch the interaction.

"Doggy's a perfectly beautiful name," Erin said, her focus never leaving Jessica's face.

Sam watched as her gaze dropped to Jessica's bandaged hand. Erin reached out and gently touched the bandage.

"What happened here?"

"Me owie," Jessica said, hugging the injured hand to her chest.

"She slammed her hand in a file drawer at my

worksite,'' Sam said, ashamed. ''She has twelve stitches.''

''Well, that's not good, is it, Jessica?''

''Not good.'' Jessie shook her head vigorously. Then, as though her brain switched gears instantaneously, Jessica ran from the room. ''Be back!''

Erin flashed Sam another crooked smile, and he averted his gaze, fighting to ignore the quick fireball of desire that rushed through him.

''She's adorable. She looks like you.''

Reluctantly, he dragged his gaze back to her face. ''Thank you.'' Before either of them could say more, Jessica bounded back into the room. Her arms were filled with treasures—a puzzle, her stuffed frog, and most surprising to Sam at least, a framed picture of Jenny. He'd framed it for her and placed it in her room just after the new house had been built, but Jessica had never acknowledged it until that moment.

She dropped everything at Erin's feet. ''Play.''

''I'd love to play.'' Erin picked up the framed photograph first. ''Is this your mama, sweetie?''

Sam momentarily ceased breathing, praying this wouldn't send Jessica deeper into her shell. They never talked about Jenny.

Jessica, true to recent form, kept her focus remaining solidly on the puzzle. ''Play puzzle.''

Sam watched as Erin carefully set the framed photograph up facing them, then reached for the frog. ''And is this Kermit?''

Jessica shook her head as she squatted down and dumped the puzzle pieces onto the rug.

Erin glanced toward Sam, one eyebrow raised.

"Froggy," he answered, one corner of his mouth lifting despite everything. "It's a pattern with her lately. Doggy, Froggy, Kitty. You get the idea."

Erin laughed, a light, effervescent sound, then set Froggy next to the photo of Jenny. Something in the way she gave all of Jessica's prized possessions equal attention without focusing on Jenny's picture, like a funeral director might, impressed him. He also liked that she hadn't pushed, prodded. That wouldn't help Jessica get over the fire.

"Okay, let's do this puzzle."

Sam watched his daughter and the unwanted nanny for a few more minutes, astounded by Jessica's reaction to Erin. His daughter acted like she'd known the young woman forever. Still, Erin wasn't right for the job, and the sooner he could get the formal interview part over, the sooner he could call the agency and ask for a grandmotherly sort. This time, he'd be a little more forceful with his request.

He cleared his throat. "So, Erin. Tell me about your professional background."

Erin caught the cue and moved to a nearby armchair. Jessica dragged her toys and her mother's photograph over to sit at Erin's feet, but kept on playing. "I have a degree in early childhood education with an emphasis on childhood trauma."

"And why that? If I may ask."

Erin nodded once. "I come from a large family. I'm one of six, actually. My oldest brother and his wife lost one of their sons to a swimming pool accident when little Bryce was two.'' As if both realizing Jessica's age, they looked momentarily at her. Erin absentmindedly threaded her fingers through Jessica's soft hair. ''I saw how it affected the other kids. Bryce's siblings and cousins. And my brother and his wife, too. I guess I just wanted to do something to help.''

''I'm sorry.'' Sam was totally taken aback by her candid sharing. He couldn't imagine what her family had gone through, losing a child. ''That had to be…horrible.''

''Thank you. It was. But being able to make a difference took away some of the helplessness I'd felt.'' She pressed her lips together for a moment, sadness clouding her eyes. ''Anyway, I started studying ways to work through the grief with my niece and nephew and found I had a knack for it.'' She shrugged, as if it were nothing. ''I spoke with my advisors and worked it into my major.'' She cut her glance away, then back, an air of determination and confidence on her face that Sam found appealing and impressive. ''I will tell you I've never been a nanny before, but I have 15 nieces and nephews and I take care of all of them. I love children. More than anything.''

He allowed one corner of his mouth to lift in a half smile. It wasn't that he had anything against Erin O'Grady. On the contrary, he was completely charmed by her. He just didn't want her sharing his home. But, he had to give credit where credit was due, and the fact that she loved children was not in question. He glanced from her to Jessica, pointedly. "It's obvious you love kids."

Erin smiled, and it truly lit up the room. "I know you wanted an older woman, but I really think I could make a difference with your daughter. If you'd let me."

"I'll think about it, Erin." He stood, hoping to give a polite enough clue that the interview was over. "Thank you for coming. I'll be in touch with the agency."

Erin studied him for a moment, then pulled in a deep breath and blew it out. It was as if she knew what his answer would be, too. He could see the disappointment like a shadow on her face, and for some reason, it made him feel like a heel.

She stood, glancing down regretfully at Jessica. "Well, you have a perfectly lovely daughter. I hope you find what you're looking for, Sam."

They shook hands, and Erin turned toward the door with Sam just behind her. Suddenly, from behind them came Jessica's anguished cry. "No!"

Both Erin and Sam whipped around to find little Jessica standing, her eyes round and moist, her hands clasped together. Sam rushed to her and knelt down on one knee, taking hold of her chubby little arms gently. "What's the matter, honeypot?"

Jessica pulled away and ran to Erin, wrapping her arms around Erin's legs. She pressed her face into Erin's thighs and sobbed. "No go. Play."

Erin seemed as startled as Sam himself was. She

blinked up at him pleadingly, then smoothed Jessica's hair back. "It's okay, angel. Don't cry."

"No go!"

It seemed like interminable minutes passed while Sam and Erin merely stared at one another. She looked torn. He felt torn. Finally, he scrubbed a palm down his face as resignation seeped through him. He had no choice in the matter. Jessica had chosen her own nanny. This was the worst set-up in the world for him, but clearly not for Jessica. He couldn't break his baby girl's heart. Not again.

"Well," he said, finally. "I'll be honest, you wouldn't be my first choice."

Erin flushed, but didn't seem to take offense. "I know. You wanted a grandmother. But keep in mind, the best grandmothers were mothers first, and before that, I'm sure they were young women who adored children." A beat passed. "A lot like me. You don't have to be an older lady to be compassionate and nurturing."

"I can see that." He offered her a sheepish smirk. "I guess there's only one thing left to do."

"What?" Erin's eyes widened, her expression an endearing mix of hopefulness and trepidation.

He shrugged. "Call the agency and tell them you're hired. That is, if you're still interested in the job."

Erin's face broke into the most beatific smile, it couldn't help but warm Sam's heart. He cut his glance away, focusing on Jessica. "Jess, baby, do you want Erin to come and live with us? Take care of you?"

"No go," Jessica said.

He cocked an eyebrow at Erin. "Well?"

"Oh, Sam. Of course I want the job."

She reached out a hand to shake on the deal, and when her warm palm slid against his, he felt another zing of recognition, a male-female awareness that left him disturbingly off-kilter. "Shall we talk about arrangements? I'd want you to move in as soon as possible. I can't afford to miss more work."

"Of course. I can move in tomorrow and be ready to take care of Jessica when you go back to work on Monday." She bent down and easily lifted Jessica into her arms.

Sam watched as his baby girl nestled her head in the crook of her new nanny's neck, and he wondered how that soft skin smelled. *Don't think that way.*

"You won't regret this. I promise," Erin said.

Yeah. Right. Sam nodded, but he wasn't so sure. If the short time she'd spent with Jessica was any indication, Erin could be just the miracle his daughter needed. No arguments there. Yes, she was beautiful, spirited, sexy, but she was also his daughter's nanny. That made her strictly off-limits. If he wasn't careful, this forced proximity with Erin O'Grady could end up being a colossal disaster for him.

Damn good thing he was a careful man.

## Chapter Three

Erin didn't release her breath until she was actually locked safely in her Volkswagen Bug, seatbelt on, pulling away from the curb. But, when she finally drove off, she threw her head back and laughed in delight. She had a job! A perfect job! Jessica was a doll, and her daddy—holy moly.

Her heart had lodged firmly in her throat the moment Sam Lowery had opened the door. Not only was the assignment perfect, but the man himself was a fantasy come to life. Tall, dark, brooding. Ultra-yummy. Her brothers *so* wouldn't approve, and somehow that made it all the better.

She laughed again, cranking her radio up louder as Sheryl Crow crooned about wanting to have fun. She planned to have a whole lot of fun with this job.

*Okay, get your brain straight, Erin.* She was only *working for* the tall, dark, brooding, ultra-yummy guy, not truly *moving in* with him, but still. It felt like a scenario straight out of one of her beloved love stories, and she couldn't help but hope that Sam had felt some of those fireworks between them, too. She'd had to focus on Jessica fully during the interview, just to keep the attraction she'd felt from exploding out of her like a big, neon sign that read, "TAKE ME, I'M YOURS!" She never had been very good at keeping her emotions hidden. Of course, Jessica was an absolute angel herself, and Erin couldn't wait to work with her. But Sam had been an extra, very unexpected but very pleasant bonus.

Even at the beginning, when she could tell he didn't want her for the nanny position, she felt an immediate bond with him. And an instantaneous attraction. He didn't look to be much older than she was. From his slightly scruffy sexiness, the sinew and muscles in his arms, to his piercing eyes, he'd been the polar opposite of what she'd imagined. Why had she automatically assumed he'd be older? The word "widower" had thrown her, she supposed. She'd been expecting a nice, older gentleman who'd started a family late and then lost his wife tragically, and instead she was faced with Mr. Utterly Perfect.

And she was going to live in his house!

"Thank you, God," she whispered, a little shiver moving through her. With any luck, she'd get to know Sam better as she cared for his daughter. She wasn't going to act inappropriately or throw herself at him or anything. But the proximity, the inevitable intimacy they'd develop because of his daughter, the whole dang situation—well, it all spelled possibility to her, with a capital P. And, in time, maybe…just maybe—

*Don't get ahead of yourself.*

Hey, she was an unrepentant hopeless romantic, but she knew when to be reasonable. Sam Lowery epitomized the word "untouchable." But things could change quickly with luck, couldn't they? And she had the luck of the Irish firmly on her side. Just that morning, she'd been unemployed and living with her parents, and now look at her.

Giddy with excitement, she slowed as she drove past her brother, Matthew, who sat hunkered down stakeout-style in his truck a few houses away from Sam's. She laid on her horn, then stuck her tongue out at her brother when he looked over. Shaking his head, he kicked his engine over and whipped a quick U-turn to follow her home.

Hoo-boy, she couldn't wait to spread the news. She was going to be living in the same house with a certified single hunk, working at the job of her dreams, and nurturing her fantasies of happily forever after at the same time. Best of all, there wasn't a darn thing her brothers could do to stop her, because despite their collective and annoying—although, admittedly, endearing—overprotectiveness, she had her own mind, and she was perfectly capable of taking care of herself.

She could hardly wait to spill her news and see the

reactions on their faces. Newsflash, world: Erin O'Grady was more than ready to grow up.

Especially in the eyes of her brothers.

As it turned out, the only way Erin could appease her brothers was by agreeing to let them ''help her move in'' the following day. The whole idea was absurd. Her rooms at Sam's house were furnished, so all she had to bring was her personal effects, all of which fit into her bright yellow Volkswagen Bug. Her parents had been no help to her; they agreed with her brothers. Maybe it was a good idea for the boys to make sure this Sam Lowery was okay, they'd told her.

Argh!

She decided she owed it to Sam to warn him before the entire O'Grady clan infiltrated his home. Dialing his number on her cell phone, she glanced at the caravan of full-sized pick-up trucks in her rear view mirror and groaned. Humiliating, that's what it was. They were undermining her professionalism.

Sam picked up on the second ring. ''Hello?''

''Hi, Sam. It's Erin. I'm on my way over.''

''Good, I have your rooms all ready for you.''

''Great. There's…just one thing you should know.''

''And what's that?'' His voice had turned immediately apprehensive, which made Erin cringe. She didn't want to get off on bad footing with the man who hadn't wanted to hire her in the first place.

"My brothers—well, four of the five—are coming to help me move in."

"Oh. That's fine."

"Yeah, the thing is, I don't have enough stuff to warrant four men assisting me." She sighed. "I'll be honest. I'm the baby of the family, their only sister, and—"

"They want to make sure I'm not an ax murderer?"

Erin laughed nervously. "Something like that, yes. I'm so embarrassed and sorry. Brothers can be so overprotective. Do you have sisters?" He hesitated for a beat too long, which left Erin perplexed. "Sam?"

"No," he said, a bit stiffly. "No sisters or brothers."

"Well, some days I'd say you're lucky being an only child."

"In a lot of ways, I'm sure you're right."

Oops. She didn't want him to think she wasn't a fan of family. After all, she was going to be caring for his daughter. "Don't get me wrong, I love my family. But, they act like I'm Snow White, running through the forest in those stupid high heels, hapless and helpless."

Sam actually made a small sound that could've been mistaken for a laugh. That pleased her.

"Look, it's fine. If you were my sister, I'd do the same thing."

*But I don't want to* be *your sister.* "You're sure you don't mind?" She bit her lip.

"Of course not. As long as they don't feel the need to beat me up or anything."

Now it was Erin's turn to laugh. "Okay, well, we'll be there shortly. Thanks for understanding."

"No sweat."

Erin hit the end button, and her phone immediately rang again. She frowned, her tone quizzical as she answered. "Hello?" Had Sam forgotten something? Changed his mind?

"This is your big brother, Patrick, behind you."

"I know who you are and where you are, Pat. How could I forget? You've been tailgating me since Mom and Dad's house. What's up?"

"Don't talk on a cell phone when you drive, Erin Marie. It's not safe."

Incredulous, she pulled the phone away from her ear and stared at it a moment. Lifting it back to her ear, she rasped, "Are you insane? *You* called *me!*"

"Yes, but just to tell you that. You were on the phone before. I saw you."

"I was speaking to my new boss. Warning him about impending O'Grady infestation of his home."

"Hang up and watch the road."

Erin muttered as she hung up, then tossed her phone in the passenger's seat and gave a surly wave to Patrick behind her. For the love of Pete, she couldn't wait to get out from under her brothers' constant watch.

The moving-in process went quickly, thank goodness, because Erin had never been a packrat. Although each of her brothers had done the squeeze handshake/suspicious size-up routine with Sam, there hadn't been any overt grilling, and they'd been polite. Hey, when it came to Eamon, Patrick, Matt, Miles, and Mick, Erin had learned to be grateful for the little things.

She let her brothers preen and puff their chests and check out the place to their hearts' content. She didn't even interfere, just sat at the kitchen table, elbows propped, chin resting in her palm. But when all the O'Gradys had left, Erin finally relaxed. Strangely, she felt like she'd come home.

The silence fairly hummed in their absence, and Erin slipped into a very un-Erin-like shyness as she glanced up at her new boss. "Well, that was uncomfortable."

Sam smirked, but didn't say a word about her brothers. She didn't know what to make of that.

"Let me show you your quarters."

"Cool, I've never had quarters before." She grinned, smoothing her palms together and scrunching her shoulders up with excitement. "Except for the round, twenty-five-cent kind."

"Well, we've got the whole shebang here." He lifted an arm, indicating the hallway off the kitchen through which her brothers had carried her belongings. Erin bounced a little on her feet, then headed off, but Sam's warm, solid, silent presence behind her made her shiver.

He cleared his throat. "If you're cold, there are extra blankets and comforters in the linen closet outside your bathroom. Feel free to take whatever you need.''

"Oh.'' Whoops. She wished she were better at reining in her emotions. ''Thanks. I do tend to be on the chilled side. You know, that female thing.''

He had no reply to that.

At the door of the bedroom, they stopped and peered in. It was the first time Erin had viewed what was to be her new bedroom, and she sighed. ''Wow.''

"I want you to be comfortable here, so feel free to change the room however you'd like.''

She glanced over her shoulder at him, then leaned into the doorjamb and wrapped her arms around herself. The room was decorated in yellows and blues, with what looked like a handmade quilt, in some sort of intricate star pattern, draping the bed. Sunlight streamed in the large windows, which were covered by gauzy, white curtains. He'd taken the time to set a vase of daisies on her hickory dresser, which touched her. They matched the daisy motif of her Bug. ''But it's so beautiful. I can't imagine changing a thing.''

Sam shrugged. ''That's fine, too.''

Erin glanced around suddenly, realizing she'd been so worried about what egregious things her brothers might do or say, she hadn't seen or greeted her new little charge. ''Hey, where's Jessica? Napping?''

Sam aimed a thumb over his shoulder. ''I actually left her at my secretary's house for the afternoon. I didn't want her upset over the moving in process.''

Erin bit her lip. "You think she would be? But we got along so well."

"I wasn't sure. Didn't want to risk it." A line of worry bisected his browline. "Sometimes it's the oddest things that set her off. I just worry. Probably too much."

"Nonsense. A child can tell when she's well cared for. But there are things you can do to help her out of her shell." Sam said nothing, so she sucked in a breath and blew it out, offering a smile. Clearly, he didn't want to talk parenting techniques. "Well. I can't wait to see her."

Sam nodded once. "After I've shown you around, I'll leave you to unpack while I go pick her up. Maybe—" He raised a hand. "Now, normally, you'll have weekends off. But I thought, tonight, maybe we can have dinner together, the three of us. A get acquainted dinner. And you and I can talk about expectations and pay, that sort of thing. I'd like to hear about your plan to help Jess get over her residual…"

"Grief?"

"Do you think it's grief? At her age?"

"Absolutely. But she can overcome all of it."

"Well. You're the expert, and you sound confident. I like that. Dinner, then?"

Erin didn't want to seem too swoony and corny, but the thought of dining with Sam and Jessica made her heart pound. "I'd love that. What would you like me to make?"

Sam blinked, appearing taken aback. "You don't

have to cook. That's not one of your duties. We'll just order a pizza.''

"Oh. Sounds fine.'' She dipped her chin. "But, you know, I will have to cook for Jessica.''

He rubbed his chin thoughtfully with the side of his hand. "I suppose so, but not every meal.''

Erin turned to fully face him. Did he have any concept whatsoever of what a nanny did? "What time do you leave for work in the morning?''

"As early as five.''

"So she'll need breakfast and lunch.''

He conceded the point with a nod.

"Do you generally get home from work the same time?''

Sam huffed. "I wish. My job can be unpredictable. I used to take her with me, so we ate on the fly a lot.''

Erin smiled gently. She had a sense that it wouldn't be smart to point out any faults in Sam's parenting philosophies—not that there were true faults. Just…adjustments that may be needed. "One of the ways we can help Jessica readjust is to get her on a normal, set schedule of meals, naps, bedtimes, etc. so she can feel secure.''

His eyes narrowed. "You think she doesn't feel secure?''

Erin's throat tightened. She still didn't quite know how to read Sam, and it made her nerves stand on edge. She didn't want to offend him, or take over too much and put him off. "No, I didn't mean it that way.

She's been through a lot, Sam. You both have. Not just the fire and losing her mother, but a move to a new house, new routines, all of it. Those schedule upheavals affect little ones.''

"I hadn't thought of it that way."

"As long as you have me here, you might as well let me do everything I can to bring Jess around. Cooking's part of that. Besides, I love cooking."

Sam swallowed warily. "Don't you want your evenings free? I mean, you're a young woman. Surely you have friends, boyfriends?"

"No boyfriends," she said quickly.

He raised one eyebrow, and Erin checked her tone, not wanting to sound like she was flirting. Or desperate. Or twenty-three-years-old and a hopeless romantic, completely crushing on her new boss. She bestowed a droll, playful look. "Hello, have you forgotten my brothers already?"

A half-smile lifted Sam's mouth. "Not hardly."

"Yeah, well, they scare every guy in the Pacific Northwest away, believe me. Any potential boyfriends meet the Evil Five and turn tail immediately."

"They just love you."

"Yeah, straight into spinsterhood."

"Oh, I think you're at least a year away from that."

She laughed. "I do have friends, but I'm Jessica's nanny. I'm here for her, first and foremost. I can go out with friends and see family on the weekends."

Sam pressed his lips into a flat line. "I don't want you to burn out, or feel like an indentured servant."

Erin scoffed at the notion. "Are you kidding? Burn out? This is my dream job, Sam. I plan to have a brood of my own someday, but for now, working with Jessica is going to be my pleasure. I promise."

Sam studied her for a few moments, then gave a grudging smile. "You know, I think this is going to work out better than I imagined. I wanted a grandmother who would treat Jessica as her own granddaughter. But maybe having a..."

Erin waited, her pulse pounding in her neck. She wondered just how Sam Lowery viewed her. New mommy? Wouldn't *that* be a fantasy come true?

"Maybe having a...big sister figure is just as good."

*Ugh.* Just what she wanted—another flipping brother. Even figuratively speaking, it didn't appeal, especially considering her wholly inappropriate and yet very real attraction to Sam. Still, she managed a weak smile. "Jessica and I will have great fun, and with time and some solid grief work, she'll come out of her shell even more."

"I want that for her more than anything." He pulled a face. "As long as you think I passed muster with your formidable brothers, of course."

Erin winked at his seemingly out-of-character playfulness. "I'm still here, aren't I? If you hadn't met with their approval, trust me, they'd have dragged me home by the scruff of my neck, job or no job."

The ice sufficiently broken by that absurd image, Erin and Sam walked down the hall toward a large bathroom. The tile was blue and white checkerboard, with the occasional yellow tile thrown in for punch. The shower curtain was blue and yellow stripes, and all the white porcelain gleamed. Erin absolutely loved it, but she bit her lip to keep her reaction composed. Instead of cheering and clapping, she said, "It's lovely."

"Glad you like it. I used to have your bedroom outfitted as a study, but I moved that upstairs to a smaller bedroom near mine. I wanted you to have your privacy."

"I'm sure my brothers approved," she said, in a wry tone.

"In fact, the dark-haired one—"

"Patrick."

"Patrick did ask me where my bedroom was."

Erin groaned and covered her face with both hands. "I'm so sorry. That was uncalled for."

"Not a problem. It's nice that you have people looking out for you."

"Yeah." She huffed. "Nice like a prison sentence."

He gave one of those almost-laughs again as he guided her toward a small sitting nook off her bedroom, and indicated a sliding glass door. "You have a small patio there. I'll be installing a Charlie Bar onto the door for safety. Your brother, Mick, suggested it."

Erin gave him an incredulous look, then squeezed her eyes shut. "Gosh, I'm really embarrassed. You must think I'm sixteen years old. God knows, they all do."

"No, it's a good idea, the Charlie Bar. If you'd like an alarm system, too—"

"No. God. No alarm system." Annoying O'Grady men. They'd ruin her entire life if given the chance. Needing space to cool down her humiliation, Erin re-entered the bedroom and crossed to the closet, opening one of the mirrored glass doors.

"Is it big enough?"

"More than." She shrugged. "I'm not one of those women who collects clothes and shoes."

"That's unusual."

"There are some of us around. Growing up with all brothers, it was hard to become a girly-girl." She grinned, proudly. "I don't collect clothes and shoes like a girl, I don't squeal like a girl, I don't take hours to get ready like some girls. I don't even throw like a girl, but that's actually a bonus."

He smiled, this time for real—albeit enigmatically. Sam never dropped that wall of emotional safety completely. "I just want you to know, the bedroom, sitting room, patio, and bathroom are yours alone. Neither I nor Jessica will come into this section of the house unless there is an emergency."

Erin crossed her arms, hoping Sam would eventually find occasion to enter her rooms. Pipe dream. The guy was so professional about the whole thing, clearly he hadn't felt spark number one during their interview. Erin really did need to rein in her romantic fantasies, because they were just that—fanciful little daydreams that would never come true. "It's a lovely design, this wing. Did you plan it?"

He nodded. ''With help from an architect friend of mine. I had…a lot of support and help from my company after the fire. My insurance didn't cover much, but they picked up the slack. This house is a real blessing for Jess and me.''

''That's wonderful.''

''I think a set-up like this is intended as a mother-in-law's suite. It's separate, but has access to the kitchen and living room. I didn't use it that way, of course.'' He cleared his throat. ''Also, if you'd like me to put a deadbolt on the outside hallway door leading in to this part—''

''Sam,'' Erin said, gravely, holding up one hand. ''Please tell me one of my brothers didn't suggest that?''

He paused, as though weighing the wisdom of his next words. Finally he nodded. ''The big one. Sorry, I have a difficult time remembering names.''

''Matthew,'' she said through clenched teeth. ''I'll be sure to kill him later.''

Sam looked amused. ''Erin, it's no problem.''

''Let me ask you something.'' She looked at him directly. ''Do I *need* a deadbolt on my room?''

He looked vaguely affronted. ''Of course not.''

''Then I won't have you bother with the expense. It's ridiculous. I'm perfectly comfortable here with you.'' She crossed her arms protectively over her chest. ''If I felt threatened in any way, I wouldn't have taken the job.''

His eyes softened momentarily, then grew remote again almost as quickly. He cleared his throat, backing away. "Good. Well. I'll just go get Jessica and the pizza, give you a little time to settle in. Anything you don't like on your pizza?"

"The usual answer. Anchovies."

"Jess would probably have a meltdown of epic proportions if I fed her furry little fish of any kind, so you're safe. She loves pineapple and ham, though."

"Cool, that's my favorite, actually."

Sam watched her intently for a moment, and it almost looked like he had something to say. But, instead of giving voice to his thoughts, he simply nodded, turned, and left. Erin sank onto the edge her bed, releasing a sigh and smoothing her palms over the softly crinkled texture of the quilt. For certain, Sam Lowery wasn't going to be an easy man to get to know, but Erin planned to do her best to bring him out of his shell, just as she hoped to do the same for his daughter. She flopped backward on the bed and stared up at the ceiling.

Miracles *could* happen. She'd seen it before.

## Chapter Four

*World of hurt* took on several new layers of meaning as Sam drove to Mia's house to pick up Jessica.

What in the hell had he gotten himself into?

Half of him pondered that question. The other half greedily soaked up Erin's sunny presence in his home, and he realized, with dismay, that he was inexplicably ravenous for the pure, platonic company of a woman like her. She was so guileless and enthusiastic, it made his heart squeeze. Her blue eyes always smiled, and she seemed genuinely happy and grateful for everything he showed her. Even her yellow Volkswagen Bug, with those silly daisy wheel covers, exuded a happy-go-lucky attitude.

Erin was so different from Jenny, who'd always been a bit of a dark soul, much like himself. Jenny had never been happy with his work schedule, never contented with their apartment, with their life, with herself. She'd never been quite happy, period, and on a lot of levels, he'd understood it. Both of them had come from difficult backgrounds. Of course, he had always hoped having each other, creating a family of their own, would help both of them heal and move on, but that hadn't happened for Jenny. Erin, on the other hand, felt like a balm to his soul in just the short time he'd known her.

Wait. Hold up. Why was he comparing Erin to Jenny?

With effort, Sam shook off the notion. Jenny had been his *wife*. Erin was his daughter's *nanny,* period, and he'd known her for exactly two days. Having met her brothers, he knew he'd be wise to remember the difference.

For a moment, knowing Erin and he couldn't get to know each other on a different level made him feel grim and bleak. Then again, hadn't he sworn off romance forever? He had, and it had been the right thing to do for his daughter's sake. He would have to settle for enjoying Erin's presence while she was around. Perhaps having a live-in nanny would be a safe, commitment-free way of enjoying the presence of a woman in his life. No ties, no lies, no complications of love and sex—no heartbreak.

And no Erin. Not really.

The thought bummed him out.

A man would have to be half-dead not to notice Erin's appeal, to be sure, and if he was picking up the cues correctly, she found him attractive as well. He'd have to watch his step. He knew damn well what her brothers feared: a guy who was out to take advantage of what their baby sister had to offer and then unceremoniously break her gentle heart.

Lucky for the O'Grady men, he wasn't interested in taking his relationship with the new nanny in that direction, because he *would* break her heart eventually. Erin needed and deserved a forever kind of guy, one who would give her that giant brood of smiling Irish babies she so wanted. He wasn't that guy and never would be. Not after Jenny, after everything that happened.

Sam groaned. Enough heavy thoughts. He just wanted to pick up his baby girl, buy a pizza, and get back home.

To Erin.

But, no. Not like that. Only, he reminded himself sternly, so that the three of them could get acquainted, and so Jessica could get used to the idea of having a stranger live with them. As the *nanny*. He'd take on the role of looking out for Erin just like her brothers did, and he'd protect her from himself.

Suddenly the thought of Lissa Cartwright intruded on his ruminations. She was *his* sister, like it or not. Did she have an adoptive brother to look out for her? To keep her away from the less than honorable men?

Then again, he didn't care, right?

He pushed the thought of Lissa out of his mind. Why was he thinking of *them* again? Lissa and Adam, Jared Cambry and his new little son, Mark, who'd received the, hopefully, life-saving bone marrow transplant from Adam. They had no place in his thoughts. It was just the O'Grady family closeness he'd witnessed making him think crazy about all the rest. It didn't help, of course, that the news show about the reunited twins had sparked a media frenzy of follow-up stories he couldn't seem to ignore. He felt as drawn to the story as half of America was, it seemed. More so because they were—no. He stopped himself, gripping tightly to the steering wheel and clenching his jaw.

They weren't and would never be his family. Not really.

He couldn't think that way, now or ever.

He had family, and her name was Jessica.

With determination, Sam sped up slightly. All of a sudden, the tumultuousness of the past few days pressed down on him and made him crave a touchstone of sanity. He needed to hold his daughter, breathe in the sweet baby scent of her hair, and remind himself of what mattered. Not a sister and brother he'd never known, nor a "father" who'd given him up. Not a nanny who was too enticing for her own good, and already too imbedded in his world for his peace of mind.

Just Jessica. His daughter.

She was all Sam needed in his life. End of story.

It didn't take long for Erin to unpack and settle in, and by the time she was done, Sam and Jessica still hadn't returned. Edgy and anxious to see them, she went into the kitchen, turned on the Bose under-cabinet radio to her favorite light rock station, and set about tossing a salad to go with the pizza. When she finished that, she whipped together a batch of no bake lemon bars from a mix she found in the cupboard. Sam and Jessica still hadn't returned, so Erin filled her time by unloading the clean dishes from the dishwasher, reloading it with the few dishes she'd used, and wiping down all the surfaces with kitchen cleanser. She found a simple, white emergency candle in a drawer and placed it into a taper holder on the table, lighting it. Might as well make their first dinner together festive.

She peered into the large laundry/mud room, which angled off the kitchen and led to the three-car garage, and noticed a hamper filled with toddler clothes that needed washing. Humming as she worked, she loaded the washer and got that task underway as well. She'd just as soon fill idle moments with productive work than sit around doing nothing. She'd learned that from her mother.

Smiling sadly, she realized she already missed her parents, despite the fact she'd been so eager to move out of the house. Hey, she was a young woman now. Yearning for independence wasn't a commentary on her parents or how much she loved them. It was a normal growing process. Crossing to a wall-mounted phone in the kitchen, she dialed the familiar number without even thinking. Mom answered on the first ring.

"Hi, Mom. It's me."

"Erin, honey! We're missing you already here."

"I was missing you, too. That's why I called."

"Oh, dear. Are things not going well? The boys called and said this Sam Lowery seemed like a decent enough fellow. I thought surely things would be okay."

"No, no. Things are going fine. My rooms are gorgeous, and Sam has been very polite and cordial." She twirled the cord around her finger, inexplicably charmed that Sam still used at least one phone with a cord. "It's just…he went to pick up Jessica, the baby, and I'm waiting for them to get home so we can eat dinner. I'm not used to having a quiet house."

Sarah O'Grady laughed softly. "No, I suppose you aren't. You know you can come home any time, if things don't work out."

"I know, Mom. But I'm determined to make it work." Suddenly, she heard the garage door lift. "Oh, they're here. I'll call you tomorrow, okay?"

"Be careful, sweetie. And bring that wee baby over to meet your family some time."

"I'll try, but it might be a while." She glanced toward the mud room door that led to the garage and lowered her tone. "Sam's pretty overprotective over Jessica. Of course, it's understandable, with the fire and all. But…I'll work on it."

"I'm sure you'll do a wonderful job."

"I love you, Mom."

"I love you, too."

Erin rang off just as Sam and Jessica entered through the mud room. Sam held a large, white pizza box in one hand, and Jessica toddled beside him. When she saw Erin, she broke into a wide, albeit shy, grin and hid her face in her father's leg.

Sam touched her head. "Honeypot, do you remember Erin?"

Erin squatted down and opened her arms for a hug. "There's the pretty little miss. Hello, Jessica!"

Jessica didn't speak, but went slowly into Erin's embrace and nestled her soft baby head into Erin's neck.

Erin smiled up at Sam, who was peering around the kitchen with a surprised look on his face. The washing machine hummed from just behind him, and the smell of lemon and crumbly, buttery crust permeated the air.

Finally his gaze settled on her. "Erin, you didn't need to clean up or start the laundry. And—" He glanced toward the countertop. "—did you make dessert?"

Erin nodded. "And a salad." She shrugged. "I had time. It's no trouble." She lifted Jessica, settling her onto one hip, moving further into the kitchen. "You're going to have to get used to me doing things around the house, Sam. I'm not one to sit around idly."

He set the pizza on the counter. "But, you were supposed to unpack. Get settled."

"Done."

He cocked his head to one side. "Where'd you learn to be so efficient?"

"From a mother who had to raise five slob brothers."

One corner of Sam's mouth quivered up. "Well. Okay. Thank you." He glanced at the dessert. "I say, let's eat the pizza so we can get to the lemon stuff."

"Why, Sam Lowery." She turned her head to the side and peered at him out of the corner of her eye, playfully. "Would it be fair to say you have a sweet tooth?"

He opened the pizza box, watching her over it thoughtfully. "I do like sweet things. Yes."

Erin's heart fluttered, and she focused on settling Jessica in her high chair, unable to maintain eye contact with Sam. She knew her Irish complexion all too well, and she was most likely crimson right then. "What would you like with dinner, little miss? Milk, juice, or water?"

"Milk," murmured Jessica, squirming to get down. "I pour."

Erin glanced at Sam for confirmation. He shook his head slightly. "Let her T-H-I-N-K she's pouring."

"Gotcha." She lifted Jessica back out of the high chair and set her on the floor. The little girl dashed toward the fridge, going on tippy-toe to pull the door open and wrestle the milk out of the door. Erin rescued the carton from Jessica, who was walking with it, half-tipped, toward the table.

He lifted a chin toward the cabinet closest to the fridge. "Sippy cups are in there. And, how about you? Care to join me in a beer or a glass of wine? I have a good Chianti. It goes great with pizza, and I sure could use it.''

''I'd love a glass, if it's okay.'' She glanced at Jessica.

''It's fine. I'm certainly not suggesting we get plowed. Just a nice, civilized glass of wine with dinner.''

She inclined her head. ''Sounds wonderful.''

''How about you serve the pizza and I'll pour?''

''Deal.''

For several quiet moments, save the radio music, they moved easily around one another in the kitchen, preparing dinner. The opening and shutting of cabinets, sounds of a cork being pulled and the subsequent glug, glug, glug of wine filling goblets, Jessica's quiet little chatter to her beloved Doggy—it all seemed so comfortable, so warm. Happiness filled Erin until she thought she might burst. She said a silent prayer that she, Sam, and Jessica would share a lot of intimate meals together in the days to come. She wouldn't say for sure that doing so would warm Sam up, but it certainly couldn't hurt.

Erin awoke the first morning in Sam's house while dawn was still hazy and blue. She listened to a sound she couldn't quite place, then realized someone was prowling the kitchen.

Sam.

Despite the early hour, she couldn't pass up this chance to speak with him alone. They hadn't really discussed much about her plans for Jessica's treatment at dinner the previous night, but she wanted to get started as soon as possible. Six months had already passed since the trauma. Time was of the essence. Tossing off the quilt, she wrapped herself in a blue, fleece robe, brushed her teeth and finger-combed her hair, then made her way down the hallway into the kitchen.

When she opened the door, Sam spun to face her, a butter knife in one hand and a jar of mayonnaise in the other. He looked momentarily stunned, but recovered in short order. "I'm sorry. Did I wake you?"

Erin crossed her arms and smiled. "No. I'm an early riser. I wanted to come out and chat with you before you left, if it doesn't disrupt your routine too much."

"Oh. Well." Sam seemed at a loss, then he indicated the coffeemaker with the butter knife. "Join me in a cup of coffee. If you'd like. Are you a coffee drinker?"

"Thank you. Yes," said Erin. "Don't mind if I do." She crossed to the cupboards, opening two before finding mugs inside the third. "What time does Jessica usually get up?" she asked, as she filled her mug with the aromatic brew.

"There's a question that should be easy to answer but isn't. I used to have to wake her and get her ready before I left for work, poor thing." He pulled a face. "She didn't like it one single bit. I don't think she's going to be a morning person."

"I can imagine, and I can't blame her, either." Erin took her mug and sat down at the table. "I'll wait until seven-thirty to wake her, I think."

Sam worked on his lunch in silence for a few moments, then sealed it all in a black lunch container. He poured himself a cup of coffee, then turned toward Erin. With his hip propped against the counter, he studied her but said nothing.

Erin tried not to squirm beneath his scrutiny as he eyed her over the brim of his mug while he drank. She swallowed thickly, curling her fingers around the warm comfort of her own mug. She had to say something. Anything. This silence was like a big elephant hunkered in the corner of the kitchen. "So...um, should I hold dinner for you tonight?"

"Never any need for that," Sam said, with a decisive huff. "I don't ever know when I'll be home, unfortunately."

She bit her lip and nodded, her gaze drifting slowly down toward the steaming dark brew in her coffee cup.

"But...I'll call if I'm going to be home at a reasonable hour. If you want."

"Yes, please. I'd like to feed Jessica dinner at six o'clock in the evenings. So, if it's not by then, I'll have to save you leftovers."

"Duly noted."

She dipped her chin slightly, but kept her tone light. "It would be good, too, if you maintained her meal schedule as much as possible on the weekends if I'm not here."

"Okay, you'll have to remind me..."

"Maybe I can type up some sort of schedule for the fridge."

"Great idea. You're welcome to use my computer. It's in the den, upstairs. Second door on the right."

Erin almost told him she had her own laptop and printer set up in her sitting room, but what was she—crazy? He was giving her free rein to enter his private area of the house. "Thanks. I appreciate it."

"So," Sam asked, "is that what you wanted to talk to me about? Dinner? Or…schedules?"

"No." Erin lifted her shoulders and let them drop. "I just have a few questions, so I can start working with Jess in the way that will help her best. I don't mean to be overeager, but—"

"Fire away. I'm eager, too."

Erin cleared her throat. "How does Jessica react when you share your feelings about what happened to your wife."

A muscle in his jaw ticked, and he looked away. "This isn't about me. It's about my daughter."

"Well…yes. But you're grieving, too. Right?"

He paused for an uncomfortably long time, then gave a grudging half-nod.

"At her age, Jessica is just learning how to deal with emotions, Sam. She's going to take all her cues from you."

"Meaning what?"

"If you want her to come out of her shell, you'll have to venture out of yours a bit."

"I don't have a shell," he said, sharply.

Erin softened her tone, but her heart started to pound. She hated confrontations. "I'm not trying to pry, Sam. But, we're going to have to work together on this. You're the closest person to that baby girl. I'm just here to help. I need to know how she…and you…handle the tragedy.''

His face took on a pained mask. ''I know. Okay, fine. What do you need from me?''

''Well, basic information so I know how to approach Jessica.''

Sam spread his arms. ''I'm right here listening.''

Erin fought back the urge to roll her eyes, then adjusted in her chair and met his gaze directly and repeated her question in a slightly different way. ''How does Jessica act when you talk about her mother?''

''I don't talk about her mother.''

A frisson of shock spiraled through Erin, and she had to blink a couple times to keep it off her face. ''Ever?''

Color rose up Sam's neck at her incredulous tone, and he cut his glance away. ''I don't want to upset her. I'm trying to help her get over the whole… thing.''

*Thing.* He was so deep into denying his own pain, he couldn't even say the words. Erin pressed her lips together, then bought a bit of time by taking a sip of coffee. Maybe she needed to come at this topic from another direction. ''What about looking through her pictures? Family photos of good times, memorabilia, her mother's clothing, that stuff?''

''I actually put all the pictures of Jenny away, except for the one I framed for Jessica's bedroom. Same deal with her clothes, perfume, and any stuff that wasn't lost in the fire. I didn't want—''

''To upset her.''

He muttered an exasperated sound. ''I'm trying to be strong for her, Erin, after all she's been through.''

''I understand. I'm not judging you. I'm simply trying to gather information about what's been done so far.'' Erin blew out a small breath. ''Does she cry about the fire? Or about losing her mother? Any of it?''

He considered it. ''No. I mean, sometimes she seems withdrawn and glum, but I just let her be. She might not even be thinking of Jenny. Who knows what her moods are about, really?''

*Not you, if you don't ask.*

''I don't want to interfere or pressure her if she's feeling...however a two-year-old would feel about such a thing.'' He looked puzzled suddenly. ''How *would* a two-year-old feel about such a thing?''

Erin flipped her hand. ''As many different ways as there are children. It depends on the child. All people handle loss differently, even tiny people.'' She sipped, gathering her courage to get back to the central issue again. ''What do you do when you feel especially upset about what occurred?''

A muscle in his jaw jumped, and his gaze drifted to somewhere above her head. ''I guess I...leave the room. Take some time alone to get my head straight.''

''Just...leave?''

He hiked one shoulder, a tense jerky movement.

"No sense laying that rap on a tiny child. She doesn't need a weak father on top of everything else."

"Mmmmmm." Her non-answer visibly agitated him.

"We keep busy, you know? Try not to think about it."

Erin peered up at him from beneath her lashes.

"What? Am I doing everything wrong? Great. That would be about par for the course," he muttered, almost to himself.

She tilted her head side to side, slowly. "Not *wrong*. But I think there are things we can do...together...to make it better for Jessica. We need to start with you, though."

"This isn't *about* me," he said, voice slightly raised.

"It's very much about you, Sam. Your wife died."

"Jessica's *mother* died."

"Jessica's mother, who was also your wife."

"I don't understand where we're going with this."

The exasperation in his words was palpable, and Erin decided she'd pressured him enough for one morning. She eased back. He hadn't given her much information, but his reticence spoke volumes and gave her a place to start. He probably had no idea. Erin wrapped her fingers loosely around her mug and gave him a bland smile. "Someday soon, when you're ready, I want you to tell me the details about the fire. That'll help me."

"O-okay. But, I'd really like you to focus on my daughter. You're *her* nanny. I'm doing just fine."

"I understand."

He turned and gathered his lunchbox and Thermos, and Erin sucked in a deep, calming breath. She had her work cut out for her with this little family, especially starting with papa bear.

She centered her mind and squared her shoulders for confidence. So much of his attitude mirrored her brother, Eamon's coping method when little Bryce had died. Fathers often felt they had to be the pillar of strength for everyone else, without understanding what kind of an example that set for the very children they wanted to help, and without ever coming to terms with their own private pain.

"But, I want you to know, Sam, that I'm very focused on Jessica. Please don't ever doubt that. That's why I'm asking these uncomfortable questions. I apologize for having to do that, but we're going to have to work together, and I know I sound like a broken record. Unfortunately, it's true." She tilted her head apologetically. "I can't make big changes in Jessie's life without you. I'm a stranger, though hopefully not for long. Still, you're her parent. Your impact is greater."

Sam turned, appraising her through an inscrutable expression. "I hear you," he said, finally, in an oddly gentle gruff tone. "I'm not trying to be difficult."

"Comes naturally, huh?"

His momentary surprise was replaced with a sexy half-smile.

Erin stood, smiling back and hoping to leave the conversation on a light note. "I'm just kidding. Anyway, we can talk about it more later. I didn't intend to make you late for work."

Sam swallowed thickly, seeming to accept her olive branch. "It's okay. What are your plans today?"

Erin shrugged, glancing around the pretty red and cream kitchen. "I thought Jessica and I would just hang out around the house, get used to each other."

Sam nodded. "I'd like to install a carseat in your Bug before you drive anywhere with her."

"Of course. I'd never take her out without proper child restraints." Her brow furrowed, and she tapped her bottom lip with the pad of her index finger. "We should do that soon, though, in case there is some emergency."

Sam got a distant, haunted look in his eyes for a moment, then nodded. He set down his Thermos and lunch container. "You're absolutely right. I'll do it now."

"Oh, but—" Surprised, Erin stood and pulled the lapels of her robe around her more tightly. "You'll be late."

"Doesn't matter."

"Yes, well, like I said, we're not going anywhere today."

"I know. But like you also said, you'll need that car seat in case of emergencies. You never know when something will crop up, which is why they're called emergencies. Believe me, I know that all too well."

Respecting his pain, Erin knew better than to argue the point. And, anyway, it was true. Who's to say she and Jessica wouldn't run into some sort of crisis on day one of the job, and she'd absolutely hate to be stranded. "Okay, well, let me just get dressed and get my keys, and I'll help you."

"I'll meet you outside. Incidentally, you're welcome to park your car in the garage. There's plenty of space."

She smiled. "Thank you, Sam. That's very considerate. Daisy Mae will love living inside."

He narrowed his gaze, studying her as if she were crazy. "You named your car?"

"Doesn't everyone?" Sam shook his head, and Erin headed off toward her wing, happiness and hopefulness making her footsteps light as air. First she moved in, and now her VW Bug, Daisy Mae, would be moving in, too. Other than pulling teeth when it came to getting any help or information out of Sam, Erin liked the way their relationship was progressing so far. Yes, indeed, she liked it a lot.

*Chapter Five*

Sam was in a full-blown brood by the time he reached the worksite, complete with dark thoughts, ''buyer's remorse'' in the nanny department, and a whole-face scowl that would bring small children and tender-hearted women to tears. He stomped his way into the trailer that held the site offices, slamming the door behind him and then setting down his metal lunch container harder and louder than necessary. He shouldn't *be* this angry, but he couldn't seem to shake it.

''Wow,'' Mia said, used to his mercurial moods and nonplussed by them, as always. Sam liked that about her. ''Did you find a rock in your cereal bowl this morning, or what?''

Sam deepened his scowl, ignoring the question

while he hung his jacket on a hook by the door. He stalked over and warmed his coffee with fresh, hot brew from a pot Mia had just made, taking his time to formulate an answer. Other men might take a problem like this to family to discuss, but Sam had no one. He'd had Mia available as a friend and sounding board for several years now, although he still held her at arm's length—to the extreme. He'd always been a lone wolf, but Erin's questioning had him spooked, and right now he really did need to vent to someone. Mia was it.

After a fortifying sip of coffee, he turned toward Mia. Leaning his back against a four-drawer file cabinet, he hooked his legs at the ankle and studied his secretary from beneath his furrowed brows. He had so much to say and no skills for molding it all into logical conversation. Defeated, he settled for, "I don't know about this nanny thing."

"Second thoughts already?" Mia sank into her desk chair, pulled out a file drawer, and propped her feet on it. She didn't look the least bit surprised by his comment. "Well, I'm all ears. What did the poor girl do? Breathe in your air space?"

"Very funny." Sam filled her in on the grilling he'd received in the kitchen that morning.

To his surprise, Mia didn't look horrified. Baffled was more like it. "And what exactly do you have a problem with, Sam? The fact that she asked the questions? The way she asked them?"

He bugged his eyes, unable to grasp that Mia couldn't see the wrongness of it all. "I can't seem to make her understand that it's Jessica's pain and suffering I'm worried about, not mine. This has nothing whatsoever to do with me."

Mia fussed with the buttons on her blouse, avoiding eye contact and saying nothing. Her lips were pursed in that way that told Sam she had a lot to say but didn't plan on saying a word of it for fear of his wrath.

"What?" Sam spread his arms. "I know you have an opinion on this, so go ahead. God knows, the women I've been around lately aren't exactly holding back."

Mia peered up at him for several long, scrutinizing moments. "Everyone's pain and suffering deserves validation."

"Geez." He snorted. "Is that from some feel-good wall plaque down at the Hallmark store?"

Mia rolled her eyes. "Seriously. Have you ever talked with anyone about Jenny's death? About how *you* feel about Jenny's death, the fire, any of it?"

Sam hung his head back and stared at the ceiling, not liking the ninety-degree turn of this conversation any more than he'd enjoyed the discussion with Erin earlier that morning. He didn't need to be double-teamed right now. "Not you, too."

"There is absolutely nothing wrong with the question I just asked," Mia said, in a prickly tone. "It's a simple question about a complicated and emotional situation."

"Doesn't mean I want to talk about it."

She sighed and gentled her words. "Sam, I know

you're the strong, silent type, and I also respect that you're a private person. I'm not prying, nor am I asking you to talk to me. Unless you want to, in which case you know I'm always here."

"I do know that."

She dipped her chin and gave him a reproachful look. "But, maybe you should give this Erin a fair shot before you write her off. She's only been there a day, and although she's not the sweet, Gingersnap-scented Grandma you'd hoped for, she seems to have your best interests at heart—"

"I want her to have Jess's best interests at heart, that's the problem."

"Your best interests *are* Jessica."

She had a point. He rolled his shoulders uncomfortably. "Still. There is no sense in me discussing Jenny's death. I'm an adult. I can handle what happened better than Jessica can."

"Says who?"

He spread his arms wide. "What's talking about it going to do—bring Jenny back?"

"Of course not, but that's not the issue."

"I wish I knew the issue, then, because I don't see one."

"Didn't you listen to what you just told me? All the questions Erin asked you were directly related to Jessica."

He cocked his head to the side and narrowed his gaze. "How so? She seemed to be asking a whole lot about yours truly."

"Yes. *Because* you're Jess's parent. And this Erin is also some sort of an expert with this kind of grief, right?"

"Right, but—"

"Humor me here." She held up a finger and moistened her lips. "Could it be that she knows a little something about the recovery process that you or I don't?"

His jaw ticked, but he nodded. Grudgingly.

"Well, then. Set limits with your sharing if you need to maintain your personal space. That's fine. But give Erin every advantage in working with Jessica the best way she knows how. Jessica deserves that much, Sam, and it's what you want." He started to protest or defend, he wasn't sure which, but she held up a hand. "Giving Erin total support in this might mean touching on uncomfortable topics for you. Buck up and accept it. You can take it. God knows, you've suffered through worse."

He chewed on that for a few. "I don't feel comfortable discussing my life with...the nanny."

"Ahhhh."

His gaze shot to her face and narrowed. "What's that supposed to mean?"

"Could it be—and I'm musing to myself, now—that you're simply looking for reasons to be dissatisfied with Erin because she's gotten under your skin a little bit?"

"Mia," Sam warned. His matchmaking secretary had been sniffing the romance trail since the moment he'd called and told her he hired a twenty-three-year-old, single, Irish beauty to care for Jess instead of the elderly woman he'd envisioned. "Don't even go—"

"Just food for thought, and the question was rhetorical anyway. I have my theories, you have your denials." She flicked her hand as though shooing away a fly. "Bottom line, though, is that Erin has a job to do and you shouldn't stand in her way."

"I'm not trying to."

"Then answer her questions."

Sam threw his arms up in the air. "Fine, fine. I'll try and be more...forthcoming if she corners me again."

"*Corners* you. Probably not the most effective way to frame the whole thing in your mind, but I've done all I can for one day." Mia flipped her feet off the file drawer and swiveled her legs under her desk. "Now, with that, kindly remove yourself from my office. I've got work to do, as do you, so put on a hard hat and get out there, will you? This place isn't going to run itself."

Sam shook his head and hid a half-admiring, half-exasperated smile as he donned his yellow hard hat and gathered his supplies for the workday. Fine, he'd talk to Erin a little bit. Clearly Mia saw it as a positive step toward helping Jessica, and he was all about Jessica. Plus, he trusted Mia's advice. She wouldn't lead him astray.

It wasn't until he was out on the site, contemplating Mia's words, Erin's questions, and his uncharacter-

istic capitulation in one big jumble, that he realized
he'd been railroaded by females twice already that
day, and it wasn't even 7:00 a.m.

After Sam had left, Erin took a quick shower and
dressed in comfortable, staying-at-home clothes. Jessica was still sleeping, so Erin took the opportunity
to walk through the house and acquaint herself with
her surroundings.

The house was good sized and decorated in a comfortable, warm style neither too feminine or too masculine. The upholstered pieces sported a lovely plush,
plum fabric and appeared big enough to sink into. The
wood pieces were in a clean, Shaker style and stained
a light cherry. From the lemon and pine scents, it was
clear to Erin that everything had been freshly cleaned.

It should've seemed like a very inviting house.

But, something was missing.

Erin stopped in the doorway to the living room and
rubbed her chin thoughtfully. She took in the oval
shaped rag rug, the corner toy box. Studied the furniture and smiled at the angled sunbeams reaching
through the south-facing windows.

Plants.

She peered around and spotted a healthy spider
plant in one corner and a potted fern by the sofa. He
didn't have a lot of plants, but he did have those two,
and they didn't look beleaguered like so many plants
in households without women. So, that wasn't the
missing puzzle piece.

Erin moved further into the room and focused on
the electronic equipment. A decent sized television,
along with all the accompanying black boxes of mod-

ern entertainment, held court with a large stack of colorful children's videos in a sleek entertainment center. All very homey, very normal. So, what was it? What felt...off?

Turning her attention to the walls, it struck her like a blow. Sam had no family photos displayed. In her parents' house as well as each of her brothers' homes, framed family photos brought life to the walls and chronicled the passing years, the joy of family life. She was used to seeing that kind of thing, but in Sam's house...nothing.

Four framed photographs adorned the mantel, but they were all of Jessica. None of him, none of his late wife, and not a single photo of any cousins or uncles, grandparents, or other extended family. It struck Erin as rather sad.

Then again, not everyone liked to decorate with personal photographs, at least not in common areas. Surely Sam would have his study more personalized. Lucky for Erin, she had carte blanche to enter his private space and use the computer, and while she was there, if she happened to peek around for pictures, well, it wasn't really *snooping*. She was merely trying to get a handle on this very confusing, intriguing man.

She quickly refilled her coffee mug, then took the stairs two at a time. No staggered photos in the stairwell, she noted in passing. The upstairs hallway was similarly bare. She peered into Jessica's room, pleased to find the baby sleeping soundly, then moved on to the study.

A desk and credenza. Two bookshelves. Filing cabinets and a nice computer system.

No family photographs.

Intrigued, Erin sat in Sam's office chair and smoothed her palms over the hunter green leather desk blotter. One thing she could give Sam, the man was neat. But, some instinct deep inside her said there were more layers to Sam Lowery than met the eye. He might be a successful construction foreman with a strong work ethic, he was certainly a devoted father. But the Sam deep inside held secrets Erin couldn't begin to imagine.

She sat back, rocking in the office chair with her hands folded over her torso. He was a puzzle, and she was going to enjoy every moment of piecing him together. Another instinct, however, told her she'd be unwise to let him know he was as much her personal project as caring for Jessica was her job. Sam and Jessica had suffered a tragedy, losing Jenny, but Erin felt pretty sure that Sam had suffered loss long before the fire. What type, she didn't know, but she aimed to find out. Nonchalantly, of course. She didn't think the very private Sam Lowery would appreciate his nanny's scrutiny of his life, but hey, with five brothers, Erin was nothing if not stealthy. Sam Lowery would never know what hit him. And someday, if things went well, he might even thank her.

With a smile on her face, Erin booted up Sam's computer, hoping to knock out Jessica's schedule before the baby awoke and they started the day. She was going to prove her worth to Sam no matter what it took.

Sam arrived home that evening fully prepared to buck up and replay the conversation with Erin, this time answering at least the questions that didn't make him feel sick to his stomach. He figured he could start there; Jessica was worth it. He entered through the mud room, like usual, removing his steel toed work boots and shrugging out of his jacket. He paused, remembering suddenly that he'd forgotten to call Erin about dinner, and a little knife of regret stabbed him. He pressed his lips together and checked his watch. It was past six anyway, but he could smell dinner wafting on the air, and his mouth watered. It would've been nice to share a meal with Jessica.

And with Erin.

The door into the kitchen was almost closed, and the dryer tumbled and emitted the smell of fabric softener, which, combined with the enticing kitchen smells, made coming home feel pleasurable for the first time in a long time. He reached for the doorknob and stopped short.

What was that sound?

He eased the door open slowly, cocked his head, and listened. Laughter. Jessica's laughter mingling with Erin's, and in the background, one of those teeny-bopper singers playing on the stereo. Was it Britney Spears? He smirked, shaking his head. Even that music was preferable to entering a silent, dark house night after night.

He walked on stocking feet through the kitchen and into the dining room. From there, he could see into the living room, where Erin and his sweet baby girl danced with wild abandon to the music. Both of their faces shone with happiness, and Jessica's cheeks were pink and chipmunk-chubby with her grin. A wild curl of poignant happiness twisted his middle. He didn't want the moment to end, and on the other hand he desperately wished he were a part of it. He crossed his arms and leaned one shoulder against the door jamb, hoping to watch them longer, but the hardwood floor beneath him creaked. Both Erin and Jessica spun toward the sound. Erin had a palm against her chest, eyes wide with alarm.

"Oh, you scared me."

"Daddy!" Jessica toddled toward him with her arms raised.

"Hi, honeypot." He bent and lifted her, planting big kisses on her face. He glanced up at Erin, twisting his lips to the side. "Sorry, I didn't mean to scare you."

"Me dance." She pointed toward Erin.

"Yes, I saw you. It looked like fun. Was it fun?"

Jessica nodded, then nestled her head on his shoulder. She smelled of baby powder, shampoo, and healthy exertion. His gaze lifted and locked with Erin's, and something raw and real clutched his insides. God, she was beautiful and vibrant and…so off limits. He swallowed hard. "Hi."

She ran her long, slim fingers through her hair and

laughed a bit self-consciously. "Hi. I didn't even know you were there. How embarrassing."

"Don't be embarrassed. You looked…free."

"Like someone who might drive a car named Daisy Mae?" She winked, then set about straightening the living room. There were toys, coloring books, puzzles, stuffed animals, and again, Jenny's framed photograph strewn everywhere.

"Definitely like that." He kissed Jessica and set her down and gave her a playful smack on the rear. "Help Erin clean up, honeypot." Jessie immediately squatted down and started picking up primary colored blocks. She was a good girl.

Erin glanced up from a stooped position. "There's meat loaf and mashed potatoes on a plate in the fridge. Vegetables, too." She crinkled her nose. "Are you a veggie eater?"

"I eat anything."

"I wish we could say that about the little miss, here."

"Yeah, vegetables are not her friends. She does like green beans, corn, and tomatoes."

"Okay. Good."

The living room was sufficiently neat, so Erin stood up and pressed two fists to her lower back. "Why don't you eat while I give the wee one a bath."

"Actually, if you don't mind, I'd like to tend to her bath and get her ready for bed. I feel like I haven't seen her for days."

"Of course. I'll just head off to my room, then, unless you want me to heat up your meal."

"No, Erin. You don't need to do that. Believe me, I've been taking care of myself for a long time." He scooped Jessica into his arms. "I'll eat after this one is down for the night."

"No!" Jessica protested, even though her little fists kept finding their way to her eyes to rub away the sleepiness.

"I've set bedtime for 7:45 p.m., if that's okay. She's a sleeper, this one."

"That's fine." He hitched her higher in his arms. "Did everything go well today?"

Erin nodded. "I've completed a schedule. It's posted on the fridge. We walked to the park, had a couple of naps, and got the laundry done."

Sam shook his head slowly, his approval for the nanny growing exponentially the more he was around her. He didn't want to feel these waves of affection and respect, but they just seemed to come without warning. "You're a pretty amazing person, Erin O'Grady."

Her face flamed immediately, and she cut her glance away. He could tell she was pleased by the compliment, though. "Thank you. It was easy. Jessica is a very amenable baby."

"She's my little honeypot."

Erin met his gaze directly. "I really think we're going to be able to work with her, Sam. It'll take time, but—"

"I'd actually like to talk to you about that. You caught me off guard this morning, but—"

"I'm sorry."

"No. It's okay. I'd like to talk to you more about it. Do you mind sitting with me while I eat dinner, so we can pick up where we left off?"

Erin's whole face lit up at this small concession, and darn if it didn't make Sam's heart lift. She had the knack of making a man feel like an absolute knight on a white horse. Danger.

"I'd love to. I'll meet you in the kitchen in about forty-five minutes?"

"Deal. See you there."

Erin was freshening up in her rooms when her private phone line rang. She checked the caller ID and smiled. It was Karla, from the agency. "Hello?"

"Erin! How are things going so far?"

She sank onto her bed and wrapped an arm around her torso. "Oh, I can't even tell you. Jessica is a great baby. We have so much fun together, and I can tell she's starved for female attention, poor doll."

"And what about Sam?"

Erin flopped back on the bed. "He's a tougher nut to crack, but I'm pretty determined."

Karla laughed. "I knew you'd be right for this job."

"Thank you for your faith in me."

"It's well-deserved, sweetie. Well, I just wanted to give you some moral support. I know it's hard taking a new assignment. And if you have any trouble at all—"

"Believe me, I'll call."

"Goodnight, Erin."

"Nighty-night."

After she'd hung up, Erin studied the texture on the ceiling and thought about Sam. Was there anything sexier than a man who did hard physical work all day long and slipped into daddy mode so easily the moment he entered the house? His well-worn jeans and fitted T-shirt molded to a body honed to perfection by hard work, not gym visits. His beard had started to come in, and his hair bore the telltale hard hat dent. But he'd cradled his baby daughter like she was made of spun sugar, and Erin didn't think anything in the world could be sexier.

How could she be crushing so hard on her boss this soon? She'd only just met the guy, but then again, she believed in love at first sight, kismet, soulmates—even faeries and sprites. She really was a hopeless, daydreaming romantic.

A light knock on the outer door to her wing startled her, and she shot up into a sitting position, heart lodged in her throat. "Yes?"

"Jess is out cold," Sam said, through the still closed doorway. "I didn't even get to read her a story. I know we said forty-five minutes, but if you're ready to talk, I'm ready to eat."

Erin fluffed her hair nervously. "I'll be right there." She waited until she heard him retreat, then stood, smoothing her moist palms along the legs of her jeans. Gosh, it felt like a freakin' first date. She needed to shake these schoolgirl jitters if she was going to be effective as Jessica's nanny—regardless of how sexy Jessica's daddy was.

As she brushed her teeth and slicked her lips with gloss, she decided the questioning method wouldn't work with Sam. Instead, she'd show him by example. She'd suffered a loss in her family, too, with little Bryce. If she opened up to Sam, maybe he'd reciprocate. Eventually.

## Chapter Six

"This is really good," Sam told Erin almost sheepishly, after swallowing his first bite of meat loaf.

"Thank you." Erin flushed with pleasure at his words and fiddled with the cup of tea she hadn't really wanted, but had made for herself, anyway, so he wouldn't have to eat with an audience. She could see he was conflicted about "taking advantage" of her cooking skills. Clearly, Sam Lowery was a man unused to accepting help, and every step was going to be a struggle. She wondered if he knew how much information he telegraphed about himself just by *being* himself.

"No, thank *you*. You've managed to make a meal that Jessica and I can both enjoy. How'd you do that?"

"I told you, Sam, I have tons of nieces and nephews, and I'm the favorite sleepover aunt." She shrugged. "I know my way around a child's palate. They can be picky."

"Don't I know it."

Erin laughed softly. "I've learned ways to trick everyone. With a big Irish Catholic family like mine, it's almost inevitable that the adults and kids will eventually eat together, and the thought of making two separate meals is wholeheartedly unappealing, even to someone like me who likes to cook."

He inclined his head. "Well, my compliments to the chef."

Her pulse quickened, in part because Sam was so darn sexy without even trying. In part because she knew she had to bring up Jessica's treatment again, and doing so could snap the little thread of companionship that stretched tenuously between them. Now was her chance, though, and she had to take it. If she was going to broach this difficult topic, she'd have to do so with a believable and logical conversational segue. Sam might be a man who worked with his hands, but he was sharp of mind and wiser than his twenty-seven years might indicate. She wouldn't be able to railroad him, and didn't even want to. Games weren't her style.

She cleared her throat and tossed her hair. In as breezy a tone as she could manage, she asked, "What about you? Do you have nieces and nephews?" Her stomach plunged when Sam went very still, his eyes focused down on his plate rather than across the table toward her. She thought she saw his forearm tighten and wondered if she'd blundered again.

Finally, he glanced up. "Only child. Remember?"

"That's right. Well, bummer. I really enjoy my brothers' kids. I can rattle their cages, get them really riled up and then hand them over to mom and dad. It's awesome." She winked. "I consider it paybacks for the hell my brothers put me through on a yearly basis."

To her relief, Sam's muscles seemed to relax.

"Being an aunt is really cool." She was rambling and she knew it, but she needed to forge ahead into more dangerous territory before she lost his attention. Glancing across the kitchen toward Jessica's schedule posted on the fridge, she swallowed, then said, "And, it was nice to have a huge support system when little Bryce died." Her fingers tightened on the tea cup. "Does it bother you if I talk about it?" She ventured a peek at his face.

"Not at all," Sam said, continuing to eat, but with his focus firmly on her.

She squeezed her eyes shut as the whole unspeakable tragedy came rushing back as if it had happened yesterday. "It was awful, Sam. Unbearable, really. There were some days when I could hardly drag myself out of bed, and it was a million times worse for Eamon and Susan."

"Your brother and his wife? The parents?"

She nodded. "And the kids, too. But, Eamon is a typical first born, too. Know what I mean?"

Sam sort of shrugged, noncommittally.

"He felt like he had to keep the world spinning for everyone, even though he'd gone through the biggest crisis any parent can face." She shuddered involuntarily. "It took a lot of time to convince him that his feelings and grief were just as valid as everyone else's, but he finally released a lot of that. It felt good for me to be his shoulder to lean on."

Sam's eyes narrowed just slightly, but he nodded.

Her nerves were on edge, but he was listening. Good sign. "A-and, once he worked through some of his grief, it was like the whole family was able to do the same. It's a strange phenomenon, how family members look to one certain person in order to school their own reactions. But, sometimes people don't know exactly *how* to react after a tragedy. We all do our best."

"Erin?"

"Yes?"

"Are you, by any chance, talking about me here?"

Whoops, busted. Her throat constricted, but she was able to maintain her expression. "No, of course not. I'm talking about Eamon. And maybe about me, about how I came to do what I do. I…just want you to understand my motives better."

After a moment of looking suspicious, he nodded once.

*Phew.* She moistened her suddenly dry lips. "It was a real trial and error learning experience for me when Bryce died."

"I can't even fathom how any of you held it together."

Good, he was starting to talk, at least, and his suspicions seemed in check. "Sure you can. Grief is grief, and you seem to have held together just fine."

He cocked an eyebrow, but said nothing.

She cleared her throat and fiddled with the woven placemat at her spot. "So...did your family rally around you after...?"

An odd shadow moved across Sam's face, and for several long moments, Erin felt certain he wasn't going to answer. Getting through to Sam was like tiptoeing through a minefield in the pitch black of a moonless night. She never knew if her next step would be the fatal one.

Finally, he set his fork aside and wiped his hands on the napkin in his lap. "No."

"I'm sorry."

"Don't be. Just count yourself lucky to have all those brothers who annoy you so much. And parents who love you."

She wondered what that meant. Did he have unsupportive parents, even during a tragedy so large as a fatal fire? She couldn't imagine, but she knew examples of that kind of familial distance happened with disturbing frequency in today's society. "My parents are great. And, I really do love my brothers, the big, annoying lugs. I just wish they'd see me as a woman and not a little girl sometimes."

His gaze darkened into something that made Erin's tummy swirl. For a moment, she forgot her mission to get Sam to loosen up and found herself fully suspended in a net of attraction for this man. She could hear a subtle whir of the kitchen clock, the ticking of the dishwasher on the dry cycle. Most of all, she could hear and feel her blood pulsing through her veins and traveling to various pertinent parts of her body. Her response to a simple look from Sam left her off-kilter and disconcerted. Gosh, she was in trouble.

"I can't imagine anyone not seeing you as a woman," he drawled.

Her heart fluttered, and white-hot embarrassment rushed to her face. "Well, thank you, but—"

"Then again, if I was your brother, I'd probably protect you just as ferociously as they do."

Erin bit her lip and tilted her head to the side. "You're a good man, Sam Lowery. But, thank you very much, the last thing I need is another brother."

He snorted, scooting back his chair to stand up from the table, then turned to carry his dish to the sink. "Thank you again for dinner, Erin. I really appreciate it, and I certainly don't expect it."

"It's no problem." She settled in and listened to the comforting kitchen clean-up sounds for a moment...water from the faucet, the clink-clank of dishes and silverware in the stainless steel sink. With effort, she shook off her distracting attraction to Sam and decided, once and for all, she needed to broach at least one difficult topic head on. "Can I ask you something, Sam?"

His shoulders braced from behind, she noticed. "Shoot."

"Jessica carries around the photograph of her

mother, but she's never said a word about it. Even when I ask her directly, she simply doesn't answer. Has this been your experience?''

Sam placed his plate in the dish drainer, along with his silverware, then turned, drying his hands on a thick, white bar mop towel. ''Not exactly.''

''How so?''

He pursed his lips, then sighed. ''Honestly? She never touched that photograph until you came into our lives.''

Shock zinged through Erin, and she sat back. Blinking a couple of times, she shored up her composure. ''Really?''

''Yep. I don't know what to make of it.''

''Sam, I think that's a positive sign. She remembers, but maybe she doesn't feel able to talk about it. Maybe—'' she held up a hand ''—and this isn't, in any way, a commentary on you.''

He nodded once.

''But maybe having a woman here is sort of…freeing her up to remember Jenny. To acknowledge that she misses the mother she loved so much.''

A pained look crossed his face, but he propped the heels of both hands on the counter at his back and set his chin. ''She did love her. And Jenny loved that baby enough to die for her.'' His voice went husky with pain. ''There's no greater love than that.''

Erin's eyes stung with tears, and she lifted her clasped fists to her chest. ''God, Sam, I'm so sorry.''

''I am, too.'' A tense beat passed. ''So, what do we need to do about Jess?''

Stunned that he asked, she didn't answer right away. Instead, she thought about it a moment, tucking her hair behind her ears so she could rein in her emotions. "Do you...can I have access to some additional photos of Jenny? Maybe you and Jenny, or Jenny and Jess?"

Sam got that oh-so-familiar distant look in his eyes and rubbed the back of one hand thoughtfully against his jawline. "For what?"

She shrugged one shoulder. "Well, to tell you the truth, I'm not sure yet. Maybe I can scrapbook them for you, or maybe she and I can just go through them. She just seems so attached to that one photograph, maybe it will help to see how she reacts to some others."

He crossed his arms over his chest. "And if it upsets her?"

"Then I'll stop immediately and try another path. You have to know I would never do anything to hurt Jessica," she implored.

The faint lines around his eyes from working out in the weather seemed to deepen. "I just want her to be happy."

"I want that, too. So much. And I want her to be free to express her emotions. About everything. It's so necessary to the healing process." *I want it for you, too, Sam.*

Their gazes locked, and Erin could sense his internal war. It almost made her feel guilty pushing him like this, but he'd hired her for her expertise and her ability to connect so easily with Jessica. She'd been through the overwhelming fatherly grief ordeal with Eamon and she knew this prodding needed to happen. If she didn't force the issue a little bit, he'd stay locked up forever, and if that happened, little Jessica would stay just as tightly wound.

Finally, he expelled a breath through his nose and looked resigned. "I'll pull the box of photos down from the attic before I turn in."

"Thank you." She breathed easier, and her shoulders relaxed. She hadn't even realized they were so tense. "I know this is difficult for you. Understatement."

A muscle in his jaw jumped, and he looked away.

"If things go well with the photographs, perhaps we can introduce some of Jenny's clothing into Jessica's life."

The wariness returned. "There's not a lot. The fire…there was smoke and water damage to a lot of…well, everything. Especially the things in our bedroom."

"But you have some?"

"Yes."

"Any of her favorite comfy clothes? A sweatshirt, maybe?"

"Yes," he said, his voice choked.

"I have some ideas I gathered after watching other children grieve for their parents." She flipped her hand. "But one step at a time. Let's save the clothing issue for another day. We can start with the photographs."

Sam eased his muscular neck side to side. "Okay."

He glanced at the wall clock, then pushed away from the counter and stretched. "I'd better get to it if I want to be worth a damn at work tomorrow. Four-thirty comes early." He headed toward the dining room, with a friendly but dismissive nod.

As he passed her, Erin reached out and touched his hand. "Sam, wait."

He stopped, turning toward her with trepidation clear in his expression, his body language, everything. He was a bundle of nerves around her, and she wasn't sure if it was because he didn't like her or because he *did* like her.

Hoping to ease his mind, she smiled. "Thanks for talking."

Sam rested his free hand on the doorjamb. He hung his head. "Look, I've never been much of a talker. But I want to do everything I can to help my daughter, and I know you're trying to help, too. I'm sorry if I was…"

"Stubborn?" Erin teased, lightly.

One corner of his mouth lifted. "Yeah, that. This morning. I don't mean to stand in your way with this."

"We have plenty of time, Sam. No harm, no foul." She grinned. "Deal? We're in this together, and having been through a major loss myself, I know there are going to be advances and setbacks along the way. Don't worry. I'm not expecting you to be superhero."

"That's a damn good thing. If there's one thing I'm not, it's a superhero."

"Oh, don't be so sure."

He studied her briefly, his eyes both expressive and searching. Hopeful and bleak. Vulnerable and yet incredibly strong. The rest of his expression remained inscrutable. "I'll go get that box and leave it here in the kitchen for you. Goodnight, Erin."

"Night, Sam."

It hadn't taken Sam long to find the box of photographs up in the attic, since he was the only person who'd ever been up there, but he hadn't quite made it all the way downstairs yet. Instead, he'd been sitting numbly on the edge of his bed with the box on his lap for—he glanced at the alarm clock—a little over half an hour. Sweat slicked his palms and his heart pounded out a dull, dread-filled rhythm in his chest.

He wanted to look.

He wanted to never look again.

Why was he so afraid to open the box? To revisit his life before the fire had left it in tatters? More guilt? Sad evidence of the family he could've built but didn't?

And, if he couldn't bear to confront the old photographs, why didn't he just take the box downstairs and leave it in the kitchen for Erin like he'd promised? This box held captured moments of his family life, short-lived as it was. He shouldn't be afraid of them, he should cherish them, but the notion left him cold and distant.

Without warning, Sam's thoughts veered sharply toward thoughts of Lissa and Adam, his *other* family. Little Mark, too, with his grave health problems. He even thought briefly of Jared Cambry, who could've been a father to him, to all of them, but thoughts of that man just made him clench his jaw. Sam hated to dwell on what could've been. But, sitting there alone in his room, with a wife gone and buried, a traumatized daughter, and siblings who didn't know he existed weighing on his mind, he couldn't help it. Things might have been so different for him if Cambry had stepped up to the plate after their young mother had been killed. Who knows, Sam might have even been part of a family like Erin's.

His hands balled into fists.

He had built a good life for himself and Jessica. He shouldn't be feeling this way, but he couldn't deny it. A seemingly bottomless well of sadness opened up inside him, sucking him in. He set the box aside and laid back on his bed, propping his hands behind his head. Above him, the ceiling swirled in and out of focus as he ruminated about the whole, incredible mess.

The last news article he'd read about the blissfully reunited Lissa and Adam said the doctors were still waiting to see if little Mark's body had accepted the bone marrow transplant. Sam had never given much thought to a rejection. An image of Jessica floated into his mind, and to his surprise, he felt a sharp surge of compassion for Jared Cambry and the rest of the family. His heart ached for any parent who might lose a child. He hurt for Erin's brother and sister-in-law, for the scare he had with Jessica on the night of the fire, even for Lissa and Adam…and for himself. But, he came to the realization that, no matter how bitter he was about having been abandoned by Cambry when he was a baby, he still couldn't wish for anything but good health for little Mark.

His brother. God, he was just a kid.

He squeezed his eyes shut and felt tears threatening. *God, let Mark Cambry live. Let…my little brother…live. Please.*

After several silent moments of prayer, a weight seemed to have been lifted from his soul, and Sam sat up slowly. With a little lingering trepidation, he opened the box of photographs and started sifting through them. Photos of him and Jenny at the Justice of the Peace. Their first Christmas, with the mother of all Charlie Brown trees. They hadn't even been able to afford lights, and all the ornaments were handmade, but he'd thought it was beautiful. In lieu of a stand, the forlorn little tree sat in a bucket of generic kitty litter and was anchored to a nail in the wall with a length of red yarn. It had been one of the best Christmases he could remember.

He pulled a particular snapshot from the stack and his chest squeezed until he felt like he couldn't breathe. Moving to the side of the bed, he studied it under the light of the bedside lamp. A hospital photo from the day Jessica had been born, after a grueling twenty-six-hour labor. Jenny looked exhausted, like she'd run a marathon…or been hit by a bus.

But she also looked happy.

He hadn't remembered her being happy for so long, but on this day, during this captured moment, she had been. On one day, at least, Jenny Lowery had been happy, and the knowledge brought him a small measure of solace. A melancholy smile lifted his mouth and thawed some of the ice encasing his heart.

Erin was right.

It would be good for Jessica to have an album of these photos. In general, people only photographed the good times in life, and it would certainly help his daughter to be able to see snapshots of happiness from a babyhood she wouldn't remember otherwise. Who knew? Having his short marriage and Jessica's first few months of life chronicled might be therapeutic for him, too. He wondered if Erin truly wanted to tackle the project. If so, he'd have to tell her to keep all the receipts so he could reimburse her for any costs. He'd probably have to assist with the sorting anyway. And if Erin wasn't up for it, maybe it was time for him to undertake the job himself, to stop hiding from the past and begin looking toward the future.

Feeling better, Sam returned the photos to the box and carried them down the stairs. He left them on the kitchen table with a short note.

"Erin—Here you go. If you truly want to work on an album with Jess, let me know and I'll buy whatever supplies you need. A lot of the photos are labeled by date, but I'll help you sort the others. Thanks. Sam"

For the first time in six solid horrible months, Sam slept soundly.

## Chapter Seven

Erin's first week as a nanny seemed to fly by once she and Jessica had a project to work on together. They spent every morning until naptime sifting through the photo box, an activity as enjoyable for Erin as it was for Jessica, although at twenty-four months, she had a limited attention span. They worked in fits and spurts, which was fine. It allowed Erin to get lots of other things done around the house, and it also allowed her to scrutinize the photographs at her leisure during the times when Jessica lost interest.

Erin noted that Jenny Lowery often seemed overly serious in the photos. She wondered why. What kind of woman had Jenny been? And why weren't there any photos of extended family? Not a single picture.

Maybe they were kept in a different box; Erin couldn't be sure. But it would be nice to incorporate multiple generations in the scrapbook project. She thought about asking Sam about it, but decided she'd pressed enough for one week. Maybe later, when he trusted her more, the conversation would come more easily.

Afternoons were dedicated to trips to the park, playing Barbies, fingerpainting, doing puzzles, baking cookies, and other fun Jessica-focused activities. Occasionally, they'd spend a half hour or so on the photo book project. Through it all though, Jessica still wasn't talking about her mother. Not one word. She would happily exclaim "me!" or "daddy!" when she came across pictures of herself or Sam, but photographs of Jenny were set quietly aside in a private pile. No one but she touched the precious photos; Erin didn't even attempt to work them into the layout. The one time she'd reached for the stack, Jessica had snatched it away, holding it against her little chest while tears welled in her eyes. Erin asked Jessie light, nonthreatening questions about the photos, but all were met with absolute silence.

That was going to have to change.

The thing was, Sam needed to be the one to change it, but he was still as closed off as his daughter when it came to the topic of Jenny Lowery, and none of Erin's attempts to bring them out of their respective shells had been successful. She was beginning to think she might be a fine "surrogate aunt," but she was proving to be a mediocre grief counselor, despite years of school and personal experience. The whole debacle was disheartening, to say the least.

On Friday afternoon, after putting Jessica down for a much-needed nap, her beloved stack of pictures within clear view on her dresser top, Erin settled onto the couch with a cup of orange pekoe tea and dialed her sister-in-law, Susan. She'd reached her wit's end and needed a brainstorming session big time. Her usual methods were falling flat. Most days, she prepped dinner during Jessica's early nap, then finished it during her afternoon nap, but that morning while Jessica still slept, Erin had whipped together chicken chili in the crock pot. She had at least ninety minutes free to ponder her dilemma and come up with a new and better strategy.

Erin had always marveled at the fact that Susan had lost a child in a most heartbreaking way, and yet she was able to come back to a place of serenity and continue raising the other kids. She was an amazing woman, and if anyone could help Erin figure out this situation, it was Susan. The phone only rang once before her vibrant sister-in-law picked it up.

"Hey, Erin! How's the new job?"

"It's absolutely wonderful," she said, with slightly feigned enthusiasm.

"Hmmm. Sure doesn't sound like it."

"Am I that transparent?" Erin sighed, running her fingers through her hair. "In so many ways, it is wonderful. I wouldn't trade this job for the world. But I'm just not making the progress I'd hoped with Jessica. I have a lot of work to do to get this baby—and her father—past their locked up grief and onto the path of healing. I'm pulling everything out of my bag of tricks but everything fails."

Her selfless sister-in-law was always ready to lend a hand, and her voice turned all business. "How so?"

She filled Susan in on every aspect of the situation, then said, "I can tell that little girl has all her feelings about her mommy bottled up somewhere I can't quite reach."

"Of course she does. She was so little when it happened."

"Yeah. But if she doesn't let it out in a healthy way, it's going to explode out sooner or later." Erin bit her bottom lip, wondering about the wisdom of forging ahead with her query. She decided to go for it. "Listen, I know it's hard for you to revisit, but do you remember how we got the kids to start talking freely about Bryce? I mean, Kellan was about Jessica's age, and if I remember correctly, he opened up after I started working with you guys. I just don't remember exactly how we made that happen."

"It's not so hard for me to talk about, hon." Susan sighed, but it was a sigh of peace, of contentment. "I've come to a place where I can celebrate Bryce's life rather than feeling bitter about his death. I miss him every day, no doubt about that. And I'll never fully heal from the sheer trauma and pain of it. But, I think of Bryce and smile now, whereas I used to think of him and weep."

"You're an inspiration."

Susan laughed. "Get out. It's called living one's

life. I'm dedicated to living my life because my son was denied that privilege. I live for him. Besides, we wouldn't be anywhere near this level of recovery if it weren't for you, so you're the inspiration."

"If I'm so great, what am I doing wrong here?" Erin flopped her head back against the plush upholstery of the sofa. "Sam—he's the dad—is still so closed off and self-protective. It's like he's always on guard. Without him, I can't get Jessica to open up. She takes every single emotional cue from him."

"Of course. Is he completely uninvolved?"

Erin felt terrible, like she'd inadvertently been bashing Sam. "Oh, not at all. He's a great father." Erin regaled her quickly about the scrapbook project. "I mean, he stretched his boundaries giving me the photo box in the first place, and he helps me sort photos into chronological order in the evenings. It's relaxed enough. Sam is—" She couldn't hold back a sigh. "—such an amazing man, really. A truly good guy."

"But overly guarded?"

"Yeah. I have a sense his little fortress of emotional safety was erected long before the fire, though. That tragedy just reinforced the walls. I'm struggling so hard to get through to him."

"How do you know?"

"How do I know what?"

"That he went through some kind of trauma before the fire. That's what you meant, right?"

"Yes." She ruminated a minute. "I can't really say. Getting to know him, I just have a sense about him. He's so self-protective and such a loner. A little haunted, I guess. He epitomizes the strong, silent type, and I'm sort of piecing his psyche together as I go. He sure isn't telling me anything without my handy Erin pry bar, and even then, the information is scant at best.''

Susan was quiet a moment. When she finally spoke, she was hesitant. ''You know, when Eamon was so closed off, nothing I did could bring him out.''

Erin frowned, confused by Susan's comment. ''I know. But he's your husband. Sam's my boss. It's a totally different situation.''

''Well…could it be that you're feeling a little something for this boss of yours? That you've become emotionally invested on a romantic level, and it's getting in the way of your work with the two of them?''

''What?'' Erin protested.

''Just listen. Caring deeply can do that sometimes. God knows, I wanted to help Eamon, but I just couldn't.''

Erin sat up straight, eyes bugged. Mostly because her sis-in-law was so darned astute…or Erin herself was completely transparent. That scared her. If Susan could see it, Sam would surely catch on sooner or later, and she'd die if he knew of her crush when he didn't feel the same. She didn't want to out-and-out lie to Susan, so she settled for a half-answer that held some truth. ''Susan, for goodness sake, I am not having an affair with my boss.''

''Of course not, hon. That's not what I meant.''

She paused, and her voice softened. "But, you are attracted to him, right?"

Erin groaned. Darn, intuitive women. "Ugh. How did you know? I can't hide anything."

Susan laughed softly. "Well, it is pretty obvious."

"That sucks."

"No it doesn't. But, all I can say is, you'd better work on your poker face tomorrow morning at brunch. You know they're all going to grill you anyway, but Eamon's back from his business trip and he'll watch you like a hawk. He'll see it, Erin."

"Yeah, what's new? It's the bane of my existence. I can't blush without people in three counties knowing it, I can't hold back my emotions, and I can't evade my brothers. I'm a mess."

"Not even. You're refreshing and charming. It's better than being locked up and closed in."

Erin slumped in her seat. "I guess."

"Hey, look at it this way. You like this Sam guy. You know and I know there is absolutely nothing wrong with attraction between two consenting adults. Right?"

"Right, except my attraction isn't reciprocated."

"Give it time."

Erin bit her lip and tamped back a bit of hope. "You really think so?"

"Sure. Why not? But, for now, hide it. If your brothers get an inkling that you have a crush on your very eligible boss, they'll make your life miserable."

"They already do make my life miserable," Erin

said, with a grudging smile. "The jerks." A worrisome premonition tickled her spine. "Maybe I should skip brunch."

"That would be even worse, and you know it. Plus, the kids would really miss you."

"Good point. I'd miss them, too. I miss them already! But enough about my ill-fated and nonexistent love life. What about getting this little baby to open up about her mother?"

"Erin, I reiterate my advice. Give it time. Give Sam time, too. You've been there, what? A week?"

"Yes."

"You're trying to undo six months worth of pain and grief, and one week isn't going to cut it. Just relax."

Erin twisted her mouth to the side, wondering how much she should share. Sam was such a private person, and she didn't want to breach that confidence. Then again, if she could confide in anyone and have it go nowhere, Susan was the person. "You know, sometimes I get the feeling that family just isn't important to Sam, but then I see him with his daughter and I know that's not true. Well...at least with her. But he never talks about other family. Ever. Not even his late wife, if you can believe that. I just can't figure the guy out."

"So, don't try. If anything, show Sam how important family is by using our family as an example. Subtly, of course."

Erin tilted her head to the side and considered the advice. "That's a good idea, actually."

"Of course it is. That's why you called me," Susan teased. "I'm full of good ideas about how to fix other people."

Erin laughed. "So true."

"Bottom line, little sis, enjoy that baby girl and give her lots of love and hugs. She'll come out of her shell eventually. I can't imagine anyone resisting you forever."

Erin felt warmed by the love of her family. "And Sam?"

"Well, hey," Susan said, wryly, "if you get the opportunity to give him love and hugs, too, I say go for it. You're a modern woman, and it's high time you found the man of your dreams. Or at least *did* the man of your dreams."

"Susan! That's not what I meant." But Erin's tummy flip-flopped at the thought, and mental pictures of showering Sam with love and affection left her distracted and grinning like the village idiot. Her brothers were so intimidating to any possible dates, she didn't even have experience with men. Oh, what a joy it would be to gain that experience with Sam. "But, what a decadent, wonderful thought."

"I have to go," Susan said, through a laugh. "Kellan is wailing like he just lost a limb in a wood chipper, but I'm sure he just lost a toy to his brother. Kids." She sighed. "Call me any time you need to commiserate, okay? I'm here."

A horrible thought entered Erin's head. Didn't husbands and wives share everything. "But, don't—"

"Not to worry. I wouldn't rat you off to your

brother, hon, whether he's my husband or not. If it was up to the O'Grady boys, you'd be safely in the convent already.''

"How did you know that's what I was going to say?''

"Duh.''

Erin breathed easier and also found herself cheered by Susan's intuitive sense. "Thank you for understanding.''

"Understanding?'' Susan laughed again. "Hey, your brothers may keep you in a glass box like some untouchable princess, but your sisters-in-law have your back, girl. Don't forget that. And don't forget us when the wedding rolls around, either. No ruffles on the gowns!''

"Oh, be quiet!'' Erin chastised. But, she hung up with a smile on her face, the glow of familial love in her heart, and a renewed hope that she could make a difference with Jessica and, God willing, with Sam, too.

It had taken a full week of Erin's exuberant, nurturing presence in his world, but by Friday, Sam reluctantly admitted to himself that he enjoyed coming home to help her and Jessica with the scrapbook project—almost too much. Not that he did much more than put things in chronologial order, but still. It was getting easier and easier to look through the photos and remember the good times rather than focusing on the loss or the guilt, which seemed sort of amazing when he thought about it. He hadn't been able to get to that point for six months, then Erin shows up and things start to change in a matter of one week.

Most surprising of all, he simply looked forward to coming home now. Walking into a house redolent with the aromas of home cooked meals, soft lighting, and the sounds of music, laughter, and baby chatter smoothed out the sharp edges of a life that had always felt so cutting. Erin was like a sunbeam, warming and lighting the dark corners of his world.

He could seriously get used to the routine.

He found himself secretly glad that Erin wasn't involved in a relationship at the present time—not because he was interested himself, of course. He'd sworn off love and meant it. But, any smart guy would recognize the gem he had in Erin and secure a ring on her finger before she could blink. The happy couple would be off to the church, and he and Jessica would be back to square one. Alone. Floundering in the cold and dark.

He knew these thoughts were unfair. More than anyone, Erin deserved to find love and start that family she had her heart set on, but he didn't want to let her go now that she was here. He hoped she realized she had plenty of time. She was a young woman, only two years older than he'd been when he married Jenny, and Jenny had been a mere nineteen at the time. Looking at it from his current perspective, they'd been veritable children, far too young to take on the daunting task of marriage and family. Certainly he would've waited to marry until he was older if he hadn't been so damned lonely and alone.

He didn't want Erin to make the same mistake, rushing into a marriage before she'd gotten to fully know herself.

*Who are you trying to kid, Lowery?*

Altruism aside, he was beginning to need Erin, in so many ways. Not just for Jessica—although Erin's caring for his daughter had lifted a huge burden from his shoulders—but for himself as well. In the evenings after Jessica was down for the night, he and Erin had taken to sitting in the kitchen chatting about the day's events. If Erin had been too busy to clean up, they shared the task. If not, he sipped a cup of coffee or a beer, while she indulged in her favorite citrusy-scented herbal tea and regaled him with...well, anything and everything, if he thought about it.

Erin, in fact, did most of the talking. But, never having been much of a conversationalist, he preferred it that way. He loved the melodious tone of her voice, her easy windchime laughter. And he liked listening to all the stories about her full, fun days with his precious Jessica. Through the ages, men could never reach a consensus about the sexiest aspect of women, but he was beginning to think there was nothing sexier than a woman who loved a man's child like Erin loved Jessica.

He enjoyed hearing about her big, colorful family, too, although she didn't talk about them too much. In a way, he lived vicariously through her. Her life seemed foreign and exotic to him, but unfortunately, hearing about her siblings made him think about his own. He knew Adam and Lissa both had recently married their true loves. Soon they'd start families of their own, adding another layer to his secret, another level to something he'd never have. Not only was he a brother, but he might very soon be an uncle. The thought was, frankly, overwhelming.

Thankfully, he and Erin had moved away from the really hard topics—like his feelings—and he appreciated that, too. He'd learned young that being under the microscope's probing lens was not a place he enjoyed, so he'd honed his aloof, private persona until it had become second nature, until it had become the core of who Sam Lowery was. Erin was the first person ever to almost crack through it, and he had to admit, that made him nervous.

But, he still loved their lopsided conversations. Oftentimes, he had a hard time breaking away to go to sleep, even knowing he had to be up at the crack of dawn to start the grind all over again. Sleep deprivation was worth spending time with Erin O'Grady. He could listen to her talk forever, could stare into her brilliant blue eyes and bask in the warmth of her endearingly crooked smile until the sun came up and beyond. Oh yeah, he had it bad for Erin O'Grady, as much as he struggled against it. Her vibrancy was like a vortex, pulling him toward her every time they were together.

Luckily, he'd been able to keep his wholly inappropriate attraction under wraps, despite how long it had been since he'd shared intimacy with a woman. He couldn't say he didn't entertain notions of taking things a step further with Erin, wouldn't deny he fantasized about making love to her in the dark privacy of his own room at night, but he'd been able to resist. All he had to do was think of Erin's brothers and their low expectations of him—and any other guy interested in their baby sister—and he was able to say goodnight and escape to his bedroom without giving in to the singularly powerful urge to taste those beautiful lips of hers, to touch her skin.

It made for some relentless toss-and-turn nights, but at least his conscience didn't have another black mark on it.

His confusing feelings warred inside him that Friday as he pulled his truck into the garage. He sat in the cab for a moment, listening to the hot tick of the engine and strengthening his resolve to keep things professional. He was so glad to be home, he wanted to run up those steps and call for Erin and Jessica, pull them both into his arms and rain kisses on their faces. Bad choice. He could shower affection on his daughter all he wanted, but when it came to Erin, polite, platonic distance was his only choice.

Once he'd tamped down his eagerness enough to stay in control, Sam entered the house the same as always, but to his surprise, Erin and Jessica were waiting for him in the mudroom doorway, all smiles and shining eyes. His stomach contracted painfully, and he stopped short and glanced around. "What's with you two? Did someone win the lottery?"

"Daddy!" Jessica exclaimed, toddling over and lifting her arms toward him.

He swung her into a big bear hug, planting kisses on her face and reveling in the feel of her embrace. "How's my honeypot? Were you a good girl for Erin?" As per usual, she didn't answer, choosing instead to nestle her sweet smelling head into his neck. He glanced up at Erin, cocking one eyebrow questioningly.

"She was a perfect little girl, like always." She bounced on her heels, something she did when she was holding in good news, he'd come to learn. "And we have a great surprise."

"Yeah? What's that?"

"We finished the scrapbook," she said, with the same pride she might've shown for winning a marathon. Her face absolutely glowed with excitement. "Well, the first one, at least."

"That's great. I didn't realize there'd be more than one." He gave Jessica one last kiss on the top of the head, then set her down. She immediately became occupied with a used dryer sheet that had fallen onto the mudroom floor while he stooped over to remove his dusty, muddy workboots.

"Yeah, there will be a second one," Erin said, rather cryptically. "I hadn't planned for it to be that way, but…" Her eyes darted to Jessica. "We can talk about it more later."

Her words sent up a red flag in his mind, but he wanted to revel in the moment and worry about any problems as he came to them. "Okay." He stood and glanced over her shoulder toward the kitchen, inhaling deeply. "Something smells great. Did you cook again?"

Erin rolled her eyes playfully. "Don't pretend you're surprised. Need I remind you, I've cooked dinner every night since I've been here? Except that first night, when we had pizza."

"Yes, but—"

"I don't have to. I know, I know. We've been over this." She winked, beckoning him in with a sweep of her arm. "Come on. Let's eat before it gets cold."

He couldn't argue with that. His stomach growled in response to the enticing scents wafting out from the kitchen, and the whole tableau of "welcome home" warmed his soul. "What's on the menu tonight?"

"Chicken enchiladas, salad, and, to satisfy the sweet tooth in you, double chocolate layer cake."

Sam groaned, shrugging out of his jacket and moving over to the sink to wash his hands. "You know, if you keep this up, I'm going to get used to it."

"One would hope. Then you might stop telling me daily that I don't need to cook."

"That won't happen."

Erin looked pleased. "It's a celebratory dinner, anyway. When we're done, we'll unveil the scrapbook."

"Sounds really great, Erin," he said sincerely. "Thank you." He indicated his work clothes. "Do I have time to change? I hate to come to a special dinner with construction dust ground into my clothes."

Erin crossed her arms and tapped her foot playfully. "Oh, if you must, but hurry up."

Sam raised his eyebrows and stifled a smile. He liked the playful ease of their interactions. Such a change in a week. He'd gone from guarded to greedy for her attention. He wondered if she could read that about him and hoped not.

Forty minutes later, they'd finished the excellent dinner and had moved into the living room for the presentation of the scrapbook. Jessica's attention waned pretty quicky, so Erin laid down a nap mat and blanket in front of the television and popped in *Mulan*, Jess's favorite video du jour. When the baby was settled in and drowsy, Erin sat next to Sam on the sofa with a thick, maroon book clutched to her chest.

She peered over at him expectantly. "Okay, here it is. I hope you like it."

"I'm sure I'll love it." He held out his hand, tapping his fingers to his palm in a give-it-up motion. His heart began to pound, though. Sure, he'd grown more used to viewing the photos each day when he'd helped Erin sort them, but seeing them like this—a chronology of his married life—set his nerves afire.

Erin took in one big breath and released it, then presented him with the book. His throat constricted, and he took a moment to marvel about the fact that, less than a week earlier, he wasn't sure he could look at these photos ever again. The change wasn't his doing, for sure. He couldn't have reached this point without Erin's gentle prodding.

Bracing himself, he opened the cover.

"Daddy & Jessica" read the title page, in colorful cutout letters and framed by little matching squiggles and swirls. What about Jenny? he wondered. He peered over at Erin, but her gaze stayed firmly on the book. She had one corner of her bottom lip clamped between her teeth, and she looked uncharacteristically nervous.

Sam pushed away his confusion, cleared his throat, and turned the page. The photos, decoratively framed with pink, green, and yellow cutouts, were all of Jessica as a newborn. He smiled. "Isn't she a doll?"

"Oh, yes."

He turned the page again to find photographs of himself. Next page, photos of him and Jessica together. A curious frown bisected his brow, and he peered up to meet Erin's cautious gaze. "Where are the pictures of Jenny?"

Erin tilted her head toward Jessica, who was sucking her thumb, lids heavy, and rapidly heading toward dreamland. "Later," Erin said softly. "After she's asleep, we'll talk."

Worry pricked at Sam's soul. It obviously wasn't anything serious, or Erin wouldn't have thrown the celebratory dinner, but he still worried. When it came to anything having to do with his daughter, he always worried. He couldn't seem to help it. Hadn't Mia told him he acted like a mother to Jessica? Hey, he didn't take that as an insult. Quite the contrary.

"Is everything okay?" he whispered.

Erin's gaze slanted toward Jessica and back. "In a

global way, yes. But…well, give it a few minutes, and I'll try and explain.''

Sam nodded once and continued perusing the book. It didn't take long before Jessica's eyes were closed, her breaths coming steadily through a slightly opened mouth. She looked like an exhausted little angel who'd tucked her wings away for the night. Sam set the scrapbook aside and stood. ''Let me just get her off to bed,'' he said in a quiet tone.

''Okay. Can I get you anything?''

''You've done enough for one night, Erin. Just relax.''

''Relax? What's that?'' she teased.

He scooped Jessica gently off the floor, waking her just enough so she could squawk her meek, sleepy protests. He started off toward the stairs with Jessica resting against his chest, but suddenly she reached out over his shoulder. ''Erin, night-night.''

Sam held her from him slightly. ''What, honey-pot?''

''Erin go night-night.'' She stretched her little arms toward Erin and whimpered a little. It reminded him of the day Erin came for her interview, which seemed light years ago. Even then, Jessica had demonstrated an unusual attachment to Erin. The woman was like the pied piper of kids.

Sam pressed his lips together for a moment, but turned toward Erin. It's not like he could blame Jessie for falling in love with her. ''Care to join us for a tuck-in?'' he asked.

Erin sat forward on the couch, her eyes troubled

but hopeful at the same time. "Oh, Sam. I don't want to infringe on your routine or your time alone with her."

"Erin, go night-night," Jessica said again, more demanding this time. She was starting to wake up fully, and neither of them wanted that.

Sam smiled gently. "It looks like you've been out-voted. And it's okay. I don't mind."

"Really?"

"Really."

"I'd love to, then." Grinning at the baby, Erin stood and smoothed her palms down the sides of her jeans. She grabbed a packet of photographs in a plastic bag, waggling them at Jessica. "Okay, little miss. Let's go night-night."

Satisfied, Jessica relaxed against her father's shoulder, and together, the three of them ascended the stairs.

Sam might've been imagining it, but he could sense Erin's heat behind him. Her perfume wafted in the air, something vanilla and youthful. It felt right, he and Erin carrying Jessica up to her crib. He couldn't help but think, this is the way it's supposed to be. Two people who love a child, a man and a woman, tucking her in for a night of sweet dreams.

For the second time that evening he thought to himself, I could certainly get used to this, and it sobered him. Sure, he could, but he needed to resist the urge. He absolutely, positively had to pull back from Erin's magnetic draw. The last thing he wanted was to hurt her, and giving in to his attraction when their relationship was a guaranteed one-way ticket to hurtsville was one hundred percent wrong.

She wanted forever.

He wanted never again.

If that wasn't a big enough indication that they weren't meant to be, he didn't know what was.

# Chapter Eight

It was probably ridiculous, but Erin could think of nothing sexier than a man who adored his child like Sam obviously loved Jessica. She'd been flattered to be included in the bedtime ritual for the first time, but she hadn't expected it to affect her feelings for Sam so profoundly. Before they left the nursery, she made sure to set up Jessica's stack of mommy photos where the baby could see them if she needed to, and then it took everything within her to walk on wobbly legs down the stairs, all while acting like everything was status quo.

Sam walked behind her, and a crazy part of her wanted to stop and just lean into his chest. She straightened her back and sped up.

"What's your hurry?"

She laughed nervously. "Oh, I just want to get things cleaned up and ready for you for the weekend, so you can enjoy your time with Jessica."

"I appreciate that, but you've done enough for one week. Let's talk instead and I'll clean up later."

"O-okay. I hate to leave a mess, though."

"I've got to meet this mother of yours," Sam joked, wryly.

"Well, she did have a big influence on me when it comes to housework." She flashed him a smile.

Sam settled back onto the sofa, so Erin chose an armchair across the room. Juvenile, she knew, but she didn't think she could trust herself sharing the same piece of furniture with the guy at the moment. Hey, she was only so strong, and he had her emotions in a delicious tailspin.

"So," he said, crossing one ankle over the opposite knee, "what's with the multiple albums? Something to do with that stack of photos you left on Jessie's dresser, I assume?"

Erin sighed, running a hand through her fiery hair. "Yes. She seems to be hoarding the photographs of Jenny."

He cocked his head to the side. "Hoarding them?"

"Yes. She pulls them out and keeps them in her private stack, then carries them around all day. I've tried to talk to her about them, but—"

"She doesn't respond."

Erin sat back in the chair and nodded regretfully. "Nope. And don't even try to take them from her."

Sam pondered this, feeling somehow like it was his

fault. Again. "Do you think it's just going to take time? I mean, she hasn't seen but the one photograph since that night."

Erin tilted her chin down and gave him a direct stare. "I think...Sam, I think you need to talk to her about the photographs. Not just the photographs, but about her mother."

"This again, huh?"

"Yes, this again. Let her know it's safe to love them—and Jenny—but also safe to let them go. Enough to preserve the pictures in a book and to mourn her mother however her emotions dictate. Then she can enjoy the album every day if she wants, and she can feel however she feels about her mother without thinking it's wrong or bad. Plus, the photos won't get damaged from being carried around."

Sam's eyes clouded over, and for a moment Erin thought she'd lost him. She'd said her piece, so she just waited.

He covered his face with both hands, pulling them down slowly. "God, I really messed things up by not talking about Jenny with her, didn't I?"

A rush of compassion filled Erin, and without worrying about her earlier skittishness, she moved to sit next to him on the couch. "No. You did what you needed to do, and there is no crime in that. Don't berate yourself."

He looked weary, older. "I don't know how to do it. I don't even know how to talk about her to...you. Or anyone."

Erin laid a palm on his knee. "It's okay. Just take

your time. Speak from the heart. You have all week-end. Well, frankly, you have your whole life, but…I'm sorry to push so much…the sooner the better. Jessica is fine on the surface, but she needs to learn that emotions are okay to express, even if they're difficult.'' A beat passed, during which she searched his face. ''That's going to be up to you.''

''Can I just tell her?''

''You have to show her.''

Sam's conflicted gaze raised. He hated to ask for help of any kind, in fact he rarely did. But this situation was beyond him. ''Will you help me figure this out? I've held my emotions in for so long, I hardly know how to show them.''

''Of course, Sam. I'll do anything. But I think you'll be surprised. You're showing emotion right now. You just need to let it carry over into every part of your life.'' She gentled her tone. ''Were your parents the unemotional sort?''

''Oh, Erin,'' he said, blowing out a breath. He sat forward, elbows on his knees, fists clasped beneath his chin. A muscle in his jaw flexed, and his eyes looked distant and haunted. Something told Erin to sit quietly and wait. If Sam wanted to talk, she needed to give him the room to do so.

''We weren't getting along, Erin.''

She gulped. ''You and…your parents?''

He shook his head. ''Jenny and I,'' he answered, through gritted teeth. ''Not just on the night of the fire, but for…God, for years before that. I can't believe I'm even saying this. She's dead and buried, for God's sake.''

''It's okay.'' Surprise zinged through her. He'd seemed so torn up about his wife's death, she felt sure he'd lost the love of his life. To learn it was otherwise came as a shock. But did anyone really know what went on behind the closed doors of a marriage? ''I'm sorry, though.''

Without acknowledging her words, he went on. ''I was working overtime the night of the fire. I didn't have to, but…man, this is hard.'' He grimaced, and his handsome face looked suddenly haggard and guilt-etched.

''It's okay. Take your time.''

''I didn't want to be home,'' he said simply, turning to look at her directly. ''There's the plain, ugly truth. Jenny wanted me home that night, and I told her I had to work mandatory overtime on the job.''

''Well, you can't help it if you had to work.''

''It wasn't mandatory.''

Erin swallowed, trying very hard not to move. She felt a thud of realization in her gut, but didn't want to do anything to interrupt Sam's revelations.

''I told Jenny I didn't have a choice about working when I actually did. Overtime was voluntary, and I rushed to volunteer, just so I didn't have to be home. That night she died saving our daughter.''

''Sam…I'm so sorry. Can you tell me…what happened?''

Sam's Adam's apple jumped a few times, and he curled his hands inward, rubbing the knuckles together. "From the fire investigation, it all started with a candle. Jenny—" His voice caught, and he pressed his lips together until he'd regained his composure. "Jenny loved candles. Burned them all the time. So much that, at eighteen months, Jessica already knew not to go near them. I hate the damn things."

Erin made a mental note to never burn candles in his presence again. She tried not to feel guilty for burning the utility candle during their first dinner together. This wasn't about her. She reached out and clasped Sam's hand in a show of support, and he allowed it.

"She and Jessica must've fallen asleep on our bed. There was a video, *Mulan*, melted in the VCR in our bedroom. I was so surprised when you put it in tonight."

"That's Jessica's favorite movie," Erin blurted.

Sam looked at her sharply. "So I noticed. She hasn't looked at it since the fire. I bought her that new copy, but—" He shrugged.

"Wow, Sam. She picked it out the first day I was here with her, and we've watched it every day since." They were both silent for a moment. "But, please, go on. I didn't mean to interrupt."

Sam nodded once. "By the time the smoke woke Jenny up, the carpet was on fire, blocking the bedroom door. There was no way out except the window." His eyes searched Erin's, and she found she was holding her breath. "We lived on the third floor."

"Oh, no." Erin released the breath in a rush and let her eyes flutter closed for a moment.

"Things may not have been perfect between Jenny and me, but God, Erin. She stood in that thick black smoke, with flames licking at her back, and held my daughter out the window until a firefighter got close enough to catch her, and then she dropped her to safety. By the time they got Jessica down and into the care of the paramedics, then went back up that ladder, Jenny was unconscious. They got her out and rushed her to the hospital, but her lungs were so burned and filled with carbon monoxide, she never recovered. She died saving Jessica. There is no bigger sacrifice a parent can make, and despite her faults and our disagreements, Jenny made that sacrifice."

"Sam..." Erin didn't know what to say.

"And I was at work. A little white lie, mandatory overtime when it wasn't mandatory. As a result, Jenny died a horrible death alone."

Erin squeezed his hand harder. "That fire wasn't your fault. You can't lay that kind of guilt trip on yourself."

Sam pulled away and stood, pacing the living room. "I should've been home. I was forever blowing out candles when Jenny left them burning." He clenched his fists. "I could've prevented the fire, or I could've found an escape route for Jenny, something. I could've done something, Erin." He spun to face her, his face ravaged, his chest rising and falling with ragged breaths. "I didn't love her anymore, but I didn't want her dead. And yet, she is. Jessica's mother is dead because of my selfish choices. I've had to live with that for six months, and I'll have to live with it forever.''

''Oh, Sam.'' Erin did the only thing she knew to do, she did exactly what anyone in her family would do. She stood and crossed the room, wrapping Sam in a hug. ''You can't blame yourself for what happened.''

''I can. I do.''

''But it wasn't your fault.''

He snorted. ''So you say. Want to know the worst part? I don't even know if I can tell you this.''

''You can tell me anything.''

He visibly struggled, clenching and unclenching his fists, which remained at his sides. ''When I'd heard that Jenny died and Jessica lived, for a split second I was relieved it wasn't the other way around. I'm a monster, Erin.''

''No, you aren't. You can work past this. I can help you.'' She felt his arms come around her and hold on, and it bolstered her courage.

''I don't know how. I don't know how to atone.''

''You don't need to atone, Sam. You aren't a monster, you're human. You need to heal.'' Erin's heart thudded, but this was her perfect opening. ''And you can do so by helping Jessica heal. Imagine how it was for her.''

''Believe me, I imagine it every day.''

''Then help her,'' she whispered.

''How?''

Erin pulled back, looking up into his tormented

face. "Talk to her about her mother. Talk to her about how much you miss Jenny, even if you don't."

"I do, just not—it's hard to explain."

"You don't owe me an explanation. But, Jessica." Erin shrugged. "Open the door for her to miss her mother, too. It's obvious she does, but she's holding it all in. That's not healthy for any person, but especially a little person."

After a moment, Sam pulled her back into a hug. They stood in silence, rocking in the embrace. Erin could feel his warm breath on the top of her head, the heat of his muscles through his T-shirt. She closed her eyes, reveling in the feeling, wanting it to never end.

"You're an amazing person, Erin O'Grady."

"So are you. And you're an amazing father. Don't you dare think otherwise."

Sam took his time reining in his emotions, but finally he released his grip on Erin and set her away gently. "Thank you for listening. I haven't told anyone…about that night. It's a bit of a relief to…admit it all."

"I'm honored you chose me."

"To dump on." He got a pained expression. "I'm sorry about that. I didn't mean—"

"Don't ever apologize for feeling, Sam." She smiled at him gently. "You're allowed to feel whatever you feel."

His eyes searched her face until his expression went from ravaged to resigned, then finally he reached out and tucked a lock of hair behind her ear. "Are you busy tomorrow night?"

Erin's heart jumped to her throat, and she blinked a couple times. "Um...no. I have brunch with my family in the morning, but my evening is free." A pause. "Why?"

"I'd like to take you to dinner. As a thank you for this week, for the scrapbook. And...maybe we can talk about how I can go about helping Jessica." He twisted his mouth to the side. "I know I can be stubborn, but I want that more than anything in the world, you know."

Erin smiled tenderly again, her heart taking flight. "I do know that. And I'd love to go to dinner."

Sam nodded once. "Good. I'll call my secretary to babysit. Mia will jump at the chance. She misses Jess so much now that she's not coming to the worksite anymore."

"I can imagine." Erin smiled. "She's a pretty amazing little person, your Jessica."

Sam's eyes darkened in a way that made Erin's tummy swirl. He reached out slowly, almost touching her cheek. She could almost feel his work-roughened hands on her face, and her skin tingled in anticipation. At the last moment, he seemed to think better of his actions. He curled his fingers against his palm and pulled away, stepping back. His eyes darted around. "I should go to bed."

"Me, too."

There they stood, strands of the unsaid stretching and buzzing between them like power lines, zapping them to the spot. He watched her. She watched him. Tension vibrated all around them, and some unspoken connection held them like a tether.

"Erin."

Suddenly, Erin could see her dream future laid out before her. Sam loving her and Jessica. More children, lots of them. She was way out of control with her fantasizing after just one week on the job, and she stumbled backwards into the reality of what was happening. This attraction wasn't real. Sam was merely grateful she was helping him and his daughter. She needed to keep things in perspective or risk a broken heart.

Sam reached out to catch her, leaving his hand wrapped loosely around her upper arm after she'd regained her balance.

"I-I'm sorry," she stammered. "Clumsy. I...should go."

He released her...but the action seemed reluctant. "Thank you for everything. And please, don't clean up the kitchen or anything else before you turn in. I mean it. You've done so much for us already."

*Gratitude. It's just gratitude, Erin.*

"I'll take care of it."

"Okay." She ducked her head, heat rising to her face. She'd agree to anything just to escape this moment where her feelings were undoubtedly plain as printing on her face. She was all about showing feelings, but she did not want to embarrass herself in front of this man. "Night, Sam."

"Goodnight, Erin."

"Sleep well."

He released a signature Sam almost-laugh. "Oh, I don't think there is much chance of that."

As she walked on wobbly legs toward her room, she wondered if she'd merely imagined the double entendre in his words.

"What's this I hear about you working for a single man?" asked Eamon the next morning, after he'd cornered her by the tea kettle when she'd gone for a refill. It was the first chance they had to talk in three weeks, since he'd been out of town.

Erin stood on tiptoe and planted a big, noisy kiss on his cheek. "Nice to see you, too, big bro."

Eamon pretended to be grossed out, making a big show of wiping the kiss away. "I mean it, Erin. If I'd been in town when you got that interview—"

"But you weren't," she told him firmly, popping a piece of cinnamon roll into her mouth. After chewing and swallowing, she said, "And your cohorts in crime went over and interrogated him before I moved in, much to my abject horror, so you have no basis for argument. Besides, he's a nice guy."

"Hmph." Eamon snagged a piece of the communal cinnamon roll and ate it himself. "I'd still like to meet the guy and be the judge of that myself."

Erin planted her fists on her hips and lifted her chin. "Maybe someday you will, Eam, but only if it happens in the natural course of things. He's already suffered the O'Grady male presence once. You're not going to put him—or me—through it again. I'm just starting to get in the groove of the job, and I don't want you messing it up.''

He frowned. ''When did you get so uncooperative?''

''Don't you trust me, Eam?''

''I do.'' He sighed, then pulled her into a hug. ''I just want the best for you.''

Erin gave him a squeeze, then pulled away. ''I know you do. But, listen. This job isn't about Sam. It's about his two-year-old, Jessica.'' Okay, so it wasn't entirely true, but Eamon didn't need to know that. Over the week, it had become as much about the man as the child.

Eamon's stony expression eased. ''Susan told me what they went through. I'm really sorry about that.''

Erin leaned her hip against the counter. ''Yeah. I'm hoping I can help them.''

''If anyone can, sis, it's you.'' Eamon grabbed her around the neck and gave her a giant noogie.

''Cut it out!''

He released her, then bent and kissed her on the cheek. ''Just be careful and be smart. And, I'd still like to meet the guy if it ever falls into place.''

''What did the others say about him?''

''I like to draw my own conclusions about a person, Erin.''

''What did they say?'' she insisted.

Eamon grumbled under his breath. ''They said he seemed like an okay guy.''

''See?''

Eamon jabbed a finger in her direction. "Folks said that about Ted Bundy, too, you know."

"Ugh!" Erin spun around and headed off. "I'm going to go hang out with the women and children, where people are sane!"

Luckily, Eamon's interrogation was the sum total of the grilling she received that morning at brunch, much to her surprise. As she drove back to Sam's, her heart felt light, and her anticipation about dinner had grown. If things went her way, Jessica would come out of her shell, Erin herself would break through Sam's wall of defenses, and her brothers would eventually do a lot more than meet Sam. They'd welcome him into the family.

Yeah. Right. Now, where had she placed that magic wand?

"So, you're the legendary Erin O'Grady," said Mia that evening, as she opened her front door to them. Erin could smell something spicy baking inside, and the sound of children's laughter wafted out on the fragrant air. She felt right at home and offered a smile to match the other woman's warmth. Mia was probably forty, a little round at the middle and radiating love and a motherly demeanor that felt both familiar and soothing. No wonder Jessica loved her so much.

"I don't know about legendary," Erin said, laughing. "Notorious might be a better word choice." She reached out a hand, and Mia shook it with enthusiasm.

"Well, come in, please." She stepped back, opening the door wider. "Hi, Sam."

"Mia," he said. "What's baking?"

"Gingersnaps."

"Yum. Those are my favorite," Erin said.

Mia winked. "Well, I'll be sure to pack up a little gift package for you to take home."

"How sweet of you."

Mia hooked her arm through Erin's and steered them into the living room. "I'm so delighted to have Jessica for the night. I've missed her."

"Understandable. She's such a doll."

Mia's gaze flicked to Sam, who carried a sleeping Jessica against his chest. "Hand her over, buddy. You're the boss at the worksite, but I'm the boss here."

Sam smirked, but rubbed a sleeping Jessica's cheek gently with his knuckle until her eyes fluttered open in confusion. Her hair was squashed down on one side and sticking up endearingly on the other. Sam kissed his daughter's forehead, then indicated his secretary. "Look who's here, honeypot."

Jessica turned her head, saw Mia, and broke into a grin. "Mi-mi!" Suddenly awake, she reached out.

Mia grabbed hold of her, smooching her fat cheeks. "How's my favorite little rascal?"

"She's doing great, thanks to Erin," Sam said.

"Oh, come on. Don't give me that much credit."

He flashed her a look of gratitude that flamed into something deeper, scarier and more exciting, and Erin caught Mia appraising them both.

Mia cleared her throat and lifted up Jessica's still-bandaged hand. "How's the boo-boo?"

"Owie," Jessica said.

"She gets the stitches out this week, right Sam?" Erin asked.

He nodded. "That ought to be a joy. I'm sure Doc will kick me out of the suture room again."

Erin and Mia laughed, and Erin reached out and laid a hand on his forearm. "Don't worry. I'll stay with her." She and Sam shared another private look that made her middle clench, and when she looked back at Mia, the older woman's eyebrows were raised sky high, her assessment obvious.

"Well," Mia said, in a tone like she'd just heard the year's juiciest gossip. "Don't let me keep you from dinner. And, remember. There's no hurry. In fact, if you want me to keep her overnight—"

"Mia," Sam said, in a playfully warning tone.

Mia shrugged and sniffed. "I'm just saying, the option is open. If you decide the evening is…getting late."

Erin's face flamed, and she stared at her feet. Did Sam's secretary think there was more to their relationship than boss and nanny? She wished.

"We'll be back to pick her up in just a few hours," she heard Sam say, in a firm tone.

"Whatever you like," Mia replied, in a sing-song, teasing manner. "So glad to finally meet you, Erin. It's nice to see Sam without that omnipresent scowl on his face."

Erin worked to keep her expression from betraying

her feelings about Sam and offered a wide smile. "Nice to have met you, too." She leaned in and kissed Jessica's cheek. "Bye-bye, sweetie."

"Bye, Win."

Erin shrugged. "She calls me Win."

Mia laughed. "That's adorable."

Sam stooped down next, cupping Jessica's face and giving her big smoochy kisses on her cheeks. "Be a good girl for Mia, honeypot."

"Yuv you, Daddy."

"I love you, too."

"Yuv you, Win."

A lump rose in Erin's throat and she splayed a palm on her chest. "Oh." She looked at Sam with moist eyes. "That's so sweet. She's never said that to me before." Returning her attention to Jessica, she touched the baby's cheek gently. "I love you, too, sweet girl."

"My sleepover offer still stands," Mia called out as they descended the stairs from her stoop.

Erin watched Sam out of the corner of her eye. He shook his head, but at least he looked amused.

"See you soon, Mia," he said pointedly.

Once they were in the car, Sam expelled a breath and started the engine. As he pulled away from the curb, he cast an apologetic look toward Erin. "Sorry about that. Mia is an unrepentant matchmaker."

Erin laughed nervously. "No problem. Hey, it's the opposite problem I have. She wants to fix you up, and my brothers want to lock me away in a convent."

"Now, that," Sam drawled, "would be a darn shame."

A flock of hummingbirds set loose in her tummy. It sounded like he was flirting, but she just couldn't trust her instincts. "So, um, where are we going?"

"Just a little neighborhood grill I like. Is that okay?"

"Fine."

"How was brunch, speaking of your brothers?"

"Well, they didn't hammer me too badly about working for a single man. But, my brother, Eamon, is back and says he wants to meet you for himself."

"Didn't he get the full report from the others?"

"That's what I asked." Erin rolled her eyes. "He said, and I quote, 'They said he was a nice guy. But people said that about Ted Bundy, too."

Sam held a fist to his chest. "Ouch."

"I know. I'm sorry."

He glanced over. "I think it's nice that they look out for you, Erin. Maybe…down the road, we can meet."

"I don't expect that, Sam, but thank you."

He reached over and patted her hand, sending tingles up her arm and all through her body. "It's no problem. Setting your brothers' minds at ease is the least I can do for you."

Erin smiled, then turned her attention toward the window. Man, was she ever falling for this man.

# Chapter Nine

Dinner with Erin turned out to be one of the most pleasant evenings Sam had spent in a good long time. She counseled him extensively about how he should approach Jessica regarding Jenny, but she'd also shared stories of her brothers' antics and her big, raucous family life that left him smiling. Truly smiling, instead of that forced slash of a grimace he'd used in place of a smile for the past several months…or had it been years? Maybe Mia had been right—he did scowl more than smile.

Her stories also made him a little envious, and an insane part of him yearned to be a bigger part of her life. What would it be like to belong to a family like Erin's? To always know there were people who accepted you, who loved you so much, looked out for you to the point of exasperation? He'd always thought having that sort of connection in his life didn't matter to him, but being around Erin made him reconsider. Listening to her stories made him yearn for something he'd never have and made him regret his childhood in an acute, very real way.

It also made him wonder about his siblings. Lissa, Adam, and little Mark, but also Cambry's teenage children, Shawna and Chad. A whole family he'd never met, he marveled. Was he making a mistake keeping his identity secret from them?

Like it or not, Erin was melting the ice around his heart, making him question decisions in his life that had previously been cut and dried. He'd reached out for connections before, though, and been bitterly disappointed with the results. Of course, his previous attempts had always been with various foster families, not with blood relatives. Would that make a difference? He still couldn't believe he had *blood* relatives.

No one would believe it—that was the thing.

But, bottom line, he had a lot of emotional work to do with Jessica in order to get their little two-person family back on track. For now, that's all he had room for in his life. He couldn't—wouldn't—even contemplate revealing himself to Lissa, Adam, and the whole world, mainly because he wasn't emotionally ready himself. He'd seen the two of them on television enough to know they were in a whole different place in their lives than he was in his.

The discussion with Erin over dinner had made him realize a lot of things about Jessica, but even more about himself. He wasn't a cold man, or bitter. Maybe on the surface, but that was mostly a self-protective thing. Deep down, he was one big ball of fear. Fear of rejection, of losing Jessica, of living a disconnected life. But, other than with his daughter, wasn't he doing that now? Maybe. Probably. But, he feared trying again, so he'd focus on Jessica and count his blessings.

Erin helped him see that he could take this journey with Jessica one step at a time, that there was nothing to fear in that respect. He hoped she was right, and he also hoped Jessica's recovery would have a ripple effect through his life.

The dinner had been a kind of awakening for him, and he'd always be grateful to Erin for it. In such a short time, she'd become one of those blessings he'd count during times he felt alone. If he felt emotionally healthier, more prepared to risk his heart, he could fall for Erin O'Grady in a red hot minute. Truthfully, he'd already begun to.

That didn't mean he planned on doing anything about it.

He'd woken the morning after their dinner to a sunny, bright Sunday and decided he and Jessica would take advantage of the weather and enjoy a few hours outside. Erin was spending the day with her parents, so it was up to him to broach the very difficult subject with his daughter alone. That's the way it should be, though. He had a whole day with Jessica, and he planned to use it wisely. A picnic in the park sounded perfect.

As he pushed Jessica in her little stroller, going over the dinner conversation from last night in his mind, he chastised himself for feeling the pressure. How could he fear talking to a two-year-old child— his own daughter? It seemed ludicrous. But, the little plastic bag filled with photos of Jenny burned a hole in his pocket, reminding him of the difficult discussion to come. With his whole heart, he wanted it to go well. Some strange part of him wanted Erin to be proud of him for how he handled this. He gripped the stroller handles tighter and glanced up at a puffy white cloud tripping through the sky.

*Please let me do one thing right.*

He truly wanted Jessica to feel free to open up about her mother. More than anything, he yearned to be a better father than Cambry had been to him— which wouldn't be too hard. Cambry hadn't been a father of any kind. And yet, how could he judge the man? Sam might not have physically abandoned Jessica, and he never would, but Erin made him realize he'd inadvertently abandoned her emotionally by closing off after Jenny's death and "keeping busy" to avoid the difficult conversations. Jessica had probably taken his silence to mean she couldn't talk about her mother, because she never, ever did. It just wasn't natural. He needed to right the wrongs, get past the pain, and set them on the path toward a better, closer family life.

Today was his chance.

He'd packed a little lunch of peanut butter and jelly

sandwiches, Oreos, and juice boxes, and he'd planned
to broach the topic after Jessie had tired of playing
and they'd shared the meal. When they got to the
park, though, Jessica showed little interest in the play-
ground equipment or the other children. Reverting to
her post-fire timidity, she sat right next to him watching the fun from the blanket they shared. They sat in
companionable silence while he shored up his courage. The air smelled of cut grass and the sweet promise of Spring, and exuberant children's chatter and
laughter ribboned through their surroundings. Finally,
he smoothed his hand through her wispy, baby soft
hair, warm from the sun. "Are you hungry, honeypot?"

Jessie shook her head and nestled closer.

Okay, game on. He'd been stalling long enough. If
he didn't jump in with both feet, he'd never get past
his own trepidation. Taking a deep, steadying breath,
Sam asked, "Want to look at some pictures with
me?"

Jessica blinked up at him and nodded. She'd grown
fond of flipping through photographs ever since Erin
launched the scrapbook project.

He pulled the plastic baggie of photos from his
pocket and opened it, carefully removing the stack of
precious photos. "Do you recognize these?"

"Mine," she said, on the verge of a whimper. Her
eyes grew wide and troubled.

"Yes, they're the photos you collected. They're
yours." He waited until she relaxed. "Are these special pictures, Jessica?"

She nodded. On top was the photo of Jenny smiling, holding a newborn Jessica in her arms at the hospital.

Jessica pointed to the swaddled baby. "Me," she said, quietly. "Baby Jes'ka."

"Yes, that's you. The day you came out of mommy's tummy." He pointed at Jenny's face, trying not to let his hand or his voice shake. "Mommy was so happy. See?"

"Mommy," Jessica whispered, as though the word were a solemn prayer, not to be uttered aloud.

Sam's heart clenched. He slipped that photo to the back of the stack and showed her the next one. It was a snapshot of Jenny sitting with her feet curled under her on the edge of the couch in the apartment. He couldn't say when the photo was taken or why. It was just one of those photos people take to finish out a roll of film, an uneventful moment in a life taken for granted. But it definitely portrayed Jenny in her most common state. She looked pensive, darkly pretty. Deep in thought.

"Mommy," Jessica whispered again.

He swallowed, as blood pounded hot and loud in his ears. "Do you remember Mommy?"

Jessica nodded. "Our house." She pointed at the sofa.

"Yes, that was our other house." He paused. "I miss Mommy, Jess. Do you miss Mommy, too?"

"Mommy go bye-bye," she said, gravely, peering down at the picture with a calm, solemn acceptance.

Oh, God. Sam choked back an onslaught of grief. He struggled to keep his voice steady, then remembered that Erin told him he didn't need to hold in his pain. He'd do Jessica a bigger favor by showing his emotions rather than bottling them up. Tears sprang to his eyes, and he let them come, which was completely out of character for Sam Lowery. His voice remained thick with emotion when he spoke. "Yes, Mommy went bye-bye, honeypot, but she loved you very much." He reached out to stroke some wispy hair off her forehead. "She loved you as much as I love you. You know that, right?"

Jessica looked up at him, surprised. To his utter shock, she reached up and touched his cheek. "No cry, Daddy."

A tear escaped, and he sniffed. "It's okay to cry, Jessica. I miss Mommy, and sometimes I cry. It's okay."

Her tiny, chubby fingers awkwardly patted at the tear, and he could almost feel his heart expand to bursting in his chest with love for this tiny, compassionate person. "Do you miss Mommy, honeypot?" he asked again.

Jessica stared back down at the picture, reaching out one finger to touch the image of Jenny's face. "Mommy angel."

He blinked with confusion, smearing the wetness from his cheeks with the back of one hand. "What's that? Is Mommy your angel?"

"Uh huh. Mi-mi say, Mommy angel."

Sam closed his eyes for a moment. God bless Mia. At least someone had been talking to Jessica about her mother. It should have been him doing the talking, but he shoved away a pang of guilt. He needed to focus on the present and the future, not the past. God knew, there was nothing he could do about the past.

Sam pulled Jessica onto his lap, resting his chin on her head. He wrapped her in his arms and released a long, shuddering sigh. "Mommy *is* your angel, Jess. Mine, too. She watches out for us every day."

"Uh-huh."

"Do you—" he swallowed "—want to talk about Mommy?"

Jessica hesitated for a moment, then shook her head.

"It's okay if you do."

"No. I want Win," she said unexpectedly, her voice cracking as her bottom lip jutted out and trembled with emotion.

Erin. She wanted Erin. Jenny had become less real for her, but Erin was a flesh and blood woman who loved her. It didn't surprise him. This conversation was emotional, probably a little bit scary, and Jessica had come to depend on Erin. "Erin will be home tonight."

At that piece of news, Jessica began to sob. "No. I want Win now." She turned and wrapped her little arms around Sam's neck, weeping until the neck of his T-shirt was wet. He just rocked her and let her release it all. He had an inkling that she was crying for Jenny just as much as she was crying for Erin, but it was hard for her to express her pain, thanks to his piss-poor example. Finally, her sobs turned into hiccups.

"Yuv Mommy," she whispered.

He tightened his embrace. "Oh, Jess. I love Mommy, too." It wasn't a lie. He'd always love Jenny for giving him such a beautiful, special daughter.

Jessica twisted around and picked up the stack of photographs, clutching them to her chest. "Mine."

"Yes, they're your pictures. No one is ever going to take them from you, okay? You can keep them forever."

She studied his face for a moment, then nodded.

"Do you want to make a book of Mommy's pictures with Erin?"

Jessica pursed her little lips, then nodded. "With Win and you."

"Okay." He kissed the top of her head. "We'll all work on the book of Mommy's pictures together. I promise."

Jessica bit her lip for a moment, then implored him with pain-filled eyes. "Mommy scared. Mommy cry."

An anvil of dread dropped in his gut. Jessica had been little more than a baby the night of the fire. Could she possibly remember the horror of it all enough to discuss it? He almost went the route of, "Shhh, it's okay," but he remembered Erin telling him to let her talk. He swallowed back his own feelings of inadequacy and forged ahead. "D-do you mean the night of the fire, Jessica?"

She nodded.

Sam fought back a wave of nausea. "Was Mommy scared for you? Is that what you mean?"

Another nod. "Mommy cry. I fall, and—" she flipped her pudgy little hands palm up, in an oddly older looking mannerism "—Mommy go bye-bye."

Sam's tears returned. Jessica's matter-of-factness about the tragedy tore at his soul. "Were you scared, too?"

Jessica bit her bottom lip, and her big, liquid eyes met his. She nodded. "I no like fall."

It was so hard to discuss this in terms a two-year-old would understand. He felt like he was swimming in a dark ocean with a desperate need for air and yet no inkling of which way was up. "I know, honey. I was so scared when I heard that you fell, too." He smoothed the backs of his fingers down her cheek. "But you know, Mommy let you fall so the nice man could catch you. So you could get away from the fire. Mommy saved you. Do you understand what I'm saying?" Probably not.

Jessica just watched him.

"Mommy loved you so much. So much, sweetie."

Jessica nodded.

"And I love you, too." He dipped his chin. "When you get sad, when you think about Mommy, you can talk to me. Okay?"

"'Kay."

"And when I get sad, I'll talk to you, too."

"'Kay."

"And you can talk to Erin or Mia, too. We all love you."

"Yuv you," she said, squeezing both of his cheeks with her little hands. "No cry, Daddy."

"I won't cry anymore today, honeypot. But if I feel sad on another day, I might cry again. Is that okay if Daddy cries?"

She nodded, and then she smiled. "'Kay."

Sam's heart soared with love and a huge weight lifted from his shoulders. They could get through this, because they had each other, and finally, *finally,* they were talking about it. He couldn't wait to see Erin and tell her how it went.

"You seem distracted, honey," Erin's mom said. They were in the bright yellow, sunflower theme kitchen at her parents' house, side-by-side, finishing up a batch of cookies before Erin headed home to prepare for the week ahead.

"Hmm?" Erin glanced up, then checked the clock. "Oh. I guess I am."

"What's up?"

She quirked her mouth to the side. "Sam's talking to Jessica about her mother today for the first time since she died. I guess I'm just hoping everything goes well. He was pretty nervous about it."

Sarah O'Grady was silent for a moment as she dropped some dough onto a cookie sheet. "Tell me more about this Sam."

Erin tossed her a droll look. "Oh, you mean the boys didn't already give you the full run-down?"

"They did, but I want to hear it from you. You know how your brothers are." She reached out and smeared a dab of cookie dough on Erin's nose.

Erin laughed, wiping it off and eating it. "Yeah, how could I forget."

"So, come on. Dish about your boss." The older O'Grady woman slid the cookie sheet in the oven, set the timer, then turned back toward her daughter.

Erin took a seat on one of the wooden and wrought iron stools by the breakfast bar, hooking her heels on the upper rung. She rested an elbow on the counter and planted her chin in her palm. What to say? "Sam's a really good guy, Mom. Such a good father, too. But...I don't know. He has a deeply mysterious side." She looked sharply at her mom. "And don't tell the evil five that I said that, or they'll be pinning unsolved serial murders on the poor guy within minutes. That's not how I mean it, though."

Sarah laughed, but she shook her head. "Erin, they just care about you. Be happy your brothers look out for you."

"Oh, I am," Erin groused. "Thrilled to death."

"So, what do you mean, dark and mysterious?"

She squinted toward the ceiling. "It's just something I can't put my finger on. I feel like we connect on a lot of levels, but there are just some parts of him I can't reach." She blew out a breath. "I guess I have a feeling that losing his wife wasn't his first trauma, but I don't know what else could've happened. He doesn't seem to have very close family ties.''

''Really?'' Sarah pulled up another bar stool and reached for two warm cookies, handing Erin one. For a minute, they both munched on them.

''Yeah. I mean, I've been working on that scrapbook I told you about, remember?'' Her mother nodded. ''Well, he doesn't have a single photo of his parents or any other extended family. And there were none of his wife's family, either.''

''Hmm,'' Sarah mused. ''Maybe they weren't big picture takers. Or maybe they didn't have the money to take photographs, Erin. We were very fortunate in that respect, but a lot of families weren't. Do you think he came from a poor background?''

Erin shrugged. ''Could be.''

''A lot of people who've pulled themselves up by their bootstraps don't like to discuss their humble beginnings.''

''Yeah, but I wouldn't care if he was poor as a child.'' She finished the cookie and wiped her fingers on a napkin. ''I just wish I could get inside his head sometimes.''

Erin's mother sat peering at her curiously, and suddenly Erin felt like a bug under a microscope. ''What?''

''If I didn't know you better, Erin go lightly, I'd say it sounds like you're interested in the man.''

Erin bit her lip and cast her mother a sidelong glance. ''Would it be really awful if I were, Mom? I mean, I know he's my boss, but it's not like I'm doing anything unprofessional with him. I just…can't help but be attracted to him.'' She groaned. ''I never thought seeing a man be a good father would be sexy.''

Sarah laughed. ''Welcome to being a grown woman, hon. And no, it's not wrong. Just be careful. This is your job—''

''I know, Mom.''

''And you'd hate to jeopardize that for…a crush.''

Erin started to protest, but her mom held up a finger.

''However, if it's more than a crush, take it slow. Be smart. And protect your heart.'' She winked. ''You never know what might happen. Heaven knows, people have found love in stranger places.''

Erin reached across and hugged her. ''I promise I'll be smart, Mom, no matter what happens. And responsible. Jessica is my first priority.''

''That's my girl.''

''Besides, you don't really have to worry. Sam's not interested in me. This is a wholeheartedly one-sided crush.''

''Well, then, the man's got one gaping fault.''

''What's that?''

''Excruciatingly poor taste in women.''

Erin laughed, then jumped off the bar stool and started packing up her things to head home. ''I'll keep you posted on how things go with little Jessica.''

''And Sam, please. Pretty please. You're my only daughter. A old married woman like myself likes to experience things like falling in love again, however vicariously.''

"God, Mom, you embarrass me." At the door Erin and her mom embraced again.

"Embarrassing you is my duty as a mother, and my right." As Erin turned and headed down the walk, her mother called out, "Don't forget, dear. Next Saturday morning is Kellan's birthday party here at the house."

"Oh, no." Erin spun back and pressed her palm to her forehead. "I've told Sam I'll work next Saturday. He and his crew are working overtime that day."

"Well, just bring Jessica with you."

Erin thought of Sam. He probably wouldn't go for that, as protective as he was of Jessica, but it sounded like a good plan to Erin. Jessica needed to get out more and be exposed to other children. Sometimes it was better to ask for forgiveness than permission. "I will think about it. I swear, you will love that baby girl."

Sarah grinned, leaning her tall, lanky frame against the door jamb. "I have six children and fifteen grandchildren, honey. I haven't met a baby yet that didn't steal my heart."

"Now I know where I got it from," Erin said, blowing her mom a kiss.

## Chapter Ten

The second week Erin lived with him and Jessica brought one revelation after another, largely because he'd finally broken through his own barriers and talked to Jessica—thanks to Erin's wise and gentle persistence. Sam could hardly remember why he hadn't wanted to hire her in the first place…except for the overwhelming attraction part. He was doing his best to keep that under wraps.

Despite Mia putting on the full court press matchmaking scheme every day since she'd met Erin, Sam went to work feeling happier and more hopeful, and he couldn't wait to come home and work on Jessica's very special Mommy scrapbook with her and Erin each evening. He'd grown to crave Erin's smiling approval, and the more time he spent with her and Jess, the more he received it. She'd been so proud of him when he told her about his groundbreaking talk with Jessica, she'd actually gotten teary-eyed. He had marveled at how freely she could show her emotions. Would that type of expression have been easier for him had he grown up in a family like hers?

She still tried, every so often, to probe for more details about his family life, usually in the evenings after Jessica was asleep, when the two of them sat in the kitchen together, sharing conversation and companionship. But instead of seeing her questioning as an invasion of his privacy, he began to tell himself it was because family was such a big part of her life. She talked about the O'Gradys all the time, and it probably seemed strange to her that he didn't talk about anyone at all.

He'd toyed with the idea of confiding in her on more than one occasion, but ultimately, Sam couldn't bring himself to tell her about his less than pleasant childhood. The last thing he wanted was anyone's pity. Plus, telling her about his beginnings might bring the issue of Lissa and Adam closer to the surface, and he couldn't risk that. Media attention on the reunited twins had ignited into almost daily updates as the world waited to hear whether the selfless bone marrow donation from Adam had been accepted by little Mark's ravaged body.

No gut-spilling, he thought. Too dangerous.

Even as close as he'd grown to Erin, the issue of his childhood would have to remain his secret.

The following Saturday, Erin had agreed to stay

home and care for Jessica while Sam and his crew pushed forth with a project that had seen more than its fair share of rain delays resulting in hundreds of thousands of dollars spent over the budget. Sam arrived at the worksite at four-thirty in the morning, hoping to power through his work and get home in time for Erin to have the rest of her weekend off. He wanted to make sure he kept her happy, because he and Jessica both needed her around.

By one o'clock that afternoon, though, Sam had finished for the day and headed home. He drove faster than usual from the site to his house, bouncing into the driveway as he hit the button clipped to his visor for the automatic garage door.

He smiled as the door rose, unable to remember ever feeling so eager to get home before. He liked to tell himself it was because Jessica was making such good progress recovering emotionally from the fire, and that was certainly a large part of it. But, he also rushed home to be with Erin. Vivacious, guileless Erin.

Seeing her, listening to her laughter and her stories, her lullabies for Jessica—all of it. He craved it. Sometimes he found it hard to think of her as merely his nanny. That was such an impersonal title, and she'd begun to feel like such a bigger part of his life.

How had that happened in such a short time?

And, anyway, it was just his little fantasy.

After pulling into the garage and cutting his engine, Sam hurried into the mudroom and stooped over to remove his work boots. He listened, but didn't hear anything from inside the house. Perhaps Jessica was down for a nap.

He took care padding into the kitchen quietly, in case Jess was, indeed, sleeping. Crossing the room, he rapped softly on the door to Erin's wing, but got no answer. For no logical reason, an alarm bell went off inside him. Moving quickly into the living room, he checked for Erin, but the room was empty. He took the stairs two at a time and peeked in the nursery. Empty. His heart grew heavy with dread, and he bounded back down the stairs. "Erin?" he called out, his voice sounding sharp to his own ears. "Jessica? Anyone here?"

No answer.

In the doorway to the kitchen, he stopped short. Of course. Erin's VW Bug hadn't been parked in the garage when he pulled in, but he'd been so lost in his happy thoughts about being home, its absence hadn't registered. Perhaps they'd just headed out to run errands. Sam took a deep breath and huffed out a laugh. When had he become such a worst-case scenario thinker?

He started toward the refrigerator to get himself a Pepsi and a snack, and that's when the note on the kitchen table caught his eye. He snatched it up and read Erin's neat handwriting.

Hi Sam,

Jessica and I are at my parents' house for my nephew Kellan's birthday party, which runs from noon to probably four o'clock. You are more than welcome to join us if you get home in time. I know Jessica would love to have her daddy there. Directions, address and phone number are on the back. See you soon, I hope!

Erin and Jessica

Without warning, a flood of anger coursed through Sam's veins, squelching his earlier good feelings. Jessica was just starting to make progress overcoming her fears. How could Erin think she would be comfortable around hordes of people she'd never met? Strangers. Especially the undoubtedly boisterous O'Grady clan? Erin knew how skittish Jessica got simply going to the park.

Lips pressed together, he flipped the note over and read the address and directions. Tossing the note aside, he headed upstairs for a quick shower. Damn right, he'd meet them at the O'Grady's house. He'd retrieve his daughter, and later, when Erin returned home, he'd lay out exactly what he expected when it came to Jessica being thrown into strange situations or large groups of people without his approval.

A small part of him whispered, "Hypocrite." Hadn't he just been singing Erin's praises? Still, this was different. He'd been looking forward to seeing Erin, and yes, she'd begun to feel like a permanent fixture in his life. But, in reality, she was his *nanny*. She had absolutely no latitude when it came to decisions about his daughter's welfare. Dammit, she should've checked with him first.

Jessica was *his* daughter.

As he yanked off his work clothes and stepped into the hot steam of the shower, Sam watched his little fantasy life swirl down the drain like so many soap bubbles. Hey, it was his fault for playing mind games with himself, for picturing what it would be like if Erin were his lover rather than hired help. But, at the end of the day, Sam really was a single parent. Any greater connection he felt with Erin was nothing more than a figment of his hopeful imagination.

Story of his pathetic life.

All the O'Gradys, big and small, were gathered in the backyard of Sarah and Eamon Sr.'s rambling ranch style home, just the way Grandma Sarah liked it. She'd loved being a mother to babies, small children—even teenagers. But now that her kids were grown and gone, she found she loved being a grandmother even more. She enjoyed spoiling her grandchildren, thrilled to the fact that she could pass them off to their parents when they had meltdowns or potty mishaps. The grandmother perks completely validated all she'd gone through raising five rambunctious and often difficult boys and one thankfully sweet and obedient daughter.

A burst of laughter followed Sarah inside as she popped into the kitchen with an empty bowl to refill. She reached for a new bag of potato chips, tore it open, and started to pour them in, humming to herself. The buzz of the doorbell gave her a start. She glanced over her shoulder toward the living room. "Just a moment," she called out as she finished.

Wiping her hands on her apron, Sarah wound her way through a chair-filled, toy-strewn kitchen and into the front entryway. She glanced through the peephole and got an eyeful of a very handsome, albeit a little stern-looking young man. Finally, she thought, feeling self-satisfied. She knew Erin would work her magic on Sam Lowery if it was meant to be, and based on looks alone, he was quite a catch.

With a grin on her face, she pulled open the door, eager to meet the mysterious man her daughter had fallen for, head over heels and then some. After meeting precious little Jessica, all Sarah could say was, bring on the daddy. Any man who had managed to raise such a precious little gem like Jessica, with all the hardships they'd faced, had to be an amazing person. Sight unseen, Sam Lowery had her vote as a potential partner for her Erin. Still, she was glad to finally meet him.

The door opened, and Sam found himself staring into the face of Erin...in about twenty-five years. Same crooked smile, same auburn hair, albeit in a more conservative style. Same kind eyes, but a generation older. For a moment, he suffered a complete loss for words. Erin's resemblance to her mother startled the anger right out of him.

He'd always been intrigued by genetic similarities between family members, since that had never been a part of his world. Until Adam Bartlett, of course.

*Don't think about that.*

"You must be Sam," said the woman, pushing

open the screen door and stepping aside. "I'm Sarah, Erin's mother. So glad you could join us. Come in, come in."

He smoothed his palms down the sides of his jeans. Sarah O'Grady's warm welcome left him suddenly awkward and a bit sheepish about his earlier temper flare. "Thank you. I...don't mean to intrude."

"Don't be silly. We're happy to have you." She tucked her arm into the crook of his elbow. "And Jessica, of course."

"Is she okay?"

"Why, she's fine. And absolutely adorable, Sam. You must be proud as punch of that little girl."

He allowed a small smile. "Thank you. I am. I thought I'd come pick her up and get her out of Erin's hair so you all can enjoy your party."

"Oh, you can't leave yet," Sarah said, sounding truly disappointed. "Jessica's having so much fun watching the other kids, and she just adores our dog, Olaf."

"Yes, but—" He inclined his head. "I don't mean to be ungracious, but Erin's been working all week. I thought she might like some free time."

Sarah laughed and leaned in toward him as though he'd just cracked the biggest joke of the century. "Believe me, it is not a hardship for my daughter to be with your daughter. I guess she hasn't told you just how much she loves children."

"Actually, she has."

"Just stay and enjoy yourself, Sam. Erin is fine. Jessica is fine. It's about time we got to meet both of you. Erin talks about you all the time, you know. What can I get you to drink?''

All the time? he wanted to ask. What does she say? Then he remembered Sarah's question. ''Any soft drink will be fine. Thanks.''

''Ice?''

''Straight up, and the can will do.''

''You'll fit right in,'' she said, laughing. She tossed him a blue can, which he caught deftly, then picked up a large yellow bowl filled with potato chips. ''Follow me. Everyone's out here enjoying the dry weather.''

Everyone.

The entire O'Grady clan in one fell swoop.

A sudden rush of anxiety nailed Sam's feet to the floor. He felt, once again, like the little orphan boy, standing on the fringes of a huge, loving family to which he'd never belong. He'd never truly be a part of such unconditional love, and he felt it like a dagger, all the way to the core of his soul. The familiar surge of futility and loneliness reminded him all too well of his earlier years, and for a moment, he wanted to bolt. Why put himself through this again?

''Sam?''

''Sorry.'' He gave her a tight smile. ''Do you mind if I use your restroom before I join the others?''

''Of course not.'' She pointed to the left, toward a small corridor. ''Second door on the right. Just come on out when you're ready.''

Locked safely in the small restroom, Sam splashed his face with ice cold water. He patted it dry with a lavender guest towel, then stared long and hard at his face in the oval-shaped mirror. He wasn't that unwanted little boy anymore, dammit. He was a grown man with a daughter of his own. A family, no matter how small. He wasn't going to run away or be afraid of the O'Gradys. Feeling more in control, Sam left the bathroom with his shoulders back and his head held high. He passed through the flowery yellow kitchen, then pushed open the sliding screen and stepped out onto the wooden back deck.

His eyes searched for and found Jessica, happily cuddled in the arms of Erin, who was talking animatedly with another woman.

God almighty, she was beautiful. Sam's throat went dry.

Erin wore a longish, black skirt that swirled gently in the breeze, and a emerald green halter top. Her slender back and shapely shoulders were beautifully displayed in the outfit, but the sexiest thing about her was how she held his daughter on her hip as though Jessica were her own. Jessica looked nothing if not comfortable, alternately nestling her head against Erin's neck and squealing happily at a tiny Jack Russell terrier who could, no lie, spring off all four paws about five feet in the air. Repeatedly. The little dog seemed as taken with Jessica as she was with him.

As though sensing his presence, Erin stopped talking in midsentence and turned toward him. Their eyes met, and Sam could swear the entire party went dead silent. A slow smile spread across Erin's face, and Sam felt an answering smile on his. For what seemed an eternity, Sam stood locked in the warmth of Erin's gaze, oblivious to the festivities carrying on around them.

"Daddy!" Jessica cried out, breaking the spell.

He lifted a hand to wave, then held his arms out for her.

Jessica wriggled down out of Erin's grasp and toddled over, arms outstretched. Sam swung her up into an embrace, kissing her chubby cheeks until she erupted in gales of laughter.

"How's my baby girl?" he asked, softly.

Her eyes went round, and she pointed vaguely over her shoulder. "See doggy?"

"I saw him. Do you like that doggy?"

She nodded vigorously.

"He sure can jump high for a little guy, can't he?"

"He sure can," Erin said, as she approached. "And yes, she seems to love Olaf. I think you've got an animal lover on your hands there."

He smiled down at Erin over Jessica's shoulder as he hugged her. "Hi."

"Hi," she said, almost shyly. "I'm glad you decided to come. I hope you don't mind if I brought her."

He toyed with his earlier angry thoughts then decided, no, he didn't mind at all. "It's fine. I'm glad you were able to join your family."

"How was work?"

"Busy. Dirty. Over, thank goodness."

Someone cleared his throat, off to the left of where they stood. Sam glanced over and saw a row of men—Erin's brothers, aka the evil five—gathered around a massive grill. More than that, though, he saw in their stony expressions that *they'd* seen what had just occurred between him and Erin. It wasn't anything blatant, just a crackle of attraction that any man who'd ever wanted a woman like he wanted Erin would recognize in a flat minute. Great.

First time at the O'Gradys and he gets busted by the menfolk casting lustful glances at their baby sister. Sam raised a hand to the men, and each one of them either reciprocated the action or lifted a chin toward him in greeting.

Jessica reached back for Erin, and Sam handed her over.

"Come on in. I want you to meet my oldest brother, Eamon. He's the only one you haven't met, and—" she leaned in, adding under her voice "—brace yourself, he's the worst."

"I'd love to," he said, wryly. "Thanks for the warning."

"And you can meet my dad, all my sisters-in-law, who are destined for sainthood for putting up with my annoying brothers all these years—"

"I heard that," called one of the brothers from his front position at the grill. He frowned at Erin before raising some barbecue tongs toward Sam. "Hey, Lowery. How's it going?"

"Fine, thanks. You?"

"Not bad. Hanging in. You hungry? We've got burgers, brats, chicken, and steaks."

"A brat sounds great."

The grilling brother nodded, turning back toward his domain.

"Which one was that?" Sam asked, out of the corner of his mouth.

"Mick."

"I'm never going to keep them all straight."

Erin laughed her musical, windchime laughter, then reached out and grabbed another look alike O'Grady male who was probably in his early thirties. "Eamon, look alive, buddy. This is Jessica's father, Sam. Sam, my oldest brother, Eamon."

"A pleasure," Sam said, reaching out to shake the other man's hand. "I've heard a lot about you."

"Likewise. You've got a great little daughter there." He tickled Jessica under the chin, and she giggled.

Sam looked at her with love. "Yeah, I think I'll keep her."

Eamon clapped a hand on Sam's shoulder. "Listen, I'm sorry about your loss, man. We lost our son, Bryce, a few years back, as I'm sure Erin has told you. I can appreciate what you're probably going through."

Sam swallowed a couple times, unused to such blatant, honest communication. He had to admit, though, it felt good to speak with someone who could relate, even in a small way. "Thank you. I'm...sorry about your son."

Eamon nodded, pressing his lips together. Clearly, the pain was still fresh. "Life. You just never know what it's going to throw your way."

"That's too true."

Erin's father wandered over, and she went through introductions again. After that, Sam found himself passed from sister-in-law to sister-in-law, and before he knew it, he was seated in a lawn chair in the middle of this big, loving Irish family, feeling more welcome than he'd ever imagined possible.

He could get used to this if he wasn't careful.

## Chapter Eleven

That evening, when Sam, Erin and Jessica left the party, Sam was imbued with a sense of safety and well-being, and he felt closer to Erin than ever before. They'd ended up hanging out and talking with the family until seven-thirty, and Jessica was so tuckered out, she'd fallen asleep immediately in Erin's car on the way home. After they'd pulled into the garage side-by-side, Sam released her from the carseat and carried her into the house. He glanced at Erin over his shoulder. "Would you like to join me in tucking her in? Then maybe we can have a cup of coffee—"

"—or tea."

He smiled. "Or tea in the kitchen. Unless you're tired."

"Not at all," Erin said, flashing a smile. "I'd love to."

They carried Jessica up the stairs together, tugged her playclothes off and replaced them with jammies, then laid her gently in her crib. Through all of it, Jessie remained solidly asleep. Both of them stood there just watching her breathe deeply for several moments. She looked like an angel.

"She's almost too old for this crib," Sam said, regretfully. "Something about that just makes me sad."

Erin touched his arm. "Yeah. If only we could keep them young forever. But, Jess is going to be such a cool kid and an even cooler teenager. I can't wait to see her grow up."

Sam peered over at Erin, repeating her words in his head. He liked the sound of them, as though she planned on being in their lives for a good long time. "Shall we head down to the kitchen?"

Erin unfurled her arm in the direction of the door with relish. "Age before beauty," she joked.

Sam snorted. "Sadly, that's true."

Several minutes of beverage preparation later, they sat at right angles to each other at the table, Erin sipping tea, Sam nursing a mug of joe. Their silences had become companionable in the past week, and Sam loved it.

"Thanks for today, Erin. I really like your family."

"Me, too." She rested one cheek in her hand, elbow propped on the table. "You totally passed the test with the evil five."

He balked. "There was another test?"

She rolled her eyes. "There's always a test. But you're an ace at doing and saying the right thing."

"I wasn't trying to be fake, you know."

"I know," she said softly. "That's what makes it so cool. You just...fit."

He'd never really fit anywhere, and the words warmed him from his heart out through the rest of his body. "Well, I'm just glad you're still allowed to be Jessica's nanny. I wouldn't want you to stay if you didn't have your family's approval."

Erin studied him through the steam rising out of her teacup. "Sam? What's your family like?"

The easy acceptance of the day had lowered Sam's guard, and suddenly he realized he didn't want to hide from Erin anymore. He wanted her to know where he'd come from, what had made him into the man he was today. A small part of him still dreaded her reaction, but he forged ahead regardless, ready to be done with the hiding. "I don't have a family, Erin."

A small, confused frown bisected her brow. "What do you mean?"

"I mean, I was orphaned at birth."

"Oh," she said, in surprise.

"Yeah. I grew up in a series of foster homes." He watched for her reaction and braced himself for her pity, which he feared would totally shatter the sense of well-being he'd cultivated over the day. Lucky for him, pity didn't seem to be a part of Erin's extensive repertoire.

"Well, that explains a lot," she said, matter-of-fact.

He cocked his head. "What do you mean?"

"I had wondered why there weren't any photos of you as a child, or any of extended family, when Jessica and I were working on the scrapbook. That's all."

Inside, he relaxed. "Well, that's why. The whole, unvarnished truth. I don't tell many people," he said, by way of mild warning.

"Don't worry. I'm not going to take out an ad in *The Oregonian.*"

Sam smiled, cheered by her joking.

"So, what was that like? Living in foster homes?"

To his utter relief, she didn't show one ounce of pity. Mild curiosity was the extent of it. He shrugged, sipping his coffee. "Part of me wants to say it wasn't so bad, but that would be a lie. It sucked."

"How so?"

He held up a palm. "Okay, to be fair, I guess not all of it sucked. I did have a few foster homes that were…fine, I guess. Some were awful. But, bottom line, during my whole childhood, I felt like a guest who just might have overstayed his welcome."

"That does suck."

"Yeah." He stared down into his mug. "I got out of the system at age sixteen and haven't looked back since."

"Do you keep in touch with any of your foster parents?"

"No. The only ones I really connected with were the Lowerys. They were older, and Dad Lowery passed away just months after Mom Lowery had an unexpected heart attack. Just like June Carter and Johnny Cash.'' He shrugged. ''They really loved each other, and I really loved them. I was crushed. I guess I didn't let myself get attached after that.''

''I'm so sorry you lost them. But can I just say, you're an amazing person, Sam Lowery.''

''Don't be silly.''

''No, really. Look what you've done with your life, how you've raised Jessica, even after having what some might call a difficult childhood.'' She shook her head with admiration. ''You're one of those resilient types who will overcome every obstacle thrown your way. I envy you, really.''

Sam pulled an incredulous face. ''Come on, Erin. You have a great family who loves you. What's to envy here?''

''Exactly. I have a great family, and despite my constant brother complaints, I've never been tested even mildly. I wonder how I'd do.''

''You were tested when your nephew died.''

''True, but that's different. I had a whole family system for support. I'm assuming you didn't have that growing up?''

''You guess right.''

''See?'' She smiled at him. ''Amazing.''

Sam smirked, shaking his head. ''Whatever you say.''

Erin wrapped her fingers around her mug. ''It's true, so just take the compliment.''

''Undeserved as it is, thank you.''

She sipped her tea. "So, what do you know about your birth parents? Anything?"

Sam's stomach lurched, and he slanted his glance toward the floor. He did *not* want to broach the topic of his genetic origins. He wasn't sure how much attention Erin paid to the news, but the stories about Lissa and Adam were rampant. All it would take was one person who knew him putting together the puzzle pieces, and life as he knew it would be over. "Nothing much," he lied, amazed that his voice remained nonchalant when his heart pounded so incessantly. "My birth mother was a teenager who died in a car accident, I guess. I don't even know her name. No info about the father."

"Wow."

"Yep." He took in a breath and blew it out slowly through his nostrils. "Oh well, what can you do?"

Erin smiled, true approval shining in her beautiful eyes. "You can overcome, leave the past behind, and build yourself a wonderful, successful life. But I guess you know all about that, don't you? Because you're a living example."

Heat rushed to Sam's face, and on impulse he reached across the table and took one of Erin's hands in his own. "You're an amazing woman, Erin. You've already helped Jessica and me in so many ways. And now...you always know just how to say the right things. I just don't know how to thank you enough." Against his volition, his gaze dropped to those full, crooked lips of hers, and all he could think about was kissing her breathless. God, how he yearned to do that right at this moment. The kitchen remained dark, save the pendant fixture just above the table, and the low lighting set a vaguely romantic mood. He could smell her spicy vanilla perfume, and her hand felt so damn soft against his. Maybe he should just go for it and kiss her.

Yes, he should kiss her.

He leaned closer, swallowing deeply and feeling overwhelmed by his desire for this spirited Irish spitfire.

Erin cleared her throat. Sam's gaze jumped to her expression. Eyes wide and serious, she looked nervous, skittish…almost cornered. A zing of guilt struck him, and he released her hand as though it had stung him.

"God, I'm sorry, Erin."

"No. No. It's okay." She ran a hand through her hair awkwardly, then pushed her chair back and stood. "It's just, I don't—"

"Please don't explain. I should never have let my thoughts run away like that. It's unfair to you. Forgive me."

"But that's not it. I—"

"Erin, listen. It won't happen again. I am not the guy your brothers warned you about. I promise."

She sighed. "Look, I should probably turn in, Sam." She raked her bottom lip through her teeth, and he could've been mistaken but she looked like she regretted the whole thing as much as he did. "Tomorrow starts early for both of us."

Sam stood, too, feeling like a jerk of colossal proportions. He'd been so wrapped up in his attraction to Erin, he'd forgotten that he was essentially her boss. Putting her in the position of kiss-or-don't-kiss was a very real form of harassment. How could he have been such a thoughtless idiot? "Yes. Okay. You go on."

Erin nodded, then spun and headed toward her rooms. At the doorway, she spun back. She looked conflicted and remorseful. "Sam, I'm sorry, but—"

"No, Erin." He held up a hand. "It's okay. I didn't mean to make you feel—"

"No, please. Don't apologize. It's just—"

"Goodnight, Erin," he said softly, closing the conversation. He didn't want her to feel like she had to explain anything when it was he who'd screwed things up so royally. "Thanks again for today. I'll see you tomorrow."

She pressed her lips into a thin line and hesitated. Finally, she nodded, and turned into her hallway, closing the door quietly behind her.

Sam released a long breath and closed his eyes, fists clenched by his sides. He needed to rein in his wild emotions about this woman before he did something they would both regret. He'd come so close to crossing a line he'd sworn he wouldn't even approach, and he had to make sure that didn't happen again. The last thing in this world he wanted was to make an impulsive, selfish mistake that hurt Erin or prompted her to leave.

Kissing was, therefore, out.

\* \* \*

How could she have been such a gutless idiot? After Erin closed the door to her bedroom, she leaned her back against it and fought to catch her breath. God, she could've realized all her dreams and kissed the man right then, but no. She'd chickened out, and in doing so, she'd somehow given him the idea that she hadn't wanted the kiss to happen.

On the contrary. She'd wanted to kiss Sam Lowery almost since the first day they'd met. But clearly, he was a worldy man, and she was, unfortunately, as inexperienced as a sweet sixteen-year-old, thanks to the intimidation factor of her brothers. Just at the moment she'd known Sam was going to kiss her, she'd panicked. Panicked and destroyed everything, darnit.

Why, why, why hadn't she just kissed the man?

Surely the act of kissing was something that came naturally. He wouldn't have even known she was inexperienced with men. If she'd led with her feelings, the kiss would've been nothing short of spectacular. Instead she'd scurried into her rooms like a schoolgirl, all while Sam promised he'd never think about kissing her again.

Ugh, what an idiot.

She shoved off the door and scuffed through her room, removing clothes as she went. It was only when she'd changed into her nightgown and climbed into bed that she realized something incredible: Sam Lowery had wanted to kiss her!

There was hope, no matter what impression she'd left with him. No matter what he'd promised. There was hope for her and Sam, and knowing that, Erin fell asleep with a smile on her face.

## Chapter Twelve

The following evening Erin and Sam had worked their way back into a semblance of normalcy with each other, and for that, Erin was grateful. She didn't want the awkwardness of the previous evening to color every interaction. That unspoken attraction bubbled just below the surface, where they could both keep it under control.

They were busily working on the Mommy scrapbook with Jessica when the phone rang. Sam was in the midst of gluing down some decorative elements on the current page.

"I'll get it," Erin said, jumping to her feet. "Just keep going."

Sam nodded.

Erin crossed to the phone and answered on the third ring. "Lowery residence."

"Erin Marie, it's your brother, Eamon."

She smiled, leaning against the kitchen doorjamb and winding the long, curly cord around her elbow. "Hey, Eam. What's up?"

"I'd like to talk to Sam."

Her smile melted into a scowl, and she turned from the living room, lowering her tone. "Eamon, don't tell me you guys are still on a witch hunt for my boss."

"No. We aren't."

"Why do you want to talk to him then?"

"If you must know, we're having a guys-only barbecue and poker day when all you yappy women go to that craft fair next weekend, and we wanted to invite him."

Surprise and pleasure zinged through her. She straightened up and laid a hand against her chest. "Really?"

Eamon sighed. "No, I'm lying. I have a habit of that," he said, in a droll tone. "Can you put the man on, please?"

"Well...okay. Hang on." Erin held a palm over the phone and glanced toward Sam, who looked so endearing as he bent over the scrapbook, doing his best to apply the decorative elements neatly. She bit her lip and once again thought, wistfully, of the kiss that had almost happened. "Sam?"

He peered up.

"It's for you. My brother, Eamon."

With a questioning look on his face, Sam drew a finger across his neck like a knife.

Erin laughed. "Nope." She held out the phone.

Sam kissed Jessica on the head, then stood and headed over, taking the phone from Erin.

Erin went back to helping Jessica, trying not to eavesdrop on the conversation as Sam and Eamon talked, but she had to admit it was difficult. Finally, he said his goodbyes and headed back into the living room.

Peering up at him, Erin asked, "What was that all about?" even though she knew already.

Sam looked, frankly, baffled. He scratched the front of his head for a moment before sweeping his fingers back through his hair. "Your brothers are having a get together next weekend when, apparently, all you women are off to some craft fair. Does that sound familiar?"

"Yes, it's a yearly thing. The craft fair, I mean. You can, of course, join us women if you'd prefer," she teased, with a completely straight face.

Sam snorted. "Yeah. Right." He indicated the scrapbook. "That is as crafty as this guy gets, and only because it's for my precious daughter."

Erin refocused on the nearly completed book, striving for a nonchalant tone. "So, you're going to go then?"

"Yeah, I think I will." He shrugged when Erin glanced back up at him. "I'm surprised they thought to include me, but hey, I enjoy their company, so why not."

"Indeed, why not?"

"Don't get me wrong. I'm sure they called in order

to find out if I have nefarious designs on their precious baby sister.''

''Gag me.'' *Do you?* she wondered, in spite of herself.

''But, I'd still like to go. To be honest, I haven't
really had many male friends lately. Or...ever.''

''Reclusive?''

''You know,'' he said, with a look of regret on his
face, ''maybe too much so. It might be nice to go do
some guy stuff.''

Erin beamed up at him. ''I'm glad you're going.
And I hope you don't mind if I take Jessica along to
the fair. She'd love it, I promise.''

''I don't mind at all. Plus—'' he sighed ''—you're
right. She does need to get out and be around other
people. She knows your family now. I know your
mother loves her.''

''My mother has never met a baby she doesn't
adore.'' She winked. ''I think I inherited her genes.''

His gaze darkened into something that made her
pulse race. ''I can think of worse things to inherit.''

Gulp. ''Me, too.'' A pause. ''Sam?''

''Yeah?'' He took his seat on the sofa again.

''I'm proud of you for stepping outside your comfort zone. Even if it is with the evil five.''

''Thank you, Erin. That means a lot to me. And I
promise I won't let them pump me for info,'' he
joked.

The day of the craft fair/guys-only event rolled
around more quickly than they'd imagined. Sam, Jes-

sica and Erin drove to Eamon's together, and Sam
tried not to think of them as a little family unit, but
that's how it felt to him. He wouldn't lie—he liked
the feeling, and not just because he'd never had a true
family before, but because it was with Erin. He'd
grown closer to her every day she lived with him and
Jessica. She was undoubtedly the most special woman
he'd ever had in his life, and he felt lucky to have
met her. In the dark of night, he allowed himself to
imagine what life would be like if he and Erin were
a couple. She was the kind of woman a smart man
would hold on to with his whole heart and soul. That
alternately drew him and scared the hell out of him.

As all the O'Grady brothers were dutifully kissing
their wives goodbye, Sam fought the urge to follow
suit with their baby sister. In fact, he fought valiantly
to avoid even looking like the thought had crossed
his mind, when in reality, he couldn't get it out of his
head.

When the women had packed off in two minivans,
the men headed off to the backyard. Mick clapped a
hand on Sam's back as they walked. "So, what's it
like having my annoying little sister underfoot 24/7,
Lowery?"

"You know, Mick, she's not so annoying when
she's not your sister. It's a strange phenomenon."

All the O'Grady men laughed, and then they settled
down for a long afternoon of poker, grilled meat, football watching, and general guy bonding. After an initial awkward period, Sam found himself relaxing,
even enjoying the camaraderie. Having male friends

wasn't as threatening as he'd imagined it would be. In fact, he could get used to it with very little effort. Not for the first time, he yearned to be a part of the O'Grady family. But hadn't he had those kinds of wishes his whole life? It was better simply not thinking about things that wouldn't happen.

It wasn't until hours into the afternoon that he noticed Eamon watching him a little too closely for his comfort. He ignored it as long as he could, then glanced up at the man, lifting one brow in question.

"Sorry, dude," Eamon said, holding up one palm. "I can't shake the feeling that you remind me of someone."

Sam's stomach dropped, and he took pains to keep his face from revealing anything. "Yeah? Odd."

"Not so odd, actually," interjected the middle brother, Matthew. "I've noticed it myself on a couple of occasions, and I finally figured it out. I mean, it makes no sense…"

Hot blood rushed all through Sam's body as the fight-or-flight response launched, full bore, inside him. "What did you figure out?"

Matthew glanced around at his brothers. "I don't know if any of the rest of you have been following that story about the reunited twins, Adam Bartlett and Lissa Cartwright," he began.

Sam's entire life flashed before his eyes. Was this to be his undoing, then? Right here in Eamon O'Grady's home, over mugs of frosty beer and delivery pizzas? "I've seen a thing or two."

"Matt's a news junkie," Mick said. "Don't mind him."

That comment earned Mick a rude gesture on behalf of Matthew's middle finger, but he went on. "I just realized after Kellan's birthday party that you bear an uncanny resemblance to Adam Bartlett. Pretty freaky thing."

"Yeah," Sam said, playing off his horror with a nonchalant snort. "Too bad I couldn't resemble Brad Pitt instead. It sure would help me more in the female department."

Everyone laughed, but Eamon didn't let it drop. "You know, that's it. Matthew's right. You really do look like the guy."

"Huh. Stranger things have happened, I guess."

"For sure," Mick said, looking less than interested in the twin story. "And speaking of the female department, let's talk about my little sister for a bit, eh? I'm sure you know we're pretty protective of her welfare."

Relief rained through Sam at the change of subject. "I do know, and I respect all of you for it. But you don't have to worry about me. Erin is a gem, and I'd do anything to keep her as my nanny. I know that wouldn't happen if the six of you," he said, including Erin's father, "worried for her safety at my house. So let me set your minds at ease. I feel as protective of Erin as you do, and she couldn't be safer living in my household. That's a promise."

They assessed him for several tense moments, and then the party turned back into just that. Beer. Pizza.

Hot wings. Football. Adrenaline continued to pulse through Sam's veins for several minutes, but soon he looked around at the other men and breathed a sigh of relief. He'd successfully jumped through the flaming hoop of his resemblance to Adam Bartlett, and he'd passed another O'Grady men test. Now all he had to do was stay away from Erin.

That, he thought ruefully, would be an even bigger challenge.

Several days later, Matthew called Erin to see if she could babysit his son, Finn, a couple evenings later. Finn and Jessica were close in age and got along great, so she agreed readily. They chatted about family stuff for a bit, and then Matt switched topics.

"You know, we had an interesting conversation with your boss the other day at the guys-only gig."

"Yeah?" Erin was in the midst of preparing dinner while Jessica slept, so she just continued chopping vegetables, the phone tucked between her ear and shoulder.

"I don't know if you've kept up with the news lately—"

She huffed. "Like I have time."

"Well, maybe you should make time."

A niggling sense of alarm slowed Erin's movements. "Why? What's going on?"

"We think Sam bears an uncanny resemblance to Adam Bartlett, that software mogul who was recently reunited with his twin sister, Lissa Something-or-other."

"Oh, I know that story. Who doesn't? It's such a heartwarming tale."

"Haven't you noticed the resemblance?"

"I haven't really paid that much attention, Matthew."

"He looks just like him. It's interesting. You should have a look at the Adam guy and decide for yourself. I mean, it's not like they could be related. Adam and Lissa were both adopted as babies. But, still. It's just uncanny."

Erin's throat tightened, and she wobbled over and took a seat at the kitchen table. She fought to keep her tone light. "So, you brought this up to Sam?"

"Yep. He blew it off with a joke, but still it's a pretty cool thing. They say everyone in the world has a twin somewhere. I'd like to find the lucky guy who looks like yours truly."

"Yeah, I bet you would. Try the mental hospitals," she chirped. "You might have some luck."

"Very amusing, sis."

"Anyway, I'll have a look next time I see something about Adam Bartlett, but right now, I'm preparing dinner. I should go, so I can get this done before Jess is up from her nap. As you well know, it's ten times more difficult to do chores like cooking with a two-year-old underfoot."

"Okay." He paused, and Erin waited because it seemed like he had more to say. "You know, we really like this Sam guy. He's alright."

"I'm glad you approve, Dad," she quipped. "But, newsflash, there is nothing going on between us."

"I know, I know. But don't feel apprehensive about bringing him around, is all I'm saying. He's a good guy. And a good father. Fits right in with the O'Grady way of living."

"I'm glad the five of you finally realized what I've been telling you all along. Sam Lowery *is* a good guy. And I have a great job here."

"Yeah, yeah. You were right."

Erin smiled. "Mark this day on the calendar. One of the evil five said I was right!"

"Evil is a little much, wouldn't you say?"

"Talk to you later, Matt," Erin sang. After they'd hung up, she rushed into her sitting room and booted up the internet. She did a google search on the twin case and came to photos of Adam Bartlett. As the first photo downloaded, her stomach plunged to her feet. My goodness, Sam didn't just resemble Adam Bartlett, he looked like his double. She turned next to photos of Lissa Cartwright. Sure, the gender thing made a difference, but even Lissa resembled Sam around the eyes and mouth.

Erin checked on Jessica quickly—still out cold— then returned to her computer and watched a taped interview with the reunited twins. The more she watched, the more convinced she became that her brothers had stumbled onto something they didn't even realize. In addition to the physical resemblance, Sam's mannerisms mirrored those of Adam Bartlett. Lissa's slow, careful smile was uncannily reminiscent of Sam's.

Upon further checking, she learned that Adam's

and Lissa's birth mother was a teenager killed in a car accident. Their ages matched, birth dates matched.

The story Sam had told her about his mother matched.

He'd said there was no information about the birth father, when clearly Jared Cambry had come forward when his little son, Mark, contracted the rare blood disease requiring a bone marrow transplant. But maybe that said more about Sam than it did Jared Cambry. Hadn't Sam told her once that abandoning a child was the worst crime a parent could commit? Maybe he wanted to forget he had a birth father, especially now that he knew his identity.

She felt certain he knew. How could he not?

Even more curious, all the birth records for the day Adam, Lissa and Sam were born had been destroyed in a fire later that year. Could the teenage mother have birthed triplets instead of twins? Could this be one of the secrets Sam held so tightly to his soul?

Then again, if he was one of the triplets, why didn't he come forward and make himself known?

Erin didn't have answers for any of it, but she made a plan to watch Sam a little more closely and figure things out for herself. This could very well be another huge layer to the mystery that was Sam Lowery...a man she respected and cared about, a man she was beginning to love.

A man filled with secrets.

Sam couldn't stop thinking about the get-together at the O'Gradys' house in the days that followed.

Wasn't it Murphy's Law that Erin's suspicious brothers would be the ones to make the connection between him and Adam Bartlett, when neither Mia nor Erin had said word one? In any case, he'd skirted the issue as best he could, and now he needed to just lie low until the whole media circus ended. He didn't want to be ''outed'' by Matthew O'Grady, or any of them. He didn't want to have his hand forced when it came to meeting his siblings, because, bottom line, he didn't want his life exposed like theirs had been.

The whole event left him feeling like he was teetering on the edge of catastrophe…and he had vertigo. Erin had gotten him to lower his guard so much that now his anonymity, his life, his daughter's privacy—all of it was threatened. There was only one thing to do: raise that guard back up and live his life the way he had for years before Erin came along. Maybe it didn't work for her and the O'Grady family, but being a closed-off, unreachable person had served him well for twenty-seven years. It was high time he went back to his usual methods.

If it ain't broke, don't fix it.

Right?

Strangely, Sam seemed to retreat into his shell after the day he'd spent with her brothers. Gone was the open, smiling man he'd slowly become in the weeks Erin had lived there, and out came the thick shell he'd hidden behind when she'd first arrived. That would all be well and good, except his complete behavioral

180 was having a negative effect on Jessica and all the progress she'd made.

Like it or not, Sam's behavior had and would always have a huge impact on that little girl. Sam had seemed to forget that, and it was becoming increasingly more difficult to bear witness to the negative transformation in Jess's demeanor. Erin let it go long enough, until one night she'd had it.

Jessica wouldn't look at her Mommy scrapbook anymore, and she'd been teary and clingy at the park that day. Sam had stopped joining Erin in the kitchen for evening conversation, had avoided all opportunities for her to discuss Jessica's change in behavior with him altogether. As Jessica's nanny, she had a duty to keep him apprised of what was up with his daughter's life. If he planned to do his level best to avoid her, she planned to make it difficult if not impossible for him to do so.

That evening, Erin waited for Sam to come back downstairs after he'd tucked Jessica in so she could confront him, but he never materialized. That was fine. Maybe he'd had a rough day at work and wanted to turn in early. But wasn't it sheer politeness to say a simple goodnight? She *had* to talk to him about Jessica, and the sooner the better. If he was going to hide out in his room, she'd go to him. The heck with it.

Bolstered by her intent, Erin headed up the stairs and stood outside Sam's closed bedroom door. She raised her hand to knock...then hesitated. She drew her bottom lip in between her teeth and felt a twinge of apprehension. What in the hell was she thinking, coming to his bedroom like this?

Doubting herself, she padded softly down to Jessica's nursery and checked on the baby. Jessica slept on her back, mouth opened slightly. Erin looked around the room and didn't see her Mommy scrapbook anywhere. All her work, all the progress they'd made, down the drain. She pressed her lips together.

This was about Jessica, not about Erin.

She had to talk to Sam.

Whirling, she left the room, crossed the hallway quickly, and knocked on his door before she had the chance to rethink her actions, to doubt herself.

The door opened almost immediately, and Erin's throat went dry. Mistake. Sam stood before her in nothing more than his wear-softened blue jeans with the top button undone. No shirt, no shoes or socks. Her gaze dropped of its own volition to his work-honed, muscular chest, and attraction swirled low and hot in her body. *Oh, God.* Taking a step back, Erin lowered her gaze. "I—I'm sorry. I shouldn't have bothered you. I—I'll talk to you tomorrow morning."

## Chapter Thirteen

Sam's hand around her shoulder stopped her from fleeing, and she reluctantly turned back. She tried to look anywhere but at the man's bare skin, but it was difficult considering his size and proximity.

"What's wrong, Erin?" He glanced down the hall over her shoulder, concern etched into the fine lines around his eyes. "Is Jessica okay?"

"Yes," she answered immediately, but then she reconsidered her answer. "I mean, she's sleeping fine, if that's what you're asking. But…" She sighed. "Sam, we need to talk."

"Now?"

"Now." Erin watched as a mask of remoteness fell over his expression.

"About what?" he said.

He sounded closed-minded and defensive. Even his body language exuded distance. He was about as open to this conversation as her brothers were open to letting her dance naked at a strip joint, and Erin's frustration exploded inside her.

Hot, healthy anger trumped her earlier embarrassment, and she was surprised to realize she was truly upset about Jessica's reversion. This wasn't about his bare chest, or her attraction to him. It wasn't about either of them. "About your daughter, Sam. About Jessica."

"What about her?"

Annoyance coupled with a lingering but unwanted, at this point, attraction fueled her to give him a piece of her mind. Her bottom lip trembled as she implored him, but with anger rather than fear or tears. "Has it escaped your attention that she's losing ground? She's back to being fearful and less talkative." Her voice rose slightly. "She hasn't looked at her book of Jenny's photos for days."

Sam stared at her for a moment, then stepped backwards into the room, indicating Erin should precede him. She did, spying a chair and side table set into a bay window area at one end of the large, very masculine room. She crossed over quickly and took a seat in the relative safety of the chair. She tried not to notice Sam's large, mission-style bed, or the fact that the entire room smelled like the spicy cleanness of the man. This was about *Jessica*.

Sam sat on the other available surface: the bed.

When he spoke, his voice was softer than it had been. "Tell me what's happened, Erin."

Good. At least one of them was focused totally on the important matter at hand. She lifted her arms and let them fall limply at her sides. "That's what I should be saying to you."

His eyes narrowed. "Meaning what?"

"I don't know, Sam." She scooted to the very edge of the chair and leaned into her words for emphasis. "She was making such progress. You both were."

"I've told you, this isn't about me."

"And, as I've told you, she takes all her emotional cues from you. You've completely closed up, and she's feeling it."

He crossed his arms over his chest, causing his pecs to bulge in a very distracting way. "But…I'm trying. I made the scrapbook, I talked to her about Jenny. I talked to you about Jenny, for Pete's sake, which isn't something I'd do on any given normal day."

"Yes, but over the past several days, you've reverted to the Sam I first met, and Jessica is following suit." Erin shot to her feet, threading fingers into the front of her hair as she paced the length of the room. "I just don't know what I'm doing wrong, Sam. One day, you and I are getting along fine, talking openly, sharing conversation after Jess goes to bed. The next day, nothing. It's as if you're avoiding me completely." She spun to face him. "Was it something I did?"

A muscle jumped in Sam's jaw, and he let his gaze slide away. "No. It's nothing."

"So, you're not going to talk about it, huh? Just bottle up whatever you're feeling so that Jessica sees you and thinks she needs to bottle up all her feelings, too?" She waited for Sam to say something, and when he remained stonily silent, she huffed. "What am I even doing here? If you don't help me, I can't help your daughter. Maybe this is a waste of both of our time."

Sam came off the bed and crossed the room in two long strides. He cupped Erin's upper arms gently. "It's not a waste, Erin. You can't mean that. Jessica loves you."

"Which doesn't much matter if you dislike me so much you avoid me." Erin smacked the back of one hand against the opposite palm for emphasis. "She takes her emotional cues—"

"From me. I heard you." Sam studied her face for a moment, than a sad, small smile lifted one corner of his mouth. "Erin O'Grady, the last thing I do is dislike you."

Her tummy tightened, but she concentrated on making her point. She squared her shoulders and hiked her chin. "Then what? What happened, Sam, to set you back?"

"I—" He released her arms and stepped back, and she stepped forward, closing the distance.

"Don't run from me, Sam. Don't run from this."

He peered down at her, looking so conflicted, so haunted. "I don't know if I can even explain it."

"Try."

Their gazes locked for several tense moments, then

he reached out and ran the back of his fingers down her cheek. "I can't, Erin."

She thought of the timeline, and suddenly everything fell into place. He might be hiding from his past, but he'd face up to it if she had anything to do with it. Everything had already gone so wrong, what would it hurt to ask? "Does this have something to do with Adam Bartlett and Lissa Cartwright?"

His eyes widened just long enough to let her know she'd hit pay dirt. For a moment, anger glittered in his eyes and he clenched his jaw. Finally, he released a long, defeated breath. "So, they told you?"

"Matthew called me." A beat passed. "None of them know you were a foster child, Sam. I didn't give up any of what you've confided in me."

"Thank you."

"But I'm asking you to level with me. Is it true? Are Adam and Lissa really two of a set of triplets?" She paused. "Are you the missing piece of that puzzle?"

Sam held his breath so long, when he finally let go, his shoulders seemed to sag with the action. "I think so. Yes."

"Oh, Sam." She lifted her fingertips to cover her mouth.

Sam raised a finger. "I don't want anyone to know. Ever."

Surprise riddled through Erin, and she blinked back her confusion. "But that's crazy. You have family, Sam. Blood relatives. A brother and a sister who seem like delightful people. Not to mention, those half-siblings.''

"Enough."

She almost winced as he barked out the word, and then she stared at him in silence for a few moments. "Why on earth wouldn't you want to meet them?"

"I'm a private person, Erin, if you haven't noticed. I don't want my life and my baby's life laid out on television like some reality TV show." He turned back toward the bed, sitting on the edge of it. His eyes looked troubled, his body language conflicted. "Besides…"

"Besides, what?" she prompted, moving over to sit in front of him on the bed, one leg tucked up beneath her, the other dangling off the side of the mattress.

When Sam looked up this time, his eyes flashed with resentment. "Lissa Cartwright grew up on a vineyard. Adam Bartlett is some fancy CEO. Clearly the two of them were adopted by loving families. Why on earth would I want to show my face as the triplet who no one wanted?" He flicked a hand, as if he were disgusted with himself, with the whole situation. "Not even Cambry, who could've been a father to us all those years ago, but he chose to ignore we existed until it was convenient for him to start a new family, a keeper family. With family like that, who needs enemies? No thanks. I want no part of it."

Erin absolutely ached for his pain, for the scars of a childhood he had not quite overcome, no matter how much he liked to pretend otherwise. She moved closer and took both of his hands in her own. Her realization at that moment smacked her so hard, she felt dizzy—she loved this emotionally scarred man so much, respected him incredibly, and he couldn't even recognize his own qualities.

"Sam Lowery," she said, her voice trembling with emotion she didn't even try to squelch, "you are one of the kindest, most gentle men I have ever been privileged to meet. You have an amazing daughter. You've overcome so much adversity and managed to build yourself a life you should be nothing but proud of. I feel like the luckiest woman in the world to be a part of your life and Jessica's life." He glanced up, and she smiled tenderly at him. "I completely respect the fact that you aren't up for media invasion of your life, but please don't avoid meeting your siblings just because you feel lesser, or slighted. You were infants when you were split up. They had no more control over what happened to them than you did." Releasing his hand, she reached up and traced his strong jawline. "Can't you see, it wouldn't be an honor for *you* to meet Adam and Lissa, it would be an honor for *them* to meet *you*." Leaning in, Erin did what she should've done days ago. She kissed him.

The feel of Erin's lips on his own, the memory of her sweet words, ignited a fireball of emotions inside Sam that he simply couldn't ignore. He'd wanted her for too long. When she started to pull back from the kiss, he tugged her closer and deepened it instead. She made a little sound in her throat, halfway between a gasp and a moan, but after a split second of surprised resistance, she melted into the kiss. Her soft hands came up around him and tangled in his hair as her tongue slipped over his. Sam heard a sound and realized it was a groan, deep in his own throat.

Erin tasted like sugary little gumdrops, sweet and smooth. Her skin felt like satin, smelled uniquely like her spicy vanilla perfume, with a hint of her own scent underneath. Mysterious, rich and inviting.

His body ached for her, and if her enthusiastic response was any indication, she ached for him just as much.

God, what was he doing?

Feeling drunk with wanting her, Sam nevertheless pulled back, pleading with his eyes for Erin to be the voice of reason in this situation. He just couldn't pull it off. "Erin?"

"No," she lifted his hand and placed it boldly on her breast, her own hand closing over it. "Don't stop, Sam," she whispered. "Please."

Sam felt the hard jut of her nipple against the center of his palm, the round softness of the breast he touched through her T-shirt. He struggled, but later he would be able to pinpoint the exact moment he began to lose grip and fall into the liquid pool of desire that shone from her eyes. He'd gladly drown there, and yet he found himself struggling for air, for reason, one last time.

On the one hand, why shouldn't he and Erin make love? They were both adults, both consenting. He wanted her, and thank God, she wanted him, too. Then again, she was his daughter's nanny. He'd initially resisted hiring her for just this reason—his instantaneous visceral reaction to her presence. But then, over the weeks, he'd fallen under her spell just like Jessica had, and now he was too far gone to resist her.

Sam nestled his face into her neck, inhaling deeply of her scent. Dammit, he deserved this. Hadn't he had enough pain in his life? Couldn't he take this moment of happiness and tuck it away for when things got lonely and cold?

"Yes," he whispered, against Erin's neck.

"Yes?" she asked.

"Yes, I want to make love to you, Erin O'Grady." He peered into her eyes, twisting his mouth to the side. "You've got to tell me if we're not on the same page."

Erin reached her hands up and cradled his face on either side. "Sam Lowery. Make love to me."

With a groan of surrender, Sam lowered his mouth to hers. This was no test kiss, no hesitant peck. He kissed her with a lifetime of pent-up need, with an urgency he'd never felt before, not even with his late wife. He kissed her like he meant it, and she pressed against him and reciprocated.

Before long, both of them were breathing heavily, arching and lifting to remove clothes that had become barriers. Once naked, Sam cupped and lifted Erin's small, firm breasts. "Beautiful," he whispered.

He lifted them to his mouth, licking and kissing each nipple in turn until Erin writhed and whimpered beneath him. When he took her left nipple gently between his teeth, she bucked and he felt her wetness against his leg, hot and inviting.

He couldn't wait any longer.

Reaching across Erin, he opened the drawer and removed a condom. He made quick work of slipping it on, grimacing against the ache of his need. He lifted himself above Erin, and she obligingly opened her legs, looking him directly in the eyes. He rubbed against her once, twice, and then plunged into her body, hard and deep.

Erin let out a short, sharp cry, then clung against him, shaking slightly. Sam himself had been stunned into immobility.

"My God, Erin," he whispered, his heart sinking. "Why didn't you tell me you were a virgin?"

She slowly opened her eyes, and he couldn't tell if she was in pain or if she felt guilty. He smoothed her hair back with a gentle hand. "Why?"

"Because you wouldn't have made love to me," she said, her voice wavering. "I did tell you I was inexperienced with men."

"That's not the same, and incidentally, I'm not going to make love to you." He started to withdraw as gingerly as he could manage, when Erin pulled him against her.

"No!" She implored him with watery eyes. "Sam, I meant it when I said I wanted to make love to you." She began to arch and rotate her hips beneath him. "I can't imagine a more perfect man to be my first. You can't destroy that memory for me, Sam. Please...make love to me."

Sam studied her face for a moment before blowing out a sigh and resting his forehead against hers. What could he do? She was right. If he stopped now, she would always have bad memories of her first time. She should've told him, but she hadn't. There was no way to get her virginity back, he realized with a sword-stab of guilt. The only honorable thing to do was to make her first time as pleasurable as possible.

And that's exactly what he did.

After Erin fell asleep in his bed, Sam, ice-cold with remorse for what he'd done, slipped from beneath the covers, grabbed some pajamas, and retreated to the upstairs guest room. His body felt fantastic, but his heart was heavy and his conscience was even heavier. Feeling physically sated just made things worse. He climbed into the full-size bed, propped his hands behind his head, and then stared up at the ceiling in a horrified daze.

She'd been a virgin, and he'd taken it.

Just like that, and rather roughly, too.

God help him. He would never have touched her had he known. She should've saved that gift for the man she married, the lucky bastard who got smart enough to hold on to her forever and give her the brood of children she desired. She deserved a devoted man, and she deserved to bear as many of his children as her big generous heart desired.

Sam Lowery was not the man to fit that bill. He'd tried the forever thing, and it had ended in the worst way imaginable. He wasn't going to risk his heart or

Jessica's heart again, hence he shouldn't have made love to Erin. With a surge of utter devastation, he realized he was exactly the man her brothers had always feared. A man who didn't love Erin, didn't plan on creating any kind of romantic, fairy tale ending, and yet he'd taken the worst kind of advantage of her. If the brothers got wind of this…but, of course, they wouldn't. Erin would never tell them, and he sure as hell wasn't making any phone calls tomorrow.

Sam threw an arm across his eyes and silently berated himself. What a selfish idiot he was. He didn't anticipate getting any sleep, but he had a lot to think about anyway. Now that he'd crossed the line with Erin, the only way to get things back on a professional track was to pull away completely. He couldn't stand the thought of losing the friendship and closeness they'd created, but there was no other way.

Sam had taken something precious from Erin.

He'd screwed up. Again. This time, royally.

Now he had to atone.

# *Chapter Fourteen*

The morning after they'd made love, Erin woke up alone in Sam's bed, which should've been her first clue that all was not right in the Lowery household. Unfortunately, she'd still been blissfully drunk with passion, blossoming into her own sexuality, and she put his absence down to the simple fact that he'd had to go to work. In his own gentlemanly way, he hadn't wanted to wake her up, she reasoned, stretching her deliciously sore body and remembering every touch, every sound, every taste, every shudder. A thoughtful gesture, his letting her sleep. It didn't mean anything more than that.

That's what she chose to believe, at least.

By day four of Sam avoiding her at all costs, Erin admitted to herself that she'd been dead wrong. His absence that fateful morning after hadn't been a thoughtful gesture. More like panic. Remorse. Regret. Whatever you'd call it, Sam was most definitely not interested in a repeat performance of what had been the most special night of her life.

Clearly it had been a milestone moment only to her.

To him, most likely a mistake.

The crushing pain of knowing that sucked her breath away.

Men *were* cads, just like her brothers had always warned her. Maybe Sam had a logical explanation for his behavior, but as bad as she felt, she couldn't bring herself to see the situation objectively. The male point of view? Not so much. Clearly, she was Venus all the way, because it was lost on her. The house—same as always, really—seemed colder, silent, almost funereal with a gauzy film of the unsaid draping over everything like a drab, gray shroud. She had grown so comfortable living here over the past weeks, yet since she and Sam had made love, that level of easy comfort had dissipated like steam on a mirror.

Screw gender differences. It made no sense. How could a man make love to you and not *love* you? Especially when you loved him so incredibly much, loved his daughter, loved the prospect of the life you could share with them both, a life you could see in your mind like a vivid picture of perfection? How could Sam see and feel that deep, true, intense love coming from her and not reciprocate? Maybe she did see the world through rose-colored glasses, but it was a darn lovely view from where she stood. She didn't plan to change, broken heart or not.

Sam or no Sam.

Feeling hurt and a little bit depressed—and hating herself for the whole icky codependence of it all— Erin nevertheless found herself dialing Sam's cell phone that afternoon after putting Jess down for a nap. Erin wouldn't call him at work if she had any other choice, but she never saw him anymore, except in passing. He barely met her eyes then, and he always did his best to vacate the area as quickly as possible. She might be inexperienced with men and love, but his feelings were coming through loud and clear, and she was no dummy.

They were finished, even before they began.

In her heart, she knew it. But she needed to hear directly from him if what they shared had been nothing more than a one-night diversion, needed confirmation so she could move on.

The phone rang twice, all while Erin's heart did its best to pound its way out of her chest. She clenched the back of a kitchen chair in a death grip, rethinking this impulsive move. Just as she went to hang up, she heard him answer.

"Lowery," he said, in a clipped, businesslike tone.

Erin swallowed and closed her eyes, praying for strength. She never wanted to be one of those whimpery, needy women, but right now she felt like she needed something from Sam. Anything, even a polite kiss-off, if that's what it was going to come down to. "Sam? It's Erin. I'm sorry to bother you at work."

"What's wrong? Is Jessica okay?" His voice changed immediately, but not in the manner she'd wished it would have at hearing her voice. There was no private, loving tone, no indication whatsoever that they'd shared each other in the most intimate, special way possible.

Erin swallowed back a bitter pill of disappointment. "No. I mean, yes," she rushed to correct. "Jessica's fine."

"Oh." A beat passed, and when he spoke again his tone was calmer but still wary. "Okay, good. What's up?"

What *was* up? Why exactly was she calling? To confront him? She should've thought this through a little better, but since she'd always been a leap first, look later kind of gal, she fell back on the first thing that came to mind. "I was just wondering if you might be home in time for dinner?" Realizing how cloying and trumped up that sounded, she added, "It might be nice for you to have dinner with Jessica. She misses eating with you."

"I miss her, too, but I don't think so." He sounded so distracted, so not like the Sam who had whispered words of gentle encouragement in her ear as his body moved inside hers. "We're running behind schedule. I'll probably just grab something before I leave here."

Erin plunked down into the kitchen chair she'd been clutching. Exhaustion weighed on her. "But... we can hold dinner, if you can give me some kind of a time window."

"I thought you said it was important to keep Jessica on a schedule?" he asked suspiciously.

*It's also important for her father to eat dinner with her now and then,* Erin thought, quite snarkily, which wasn't like her at all. But she couldn't go back on her word at this stage of the game. "Yes, you're right," she relented. "I did say that, and it is."

"Then…go ahead and do that, Erin, okay?" Sam sounded impatient with the whole topic. "I've got a lot on my plate here at work and just about nothing's going right."

What was the point? He wasn't giving her an inch. "Okay. I'm…sorry to have bothered you." *Say something, Sam,* Erin pleaded silently, winding the long curly phone cord around her arm. *Acknowledge the fact that you and I were more than just employer and employee, even if just for one night. Something. Anything.* Tears stung her eyes, and she bit her bottom lip hard enough to cause pain. She gratefully focused on the pain in her lip rather than that of her slowly breaking heart, only easing up when she tasted blood, coppery and acrid. Reaching for a napkin from the holder centered on the table, she pressed it to her cut mouth, daubing the blood away.

"Is there anything else?" Sam asked, the trepidation and impatience clear in his question.

She thought about broaching the subject of their lovemaking and the subsequent distance, but decided his silence and irritation were comment enough. Why put herself through hearing it out loud? He didn't want her. He'd never wanted her in anything other than a physical way, and now that he'd reached that goal, he was moving on. No sense crying about it. In fact, she ought to take a lesson from Sam and move on, too. Her brothers had warned her that men did that sort of thing to women all the time. She never thought she'd admit this about the evil five, but she should've listened.

In that moment, Erin grew up just a little bit more.

"Erin?" Sam prompted.

"No. Nothing else." She paused, knowing she was about to tread on dangerous ground and not caring much. "Well, maybe one other thing."

"Which is?"

Screw caution. If a destined love affair wasn't in their future, the least she could do was continue her work with Jessica *and* Sam, help them both to heal. That's what she'd been hired to do in the first place. Feeling stronger and imbued by a what-the-hell? sort of calm, she lifted her chin. "Have you thought anymore about getting in touch with Lissa and Adam, letting them know they aren't twins after all?"

She heard Sam blow out a frustrated breath. "Erin, I'm working. We're behind schedule and it's costing thousands of dollars a day. Thousands. You can't possibly think I want to get into this subject now."

"But—"

"Or ever. I've made my wishes clear. Now I'd appreciate it if you'd just drop the topic altogether."

She cringed, knowing she was stretching, looking for any reason to keep him on the line. "You're right. This isn't the time. I'm sorry."

Annoyance threaded into his voice. "Why do you keep saying you're sorry?"

*Because I am,* she thought. Sorry she'd ever thought there could be something deeper between them, sorry she'd pinned all her hopes on a man who'd flat out told her he never planned on marrying again. After all, Sam had never been anything other than brutally honest with her. He told her on numerous occasions that his life was Jessica and he had no room for anyone else.

Why hadn't she believed him?

Her family always told her she couldn't save the whole world, and again, they were dead-on right. Maybe she was the one who needed some sense knocked into her. Sam had even given her a chance to back out on the night they'd made love, but she hadn't taken it. She'd chosen to make love to him. Really, this was as much her fault as his, and it was high time she took responsibility for her own actions. She'd wanted to feel Sam inside her, to connect with him in a deep, visceral way, and she had. The whole thing had been a grown woman's choice, and it didn't go her way. Oh well. Life wasn't always fair. If it were, her nephew, Bryce, would still be alive. Jessica's mommy would still be alive. And Sam might just love her.

None of that was true.

She was logical and intelligent enough to know that not every tryst had a romance-novel ending. And, hey, at least she'd had one night. *Be happy with that, Erin, and get on with your life.* She still had her job, and her first lover had been a man she adored. That was more than a lot of her friends could claim.

Taking a deep breath, she felt stronger, resigned, more serene about the whole stupid situation. "Never mind. Everything's just fine. Go back to work, and we'll see you whenever we see you." She hung up before he could have the satisfaction of doing it first.

Sam flipped the face of his cell phone closed and muttered a vicious curse. He'd hurt her deeply; he could hear the pain in her voice. Knowing that lanced through his soul, but, dammit, there was no other way. He wouldn't marry Erin and drag her into the dark emptiness of his life. He couldn't bear to father a passel of babies, just to flounder in parenting them like he'd done with Jessica. A large family with a devoted husband and father were Erin's dream, and since he couldn't fill those daunting shoes, he had to let her go completely. If only she could understand it. She was all about family and he had absolutely nothing to offer but shoddy genes and poor parenting skills.

Not to mention all the emotional baggage.

Aside from all that, Erin's constant prompting for him to meet Lissa and Adam had begun to needle its way inside him, stirring up trouble and guilt and curiosity he desperately didn't want to feel. Why couldn't she let it drop? Not everyone needed a close family, for Pete's sake. Lissa and Adam didn't even know he existed. No harm, no foul. What Sam needed was absolution, peace of mind, and a happy, healthy daughter. He did not need more upheaval in his life, and meeting Lissa and Adam would cause him nothing but upheaval of the most stressful variety.

So would falling in love with Erin O'Grady, which he was doing his damnedest to avoid.

No thank you. Give him peace and anonymity any day.

He didn't need love.

He didn't need a bigger family than he already had, no matter how intriguing the concept.

Too bad he couldn't expel the feel of Erin from his soul or her gentle urgings from his conscience....

"Hi, Mom."

"Erin!" Initially, Sarah O'Grady sounded delighted to have heard from her youngest child, but with that uncanny, inexplicable maternal instinct, she homed in on Erin's mood immediately. "What's wrong?"

Erin bit the corner of her mouth. She dreaded this, but she needed someone to talk to. "If I tell you, do you promise not to tell Dad or the evil five? And do you promise to listen without judgement?"

Her mother sighed. "You've fallen in love with your boss, haven't you?"

Momentarily stunned, Erin's jaw dropped. "H-how did you know that? All I said was 'Hi, Mom.'"

"Erin, doll. Before I was your mother, I was also a young woman. I'm not so obtuse."

Erin groaned, and tears stung her eyes. Instead of holding them back, she just let them slowly trickle down her face unheeded. "God, I've made a mess of things."

"Tell me about it."

Erin filled her in on the whole scenario, including a Cliff's Notes version of their impromptu lovemaking but leaving out the long-lost triplet angle. She respected Sam's privacy in that respect.

"Goodness, honey." Erin's mother sighed, but thankfully didn't lecture her about crossing the line with her boss. "I'm so sorry you are learning this the hard way, but it sounds to me like you're going to have to cut your losses. There is no other way. And look at the bright side—you still have a job you love. Jessica really needs you in her life, honey."

"I know." Erin sighed, long and full of despair. "The whole thing really is my fault, but that doesn't make it hurt any less." Her voice wavered. "I love him, Mom."

"Love is always a blessing, even unreturned love. And if you really feel that way, let him go."

"How can I?"

"You have to. Give him the gift of caring for his daughter but release the rest. That's true love, baby girl."

"Why can't it be easy?"

She heard her mother's soft laughter carry across the line. "Nothing worth having is easy. You'll find the perfect man for you someday, Erin. You're young. You don't have to push it."

Erin glumly pondered this a moment and, even though she didn't want to hear it or admit it, she realized her mother was completely correct. She did have time, and she owed it to Sam to leave him with a healthy, happy Jessica.

And since she *would* have to leave him eventually, she made another split-second decision. If she couldn't have him, couldn't live the dream of being with him and Jessica forever, then the least she could do was leave him with one gift.

His siblings.

No matter what it took, no matter how much he wanted to throttle her in the end for all her pushing, she would convince Sam that meeting Lissa and Adam was the way to go. That way, if things worked out like she suspected they would, Sam would always remember her fondly. Remember her. Which meant she wouldn't be a part of his world.

Why did life rot so much some days?

By the end of the week, avoiding his attraction to Erin had morphed into a full-time, extremely difficult job, and Sam felt ready to crack under the pressure. He wanted to get away, to run fast and far from feelings he shouldn't be having, from desires for a future he couldn't even let himself contemplate. Erin had slipped into some annoyingly serene state of mind, tending to Jessica and being faultlessly polite whenever they collided. He, on the other hand, wasn't able to be so Zen about the whole jacked-up situation. His tension manifested itself in a case of extreme edginess, and he dared anyone to cross his path and come out alive. At the worksite, he'd become growly and unapproachable. At home, he'd retreated into a brooding, remote state. Sure, everyone from Mia to his employees to his own daughter had quickly read his evil mood, and everyone was giving him a wide berth. Everyone except Erin, of course. She'd suddenly felt the need to go full court press with this "reunite with your siblings" diatribe, citing the often logical reasons why and shooting down all of his—mostly self-protective and lame—excuses.

None of it helped.

On Saturday morning, he crept downstairs early, hoping to snatch the paper and a cup of coffee, then skulk back to the safety of his room until Jessica woke up or Erin left for her weekend off, whichever came first. No such luck. His heart dipped when he saw the glow from the kitchen light reaching out into the dark house beyond. He knew she'd be there, and he knew she'd press him to talk. He'd awakened from a disturbing dream about his little half-brother, Mark, and he wasn't feeling chatty. Not in the least.

Sure enough, Erin sat at the table, nursing her own cup of coffee and perusing several papers. His burst of uncontrollable joy at her presence warred with his fear that she'd start in on him again. No, not fear, knowledge. Erin hadn't let up about his "family" since he'd admitted the truth to her. Why should today be any different?

Erin glanced up from the article in which she'd been immersed. "Good morning."

He grumbled something that could've passed for a polite reply and stalked over to the coffee maker.

*Please just let me get my coffee and go,* he prayed silently.

"You should have a look at these new articles about Lissa and Adam, Sam," she said, with an excitement in her tone that was simply too much for the crack of dawn and his state of mind. "Due to the publicity, they're uncovering more detailed records from those the adoption agency lost in the fire. It's been a win-win for everyone."

Yippee. He said nothing. Couldn't she get the hint? Didn't care, didn't want to know, didn't like talking about it. Period.

And why did she smell so damn sweet in the morning, even before a shower? He remembered the distracting candy scent of her skin, the sugary taste with a primal jolt. All of it was pure Erin. No perfume company could bottle something so insanely erotic. He didn't want to think about her in that way, but with her so near, so sleep tousled, he could hardly help it. Good thing she kept ruining the mood by yammering on about the triplet thing, or he'd be in trouble.

"They haven't uncovered anything about you being a triplet, though," she added, oblivious to or ignoring his Grinchy silence. "I think that's something you're going to have to do yourself."

His jaw tightened. "Or not do myself." He crossed to the table and deliberately ignored the feel-good human interest sections of the paper she tried to foist on him daily. Instead he pulled out the sports section, world news, and the comics, tucking them under his arm. "I'll talk to you later. Have a nice weekend off."

Sam spun stiffly and started out the kitchen door, but Erin's palm around his forearm stopped him. It also sloshed hot coffee out of his mug onto his hand and the floor.

"Dammit, Erin."

"I'm sorry." She stood, crossing to the paper towel roll mounted below one of the cabinets. "I didn't mean to spill it."

Chagrined, he bent to help her sop up the mess. "And I didn't mean to swear at you."

"Hey, that's okay." She tossed her hair back, offering him a playful half-smile. "I know how you are before coffee."

"And how's that?"

"You know...growly."

He pulled back his chin. "I have never growled."

She rolled her eyes. "I'll set up a tape recorder tomorrow morning. Trust me. You growl."

"Can I give you a suggestion then?" He smiled, but the sharp slash of his mouth felt insincere, a little anger-induced.

"Sure."

"Stop jamming the Adam and Lissa stuff down my throat and perhaps I won't feel the need to growl so often."

Erin sat back on her haunches, wadding the soiled paper towels in a ball. "I'm not jamming anything. I just think it would be really good for you, and for Jessica, to know your extended family."

"They're not my family, Erin," he said, his tone bursting out angrily. "How many times do I have to tell you that? How many ways?"

She blinked at his raised voice, but didn't falter. "Oh, but they are. You can deny it all you want, deny them if you're stubborn enough to do so, but they are and always will be your family. A family you're choosing to ignore for God knows what reason, Sam Lowery. If for nothing else, your daughter deserves to know who her relatives are."

That did it. Sam could handle being told how badly he was screwing up his life, but he drew the line at being told he was also screwing up Jessica's. "Listen, Erin, because I'm only going to tell you this once. You are Jessica's nanny. Period. Not her mother, not my wife. When I want your opinion on how I raise my daughter, I'll ask for it." He stood. "Until then, do me a favor and butt out. I don't want to hear another word about Lissa Cartwright or Adam Bartlett. Do I make myself clear?"

Erin stared at him through wide, watery eyes, her lips shaking slightly with shock. He didn't think she could look more hurt if he'd reached out and struck her. Slowly, with pained dignity, she stood, too. "Perfectly clear, Sam. You couldn't be more clear if you printed it on a billboard, and believe me, I get the message." She lifted her chin. "I'm nothing more to you than hired help. What we shared that evening meant nothing to you, either."

"Erin, that's not what—"

"And as for Jessica," she went on, ignoring his

attempts to cut in, "as much as I love her, you're right. Maybe I do need to butt out." She smoothed the front of her robe. "Unfortunately, I care too much, and this Lissa/Adam issue is too much a part of her healing process. So the only way for me to butt out is to resign my position as Jessica's nanny."

Sam's heart lurched. "Erin—"

"Don't." She held up a hand. "It's my decision and it's final. I'll have my things out tomorrow by the time you get home from work. You'd better arrange for alternate childcare for Jessica tomorrow, in case you have another late night. Because I won't be here when you get home, Sam. I can't stand by silently and watch you destroy yourself, and I can't seem to get through to you. That's probably my failing and not yours, but rest assured, I won't be here ever again."

*Chapter Fifteen*

Erin spent her first two days back at her parents' mostly sleeping and avoiding everyone and everything—primarily her bruised feelings. Her mother had told her she would always have a loving place to return to if things didn't work out with the nanny job, and in a global way, that was true. Her mother hadn't even blinked when Erin told her she'd quit her job and would be moving home. The house was warm and cozy, food was plentiful, and she was surrounded by people who loved her unconditionally. Ironically, the only loving place she wanted to be was at Sam's house, in Sam's arms.

Fat chance.

The worst thing of all was how her brothers tiptoed around her, being extra nice, super solicitous. Not a single "I told you so," had been uttered, and although part of her felt relieved to have avoided the slings and arrows she'd expected, the rest of her was simply disconcerted.

These weren't her brothers. They were some weird shell-like brother stand-ins who were eerily in touch with their feminine sides. She preferred them annoying.

Clearly Mom had talked to them and threatened them with their lives if they bothered her, but that didn't feel right either. In fact, nothing felt right without Jessica and Sam.

On day three, she was taking a nap when someone knocked on her door. Turning groggily toward the sound, Erin croaked out, "Come in."

Eamon, the worst of the worst, entered, standing just inside the door, which he'd closed behind him. "Want to talk, sis?"

"No."

A long pause ensued. Erin finally sighed, dragging herself into a sitting position, knees pulled up against her chest. She wrapped her arms around her knees and flashed Eamon an undeserved venomous glare. "Fine, talk."

"I just want to make sure you're okay. We all do."

She toyed with the idea of lying, but decided not to. "No, I'm not alright."

"What happened?"

"I screwed everything up. I had the perfect job and I fell in love with my boss."

A muscle in Eamon's square jaw jumped, but to his credit, he declined to lecture. "And Lowery?"

"Not so much in love with me."

Eamon crossed the room and sat on the edge of the bed gingerly. He cast Erin a baleful, earnest glance. "Do you want us to beat him up, sis?"

The absurdity of the question dragged Erin out of the pits of despair in which she'd taken up residence, and she laughed. "No, geek. He's a nice guy—he just doesn't love me."

"That's enough of a fault to earn a beating, little sis."

"No beatings!"

Eamon made a regretful face. "I guess I'm glad about that. I liked Lowery."

Erin bit her lip and her eyes filled with tears.

Eamon reached out and took her hand in his. "Growing up sucks, little sis—"

"I'm already grown up."

"I know. But we continue to grow all the time. It doesn't end when we're suddenly legal to buy booze."

Erin felt a wash of affection for her stern, meddling brother, and she scooted closer to him and rested her head on his shoulder. "I know. Thanks."

"For what?"

"For not annoying me."

"I didn't annoy you? What a drag." A pause ensued. "You know, that woman from the agency keeps calling. She wants you for a temporary nanny job. You should call her."

"I know." Erin sighed, but the action quickly morphed into tears. "I'm sorry. This is so stupid. I just don't know if I'm ready to jump into another job. I miss Jessica so much."

"It's not stupid. That baby was one heck of a wonderful kid. But there are a lot of children who would benefit from being around you, kiddo. Especially your nieces and nephews." He let that sink in. "You can call her back whenever you're ready, but will you do me a favor?"

"What?"

"Come back to the land of the living. Take a bubble bath, have a glass of wine, whatever you need. But, after that, rejoin the family. We miss you, Erin. The kids really miss you."

Erin realized how right Eamon was. She might not have Jess and Sam, she realized with a stab of pain, but she was missing out on what she'd always had— the love of her big, boisterous family. It made no sense to take out her pain on them. "Okay, I'll come out there."

"Yeah?" Eamon beamed.

"After a bath, which was a great idea. Make yourself useful as well as ornamental, Eam, and bring me that glass of wine. I'll fill the tub."

Eamon squeezed her against his shoulder. "That's the Erin we know and nag. And hey, the offer of a beating still stands. You say the word and you've got ten meaty O'Grady fists on your side."

Erin pulled away and stood. "Duly noted, but I'm not so into the violence thing. Now, get."

Eamon left, and Erin stood up and stretched. Crossing to the bathroom, she pulled her favorite vanilla bath foam from the cabinet and set it on the edge of the tub. As the steamy water gushed into the tub, she looked at herself in the mirror and got philosophical. So, she'd fallen in love with an unattainable man. It happened to a lot of women. She'd get over it eventually, even though it didn't feel like it at the moment. But being cocooned in the arms of her family could do nothing but help the process along. She'd loved, she'd lost, she'd mourned. Now it was time to move on.

Though it was Monday morning, Sam had taken the day off to try to get a handle on this train wreck of a life. He had tried to go back to being Superdad after Erin left, simply as a matter of pride. He wanted to show the world—or maybe himself—that he could handle a full-time job and a two-year-old on his own. Heck, single mothers did it all the time.

As he filled the washing machine with light garments picked out of the monstrous mound of unwashed laundry and simultaneously threw together some pathetic excuse for lunch on the stove, he wondered how in the hell the single mothers pulled it off. He certainly didn't have a handle on the multitasking thing, not even a fingerhold. He was chagrined to admit that he hadn't had any clue exactly how much Erin did around that house to make things run smoothly, but the past several days had given him a hard lesson in the truth.

God, he missed Erin.

And, as much as he missed her, Jessica missed her even more acutely. His baby girl was utterly inconsolable, and Sam couldn't even deny that her unhappiness was his fault. Granted, the break with Erin had to happen, and he'd stand by it. Still, knowing that didn't make the days any easier.

Just as he started the wash cycle, the smoke from the burning lunch on the stove top set off the smoke alarms, and the shrill sound startled Jessica out of her nap. As she screamed and wailed from her crib, he alternated between running into her bedroom to console her and dashing to the various smoke alarms waving a towel at them in the hopes of stopping the heinous shriek. After he'd pulled open all the doors and the smoke had dissipated enough to silence the alarms, Sam, breathing heavily, pulled Jessica out of her crib and sank onto the floor of her bedroom. He cradled her in his arms until her sobs had mellowed into hiccups, all the while deciding that home cooking was overrated.

He washed Jessica's face, combed her soft hair, and buckled her into her carseat for a quick drive to McDonald's. They used to love impromptu lunches together at McDonald's, but after they'd gotten their food and settled at a table in the Playland area, all Sam could feel was the absence of Erin. Life was staid and drab without her, colorless and humorless. He stole a peek at his listless baby girl and knew she felt the same thing.

He remembered Erin's lessons all at once, and decided to give them a try. His heart started to pound, and he swallowed once and then cleared his throat. "I miss Erin, Jess. So much. Do you?"

Jessica blinked up at him in surprise, then nodded. "Want Win home. Make Win come home." She burst into tears and reached her chubby arms out. Sam went to her immediately, pulling her into an embrace on his lap.

"I don't know if Erin will come home, baby. But maybe you can go visit her. Would you like that?"

Jessica shook her head emphatically. "Want Win home!"

Sam sighed, tucking Jessica's head under his chin. "I know. Your old dad is a champ at screwing things up, honeypot. Did you know that?" She didn't answer, and he was grateful. "I don't know what to do to make things better."

"Win come home."

That would make things better. Just like peace would make the world better. Yeah. Right. He held Jess and rocked her for a few minutes, saying nothing. Finally, he patted her on the back. Somehow, they needed to move on. "Go eat your lunch, Jess. Okay?"

"Not hungry."

Hell, he wasn't going to force her. He hadn't had much of an appetite since Erin vacated their lives, either. "Do you want to go play, then?"

Jessica nodded unenthusiastically, then wriggled off his lap and toddled toward the multicolored play station.

To pass the time, Sam pulled a newspaper off an adjacent, empty table and began to peruse headlines. Most of the world news escaped his interest, he hated to admit. He finished the first section, checking on Jessica regularly, then slipped it behind the rest of the stack.

His eyes immediately fell to the article about little Mark, and his heart leapt. Most of the other articles centered on Lissa and Adam, so this had to mean—

Scanning it quickly, Sam learned what he'd hoped: the bone marrow transplant had taken. Finally. Little Mark was on the mend and his prognosis was great. Sam released a long breath, surprised to realize how much he'd been praying for this outcome. Everyone had cause for celebration because a beloved child had a second chance at life. He grabbed his cell phone on instinct, thinking he should call Adam and congratulate him.

Adam. A man he'd never met.

Not just his brother, but a brother who'd shared a womb. What had he done? He replaced the cell phone on his belt and scrubbed his hands over his face. Yes, everyone had reason to celebrate Mark's news except Sam himself, because he'd chosen not to know these people. His little brother. He'd *chosen* not to reach out for the one thing he'd always wanted. Family.

Without warning, the sting of tears blurred his eyes. Was he the most obtuse man who ever walked the earth? Erin had been right all along, and he'd punished her for it. He *should* be celebrating with his siblings, with little Mark Cambry, who was a complete innocent in the whole drama of Sam's abandonment and childhood. If he chose to continue down this path of denial, it was no one's fault but his own if he remained lonely and bitter.

Adam. Lissa. Mark. Shawna. Chad.

How exciting would it be for Jessica to know she had aunts and uncles, even one just a few years older than she?

He'd been so selfish.

So stupid.

So deeply in denial.

Sam's hands trembled as the biggest realization he'd had in maybe forever zinged through him like an electrical charge. Part of him found it ironic, the other part found it pathetic. Only Sam Lowery would have a life-changing epiphany in McDonald's Playland.

But, surroundings notwithstanding, he couldn't deny it.

Like a sledgehammer to the chest, Sam admitted that he'd screwed up the most important chance he'd ever been presented in his life. Not the delay in meeting his siblings, which he could remedy with a little courage. But rather, his chance at a relationship with Erin. Sure she'd goaded him, prodded him, pushed him repeatedly to the edge of his comfort zone which annoyed the heck out of him, but that was only because she loved him. No one had ever loved him like that, and he'd turned that love away.

God knew, he loved her, too. With his whole heart, soul, being, he loved Erin.

He might not be the perfect man or father, but his love for Erin O'Grady was poignant in its perfection, right and whole and complete. Why hadn't he seen it before? Instead, he'd done his very best to push away the one woman who'd loved him in that unconditional manner for which he'd always yearned.

Urgency filled him. He had to make things right.

Sam hastily stacked the paper and pushed it aside. He threw away their mostly uneaten lunches and then called for Jessica. Generally obedient, she came to him immediately, curiosity showing in her expression.

Sam squatted down before her, smiling. "Want to go get Erin, honeypot?"

His little girl broke into a huge grin for the first time in at least a week, and she nodded vigorously.

"Let's go get her, then." He kissed Jessica on the temple. "I love you so much, Jess."

"Yuv you, Daddy."

And I love Erin, he thought. I am in love with Erin O'Grady and there's no going back. He squeezed his eyes shut, trepidation riddling through him. Please, God, let her be a forgiving woman. Moreover, let her brothers be forgiving men.

Sam clung to Jessica a little tighter as he knocked on Eamon O'Grady's front door. He'd called ahead and asked for an emergency meeting with all the O'Grady men, including Erin's father, and the reception had been icy and grudging, but at least they'd agreed. He didn't know how much they knew about his and Erin's relationship, but surely they wouldn't pound him into cad dust if he had a baby in his arms.

Eamon yanked the door open. "Lowery."

"Eamon. Thanks for taking the time to see me."

Eamon inclined his head and stepped aside. He gave a wink and a smile to Jessica, who giggled in response.

Sam entered the house, heart hammering in his chest. He wasn't used to opening up, but if he meant to bring Erin back to him and Jessica, he'd have to suck it up and spill his guts in order to get past the nearly impenetrable wall of brotherly protection.

In the living room, Matthew, Miles, Mick, Patrick and Erin's father, Eamon Sr., took up most of the space. He nodded to each one in turn, ending with Erin's father. "Sir, thanks for seeing me."

Eamon Sr. turned his attention to Jessica, holding out his arms. "Come here, you bonny little lass," he said in a very grandfatherly tone. "I might have a bit of candy for a pretty girl." He patted his chest pocket.

Jessica giggled shyly and looked toward her father. Sam nodded, setting her on the floor. She toddled over to the senior O'Grady male, clambering up into his lap.

"Have a seat," Matthew said to Sam, indicating a straight-backed wooden chair they'd set in the middle of the room.

Sam eyed it warily, half expecting it to be an electric chair.

"Fill us in on what this is all about. Something to drink?"

"Hemlock?" Mick suggested, in a thinly veiled venomous tone.

"Mick, watch yourself," his father admonished.

Mick held up his hands and backed down. "Just a suggestion, Dad. That's all."

"It's fine. I understand his anger." Sam took a seat, smoothing his sweat-slickened palms on the fronts of his jeans. Once Eamon Jr. had joined them, Sam leaned forward, resting his elbows on his knees. He made sure to look directly at all of the brothers as he spoke. "What this is about is the fact I've been a total ass."

"We don't know details, but we gathered that," Matthew, the burliest brother, said. "We've told Erin we'd be glad to pummel you into the dirt, but you remain unscathed at her wishes."

Sam clenched his jaw with chagrin. "I'll be sure to thank her when I see her."

"You expect to see her?" Mick asked.

"Expect? No. But I hope to see her." He paused, formulating his words. "Mr. O'Grady? Eamon? Patrick? Matthew? Miles? Mick? The truth is…I'm in love with Erin. Granted, I've screwed things up, but Erin came into my life like a whirlwind and sort of—" he shook his head "—threw me off kilter."

"Erin has a knack for that," Patrick said, and he didn't sound murderous. Sam took that as a good sign.

"I screwed things up, no doubt about it," Sam continued. "But I'd like your blessing to make it up to Erin."

"You want her back as your nanny?" Eamon Jr. asked, his eyes narrowed suspiciously. "She's already found another nanny job. She can't be bouncing back and forth at your whim."

"No, not as a nanny," Sam told him, all of them, feeling more assured about his position the more he talked. "I want to make her my wife."

"What?" Eamon Jr. asked.

Sam nodded. "I'm very serious with my intentions. I just can't stop thinking that Mrs. Erin O'Grady Lowery rolls off the tongue like poetry, but I won't propose if you disapprove." He paused, gathering the last of his courage.

"What are you asking us, son?" Erin's father asked gently.

"I'd like your blessings to propose to Erin."

Erin sat on the floor with her new charges, twin four-year-old sisters, listlessly playing with Barbies. It wasn't that she didn't like the children; Erin liked all children. But her heart had been shredded, and all she could think about was Sam and Jessica, especially after having read the update about Mark's bone marrow transplant in the newspaper that morning.

Had he gone on with his life?

Did he even care that his little brother's life had been saved? Did he know?

"Erin!" whined Britney. "Your Barbie is wearing the shoes that go with my Barbie's outfit."

"I'm sorry, honey," Erin said, slipping off the minuscule plastic pumps and handing them over. Just then, the doorbell rang. Erin turned toward the entryway with a frown on her face. She wasn't expecting anyone.

She glanced back at Britney and Blair, smiling. "Stay here, loves. I'll just go see who that is."

The girls were so caught up in their game, they didn't give the doorbell a second thought, nor did they respond to her comments.

Erin padded through the house, stopping to check her appearance in the foyer mirror. No two ways about it, she looked like death. Dark circles smudged the delicate skin beneath her sad eyes, and her cheeks seemed sunken. No surprise, since she hadn't been able to sleep soundly or eat appropriately since leaving Sam's house, but she didn't like the overall image. Her hair was wild and crazy, but then again her hair was always wild and crazy. She liked it that way.

She threw the deadbolt and pulled open the door, then stopped, stunned. Her throat closed. "Sam. What are you doing here?" The ache to pull Jessica into her arms reached all the way down to her bones. No, deeper. To her soul, her heart, her very being. She missed both of them so incredibly much, she momentarily forgot her manners. She wanted to laugh, to cry. She wanted to yell at Sam and then hold him close. Hope and wariness fought for top billing inside her. Her emotions were so jumbled, so overwhelming, she simply stood there dumbfounded.

"I need to talk to you," he said, his voice husky. He looked terrible, as terrible as she felt. Clearly, he hadn't been sleeping or eating either. Part of her rejoiced in that, another part wanted to take care of him. "You look awful," she blurted, unintentionally.

One side of his mouth lifted. "Sleep deprivation."

"I hear you." For a moment, they simply searched each other's faces.

"Erin, I—"

"Win!" Jessica stretched as far as she could without falling, and Erin glanced up at Sam for his approval.

He nodded, so Erin took Jessica into her arms, cuddling her close. She breathed in her baby smell, closing her eyes at the wave of emotions that washed over her, sucking her under. "I've missed you so much, Jessica."

"Yuv you, Win."

"Oh, gosh." Erin's voice caught, and she had to swallow several times to regain her composure. "I love you, too, Jess. So very much."

"Erin."

Sam's soft voice drew her attention back, and she read something new and enticing in his eyes. Her heart leapt with hope, fired to life by the look on his face.

"Can I come in? We need to talk."

"Of course."

They stood just in the entryway, and Sam reached out and touched her cheek. Softly, gently.

Erin swallowed. "What's this about?"

"The transplant took. Mark's. His prognosis is good."

Tears filled Erin's eyes, and she smiled up at Sam over Jessica's head. "I know. I read it this morning and thought of you. All of you."

She watched his Adam's apple rise and fall with emotion. "My first instinct after reading the story was to call Adam, Erin, and congratulate him."

"But—"

"But I don't know him. He's my brother, and I don't know him. He doesn't know I exist." Sam raked fingers through his hair, leaving some of it standing askew. It gave him a boyishly vulnerable look.

"You can know him. If you want to."

"I know." A beat passed, then he lifted his gaze to her face cautiously. "But there's one problem."

"Which is?"

"I don't want to meet...my family without you."

Her heart jumped. "W-what do you mean?"

Sam started to pace in the large foyer, and Erin moved to lean against the wall and get out of his way. "God, Erin, I've had so much time to think since you left, and everything's wrong."

"What do you mean?" She was repeating herself, she knew, but he wasn't making much sense.

Suddenly, Sam spun to face her. "What I mean is, I don't want to live without you, Erin. I'm a mess. Jessica is a mess, and she needs you."

Her stomach dropped. "You want me to come back and work for you? Sam, I don't know."

"No. I don't want you to come work for me."

"Oh."

"I want you to marry me, Erin."

The room swayed before her. "Excuse me?"

Sam moved close, smoothing his hands down her upper arms. "I'm in love with you, Erin O'Grady, and I was just too damned stupid or scared to admit it to myself. Too afraid of losing you to let you close. I want to marry you, Erin. I want you to be my wife and Jessica's new mother. Please say yes. I haven't begged for much in my life, but I don't want to face another day without you."

"Oh, Sam." Tears filled her eyes and spilled over. Jessica, confused, reached up to pat her cheeks. "No cry, Win."

Erin laughed, a watery sound, and kissed Jessica on the head. "I thought you said you didn't have room for family in your life?"

"I'm an idiot. I was wrong. Scared, maybe. I want you and Jessica. I want all the other children we'll create together. I even want the evil five, who have, incidentally, given us their blessings. Your father, too."

Her jaw slackened. "You actually went to my brothers?"

He pulled his chin back. "Come on. Do you think any guy in his right mind would get near Erin O'Grady without first getting permission from the O'Grady men?"

Erin laughed, feeling bubbly and free. "You're crazy."

Sam pulled her into his arms, Jessica cuddled between them, and he kissed her softly on the lips. "I am. Crazy about you, and crazy without you. Please take me out of my misery and say you'll marry me." He glanced at his daughter affectionately. "That you'll marry us."

Erin smiled so widely, she felt like she'd never be able to stop. "Of course I will, Sam. You know I will."

He cupped the sides of her face in his hands and kissed her so gently, her heart ached. "I love you, Erin O'Grady."

"And I love you, Sam Lowery. I'll love you forever." They kissed for several moments, then Erin pulled back. "There's just one thing."

"Uh-oh. What's that?"

"You once told me you had no room for more family in your life. You *do* realize that marrying me means marrying my family, don't you?"

"I can't think of anything better. Well, except for introducing you to *my* family as my soon-to-be wife." He smiled slowly at her. "Can you handle that?"

"I can handle anything as long as we're together."

"So can I, Erin, love. So can I."

## Epilogue

Sam's throat was so tight, all he could do was grip Erin's hand and stare straight ahead as they walked down the hospital corridor toward Mark Cambry's room. His nervous solemnity belied the cheeriness of the giant purple stuffed elephant he carried, a gift for his recuperating little brother. Finally, after twenty-seven years, he was about to meet his siblings. He could hardly believe it.

Lissa and Adam had been floored when Sam first contacted them, but after he'd outlined all the facts and mailed a photo, they couldn't wait to meet him. The human heart, he learned, had an infinite capacity for love. They welcomed him into the fold just as they'd first welcomed each other, as they'd both welcomed Mark, Shawna and Chad. Even the father who had abandoned them all, Jared Cambry. Sam wasn't sure he'd quite reached that point of altruism, but he wanted to meet Mark, wanted to tell the little guy to hang in there.

Thankfully, both Lissa and Adam respected Sam's aversion to publicity, so they agreed to meet in private this first time. No one had alerted the press that a third sibling had come forward, and the hospital business carried on as usual, with no one giving Sam a second glance. Maybe in the future, they'd decide together to let the media in on this little twist in the reunited twins story, but for now, it was a family event, pure and simple. Family. He loved the sound of that.

Outside the threshold to Mark's private room, he glanced at Erin, and she sent him an encouraging smile full of love. Jessica, all prettied up, sat happily on Erin's hip. Sam took a moment to marvel that he had more family in this moment than he'd ever had, and he adored it. He couldn't wait until he and Erin added new babies to their family tree. The more the better. Jessica deserved to be a big sister, and she'd make a great one. And as for Erin's mothering skills, well, Sam only knew that their children would be extremely lucky.

"Go ahead and knock, honey," Erin said. "We're right here for you."

He nodded once, rather grimly, then raised his fist and knocked gently. Immediately, his heart began to thud in his chest and he had to fight the urge to bolt.

"Come in," called a feminine voice.

He raised his brows at Erin and took a deep breath. "Now or never," he murmured.

Sam pushed open the door and peered in.

"He's here!" Lissa cried, jumping up from the chair she occupied next to little Mark's bed. "My God, look at you. You look just like Adam."

Sam took in Adam's tailored, undoubtedly expensive suit and laughed wryly. "I wouldn't say we're exactly twins."

Everyone laughed.

Adam rose, too, and came over. Sam handed the giant purple elephant to Erin, who hung back, then both Adam and Lissa wrapped Sam in a huge, long-overdue, swaying hug. Tears filled the corners of Sam's eyes as they clung to one another. He didn't know what to say. How did people catch up on twenty-seven lost years? They had time for that. All he knew at that moment was, this felt right—it felt like he belonged at last.

When they pulled apart, all three of them had tears in their eyes. Adam grinned. "Can I just say, I hope we're not quadruplets? I don't think I can handle another shock like this in the near future."

Sam and Lissa laughed, then Sam glanced toward the solemn, observant little boy in the hospital bed. He moved over, taking a seat on the edge. "I'm going to take a wild guess and say you must be my brother, Mark."

The little boy nodded, then reached out for a hug. Sam embraced the child, squeezing his eyes shut.

"I'm so glad you're doing well, little buddy. I read every story about you in the papers."

"Why didn't you come visit me earlier?"

Sam pulled back and sighed, holding one of Mark's hands in his own. "I was afraid. Not of you, but just—"

"Because you didn't know any of us?"

"How'd you get to be so wise in such a short time?" Sam asked, tilting his head to the side.

"I don't know." His eyes flickered toward the door. "What's with the elephant?"

Sam looked toward Erin, and she moved forward. "I brought him for you. But if you're too grown up for him, I'll get you something else. Whatever you want."

"No, he's kewl." Mark reached out for the elephant, and Erin handed him over. "Thanks, Sam." He peered curiously toward Erin and Jessica then. "Is this your wife?"

"She will be soon." Sam looked around to include Adam and Lissa in this conversation. "This is my fiancée, Erin. And Mark, this is your niece, Jessica. My daughter."

Mark looked momentarily stunned. "I'm an uncle?"

"That you are."

"That is so unreal." His little chest puffed out as he glanced at Jessica. "Hi, there. I'm your uncle Mark."

Again everyone laughed.

Jessica reached out for Mark, and Sam held out a hand. "Is it okay, Mark? Are you in pain?"

"Naw, I'm fine. She can sit on my bed."

Erin sat Jessica on Mark's bed, instructing her quietly to be gentle with her young uncle, and Jessica seemed to understand. As the children chattered, the adults gathered in one corner of the room, and Erin was hugged and welcomed into the family by both Lissa and Adam. They'd begun to talk about wedding plans when the door swung open.

Everyone turned.

Sam's gaze met that of the man who could only be Jared Cambry. To Sam's surprise, the man didn't look like a self-serving monster. He looked like a concerned father who'd gone to hell and back. Sam, nevertheless, stiffened.

Jared came right up to him and held out a hand. "You must be Sam. I'm your—" He pursed his lips. "I'm Jared Cambry. I'm so glad you came by."

Sam took the man's hand and shook it, then introduced Erin and Jessica.

Sam was shocked to see Jared's eyes moisten as he looked at Jessica. "I'm a grandfather?" Sam said nothing, and the older man cut a glance his way. "Would you rather I didn't refer to myself that way?"

Erin moved up beside Sam and curved her hand around his elbow. "Sam, wouldn't it be nice for Jessica to have another grandfather?"

"Yes. I guess that would be fine. Although you seem pretty young to fit that bill," Sam told Jared.

Jared eyed him, then laid a hand gently on his shoulder. "How about you and I take a walk, talk a little?"

Sam glanced toward Erin, feeling uncertain.

"Go," she told him softly, and the love in her eyes said she knew he'd handle everything just right. Her faith imbued him with confidence.

"That'd be okay, I guess."

Sam and Jared left the room side by side and didn't speak until they reached a private, family consultation room down the hall from Mark's. Jared peered into the oblong window in the door and, finding it empty, he opened the door. "After you."

Sam went in and took a seat on one of the plum-hued sofas. Jared chose a chair at a right angle to the sofa, and then he simply met and held Sam's gaze.

"I wanted to hate you," Sam said, through a clenched jaw. "But you're not quite the monster I'd made you out to be in my mind. You're just a father, like I am."

Jared expelled a long breath through his nose, and a lifetime of regret etched lines around his eyes. "I didn't know there were three of you, Sam. Didn't even know Olivia had died in the crash until Mark got sick and I got desperate to find a way for him to live." He wrung his hands. "There is nothing I can say to make up for not having been there when you three were growing up. But you're all adults now and you've built amazing lives. I'm proud of you, whether or not I have a right to be."

Sam swallowed thickly. "Thank you."

"Listen, can we just start from here? I don't expect you to call me Dad or to think of me as your father. But I would like to be a part of your life."

"I...I'd like that, too. I've been so damn angry at you since the stories about Lissa and Mark first hit the media."

"I understand. I don't blame you."

"But I want to let it go. I want to start fresh." Jared reached over and patted Sam's forearm, and surprisingly, the gesture felt consoling to Sam. He continued, feeling stronger. "Erin and I are getting married, and I'd like the whole family to be involved in the wedding."

"I'd like that very much."

"I may not ever refer to you as...Dad, Jared, but—"

"What is it, Sam?"

"I'd like to start anew. I'd like you to sit in the place of my father at the wedding. I've never had a father—" His voice caught, and he clenched his fists.

"Sam Lowery, I'd be honored to participate in your wedding in whatever manner you'd like. You may never consider me your father, but I think of you and Lissa and Adam as my children, just as much as I think of Mark, Shawna and Chad that way."

"I've never had a father," Sam said again, dazedly.

"Well, maybe we can start with friendship and work from there."

"I'm glad Mark's okay," Sam said.

"Sam, I'm glad you're okay."

Sam thought of Erin and Jessica. He thought of

Adam, Lissa and their spouses, whom he'd be meeting later that evening. He thought of Mark, Shawna, Chad, Jared and his wife. Lastly, he thought of Erin's family, the whole big, bustling bunch of them. And he realized, maybe for the first time, that he *was* okay. He had more family than he'd ever imagined and he felt surrounded, loved, included. "I am okay, Jared. I really am."

The two men shared a smile of understanding, then they walked, side by side, back to be with the rest of their family. They'd come full circle, and both were now ready to move forward. When they entered Mark's hospital room, Sam met Erin's eyes and shared a private look of love. Her pride and respect shone through and warmed him from the inside out. His precious baby daughter laughed happily with her young uncle on his hospital bed, and the siblings with whom he'd shared a womb for almost nine months sat smiling up at him as if they'd never been separated. Calmness and completeness knocked the chip that life had put on Sam's shoulder off, once and for all, and he smiled back at all of them.

He was crazy in love.

His baby girl was happy again.

And, most unexpectedly, he had siblings—a lot of them—bound by blood and all that kind of connection entailed. The good, the bad, the happy, the sad, all the rights and responsibilities that were part and parcel of belonging—he would gladly take all of it and give back in kind.

For so many years, Sam had built houses. It had

been his calling, his passion, to take raw materials and fashion them into houses of every style imaginable, but, standing in Mark's hospital room that afternoon, he realized he'd never built a home. Only love and family built a home, and he knew that now because he'd come home.

Finally and forever, Sam Lowery had a home—not the kind built out of brick and wood, but the kind made of love. The kind a man never lost…and never left.

The kind he never, ever took for granted.

\* \* \* \* \*

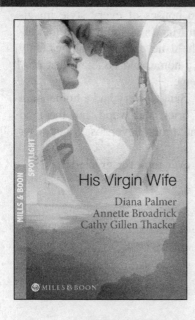

*The only woman he wanted –
and the one he couldn't have...*

When a moment of unbridled passion results in a
kiss, wealthy ranch owner Jason realises that he's
falling for Gracie. But Gracie harbours a shameful
secret that makes her deeply afraid to love. Stung by
her rejection, Jason leaves, ready to put the past –
and the one woman he can't have – behind him.

But when danger threatens, Jason will have
her heart forever!

### Available 5th February 2010

www.millsandboon.co.uk

# millsandboon.co.uk Community

## Join Us!

[th]e Community is the perfect place to meet and chat to [kin]dred spirits who love books and reading as much as [yo]u do, but it's also the place to:

**Get the inside scoop from authors about their latest books**
**Learn how to write a romance book with advice from our editors**
**Help us to continue publishing the best in women's fiction**
**Share your thoughts on the books we publish**
**Befriend other users**

**[Fo]rums:** Interact with each other as well as authors, edi[tor]s and a whole host of other users worldwide.

**[Bl]ogs:** Every registered community member has their [ow]n blog to tell the world what they're up to and what's [on] their mind.

**[Bo]ok Challenge:** We're aiming to read 5,000 books and [ha]ve joined forces with The Reading Agency in our [in]augural Book Challenge.

**[Pr]ofile Page:** Showcase yourself and keep a record of [yo]ur recent community activity.

**[So]cial Networking:** We've added buttons at the end of [ev]ery post to share via digg, Facebook, Google, Yahoo, [Te]chnorati and de.licio.us.

*www.millsandboon.co.uk*

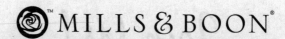